Sadie
on a
Plate

Sadie
on a
Plate

AMANDA ELLIOT

Jove
New York

A JOVE BOOK
Published by Berkley
An imprint of Penguin Random House LLC
penguinrandomhouse.com

Copyright © 2022 by Amanda Panitch
Excerpt from *Best Served Hot* by Amanda Elliot copyright © 2022 by Amanda Panitch
Penguin Random House supports copyright. Copyright fuels creativity,
encourages diverse voices, promotes free speech, and creates a vibrant culture.
Thank you for buying an authorized edition of this book and for complying
with copyright laws by not reproducing, scanning, or distributing any part
of it in any form without permission. You are supporting writers and
allowing Penguin Random House to continue to publish books for every reader.

A JOVE BOOK, BERKLEY, and the BERKLEY & B colophon
are registered trademarks of Penguin Random House LLC.

Library of Congress Cataloging-in-Publication Data

Names: Elliot, Amanda, author.
Title: Sadie on a plate / Amanda Elliot.
Description: First edition. | New York : Jove, 2022.
Identifiers: LCCN 2021027920 (print) | LCCN 2021027921 (ebook) |
ISBN 9780593335710 (trade paperback) | ISBN 9780593335727 (ebook)
Subjects: LCGFT: Romance fiction.
Classification: LCC PS3605.L4423 S23 2022 (print) | LCC PS3605.L4423 (ebook) |
DDC 813/.6—dc23
LC record available at https://lccn.loc.gov/2021027920
LC ebook record available at https://lccn.loc.gov/2021027921

First Edition: March 2022

Printed in the United States of America
1st Printing

Book design by Ashley Tucker
Interior art copyright Shutterstock / VectorMine

This book is for Jeremy.
You are why I write stories about love.

MY LIFE HAS THIS IRRITATING HABIT OF THROWING ITS biggest changes at me while I'm completely in the nude.

Exhibit one, ten years ago: I was seventeen and enamored with a boy my parents hated, all for the completely unfair reason that he skipped school most days to smoke pot behind the local 7-Eleven. I'd snuck him up to my room, deciding against the back door in favor of the tree outside my window because it seemed so much more romantic. We were in the throes of quiet passion when my door flew open.

"Sadie?" my sister said, and her mouth dropped open. She was four years younger than me, so I would've felt bad for traumatizing her if I wasn't so busy screeching and scrambling for my clothes or a sheet or anything to cover up our naughty bits.

"Get out of here!" I grabbed the closest thing within reach—an old soccer trophy—and hurled it in her general direction for emphasis. It landed with a thunk on the rug, which made her jump and blink her eyes. "Get ouuuuuuuut!"

"Okay. Fine." She blinked again and adjusted her glasses. As she turned to go, she said over her shoulder, "By the way, Grandma died."

Exhibit two, six weeks ago: I was getting out of the shower when I heard my phone ding with a text. It was charging on the nightstand, so I picked it up on my way to the dresser. All I saw on the lock screen was that it was from Chef Derek Anders, my boss, and it started with, Hey Sadie . . . I sighed, figuring he was probably asking me to come in for a last-minute shift on the line. I entered my PIN and read the whole text.

Hey Sadie, I'm sorry but we're going to have to let you go.

Exhibit three, five weeks ago: I was walking around my apartment eating Nutella out of the jar with my fingers for breakfast, psyching myself up to put on fancy professional clothes and head out for my nine a.m. interview at the temp agency. My phone rang with a 212 number, which I knew was New York City, and the only reason I picked up was because I thought that the temp agency had its headquarters in New York and maybe they were calling to cancel the interview because *what are you thinking, Sadie, all you've ever done is work in restaurants and all you've ever wanted to do is have your own, why are you trying to get an admin job at some obnoxiously hipstery tech company?*

It's not like I want to work at a tech company, I argued silently with the temp agency. *It's that I've been blacklisted for the near future from the entire Seattle restaurant scene and need some way to earn money until all this fuss dies down.*

The temp agency scoffed in my head. *Yeah, okay. Like you could do a fancy office job. All you can do is work the line, and now you can't even do that anymore. You're worthless.*

I picked up the phone, my shoulders already drooping. "Hello, this is Sadie Rosen."

"Hi, Sadie!" It was a woman on the other end, her tone far too chipper for this hour of the morning. "My name is Adrianna Rogalsky, and I'm calling from *Chef Supreme*. Is this a good time?"

I almost dropped my phone. "Yes!" I cleared my throat, trying to keep from squeaking the way I did when I got too excited. "I mean yes, this is a good time."

"Great!" Adrianna chirped. "I'm calling to tell you that the committee really liked your application and your cooking video. Would you mind answering a few more questions for me?"

My eyes involuntarily darted to my bookshelf, which consisted mainly of cookbooks. I spent too much time in restaurant kitchens to cook much from them—or at least, up until a week ago I had—but I liked flipping through them to gather ideas and marvel at the food photography. Five were written by winners of *Chef Supreme*, and four by runners-up and semifinalists. I'd watched every episode of all six seasons, seated on the edge of my couch to goggle at every cooking challenge and winning dish and contestant who cried when eliminated.

Season three's winner, Seattle's Julie Chee, was my culinary idol. Derek, my boss, had taken me by her restaurant after-hours one day. She'd laughed when I told her how I'd been rooting for her all season, patted my head like I was a little kid, and then cooked me a grilled cheese with bacon and kimchi. It was the best night of my life. Right after that, I'd started dreaming about competing on the show myself.

"Hello? Sadie?"

And if I didn't get on my game, that dream was going to evaporate like a pot of boiling water forgotten on the stove. I mean, I didn't really think I was actually going to make it on the show, but it wasn't like I was going to hang up on someone from *Chef Supreme*. "Sorry!" I said. "Bad connection for a minute there. Yes, I'd love to answer some questions." I shook my head and grimaced. Love? *Love* was a strong word. I should've said I'd *be happy* to answer some questions. Now Adrianna was probably—

Talking! Already! "Your application from six months ago says that you're a sous-chef at the Green Onion in Seattle?"

I cleared my throat. "Well, um." This was not off to a great start. "I was a sous-chef there until last week. I decided to leave to . . . um, pursue personal business opportunities." Another grimace. Personal business opportunities? What did that even mean?

I really wished I wasn't naked right now. I knew Adrianna from *Chef Supreme* couldn't see me through the phone, but I still felt way too exposed.

Fortunately, job-hopping is fairly common in the food world. So Adrianna just said, "Great. And how would you describe your personal style?"

I hoped she meant food-wise and not looks-wise, because my personal fashion style consisted mainly of beat-up Converses, thrift store T-shirts, and constant calculations on how far I could go between haircuts before crossing the line from fashionably mussed to overgrown sheepdog. "At the Green Onion, I was cooking mostly New American food with some French influences and a bit of molecular gastronomy," I told her. "But my own style, I'd say, is more homestyle, with Jewish influences?

Not kosher cooking; that's a different thing. I'm inspired by traditional Jewish cuisine."

Paper rustled on the other end. "Right, the matzah ball ramen you cooked in your video looked fantastic. We were all drooling in the room!"

I perked up. Forgot that I was naked. Forgot that lately I was a walking disaster. "That's one of my go-tos and will definitely be on my future menu. I've been experimenting lately with putting a spin on kugels . . ."

As I chattered on, I could practically see my grandma shaking her head at me. Grandma Ruth had cooked up a storm for every Passover, Yom Kippur, and Chanukah, piling her table till it groaned with challah rolls, beef brisket in a ketchup-based sauce, and tomato and cucumber salad so fresh and herby and acidic it could make you feel like summer in the middle of winter. *Pastrami-spiced* pork *shoulder? Really, dear?*

I shook my own head back at her, making her poof away in a cloud of metaphorical smoke. I had that power now that she was dead and buried and existing primarily as a manifestation of my own anxiety.

". . . so in that way it's really more of a cheesecake with noodles in it," I finished up. My blood was sparking just talking about my food; I had to do a few quick hops just to burn off some of that excess energy.

"I love your passion," Adrianna said on the other end of the phone. "So, I take it that opening your own restaurant is hashtag goals for you?"

"Hashtag goals," I agreed. And my shoulders drooped again, because that was a dream that was never going to happen now. After I got fired by the Green Onion and the chefs at all the other restaurants worth working at learned why, I became the joke of Seattle's restaurant industry. Who wanted to invest in the local joke?

She asked me a few other questions, pertaining mostly to my schedule and availability (there were only so many ways to say, "I'm free whenever you want me, considering I no longer have a job"). I continued to pace around my apartment, circling the coffee table, bare feet padding over the rug. And then, "It's been lovely to speak with you, Sadie."

I stopped short, my shin slamming into the table leg. I swallowed back a curse. "It's been lovely to speak with you . . . too?" I finished with a question, because I couldn't ask what I really wanted to ask. *Is this it? Did I not meet whatever criteria you have? What's wrong with me?*

"We'll be in touch soon," Adrianna said. "Have a great day!"

I did not have a great day. Because of Adrianna's call, I was fifteen minutes late to my interview at the temp agency and arrived all sweaty and panting from the rush to get there on time. The interviewer's lip had actually curled in distaste as she touched my damp, clammy hand. The sugar rush from the Nutella had worn off by the time I hurried back out onto the street, and I was starting to feel a little shaky, but the only place to buy food in the vicinity was a coffee shop where I was forced to choose between a stale bagel and some slimy fruit salad.

And that wasn't all. As I chewed (and chewed, and chewed, and chewed) on my stale bagel with too much cream cheese caked on, I ran into an old friend. Like, literally ran into an old friend, as in our bodies collided as I was trying to catch the bus.

"Oh!" I knew it was her as soon as I heard that raspy voice, earned from years of smoking in alleyways behind restaurants.

Her eyes widened as she took me in: the sweaty strands of hair sticking to the sides of my face, the thrift store blazer that still smelled like the eighties, even though I'd washed it twice and taken the shoulder pads out. "Sadie! How are you . . . doing?"

I gritted my teeth at the false sympathy in those big blue eyes. "Hi, Kaitlyn. So you heard?"

Kaitlyn leaned in, bringing the smell of smoke with her. I fought the urge to step back. Even after years working in restaurant kitchens, where most everybody was a smoker at least when drunk, I hated the smell. "Of *course* I heard. I'm surprised you're still here. Not here in SoDo, like, in Seattle."

"I'm still here," I said through a clenched jaw. Kaitlyn Avilleira and I had quasi-bonded in our early twenties, a little over five years ago. We were the only two women on the line at Atelier Laurent, and we had to have each other's backs if we didn't want to get banished to the pastry kitchen.

Having her back didn't mean I liked her.

"That's really strong of you." Kaitlyn pulled me in for a one-armed hug that might actually have been an attempt to strangle me. "I'm rooting for you, girl!"

I gritted my teeth in a smile. This was the song and dance of our relationship: seeing who could pretend harder that we *did* like each other, because we were busy fighting so many stereotypes about women on the line that there was no way we could fulfill the one where the only two women were enemies. "Thanks, Kait!"

An uncomfortable silence settled over us. I looked in the direction of the bus. No, I *stared* in the direction of the bus, willing it with my eyes to appear.

Alas, I had not developed any magical powers in the past few minutes.

"We have to get drinks sometime," I said. "And catch up. It's been way too long."

"*Way* too long," Kaitlyn said. She tossed her long, shiny brown hair. Her eyes sparkled, and her cheeks were naturally rosy. *She* never had to wear blush or undereye concealer to keep coworkers from asking her if she was sick. "Wait till I tell you about working for Chef Marcus. He works me like a dog." She trilled a laugh. "I almost wish I could take a break like you."

I clenched my jaw and told myself that I couldn't hit her or I'd get arrested, and going to jail was really the only way I could make my situation worse. Well, that, or moving back in with my parents in the suburbs, into my childhood bedroom with the shag carpet and no lock on the door.

"Well, I'd better be going," Kaitlyn said, just as I was saying, "Well, I'll let you go." Our words clashed, and we both laughed nervously before hugging yet again. "You should finally open that restaurant now that you're free and have all this time," Kaitlyn said as she backed away. "I'll be there opening night!"

Thankfully, she was off before I had to respond. I made a face at her back. Of course I wanted to open my restaurant now that I was *free* and had *all* this *time*. But opening a restaurant either took lots of money, which I didn't have even before the whole unemployment situation, or a bunch of rich investors willing to throw their money away on my behalf, which, again, I *wished*.

The bus was delayed, obviously, and it took me twice as long as it should have to get home, the whole time crammed in next to a manspreader who kept giving me dirty looks for trying to sit in three-quarters of my own seat. I stared hard out the window, watching the warehouses and industrial lofts turn into the residential buildings and parks of Crown Hill. By the time I stumbled through the door of my apartment, I was done with today. I pulled off my clothes, dropping them in puddles on the floor, so that I could shower the stink of failure away and then eat something for my soul. Like more Nutella out of the jar.

My phone chimed. *It's probably the temp agency already rejecting me*, I thought glumly, digging it out of my bag. Sure enough, it was an email.

But it was from Adrianna Rogalsky of *Chef Supreme*. And it started with, Hey Sadie, just like my firing-by-text. *Fantastic.* I took a deep breath as I clicked it open, readying myself for yet another important food world person to tell me how inadequate I was.

Hey Sadie, I enjoyed our conversation earlier. Upon further discussion with the *Chef Supreme* team, we'd like to fly you out to New York for some more interviews and cooking tests to determine whether you'd be a good fit to compete on *Chef Supreme* season 7. Would next Wednesday work for you?

I dropped my phone. *OhmyGodohmyGodohmyGod.* What if I'd just shattered my phone and I couldn't afford a new one and I couldn't get back to Adrianna and . . . and . . .

I picked it up. It wasn't even cracked. I opened up an email and wrote Adrianna back about how yes, I'd love to come in whenever they needed me because it was my dream to be on *Chef Supreme* and I couldn't wait to meet—

Backspace. I cleared my throat. Okay, take two, and be more professional this time. Hi Adrianna, thanks for reaching out! Yes, next Wednesday still works for me. I look forward to receiving the flight information.

I sent it off, chewing nervously on my lip even as I tried to talk myself down. *They probably have a hundred people come in to audition further for each season's twelve slots. And seriously, if they have a hundred people to choose from, why the hell would they choose you? Maybe you shouldn't even waste your time. Is it too late to email Adrianna back and cancel?*

I spilled this all on my parents the next night at dinner. I kept my eyes on my plate of eggplant Parm, and not just because my sister, Rachel, who sat across from me at our kitchen table, tended to chew with her mouth open. "So it probably won't actually turn into anything if I decide to go," I said. "But on the off chance it does, it could mean a new start for me. The goal is really not even to win, but to get noticed."

"Get noticed by who?" asked my mom. She set her utensils onto her plate with a clink. My dad followed suit. Only Rachel was left chewing. Loudly.

I let myself look up and look left, at my mom, then right, at my dad. I was an uncanny mix of the two of them: deep-set dark eyes and big boobs like my mom; a round face and thick, wiry brown hair like my dad. Unlike Rachel, who was a blond, blue-eyed giraffe. Even sitting, the top of her head nearly brushed the brass light fixture hanging over the table.

I cleared my throat. "Get noticed by anyone, really. The top four is the sweet spot. They get noticed by the public and by investors. Are offered their own restaurants and fancy executive chef gigs."

My dad shook his head. "Do you really think you're ready for that?" His eyebrows were furrowed with both love and concern, but his words hit me like a kick to the stomach. I pursed my lips and stared over his head, at the row of porcelain chickens in a perpetual march across the counter. "You've been through a lot lately. And you're still so young. I'm just worried about you, honey. Maybe going on TV in front of the whole country isn't the best idea right now."

"I'm not that young. I'm twenty-seven." I blinked hard, trying not to cry. "You don't believe in me?"

"Of course I believe in you," my dad said. He sounded wounded by my very suggestion. "I think you could win. I *know* you could win. But you've spent the past few weeks huddled up crying. Maybe next—"

"I think that's exactly why you *should* do it, Sadie." My mom's eyes were fiery as she reached out to grab my hand. Her squeeze made me sit up straight. "Follow your dreams. Why the hell not, right? Make it to the top four. Get noticed. Never work for a shithead man again."

Relief swept through me, lightening the weight on my shoulders, and that was just about enough to convince me that she was right. That I *should* do this. "I haven't even made it on the show yet," I cautioned.

"But if you do . . . This is what you've always wanted. Don't let it go."

I was pretty sure what I wanted to do, but I looked at Rachel anyway. Grimaced at the chewed-up mass of eggplant Parm that greeted me from her tongue, then the raised eyebrows of a question. She grinned without swallowing. "Do it."

So I got on that plane Wednesday with my heart hammering and my head held high. Jet-lagged and sleepless, I talked to producer after producer, random person after random person. I

cooked more of my food for other random people, and sometimes they liked it and sometimes they chewed slowly and ex-
pressionlessly and nearly made me scream with anxiety. I sat
down with a psychologist or a psychiatrist, I wasn't sure exactly,
and he introduced himself too quickly and I thought that maybe
asking him to repeat himself would get me a black mark, and I
tried to seem a lot less crazy than I actually was, which in turn
made me paranoid that he'd see right through me, so I tried to
seem a little crazy but not *too* crazy, and—

Well, anyway, they flew me back to Seattle and didn't even
make me wait impatiently for weeks and weeks before they told
me I got in. While I was changing into my running clothes, naturally.

Was it that I spent far more time naked than the average
person? Either way, nudity never failed.

TWO MONTHS LATER, I BOARDED MY FLIGHT OUT OF
Seattle burdened by three things: my carry-on bag, an unbridled
sense of optimism, and the strict instruction not to tell anybody
I met that I was going to compete on *Chef Supreme*.

I already knew that was going to be difficult, considering I
was a nervous talker and flying made me extremely nervous.
And that, against all odds, the featured TV show blinking at me
when I booted up the in-flight media center on the screen in
front of me was *Chef Supreme*. "No way!" I yelped, then immediately glanced at the seat next to me. Good. Nobody was sitting
there. Ideally, nobody would sit there at all and I'd get two seats
all to myself to stretch out and prop up my feet and pretend I was
on my couch at home, with the exception of the pantsless part.

Not that I actually needed the extra space. *Chef Supreme* had
been kind enough to bump me up to business class, which marked
the first time I'd flown not crammed up against a stranger with a
peculiar smell ranging from strong onions to dirty diapers. I had

a big, cushy blue chair the size of a recliner all to myself, with leg room for days (at least for me, who was not particularly tall) and only one person next to me on the aisle. There was enough room between our seats and the row in front of us where, every time I had to nervous pee, I wouldn't have to ask them to get up so I could get by. The height of luxury.

Maybe *Chef Supreme*'s presence on the screen was a sign. A sign from the universe, or, as my mom would say, a sign from Grandma Ruth that she was thinking of me from her heavenly abode and would probably try to rig the contest in my favor, because as small and frail as she was, she was not above arguing with the Almighty to help her grandchildren get ahead. Would help from your ghostly grandmother be considered cheating?

Hopefully not. And hopefully, I wouldn't be the chef going home first, a major badge of shame. Fear coiled cold in my heart. I would probably be the first one going home. I didn't need to actually win: while the title of *Chef Supreme* and a big cash prize would be nice, finishing in the top few or distinguishing yourself from the competition in some way was often enough to attract interest from investors, which was my goal.

But if I went home *first*? I could just see my old boss Derek shaking his head with disappointment. *I knew Sadie didn't have what it takes to survive in the food world.* Kaitlyn clucking her tongue with feigned sorrow, her eyes lit up with glee. *So sad, I was totally rooting for her.* Investors frowning and saving their money for literally anyone else.

Somebody cleared their throat next to me. "Excuse me, are you okay?"

I realized I was shaking, my elbow jumping up and down on the armrest. "Fine." My voice sounded tinny. "Just nerves."

"I'm not a fan of flying, either." My seat shifted as they sat down beside me. I turned to get a better look at my seatmate. It was a guy probably my age. A *really cute* guy. "But I find it preferable to the forty-three-hour drive from Seattle to New York."

"Wow, you've driven it before?"

"No, I looked it up beforehand to remind myself why I'm on this plane." A smile tugged at the corners of his lips. "If you're wondering, it's also a three-day bus ride, a thirty-nine-day walk, or an eleven-day bicycle trip."

He looked vaguely familiar, but that might have been because he was so handsome, and all extremely good-looking people seem vaguely familiar since they're the ones splashed all over ads and billboards and the media. He had lush black hair, eyes that suggested East Asian ancestry, and broad shoulders. The black line of a tattoo poked out from beneath his black T-shirt, which seemed almost as if it had been tailored to his trim form. I was wondering if people got T-shirts tailored, but I was wondering more about the tattoo. I eyeballed it, ready to ask, but then hesitated. Was it rude to ask people about their tattoos?

Then I remembered his comment. "I was not wondering," I said. "But thank you anyway."

He shoved his laptop bag under the seat in front of him, then straightened up, folding his hands in his lap. And smiled. It was truly a glorious smile, but it was the hands that demanded all my attention. Not that I had a hand fetish (though really, as far as body part fetishes went, I could do worse than hands). No, his were covered in scars: a ropy one probably from a knife on his left middle finger and another one on his thumb; thick, rough burn scars on the backs. A current burn, shiny with healing, winked at me from his palm. I knew those hands. They looked like mine.

"Hey, you're a chef," I blurted.

He cast his eyes downward, trailing from my face to my chest to my lap. Under other circumstances I might tense up, but his gaze finally settled upon my own hands. "Hey, so are you."

Possibilities hit me, one after the other. He was very photogenic: you might even say the perfect person to put on television. Where did chefs go on television? *Chef Supreme*, of course.

What if we were both going on *Chef Supreme*?

He was flying in the same day and time as me. On the exact same flight *Chef Supreme* had booked for me. Sitting next to each other, meaning our tickets had probably been booked at the same time.

Oh my God, we're both going to be on Chef Supreme*!*

I took a deep, shaky breath. I couldn't tell him I was going to be a contestant this year. That was breaking the rules. If I was wrong about him being one, too, or if he was a stickler for the rules, I could get kicked off before I so much as started. That would be even worse than being the first one off. I'd be negative first. I'd be a cautionary tale passed down through the seasons. No investors wanted the cautionary tale.

Bold to assume any investors will want you even if you're not *the cautionary tale.*

"I'm Sadie," I said, giving him my scarred hand to shake.

He took it. His hand was warm and dry, each scar either a ridge or extra smooth like satin. His skin told a story. "I'm Luke."

I could feel his pulse beating in his wrist. I held on for an extra moment before letting him go. "Restaurant?"

"Many," he said. "You?"

"Same." So that was how we were playing it, huh? Maybe he'd just been fired, too, or he'd quit to come on *Chef Supreme*.

That was fine. If he didn't want to talk specifics, that meant I didn't have to, either. "What are you doing in New York?"

"I live there but am leaving some business negotiations in Seattle early for a new opportunity back home," he said. "Something came up at the last minute, and I just had to take it."

"Same here." We shared a smile. It was like we were speaking a secret language.

Except we'd be competing. The smile dropped off my face. I'd be battling against him for the *Chef Supreme* title and the massive cash prize. We'd be competitors.

Except lots of *Chef Supreme* contestants had hooked up in the past. Season four, Jane Simon and Joshua Martinez had been caught on camera, and they were still together. Neither had won, but they had their own restaurant now. Maybe Luke and I would—

I jumped as the flight attendant slammed the baggage compartment over my head, then jumped again as my screen started playing the flight safety video at what seemed like an unreasonably loud volume. I turned to Luke, ready to crack a joke about how at least we didn't have any hot pans to worry about, only to find him staring intently at the screen the way we were supposed to. Though I never worried too much, considering if the plane actually did crash, we were probably all going to die anyway and no number of inflatable slides was going to save us.

Still, I watched the video all the way through, sitting up extra straight in my seat in case he looked over. Then slouched back down as soon as the video ended, because good posture was exhausting.

Of course, with the safety video gone, *Chef Supreme* was back on-screen in its featured spot. "So," I said, as casually as I possibly could. "Have you ever watched this show?" Held my breath. Stared at his face, waiting for any telltale twitches or half smiles or glances away.

But he looked me straight in the eye. "I've been watching it a lot lately, actually."

I choked on air. That was as good as an admission, right? That he was going to be on the show with me? "So have I," I told him. "But I could always go for a rewatch."

And so, once we were sailing through the atmosphere in our thin metal tube, we commenced a rewatch of the latest season. Together, we watched rapt as the Austin-based chef Kevin Harris battled his way through cooking challenge after cooking challenge and vanquished competitor after competitor, including the chef I'd been rooting for. "I really admire the risk Helen took there," Luke would say. I'd respond, "The day after this episode aired, I went to work and did a special with that carrot-tahini soup, and it sold out by the second seating."

He wrinkled his nose every time the chefs cooked with fennel. I shivered with horror whenever they were given a dessert or baking challenge. We shrieked together, exchanging wide-eyed glances, when the front-runner was eliminated based on his teammate's mistake, even though we both knew it was coming. "Not fair," I said, just as Luke said, "Not right."

We were still looking into each other's eyes. My cheeks warmed. I couldn't see them, but I knew they were redder than a stop sign right now.

A stop sign was the last sign I wanted to give him.

He cleared his throat, his cheeks pinkening, too, just the tiniest bit. "I must say, I think the judges got it wrong there."

Soon I'd be serving those judges *my* food. Another thing I'd somehow managed not to think about. The judges on *Chef Supreme* were legendary: Lenore Smith and John Waterford, two of the country's most renowned chefs. They were both older, winners of endless James Beard Awards (the Oscars of food), and joined every season by a cast of rotating chefs usually themed for the episode.

I looked away before I could throw up on him. And not because of the turbulence.

On-screen, we moved to the next episode. Kevin Harris was cooking up a pot of his grandmother's jambalaya, which would become his signature recipe. The flight attendant bumped through the aisle beside me. The booze was free in business class, which was sweet. Our tray of food was sweet, also, but not in the way it was supposed to be.

"Do you think they used molasses on this chicken?" I asked Luke, cocking my head at the glistening brown lump on my plate. They might have taken the food out of the standard metal tray and plopped it on white porcelain, but that didn't make it taste any better. "Or is it just brown sugar and salt?"

Luke poked gingerly at his own chicken with his butter knife. "I think it might just be brown sugar and corn syrup."

It was either eat or starve. To distract ourselves while we choked this meal down, I asked, "What's your favorite food?"

"My favorite food?" He blinked at me. "What category of favorite food? Like, favorite food that I've cooked, or favorite food that I've eaten?"

"The best of the best," I said.

This smile was different than the one he'd given me before. It was smaller but more genuine somehow. "When I was little, we'd visit my halmoni in Korea every summer," he said. "Her house was busy and warm, and it always smelled like food, so different from my other grandparents' in Connecticut. And I could spend as much time in the kitchen as I wanted."

I took a swallow of my drink as we swam through puffy white clouds. At least the wine wasn't terrible.

"She'd make all the ingredients individually for her kimchi-jjigae," he went on. "Anchovy stock. Her own kimchi, which made the cellar smell like garlic and red pepper all the time. The pork shoulder simmering away. And when she'd mix it all together . . ." He trailed off, tipping his head back against the seat. It was the first movement he'd made over the course of his speaking; his hands rested still by his sides. "It was *everything*. Salty, sour, briny, rich, and just a tiny bit sweet from the sesame oil. I've been trying to make it for years, and mine has never turned out like hers."

My anxiety manifestation popped up out of nowhere, hovering invisibly over one of Luke's shoulders. *The boy doesn't know that the secret ingredient in every grandma's dish is love. He needs some more love in his life*, said Grandma Ruth, eying me beadily. *Maybe yours. Is he Jewish?*

I shook my head, banishing her back to the ether. "I get the feeling," I said. "I can make a mean matzah ball soup, with truffles and homemade broth boiled for hours from the most expensive free-range chickens, and somehow it never tastes as good as the soup my grandma would whip up out of canned broth and frozen vegetables."

Damn straight, Grandma Ruth said smugly.

Didn't I just banish you? I thought, but it was no use.

"So is that the best thing you've ever eaten?" Luke asked. "Your grandma's matzah ball soup?"

I shook my head. I opened my mouth, about to tell him about Julie Chee's grilled cheese with kimchi and bacon and how it hadn't just tasted of tart, sour kimchi and crunchy, smoky bacon and rich, melted cheese but also belonging and bedazzlement and all these feelings that didn't have names, like the dizzy, accomplished feeling you'd get after a Saturday night dinner rush when you were a little drunk but not a lot drunk because you had to wake up in time for Sunday brunch service, but then everything that happened with Derek and the Green Onion kind of changed how I felt about it. Painted over it with colors just a tiny bit off.

So instead I told him about a meal I'd had in Lima, Peru, after backpacking up and down Machu Picchu. "Olive tofu with octopus, which you wouldn't think to put together, or at least I wouldn't have," I said. The olive tofu had been soft and almost impossibly creamy, tasting cleanly of olives, and the octopus had been meaty and crispy and charred on the outside, soft on the inside.

"So it sounds like your feelings about that meal are all wrapped up with your exhilaration at climbing Machu Picchu," he said. "Just like my feelings about my kimchi-jjigae are all tied up with my feelings about learning to love the kitchen and the love of my halmoni."

"We're not trying to feed people food," I said. "We're trying to feed them feelings."

It sounded a lot wiser in my head, but his eyebrows raised in what looked like an impressed sort of way. "That's true. It's so true." His mouth opened, looking like he wanted to say something else, but he closed it.

"So do you cook mostly Korean food?" I asked.

A cloud passed over his figurative sun. "No," he said. "No, mostly not."

Silence fell over our row, unless you counted the clatter of
the flight attendants cleaning up after the seats behind us in
their big metal cart. Should I press? If we were going to be living
in the same house for the next six weeks, I might as well get to
know him now. "Why not? It seems like that's where the love is
for you."

He snorted. "You've known me for all of a couple hours
and—" *How dare you presume you can tell me what to do with my life and
my career?* "—you're absolutely right."

I stared at him. He stared at me. His eyes were such a dark
brown they were nearly black, like the darkest chocolate, sweet
and also bitter, the kind of chocolate I loved to suck on at the
end of the night when I couldn't bear the thought of any other
food . . .

"Can I take that for you, hon?" the flight attendant said
loudly. I pulled my eyes away from Luke, my cheeks heating up
again.

"Sure. Thanks."

By the time the flight attendant trundled away with our re-
fuse, the mood had changed, the way creamy caramel left too
long on the stove turns into a sticky glob. "All right, then," Luke
said. "We still have half a season to go, don't we?"

We didn't make it. Not in terms of surviving the flight—the
plane landed safely and everything. In terms of making it through
the rest of *Chef Supreme* season six. We'd barely made it to the pen-
ultimate episode when the screen flickered off and the pilot came
over the loudspeaker to thank us for flying with her and to say she
hoped we had a nice day.

Luke and I walked down the ramp together, then stood next

to each other at the baggage carousel. "So do you have terrible taste, or do you think Helen was robbed?" I asked him.

He snorted. "I don't think there's a way to answer that question without sounding terrible. Would you rather eat Kevin's jambalaya or Helen's upscale Frito pie?"

The rubber belt of the baggage carousel whirred to a start as we debated; amidst all the bright airport lights and loud chatter of the crowds, our bags started rolling through. I stared at the succession of black suitcases and wished, suddenly, that they'd slow down a little. It might have been the first time that somebody in an airport ever wished for things to move more slowly, but I wasn't ready for the day to be over yet. Not ready for us to potentially become competitors.

"Hey," Luke said.

I waited for him to continue: maybe with *hey, there's my bag*, or *hey, you've got something on your face*. But he didn't say anything. It was like the rest of it had gotten stuck in his throat.

"Hey, what?" I said.

He swallowed audibly. "Hey, you said this is your first time in New York, right?"

I must have mentioned that on the plane during our *Chef Supreme* marathon. "Yup. It's too bad I won't get to see much of it."

He wrinkled his brow. "Why not?"

Because I'd be in the *Chef Supreme* house the whole time, not allowed out with the exception of official *Chef Supreme* business. Shouldn't he understand that, if he was going to be a competitor, too?

Maybe I'd gotten this wrong. Let the fantasy in my head run

away without me. Maybe he was just a normal chef in town for a while.

I cleared my throat. "I'm going to be kind of . . . um, secluded from society," I said. It was really hard to explain this without getting into it for real and potentially jeopardizing my contract. "For the next six weeks, it's safe to say I won't be getting out much."

"Interesting," he said. "Well. Then you should probably see the city now."

My bag was coming toward me, easily noticeable thanks to the big neon orange ribbon my mom had made me tie around the handle, but I didn't move toward it. "What do you mean?"

He smiled. The lights shone brighter. "There's somewhere I'd like to take you." The smile dimmed. "Did that sound creepy? It wasn't intended to be creepy. I meant, I'd like to take you somewhere and feed you." Dimmed a little more. "No, that was definitely worse."

"I get it," I said. Were those birds singing in the airport? I looked around, but the only bird I saw was a disgruntled-looking pigeon trying not to get stepped on, so it seemed more likely that the singing was all in my head.

"I would love to go somewhere and get fed by you. The only thing is . . ." I couldn't be late to the *Chef Supreme* house. Not only was I contractually obligated to be there this afternoon, but I didn't want to be the last person to choose my bunk. If Luke was a fellow competitor, wouldn't he be worried about the same thing? "Can we go somewhere near where I'm going? It's in Astoria, Queens?"

The smile was back. I tingled inside. "I know just the place."

He hadn't said he was also going to Astoria, which made me

deflate a little. The words were on the tip of my tongue: all I had to do was share the address I was going to, because if he was a fellow competitor, he'd be going there, too.

And yet I didn't say them. Maybe I didn't want to know just yet.

A half hour later, our Uber deposited us onto the streets of Queens. Well, a sidewalk. "Is it okay for me to drop you off here?" the driver said again, an apology in his voice. "All the construction on the road, it would make it difficult for me to get to my next rider on time . . ."

"It's really fine. We don't mind a little walking," Luke assured him. We thanked the driver and said goodbye as he took our luggage out of the trunk then drove off.

Luke and I trundled down the block, our bags rattling over the cracked sidewalk behind us as we passed people sitting on stoops and smoking, fruit carts piled with bright, sweet-smelling apples and bananas with ridiculously expensive prices stickered on them, and bus stops flashing the number of minutes to go until the next one pulled up. Something that sounded like a train rattled in the distance, and the sound of Spanish music floated toward us on the breeze. I bopped my head to it, then stopped when I realized how stupid I must look.

"It's just over here," he said, looking over his shoulder. Somehow he'd gotten ahead of me. Navigating this sidewalk with my bags was harder than I'd thought. "Are you okay?"

I sighed dramatically. "My bags are just trying to kill me."

And though I insisted I'd been kidding, he gallantly took my big suitcase and wheeled our two bags over the bumpy sidewalk at once, maneuvering deftly through the crowd. I kept glancing sidelong at him to check out those muscled arms pulling on the

bags, or the way his chiseled jaw cut a line into the sky, only to
catch him glancing sidelong at me, too.

My romantic history was, to put it nicely, a bit of a disaster.
Take your pick of failed relationships. My pot-smoking beau in
high school, who ghosted me before ghosting was even a thing
after I burst into tears mid-coitus (RIP, Grandma). The guy I
went out with in the two years of college I attended before dropping out, who made no secret of the fact that he thought I was
stupid (and went on to get rejected by every law school he ap-
plied to, which to this day brings me great pleasure). The wait-
ress at Atelier Laurent who made me realize that maybe I wasn't
entirely straight . . . but that she was. The series of hookups in my
early- to mid-twenties that weren't all that satisfying but that
were the only thing my schedule would support, considering I
was working pretty much every night until two a.m. To put it
kindly, I had a history of making bad decisions when it came to
romance.

And, depending on who you asked later, Luke would be no
exception.

3

LUKE ROLLED OUR SUITCASES TO A STOP IN FRONT of . . . a convenience store. The front windows were bright with orange signs advertising fifty percent off milk and eggs, the spaces between them offering glimpses of shelves stocked with basics and cigarettes piled behind a bulletproof glass enclosure. "Here," he said.

I eyed it dubiously. I could hear the fluorescent lights buzzing from the sidewalk, see the black specks where flies had gotten stuck inside and died. "Here?"

He was already wheeling our luggage inside. "Trust me."

"I just met you," I said, but I wasn't about to lose all my best clothes or my retainer, which to be honest probably cost more than all of my clothes combined, so I followed my suitcase inside.

Which did not clear up my confusion. I trailed my fingertips along a shelf of soup cans and came away with dust. The young man sitting behind the glass partition, staring down at his phone, didn't so much as look over at us.

I followed Luke back to the beer shelf. Did he think I was that cheap a date? The beer wasn't even cold. I wished I could say this was a new low. "Maybe I should get going after all," I said.

He grabbed the shelf and pulled. I jerked back, ready to shield my head from the torrent of beer . . .

. . . but the shelf had shifted smoothly to the side. A door. A secret door in the back of the convenience store. I leaned forward, curious. Laughter floated out from the doorway, mingled with the clink of glasses.

Luke glanced at me sidelong, his lips twitching with a smile. "It's a speakeasy. Pretty cool, right?"

The space inside was dark, but not in a way that felt menacing or creepy: with its small leather booths, TVs hanging over the bar, and paintings of foreign landscapes, the room was cramped yet cozy. There weren't many people in the room, which wasn't that surprising considering it was still afternoon on a weekday, but the few people who were there were men in their sixties or seventies. Including the bartender, whose face split into a wide grin as he saw me and Luke. "Luke! Luke, come in."

I floated behind him as he walked up to the bar and hugged the bartender over the polished wood. "This is Sadie," Luke said, touching me gently on the shoulder. My whole arm buzzed with the connection. It was so busy buzzing that I missed the bartender's name, which made me feel bad as he reached over to shake my hand. His was rough and dry and maybe even more calloused than mine.

"It is a pleasure to meet you, Sadie," said the bartender. I went to pull out a stool, but he shook his head, the corners of his eyes wrinkling even more than the rest of his extremely wrinkled face. "No, you two will have the booth of honor."

The booth of honor turned out to be the booth tucked into the corner of the bar, secluded from the one next to it by a wooden screen. "The booth of honor," Luke said, sounding amused as he looked over. "How kind of you. Well, let's get drinks first. Sadie, is there anything you want?"

I opened my mouth to request a sparkling water, then hesitated. I wouldn't let anything slip after just one drink. I could use a drink, really, to tamp down that voice in my head that kept insisting I wasn't good enough for this. For *Chef Supreme*. For a good guy who liked me. "You know what's good here. You tell me."

"Yes." Luke clapped his hands together. "You will not regret this. Sadie and I will have your special, please."

We stood and watched together as the bartender mixed up something clear and green and packed with green leaves that looked like mint or basil. I craned my neck, trying to catch sight of what he was pouring in, but none of the bottles were labeled.

Luke caught me craning. "I think he makes all his liquor in his bathtub," he said, grinning.

The bartender spun around. "I do not!" Then beamed, exposing a missing canine tooth. "Only the finest buckets for *my* liquor."

Whatever he'd put in it, it made me swoon. Both because of how strong it was and how good it tasted. Fortunately, we were already seated in our booth of honor, so I only slumped back against the cracked leather banquette and not off a barstool. "Damn. That's good stuff."

"Right?" Luke slurped his appreciatively. I wished I knew what was in it so I could replicate it myself—it was sweet and tart and a little sour, with fresh herbaceous notes from the mint and basil and some other curly herb I couldn't identify in concert with everything else—but when I'd probed the bartender, he'd just given me his gap-toothed smile and told me the recipe was a family secret. "I've never seen it anywhere else. It's like a mojito on steroids."

"It's what a mojito grew up dreaming it would be," I said. "The way kids in culinary school assume they're going to graduate and get their own cooking show on TV and immediately become a superstar."

Luke chuckled dryly. "Well, this mojito made it. Unlike Brian, who thought he could leap directly from garde-manger to creating his own specials. In three days."

We took some time trading stories of our worst interns and stages before Luke's tone sobered up. Which was kind of funny, considering our glasses were mostly empty by this point. "I haven't fulfilled my own dreams yet," he said. "And that doesn't count my dream from age five, when I decided I wanted to become a fire truck."

"Not a fireman?" I asked.

"No. The truck itself."

"Sounds fun."

"Right?" he said, perking up a bit . . . then drooping again. "I've been working in fancy, expensive restaurants all my life, but all I've ever wanted was to cook my halmoni's food."

"Could you cook her food in a fancy expensive restaurant?" I asked. "Somewhere like Atomix?" That was one of the buzziest restaurants right now, a high-end Korean restaurant in the heart of New York I'd been dying to go to.

Luke shook his head. "Atomix is great. I've been there several times, and each time it wows me. There are so many fantastic upscale Korean restaurants in New York. But I don't love cooking high-end food only for people who can afford the prices. I want a place that welcomes everyone. Where everybody can be comfortable. Where I can cook exciting, experimental food for anyone who wants it." He paused. "It's not about the market. It's about me."

I wanted to say *then do it*, but I knew more than anyone it wasn't nearly as easy as that. "I hope you get to do that someday," I told him sincerely.

"Me, too," he said. "My father doesn't, of course."

I waved a hand in the air. "Fuck your dad," I said, which was maybe not the best thing to say. *Thanks, delicious green drink.* "I didn't mean that. Of course you shouldn't fuck your dad." *Aaaaand that made it worse.* "Okay, I really didn't mean it *that* way. I—"

"I get it," Luke said dryly. There was a bit of a British affect coming through his voice now, the way my mom's vowels rounded New Yawkily when she got drunk or really angry. "Let's change the subject."

Had I already messed this up? Well. It wasn't surprising. Another one of my terrible romantic decisions had been dating my boss at the Green Onion. Chef Anders. Derek. And we'd already seen how well *that* turned out.

"Hello? Earth to Sadie." Luke was waving his hand in front of my face. "I think we could both use something to eat to absorb some of that drink. Is there anything you don't like?"

A warm glow suffused me. Okay, maybe I hadn't entirely fucked this up. Yet. I'd better stay away from the topic of his father. "I like everything. Is there a menu?"

"Menu?" He sounded shocked, though his lips quirked playfully. "I don't need a menu. It's a bit early for dinner, but we could do a full meal anyway? The banchan here are excellent."

I did love all the small dishes that came with a traditional Korean meal, and I *was* pretty hungry, but I couldn't stay that long. I was pushing it as it was. I was already definitely not going to be the first person at the *Chef Supreme* house; I might actually end up the last one there, relegated to the least desirable bunk bed above the designated snorer of the season.

And yet somehow this all seemed worth it.

Still . . . "Let's just get some snacks," I said. "I should really get going soon."

"We can do snacks," Luke said, and the way his face drooped just the tiniest bit was maybe the most adorable thing I'd ever seen.

"Let's do snacks."

And snacks, we did. We consumed japchae, stir-fried sweet potato noodles with shredded veggies and beef, that were sweet and savory and wonderfully chewy. Ddukbokki, chewy cylinders of rice cake, soft and springy cakes of sweet ground fish, more veggies, and sweet and spicy gochujang sauce. Soondae, a sausage stuffed with noodles, barley, and pig blood, which I had to say gave me slight pause (and made my Jewish grandmother shriek with terror), but which had the most interesting mix of textures. We cleansed our palates with hobakjuk, a porridge made from glutinous rice and the sweetest steamed pumpkin I'd ever tasted, and finished up with hotteok, sweet, crunchy fried pancakes filled with cinnamon, honey, brown sugar, and peanuts.

I was glad I'd worn leggings for the flight, because my belly was definitely rounder than it was when I left. I pushed the last bite of hotteok into my mouth anyway. "Mmmmph," I said, because I couldn't exactly do words right now. "So good."

We both marinated in our fullness for a minute, enjoying a

comfortable silence over the table. Finally, I said, "Is this the kind of restaurant you want?"

Luke shook his head. "I love what they're doing here, but I want to play with tradition more," he said. "Don't you?"

That was what dishes like my matzah ball ramen were all about. "That's the fun of food, to me. I want to take things my grandma did, or my ancestors did, and make those things new and fresh and exciting."

His smile broke over his face like the dawning of the sun. I smiled back, and it felt like the dawning of the sun inside me, too.

And then my phone buzzed in my pocket. As much as I wanted to ignore it, I slipped it out and took a quick look. My sister, Rachel: Are you there yet???? What's it like??

Forcing myself to ignore her total ignorance of punctuation mark etiquette, I texted her back. Not yet. Soon. And in there I won't have my phone, so I won't be able to tell you!!!!!!

It was with great reluctance that I looked back at Luke. Not reluctance to look at him, because I could put him in a frame and hang him over my couch and never get sick of looking at him. Reluctance to tell him what I knew I had to say. "I have to go. I'm already late."

"No problem," Luke said. He pushed himself out from the bench and held his hand out for me.

"Don't we have to pay?" I took his hand. Squeezed extra tight as I left the booth so I could feel every callus, every scar, try to learn their stories.

"I'll come back and pay after. They know me." Luke gallantly grabbed my luggage again. "I'd rather not make you late. Then you won't want to see me again."

He . . . wanted to see me again?

Maybe I wouldn't have to frame him and hang him up after all. Maybe he'd be sitting there on the couch with me under the frame, his feet kicked up on the coffee table, not wearing a shirt. All the time. That would be my new house rule: no shirts allowed if you're Luke.

I let myself fantasize about it until we left the bar and were walking out through the convenience store, where one befuddled-looking young man was browsing through the shelf of vitamins. Outside, I stopped. Looked at Luke. This was the moment of truth: either he'd be a fellow competitor or he wouldn't. "This is where I'm going," I said, and told him the address, and held my breath. *Please be going to the same address, please be going to the same—*

"I'll walk you there and then grab an Uber the rest of the way into the city," Luke said. He grabbed his phone.

All of my hopes crashed at once, deflating me like a popped balloon. Maybe this was why I hadn't asked earlier: because I hadn't wanted to hear he wasn't going to be with me for the next six weeks.

"I think I have to go the rest of the way on my own," I said. If he wasn't going to be competing with me, then I didn't think I could bring him to the house. I couldn't take the chance of breaking my contract. "I'll explain later. Right now I'm bound by a nondisclosure agreement."

A gritty wind ruffled his hair. Behind him, music blasted bright and brassy through an apartment window. "All right. So this is goodbye."

"Goodbye for now," I said.

He already had his phone in his hand. As he finished making his Uber request, he asked, "Can I give you my number?"

"Definitely!" I said, taking my phone out and quickly entering it in. Then I deflated a little bit. "Just . . . for the next six weeks or so, I won't be reachable. I won't have my phone or my laptop or any access to the Internet. I swear I won't be ignoring you."

His eyebrow was raised a bit skeptically. When he spoke, he had that British trace to his words again. "Right, you mentioned that on the plane. That's . . . interesting."

I could practically see his thoughts. *This is a weird way to let me down. To say she doesn't want to see me again.* And I couldn't let him think that. Not when I was picturing his feet propped up on my coffee table.

"Say—" He was starting to say my name when I kissed him. His lips rested still against mine for a moment before beginning to move, and then there was another explosion. Internal, this time, of sparks and heat and sheer, growling *want*. He cradled my face in his hands; I could feel every ridge and smooth burn scar against the soft skin of my cheeks and jaw. He pulled me into him, nipping gently at my lower lip before his lips melted again into mine.

He gasped as I sank my fingers into his hair, and then I gasped as he pressed a line of gentle kisses over my jawline, and he shivered as I flicked my tongue against his earlobe, and I shivered as he—

"Uh, hey, man? You Luke?"

We broke apart, panting and flushed. There was a black car. Luke's Uber. The driver hung out the window, gaping at us. A woman walking a fluffy white dog passed by, and both she and the dog stared at us, too.

"Um, yes," Luke said, his cheeks a deep pink. "I'm Luke. That's me." His eyes flicked to me apologetically. "Er . . ."

"Go ahead." I smiled bravely. "I'll call you. In six weeks. I promise I'll explain everything."

"Um . . . okay." He hesitated for a moment, then leaned in for one more kiss. I drank in the feel of his rough jaw against my smooth skin, the feel of his mouth on mine . . .

And then he was loading his suitcase into the trunk, opening the back door of the car. Looking back over at me. Running over for a final kiss, just a brief brush of his lips on mine, one that left me wanting more and more and more and more.

And then he was gone, off into the hazy afternoon. I stood and watched him go, feeling like a fourteen-year-old girl who'd just been kissed for the first time, blushing, wondering if he still felt my lips on his, too.

4

I FOLLOWED THE GPS ON MY PHONE AS IT DIRECTED me down a few blocks, bodegas and buses fading into big brick apartment complexes and shady garden plots and playgrounds swarming with cheering kids. By the time I arrived at the *Chef Supreme* house, I'd talked myself down a little bit. I couldn't afford to spend this entire competition yearning for Luke when I had to focus on the food. *He was just a guy,* I told myself, which was not convincing at all, because he wasn't just a guy. Not to me, even this quickly. So then I argued, *You are about to arrive at the* Chef Supreme *house. It's been your dream to be on* Chef Supreme *for years, and placing might be the only thing that could possibly dig you out of your hole and even get you your own restaurant. So buck up and focus on that.*

I took a deep breath as I paused outside the building's doorway. A concrete gargoyle glared down at me from an alcove above, as if judging my T-shirt and leggings. I'd packed my favorite clothes and shoes, things much nicer than my plane outfit, but Adrianna had advised me that wardrobe would fill in "as suitable." Meaning, basically, if wardrobe thought you dressed like garbage, they'd take care of it themselves.

Chef Supreme was supposed to take care of everything else, too. They provided toiletries and entertainment: cable TV, board games, and lots of books to fill our minimal free time. They'd be stocking our kitchen and giving us limited funds to order in, too. We wouldn't have our phones or Internet access.

That reminded me. I slipped my phone out of my pocket. It was at thirty-three percent battery, which I took as a good omen. Three was my lucky number, and the only way you could get better than two of them in a row was three, but my phone didn't go up that high. I sent my sister and parents a quick message in our group chat. About to go into the *Chef Supreme* house! They're going to take my phone. Wish me luck!!!

My parents took forever to respond to texts, but Rachel responded immediately. Omg Sadie!!! All the good luck!!! Don't cut your finger off on the first day!!!

Now I was worrying I would cut my finger off on the first day. I could just imagine the judges, stately Lenore Smith and John Waterford with their old-school training and helmets of silver hair, frowning down at my dish. *Do you expect us to . . . eat this finger? Why would you put an inedible garnish on the plate?* My battery was now at thirty-one percent, which added up to four, which was not a lucky number. I took another deep breath. This was going to be my legacy. The four-fingered *Chef Supreme* loser.

I messaged Rachel back, Gee thanks!!! You're the worst!!! then powered my phone off before she could reply.

The *Chef Supreme* house was not technically a house, merely a very large apartment. I entered the lobby of the large brick building, passed a line of brass mailboxes and a few beat-up leather chairs, and was directed by a peppy *Chef Supreme* assistant to the penthouse.

I ran over the facts I already knew as I rode up in the elevator to the fifteenth floor. Every season of *Chef Supreme* had twelve contestants flown in from all over the country. They were professional chefs in some capacity, but not celebrities or big award-winners yet. I'd likely be one of the younger contestants at twenty-seven, but not as young as the youngest contestant ever, who'd taken part at twenty-two right out of culinary school (and gone home first, to everyone else's satisfaction). The gender breakdown was usually slightly in favor of men, so we'd probably have something like seven or eight men and four or five women.

The elevator opened. I stepped directly into my new home for the next (hopefully, hopefully) full six weeks.

The first thing I noticed was the light. The entryway led into an enormous, two-story great room, with brushed concrete floors and huge windows that poured in the sun. At one end sat a grouping of couches and armchairs around a coffee table and TV; at the other end was a shiny chrome kitchen, breakfast bar, and long, sprawling table with seats for twelve. Above, I could just see a railing, suggesting that there was a space on the second floor that looked out over this central area.

The second thing I noticed was the people. I counted them quickly: six. So I was here about halfway through the arrivals, which wasn't terrible—I wouldn't get the best bunk, but I wouldn't get the worst one, either.

As if she could read my mind, the closest woman to me said, "You should go pick your bunk. The emptiest room is upstairs to the left."

I nodded in thanks and climbed the steep spiral staircase that led up to the second floor. Up here, exposed pipes ran along the ceiling, and the walls were hung with the kind of art I'd never really understood, abstract splotches of color that looked like paint randomly thrown on a canvas. I didn't really think of art as art if I could do it myself. And the only art skills I had were on a plate, so it wasn't like the bar was so high.

The hallway split in two with a huge mural of blue and silver slashes; as instructed, I turned left. There was a full bathroom, then the bedroom. It looked much the same as it had on previous seasons of *Chef Supreme*, only smaller because it was squashed into an apartment. Plain white walls. Three sets of bunk beds. A double closet. Some drawers.

I did a quick calculation of the situation. The middle bunk was clearly the worst place to be: less privacy than the others, the light from the door glaring you in the face, people stumbling by you on their way to the side bunks. The two people who'd chosen already had clearly made the same calculation, since the left top bunk was taken, as was the bottom right one. I preferred a top bunk to a bottom, so I tossed my bag up there on the right and claimed it. Claimed some closet space and a couple drawers, too.

Maybe my roommates would go home first and leave me some extra room.

Back downstairs, nobody new had arrived. I took a seat at one of the breakfast barstools and grabbed some cheese and crackers off a platter to give me something to do with my hands. Everybody was engaged in a debate about whether culinary school was necessary or not, which seemed mostly to be them trashing their straight-out-of-culinary-school interns, but as soon as I sat down they stopped mid-sentence, and all of their eyes swiveled to me like I was their straight-out-of-culinary-school intern and I'd walked right in on them trashing me.

I opened my mouth, ready to introduce myself, but someone else beat me to the punch. "Sadie Brooke Rosen," she said. The girl who'd pointed me toward the bedroom. She was small and pointy everywhere, with deep brown skin and black hair shaved close to her head. "From Seattle. Cooked at the Green Onion, focuses on food with a Jewish twist."

She stopped and stared at me again, as if waiting for a prize. How did she know who I was? "Um, yes?" I said. "That is me?"

She clapped her hands together. No smile, just satisfaction. "I knew it. I researched every chef I could find who might possibly be on this season, along with their cooking style, so that I'd be prepared."

She blinked at me, eyes dark and round and serious. I had no idea what to say. That must have been hundreds, if not thousands, of chefs. And how had she even found info on us?

"It's okay to be creeped out a little," someone else volunteered. "We all were, but that's just Nia. She has a photographic memory or something." Stuck out a hand for me to shake. "I'm Kel. Pronouns are they/them."

Kel's words had a rote, rehearsed sort of feel to them. They must have said their pronouns a lot to people prying about their gender. "Nice to meet you."

"Likewise." Kel leaned back on their stool, grinning, and clasped their hands behind their head, nestling their fingers in their pale purple hair. Piercings were scattered all over their face, nose, lip, and ears, glittering under the lights.

I turned back to Nia, who was still watching me with those solemn eyes. "So what does Kel cook?"

Nia's eyes lit up. She ran a hand over her head. "Upscale Appalachian food!"

"Appalachian food?"

"It's not given its proper due," Kel said. "But it's just as rich and diverse and interesting as every other cuisine."

I didn't know a ton about Appalachian food, but I knew it incorporated foods native to the Appalachian region and was sometimes stereotypically associated with times of hardship, when families had to feed a lot of people with very little. Buckwheat cakes. Vinegar pie. Stews and rabbits. Vegetables like morels and ramps eaten fresh, or others canned in creative ways. "I can't wait to see it," I said, then turned to the silent majority. Four guys, sitting side by side on the couch. Two smiled and waved at me, the others gave me bro nods. "Hi, I'm Sadie."

"We're Joe," said the guy on the right. He looked to be somewhere from twenty-five to thirty-five, with hair of no distinguishable color, with a potbelly and loafers. He reminded me a little bit, looks-wise, of Bobby Flay.

I blinked at them. Was this some joke I wasn't getting? I glanced down, seeing if maybe they were a single four-headed organism connected by the legs, but no.

"We're all named Joe," said the guy on the left. This Joe was older than the other three Joes, with leathery skin and a thin mustache.

"We gave them nicknames," Nia said brightly. "From right to left, we've got Vanilla Joe, Bald Joe, Kangaroo Joe, and Old Joe!"

Old Joe took a long drink of something brown. "I did not get any say in this nickname."

"Neither did I," said Bald Joe.

"Okay, this is going to require a little explanation," I said. "Bald Joe and Old Joe are pretty obvious, but . . ."

"I gave Kangaroo Joe his nickname because all I could find when I looked him up was that he'd won a kangaroo cooking challenge at one of those bars that specializes in cooking exotic meats," Nia chirped.

"Kangaroos are the deer of Australia," said Kangaroo Joe.

"Okay." I glanced over at Potbelly and Loafers. "And Vanilla Joe?"

"His signature recipe on his food truck involves a vanilla sauce on a hot dog," Nia said.

"It's an artisan sausage, not a hot dog," said Vanilla Joe. "And the sauce is technically an aioli."

"Okay, Vanilla Joe," Kel said. Their lips twitched, and I suspected the reasoning behind his nickname had nothing to do with the vanilla sauce on his food truck.

"It's the season of the Joes," Nia said. "Oh! I think I just heard the door open."

Over the next couple hours, I ate my weight in cheese and met four of the other five contestants. There was Ernesto, a serious-looking guy in his thirties who cooked Tex-Mex, heavy on the Mex. Oliver, who cooked California cuisine. Mercedes, who cooked modern Filipino food. Megan, a solidly built woman with a buzz cut who cooked what she called "eclectic food" with a Chinese twist.

I was absolutely going to forget everybody's names. The only ones who were really sticking so far were Nia and Kel, who both still sat by my sides. I'd watched with fascination as Nia named every contestant down to their cooking styles and last names. Probably a good one to befriend, her.

"Have you noticed?" said Nia. Her hands were folded in her lap, but they fluttered up often to rub her head, twist an earlobe, or chew on a fingernail. "Have you noticed that there are as many Joes in this room as women right now?"

We all exchanged glances. It was true. Four Joes, four women: me, Nia, Mercedes, and Megan.

Each of the Joes had a different reaction. Kangaroo Joe looked apologetic. Old Joe, tanned and leathery, shrugged with his palms up like, *well, that's the way it is*. Bald Joe, who had a goatee thick enough to make up for his lack of scalp hair, raised his eyebrows.

And Vanilla Joe smirked. It wasn't his fault that the number of Joes and women in this room was equal, but that stupid smirk made my blood run hot anyway. How hard would it be to show some surprise or sympathy at how women were still under-represented in the culinary industry? How our labor was valued in the kitchen at home, but devalued professionally? *Cooks are women, but chefs are men.* I couldn't count the number of times I'd heard that lobbed at my back. At my first job on the line, Atelier Laurent, Kaitlyn and I had spent half our nights rolling our eyes at each other, silently reminding the other that it wasn't us who were crazy, it was the industry that—

The front door flew open, banging into the wall. My attention immediately turned to the entryway. This had to be contestant twelve, the last person we'd be competing against for the title of Chef Supreme, the fame, and the prize money.

And there in the doorway stood Kaitlyn Avilleira, her light brown hair mussed, panting and out of breath, probably because she'd just smoked at least two cigarettes downstairs. I blinked with surprise. Had I literally just summoned the person I'd least like to see?

Arghhhhhhhhh.

I came back to the situation in time for Kaitlyn to notice me. She didn't look any more thrilled than I was. First there were the telltale signs of unpleasant surprise—those plush lips widening in a hint of a grimace; pert nose wrinkling at the tip—and then the cover-up—lips widening further into an enormous gummy smile. "Sadie, fancy meeting you here!" she exclaimed.

The wheels of her rolly bag made almost a roar against the brushed concrete floor as she moved toward me to swoop me into a hug. I let her do it, preparing my lips for just as fake a smile as soon as she pulled back. "Kaitlyn, great to see you!"

There was steel in her blue eyes. "I hope you get second place." A laugh went up around the room, but she was deadly serious. Then again, that's something I would say to everybody else here except maybe Vanilla Joe.

I hoped he went home first.

It took a while for her to introduce herself to everyone. She repeated everybody's name after each person said it to her, pausing for a moment after as if scrawling it down somewhere in her memory, then flashing a brilliant smile at them. Everybody smiled back, of course. It was really amazing how she did this, immediately getting everybody to like her so easily.

It just made me dislike her more.

After that, I expected her to head upstairs with her bag and put her stuff away, but she just looked around at us with a smug expression on her face. "Have you guys heard the big news?"

I hated when people said things like that. How were we supposed to know what the big news was? So I didn't say anything as the others shook their heads, saying that we had no phones, how could we possibly have any news.

"It broke late," Kaitlyn said, leaning in to give the feeling that her words were a big secret. "Like, right before I came up. That's why I'm so late. I couldn't get off of Twitter!" She let out a brittle laugh. "John Waterford had a heart attack a week ago."

Gasps sucked all the air from the room. John Waterford had been a mainstay of *Chef Supreme* since season one. Alongside Lenore Smith, his honed palate had judged every contestant on *Chef Supreme*.

We all wanted to ask it, but the only one blunt enough was Nia. "Is he dead?"

Kaitlyn shook her head, which made me breathe a sigh of relief. Even more than Lenore Smith, I'd so looked forward to John Waterford's thoughtful chewing of my food. And then she said, "But . . ." and my heart dropped, because nothing good ever came after a but like that. "But he had to bow out this season. At least that's what all the rumors are saying. Obviously, the official *Chef Supreme* account is saying nothing but giving good wishes for his recovery."

Silence hung heavy over the room. Was *Chef Supreme* even the same show without John Waterford?

"Who are they replacing him with?" Kel asked. "Any rumors to that regard?"

Kaitlyn shrugged. "A million. But nothing definite yet."

My fingers twitched, wanting to google and check for myself. I hadn't realized how strange and alienating it would be not to have my phone. To not have the information of the world on demand, as usual. We really took it for granted. It was like we were on another planet in here.

So we took it in the only direction we could: speculation. Kel leaned in, crossing their legs. "Because they already have Lenore, it's got to be another man, because God forbid a man doesn't get to judge our food." Besides the host, who was also a man and judged the food but wasn't officially considered a judge. It was complicated.

Vanilla Joe, steadily becoming my least favorite person in the room, snorted and rolled his eyes. Kangaroo Joe glanced at him sidelong from their positions on the couch, then said extra loud, like he wanted to show us that all Joes weren't the same, "I think equal representation in the culinary world is *important.*"

"At least we have more women than Joes now," Nia said.

Kaitlyn cleared her throat. "*I* bet they'll choose somebody young and hot."

Old Joe gave a disgusted-sounding sigh, but that didn't stop Kaitlyn from going on.

"They've already got the establishment vote with Lenore Smith. I feel like they're going to want someone more hip."

From there the conversation went wild, with us naming pretty much every young, hot chef we could think of. As we spoke, the sun outside our enormous window went down in spectacular fashion, showering pinks and golds and blues all over the New York City skyline. I spared it only a glance or two. We had more important things to think about.

Eventually, everybody started yawning, and the assistant popped up from the lobby to let us know we'd have to be up at five tomorrow. "You'll need to be outside at a quarter to six to be driven to the *Chef Supreme* studios for your first day," she chirped. "Have a good night's sleep!"

Like there was any chance of that. Still, the group broke up as people called dibs on the shower and went to change into pajamas. Kaitlyn, though, went the opposite direction, toward the terrace for what I could only assume was a cigarette break.

I followed. Our building wasn't right on the waterfront, but we were high up enough where we could see the river from here. Manhattan's lights sparkled against it, red and yellow and green. Megan and Ernesto were out here already, thin coils of smoke stretching above them into the clouds, so I pulled Kaitlyn to the side. She looked remarkably chill about being manhandled like that. "Hey, I didn't know you smoked," she said, pulling out a cigarette. "Want a light?"

"No, thanks." I watched as she inhaled, her shoulders visibly relaxing. Maybe I *should* take up smoking.

No. No, that was not the point of being out here. I leaned in even closer, so that I could see every pore on her face. And there were a lot. Everybody was better-looking from far away. "You're not going to tell anyone about what happened with me and the Green Onion, are you?"

She exhaled in a low whoosh, enveloping us both in a cloud of smoke. Now we were really hidden from view. "Of course not," she said. "Who do you take me for?"

Someone who really wants to win, I didn't say. She was in possession of information that could, if not get me disqualified, at least shake the foundation of where we stood to compete. She could make it hard for me to advance in this competition. And one less person advancing in the competition left one less person for her to beat.

"I just wanted to make sure," I said, but she wasn't done. She stood up straight, her eyes blazing. With the cloud of smoke and her angular bone structure, she made me think of a dragon. Next, puffs of flame would come shooting from her nostrils.

"It's none of my business, and certainly none of theirs." Now she was loud enough that Megan and Ernesto both looked over, then looked away. I didn't blame them. I wouldn't want to challenge the dragon. "It's up to you if you want to say something. *I* think you should. It's not your fault what that asshole did." Of course she would say that. She wasn't the one who'd face consequences. "I'm here for you if you do, girl!"

The thought of telling anyone the details made the skin crawl all over my back. Or maybe it was just the rasp in her voice when she called me "girl." I wasn't her girl. Or anyone's girl, really. Neither of us had been girls in years. "Thanks," I said anyway. "And hey. Good luck."

She gave me a very dragon-like grin. Had her teeth always been this pointy? "Same to you."

5

AS PROMISED, A CHORUS OF ANALOG ALARM CLOCKS shrieked as soon it hit five o'clock the next morning. Kel groaned in the bunk under me. I rolled over in my top bunk, swearing under my breath at the hour, swearing even more as I almost rolled right off the bunk and went crashing to the floor. Showing up for the first day in a cast: that would be a way to make an impression.

Half asleep, I threw on the outfit the assistant had advised us to lay out the night before, then stumbled out into the kitchen, following a wonderful trail of coffee smell. There a woman was waiting for us, a tray of paper cups sitting before her on the breakfast bar. My memory for faces isn't the greatest, but I didn't think she was one of us.

"Good morning," I mumbled, reaching for a coffee. The woman stared at me with far too much thought for this hour of the morning.

SADIE ON A PLATE

"Sadie," she said, and just like that I recognized that too-tight ponytail and those absurdly high cheekbones. I stumbled back a few steps with my coffee, dribbling some precious brown liquid over the rim.

"Oh my God, Adrianna!" I said. "It's you. I'm sorry." I remembered her from the phone call asking those initial questions, and later from her actual face asking me questions during my in-person interview. "Good morning."

The world around me pulsed in time with my head—not in pain, but in recognition that this was an hour of the day I should not have been awake. My eyes felt almost as if they were too open. I was a chef. Made for working till two a.m., staying out till four at someone's restaurant or a chef bar, stumbling into bed, and rolling out of it in early afternoon. My schedule had been completely reversed.

But then I looked at Adrianna's serious face, took a sip of the lukewarm coffee in my hands, and remembered that today was my first day on *Chef Supreme,* and all my insides seized up into one cold concrete block. I'd felt like I had to use the bathroom just a little while ago, but I was pretty sure nothing would come out if I tried now.

"No worries," Adrianna was saying, which was the exact opposite of how I felt. "It's extremely early. I mean, I usually wake up around four to get in a good workout, but I know *most* people don't do that."

Normally, I would've immediately hated someone for saying something like that to me, but somehow I couldn't glare at Adrianna. Maybe it was because of her absolutely matter-of-fact tone, like she was only stating something everyone already knew. Maybe it was because even the sleepiest parts of my brain realized that part of my future in this competition depended on Adrianna liking me, so I couldn't afford to be an ass.

I still wasn't actually sure what she did here, though. I was about to ask, even though odds were she'd already told me at some point during my in-person interview, but then she told me anyway. "I work in production on *Chef Supreme*, as a reminder. I'll be your point person for the show: doing your confessionals; getting you dressed; basically, making sure you have everything you need before you need it."

I nodded to show I understood, taking another sip of my coffee. It was tasting worse and worse, the sign that it was working. It was like Adrianna was psychic.

Adrianna cracked a smile. "I'm not psychic."

That's exactly what a psychic would say. I beamed as hard as I could in her direction, but she only continued on smiling, and then the Joes entered the kitchen and took it over, leaving me to retreat to a corner and sip my coffee and try to psych myself up for whatever challenge we were going to do that day.

In the corner I found Nia curled up in an armchair, her head propped up on an armrest. I started to quietly back away, thinking she was sleeping, and then she raised her head and blinked at me, her eyes huge and dark and liquid. "I suppose it's morning," she said.

"Yes," I said back.

She uncoiled herself, stretching her long, thin arms over her head, yawning so wide I thought she might actually crack her face in half. "I was too nervous to sleep, so I came out here to read, but I guess I must have fallen asleep eventually. Where's my book?" She uncoiled a little further, revealing a book open in her lap, a damp half circle of drool on the pages. Her eyebrows raised as she examined it. "Well, at least it's not a library book."

As she sorted herself out with various stretches and little warm-ups that I forsook in favor of coffee and a body that will definitely fall apart by the time I'm forty, I speculated on what the first challenge was going to be. "Maybe they'll give us something nice and easy to smooth our way in, since we won't be comfortable in the kitchen yet," I mused. "Or maybe they'll really hurl us into the deep end. Like the time they threw the contestants into Central Park and made them do a scavenger hunt to find their ingredients, and then they had to cook everything over an open fire."

Nia shook her head. "Pretty sure they got fined for cooking on an open fire," she said. "So we don't have to worry about that."

Cold comfort.

"I watched all six seasons before I came and took careful notes, obviously," she continued. "All first challenges so far have been held in the *Chef Supreme* kitchen, and I haven't rated any of them above a seven in difficulty. Though I'm sure the difficulty level increases once you're the one on camera under the lights working with a time limit."

The back of my neck started to sweat, as if I was already under those lights working with a time limit. My stomach squirmed. I went from being unsure anything would come out if I got on the toilet to being positive all of my insides would flow right out of me.

And yet Nia's face held a supernatural calm. "Aren't you nervous?" I asked her.

She gave me an elegant shrug. "I'm going to win."

Before I could probe more into her mindset and hopefully

get some pointers on how to be that confident, the *Chef Supreme* assistant I'd seen yesterday—maybe another production person/ handler like Adrianna—called us out to the entrance. It was time to go.

Three boxy black cars, shiny and polished, were waiting for us on the street. "They're one of our sponsors, so it would be great if you could organically mention how smooth your ride is or how safe you feel in the back seat," Adrianna informed us as she ushered us into the cars. "See you soon!"

I crammed into a back window seat with Nia beside me, then Kel at the other window. Vanilla Joe took the front. Our driver nodded at us, and then we were on our way, driving sleekly and silently over the dark, quiet streets of Queens. The fruit cart sellers weren't out yet, but people were waiting for the bus. Coffee carts were setting up, handing steaming to-go cups to people heading out for work as the train rattled by somewhere in the distance.

We spent the first few minutes of the ride giving one another furtive looks, all of us maybe too nervous to share exactly how nervous we were. And then Vanilla Joe spotted the camera on the ceiling. "Hey, look," he said, pointing right at it. It hung down from the ceiling, its black lens glittering in our direction.

We shouldn't have been surprised, given not only how Adrianna had told us to talk about the car in the back seat but how we'd literally just signed a contract consenting to being filmed at all times outside of the bathroom, and yet somehow we all stared dumbly at it. Maybe it was the hour of the morning. Maybe we were all too dumb to be Chef Supreme and that dumbness was being recorded for all the producers and showrunners to cluck their tongues at.

Nia broke the tension first: she stuck her tongue out. Right at the camera. And then the smile unfurled over her face, outshining the sun at high noon.

The cameras were going to love her.

Even Vanilla Joe cracked a smile, and I hated to say—well, think—it, but his smile wasn't too bad, either. Cheekbones emerged from his pale face like sunken mountaintops cresting forth with the tide. His blue eyes crinkled merrily at the corners, and one of his front teeth was crooked just enough to be charming. The cameras would love him, too. And Kel, I realized as I glanced over at them, at the light glinting off their facial piercings.

I prodded my cheeks and my teeth as I smiled. Would the cameras love me? I couldn't see it, with my wild hair and bit of a tummy, but the producers must have thought so. There was a reason none of us in the *Chef Supreme* house were too old (even Old Joe, I suspected, had been aged up in my mind thanks to over-tanning) or missing too many teeth or pitted with too many acne scars. We'd been chosen partially because of our cooking skills and partially because of our appeal to the American public. We were all just a little bit shiny.

"Are you okay, Sadie?" Nia asked, her smile disappearing. I realized I was still poking at my bared teeth, long enough that they felt cold now. Cold and slick.

I dropped my arm into my lap, letting my mouth close. "I was just thinking about how much I *love* this *car*." I projected my voice like I was the *Chef Supreme* host pitching one of their in-house products. "Can you not feel how *smooth* this *ride* is? Why, I hardly feel as if I'm in a car at all!"

"You sound so natural," Nia said dryly, but Kel took my words and ran with them.

"I don't know if I'd call it smooth," they said, then let out a breathy-sounding moan and bounced up and down a little in their seat. "I'd call it a little bouncy. *Pleasurably* bouncy, as a matter of fact. Who needs a vibrator when you've got a car like this?"

Nia looked a little like she'd seen a ghost, but Vanilla Joe cracked up. He cocked his head at the camera, pushing his beige hair off his forehead. "Fellow gentlemen, purchase this car and forget about lengthy foreplay when you get home from a date. Your lady will be ready *immediately*."

If the car had been riding smoothly before, now it shook with laughter. Even Nia's. She wiped tears from the corners of her eyes and said, "Yes, this car has brought me as well to orgasm!"

The laughter halted. She blinked. "Did I just kill the fun?"

Fortunately, just then we pulled up to the *Chef Supreme* studio. It was an unobtrusive brick building on the far west side of Manhattan; it looked like it might have been nothing more than a warehouse or a loft among a street of similar warehouses or lofts, if not for the small sign over the main door. Adrianna and the others ushered us inside through a generic taupe lobby, stopped quickly in wardrobe where they brushed some makeup on my face but didn't make me change out of my mom jeans and flowered blouse (which gave me a surprisingly big ego boost), and then pushed us into a different world.

Seriously, it was like we'd been sucked through a portal. I'd only ever seen the *Chef Supreme* kitchen on TV, and now here I was, standing in the middle of it. It didn't feel at all real, bigger and smaller at once than I remembered, quiet and echoing without the cheery and/or tense *Chef Supreme* theme music playing in the background.

Adrianna popped into being in front of us. I had no idea how she'd gotten ahead or what door she'd come through. "Welcome to the *Chef Supreme* kitchen, everyone!" she proclaimed, clapping her hands together. "We're thrilled to have you here. I'd like each of you to please find your stations. Your name will be on the handle of the oven."

The room itself was a long rectangle with a high ceiling and brick walls. Set up lengthwise were twelve miniature kitchens, one across from the other, each shining chrome with an oven, a stove top, counter space, and room underneath for shelves and a small fridge or freezer. I found mine right in the middle of the pack and took a moment to open the fridge or freezer (it was a freezer), turn the stove on and off (it was gas), and spread my hands out on the counter, imagining myself cooking and sweating and winning.

I know I kept thinking it over and over, but it came to mind again. *I can't believe I'm here.*

Seriously. What the hell was I doing here? My legs began to shake like an earthquake was rumbling beneath us. I'd just been fired. I had no business thinking I could be Chef Supreme. I was going to bomb out in the first challenge. Worse, I was going to bomb out *in front of the entire country.*

"Hey, neighbor."

I looked up. Across from me was Bald Joe, waving genially. I hadn't talked much with him, but he seemed nice enough. Somewhere between thirty and fifty in age. Bald of course, by choice or genetics I couldn't tell. Muscles bulged from his upper arms, and his ring finger was bare. I couldn't help checking. It was a compulsion. Not that it meant anything conclusive among chefs; many didn't wear wedding rings at work because our hands were

constantly getting dirty and kneading dough and washing themselves and doing all other sorts of things. "Hey there," I said.

He didn't seem to have anything else to say, just a kind head
bob, so I looked from side to side. On my left was Nia, who was
busy surveying every inch of her station with a beady eye, probably translating it real-time into mental blueprints marked with
numbers and everything. Across from her, Kel was setting up,
the silver of their facial piercings gleaming against the heavy TV
lights above.

Kaitlyn's station was to my right. She'd tucked her light
brown hair into a no-nonsense ponytail as her fingertips tap, tap,
tapped away on the edge of her stove. Jitters, or cigarette crav-
ings? She kept glancing at and then away from Megan, who was
across from her.

Something about the tapping reminded me of a conversation
we'd had way back when we were on the line together at Atelier
Laurent. Not on the line itself, of course: the dinner rush didn't
exactly lend itself to introspective conversations. We were on
break at the end of the night, when the rush was dying down and
it was more important that somebody take out the trash than
stand at their station. I hoisted the bag of garbage before me,
turning my head in a vain attempt to escape the smell, realizing
too late that Kaitlyn had followed me outside.

"Cigarette break?" I'd asked her.

She'd shaken her head. Her fingers were tap, tap, tapping
against her side the same way they were doing now. Her empty
fingers. That could definitely have held a bag of trash so that I
didn't have to make two trips. "Trying to quit." She was quiet for
a moment, but before I could ask her to help me with the garbage, she asked, "Sadie, why'd you become a cook?"

My eyes lit up at my favorite topic. The words just started spilling out for what felt like hours: how putting ingredients together sometimes felt like magic, and who didn't secretly want magic; how I found experimenting with food and all it could do the most fun I've ever had; how I loved seeing the look on people's faces when they ate something I was especially proud of; how a knife in my hand and the rush of a kitchen just felt like *home*. "How about you?" I finished, now so exhilarated I barely noticed the reeking hot garbage smell of the narrow alleyway.

She hesitated for so long I started to wonder if she'd heard me. "Because I didn't want to go to college, and being a chef seemed glamorous," she said quietly. The Food Network effect— even I'd fallen victim to it at times. "When does the glamorous part start?"

I shook my head, shaking the memory away. Good for Kaitlyn: she'd finally found her glamour. I turned back to Bald Joe. "So, where you from, what do you cook?"

Bald Joe was from right here in New York, he told me. Grew up somewhere in Manhattan, where he started in the kitchen at a pretty young age. "Found my first job washing dishes at Kimoto and rose through the ranks," he said. Kimoto, aka one of the most famous Japanese restaurants in New York City. No, the world. On par with Nobu or Morimoto, with how many Michelin stars again? "Chef Kimoto became a mentor to me," Bald Joe continued. "Almost like a father. So I cook Japanese food."

"Japanese food, huh?" I tried not to blink in surprise.

"Japanese food." He cracked a smile. "Yes, I know it's uncommon to see a Black guy making sushi."

"Chefs, you may now take some time to familiarize yourself with the equipment on offer and with the pantry," Adrianna announced from the front of the room. Either she had a naturally loud voice or else her projection was on point, because I didn't see a microphone. "You'll notice we have all the most common ingredients available—if there's something you don't see that you think you'd like to cook with in the future and that you didn't include on your application, please let me know and we'll try to special-order it for you—and all types of kitchen equipment. Everything is first come, first served, so if you think you'd like to make ice cream, you'd better be first to the ice cream machine.

"Oh, and you'll notice it's all Cooking-at-Home brand. They're one of our sponsors, too," she added. "So if you'd like to organically mention at any time how quickly your oven heats up or how evenly the stove top cooks, please, feel free!" A small, wolfish grin. "It'll get you more camera time."

I spent the next twenty minutes wandering around the equipment and the pantry, taking mental notes on where everything was. The blenders were over *here* in the corner. This was the meat fridge, and *that* was the dairy fridge, which reminded me of my synagogue growing up where meat and dairy were never cooked together in order to apply with the rules of kashrut, or kosher cooking. Spices were arranged in alphabetical order on *this* shelf.

When Adrianna called us back to our stations, my head was spinning, and I had no idea where anything was.

"I'm sure it all feels overwhelming right now, but rest assured, your first challenge won't be so bad," Adrianna said. My stomach gave a flip. I wondered how this was all going to work. On TV, the host showed up, gave the chefs their task, and then immediately the contestants were running through the pantry, stealing all the eggs and fighting one another for the last bundle of parsley. But surely they couldn't— "I'm going to tell you your task, and then you'll have time to plot out your dish before Maz comes in and we do it for the cameras."

My stomach probably should've relaxed, but instead it did a few more backflips. Because this was really happening. Soon enough, Maz Sarshad, the show's host, would be here right in front of us, and I might go home—

"As I said, your first challenge won't be so bad," Adrianna said with another grin, this one more shark than wolf. "Since this is our first episode, we'd like to introduce our judges and viewers to *you*. We want to see *you* on a plate. Your cuisine, your favorite ingredients, whatever. Someone should take a bite of whatever's on that plate and be able to see how it connects to you and your life."

I began to breathe a little easier. That wasn't so bad. Of course, the seemingly "easy" challenges meant you had less room to mess up. If you were running around Central Park trying to find your ingredients and then had to cook them over an open fire, it wasn't so bad if you were missing an ingredient or something wasn't quite cooked right.

In this, everything had to be perfect.

But could it ever be perfect with *me* on that plate? Would anyone even want to eat it?

"Remember, we want to see *you* on a plate. You'll have ninety minutes to prepare four plates," Adrianna said. "I'll give you some time to plan now. Try to remember everything you're doing, because you'll be asked to recount it all and answer questions tomorrow when you come in to tape your confessionals."

Right. The sections of *Chef Supreme* where they cut to a chef sitting in front of a neutral backdrop explaining the thought process or feelings behind whatever we'd just watched them do or say. I hadn't realized they'd been filmed on a different day from the actual event until I'd come for my auditions. Though it did make sense. You couldn't pull someone off the line to talk about what they were doing without risking things getting burned.

I focused back on the challenge. "Me on a plate," I murmured. A dish that represented me somehow. Sadie on a plate. So what represented me?

There had to be some kind of Jewish twist, obviously. That was both my cuisine and my heritage. But it had to be elevated and interesting and impressive, too. I racked through my mental menu, which was updating itself all the time. I'd only have an hour and a half, so unless I wanted to mess with the pressure cooker, which I didn't first off—no matter how much I'd practiced with it at home—anything that had to braise or marinate for a long time, like brisket, was out of the question. Chicken routinely got sneers for being too easy, so chicken was out, too, at least for this first challenge.

All I'd scribbled so far in my notebook was an elaborate question mark. I peeked up. Bald Joe was nodding to himself as he wrote. Nia was smiling and muttering under her breath, straddling a tight line between genius and serial killer. Kel was scratching away furiously, and Vanilla Joe had already stepped back from his station, surveying us all with a smug look. I evaded his eyes and got back to work on my question mark so that I'd look like I was doing something, at least.

Maybe I should do a play on pickled herring: that was delicious and didn't take too long to cook. It was also flexible, could be done with most whitefish in the event they ran out of herring or didn't have it in the kitchen. And you know what would go well with that? My breaths grew faster and faster with excitement as I wrote over my question mark. My knish: a crisp fried pocket full of the smoothest, creamiest potatoes you've ever met. Except mine wouldn't just be potato. It needed something to lighten it up. I'd have sour with the herring, so maybe something bitter . . .

I scribbled away furiously, but my attention kept getting called away by things happening around the room. Camerapeople were making their entrances, setting up their equipment and squinting around at all the angles. And then . . .

"That's Maz!" Nia said in a furious whisper.

Sure enough, the host stepped through the main door. He looked just as he did on TV: a wave of dark hair cresting over his tan forehead; bright green eyes—perhaps colored contacts?—surveying the room from beneath his sculpted brows; perfectly tailored suit hugging every curve. Except he was definitely shorter in person. Adrianna wasn't especially tall, but he only came up to her nose. And from this angle, I could see the small black earpiece in his ear. According to some podcasts I'd listened to and articles I'd read for research before boarding that plane, it was so producers could feed him lines in the moment and give him questions to ask contestants.

For some reason, seeing Maz here made it all feel more real. Like, this was actually happening. I gaped at him.

Naturally, he glanced my way just then and noticed me staring. He winked. I blushed. He wasn't my type—way too polished—but there was still something about him. Something that drew people to him, made them have to stare. I guess that's why he became a TV show host.

"Guys, we're filming in a few!" Adrianna announced. "We'll

do multiple takes to get every reaction and angle. You'll want to look attentive and relaxed while Maz talks."

So I did. Or I tried, anyway. The thing about trying to look relaxed is that the very act of trying negates the relaxedness. I definitely nailed the attentiveness, though, as he basically repeated what Adrianna had told us earlier. By his fourth run-through, I was pretty sure I could recite his lines myself.

They finally had enough takes. Adrianna stepped forward again. "Maz's going to segue into a count this time, and you'll all run for the pantry to collect your ingredients. For this challenge, you'll only be able to use what you grab during your five-minute shopping time, so make sure not to forget anything!"

I was glad I'd prepared a list, but I ran through it again quickly in my head. Couldn't forget the fish. Couldn't forget the potatoes. Couldn't forget the—

"Go!"

My feet lurched forward, pulling the rest of me along. The scene at the pantry doors was something like a stampede: people cramming through the doors, arms and legs flying everywhere. I half expected to watch someone go down, hear the crunch of bone beneath our comfortable sneakers. Somehow we all made it through, and with the *Chef Supreme* wire baskets in our hands, no less.

At home I would scream at the chefs in the pantry. *What are you doing? Go for the shrimp first before it's gone! You're forgetting the basil!* But it was easy to say those things as I was sitting at home on the couch, stuffing caramel popcorn into my mouth.

Now the room spun around me, my ears attuned to every thirty-second chirp from the timer. I'd just spent fifteen minutes poking around the space, yet I seemed to have forgotten where everything was. I was first to the seafood fridge, which let me grab the herring without competition, but the crowd was thick over by the potatoes; it took me so long to select a few good taters that I had to scramble for horseradish root and beets before the timer ran out.

Back at my station, I found myself gasping for breath like I'd just run twenty miles instead of twenty feet as I surveyed the basket in front of me. It was a good thing the basics shelf was always available, stocked with things like olive oil and spices, because I'd totally forgotten any fresh herbs. But that was okay. I'd managed to get everything else I—

"Attention, chefs!" Maz was at the front of the room, a big shit-eating grin curled over his lips. I tensed as I realized the cameras were on us, their red eyes staring. "I'm afraid I have one of *Chef Supreme*'s signature twists in store for you."

I didn't have to fake my shock. Of course I knew *Chef Supreme* liked to surprise the contestants, but here, in the first challenge . . .

"We'd still like to see *you* on a plate," Maz proclaimed. I relaxed a tiny bit. At least I didn't have to totally reevaluate my dish. But what were they going to do to us? Take away all our access to heat sources? Make us transform our meal into a dessert?

He paused for dramatic effect. I could only assume the cameras were swooping around to get all of our genuine surprise. They'd probably make us do a few more takes, but there was no way I'd be able to look this stressed-out on command.

"So, chefs," Maz said. "I'd like you to trade baskets with the chef across from you."

No. Oh no. I met Bald Joe's eyes; they were staring at me with just as much dismay as I assumed he was getting from mine.

He cooked Japanese food. How in all the hells Judaism didn't believe in was I going to make my dish out of miso paste and seaweed and rice? Bald Joe was probably thinking the same thing—how could he make sushi or whatever out of my herring and potatoes and cornmeal?

But this was what we'd signed up for. I gave him a tight smile as we swapped, just in case the cameras were on me. I had just enough time to take a cursory look over everything inside— some sushi-grade salmon; rice; sesame oil and seeds; dried seaweed—between each take. My mind spun its wheels, but it was like trying to drive in the sand. Nothing was coming up. *At least it won't be totally embarrassing when I go home first*, I tried to console myself. *People will understand what an impossible task this was.*

On my left side, Nia and Vanilla Joe looked slightly happier than I felt—she'd clearly been planning on fried chicken and biscuits, while he had shrimp. On my right, Kaitlyn was literally scratching her head over Megan's basket of various Chinese sauces and vegetables. Maybe she'd go home first and I wouldn't have to worry about her anymore, I thought hopefully. No, that was mean.

"One more take," Adrianna called out. I shoved Bald Joe's Japanese basket back over to him and took my herring and potatoes lovingly back into my arms. *I wish you could stay*, I thought, rocking the basket like a baby. *You were going to be so delicious on my plate.*

And then they were gone. I literally almost cried.

"Good," Adrianna said with a brisk clap. "You have fifteen minutes to plot out your new dish while we come around to chat with you. Good luck!"

My mind whirled through all the options—or, really, the lack of options—as Maz walked around with the cameras. I heard him laugh at something Vanilla Joe said, then express sympathy for Nia. I couldn't stop listening. I couldn't focus.

And then suddenly he was in front of me, flashing me a very white smile. "Chef Sadie," he said. "How are you doing?"

I couldn't formulate a response. My mouth hung open a little bit, and I just stared at him, mute and desperate, probably looking like I'd been electrified.

Which made him laugh. "That was golden. We'll definitely be able to use that," he said, seemingly to nobody. Maybe to the producers through his earpiece. "And Chef Sadie, I'll let you get back to what you're doing, but who do you see as your biggest competition so far?"

That answer came immediately. "I guess I'll see after I've watched them cook," I said. "Right now, I just need to focus on my own plate."

That polished smile again. "Brilliant answer. Well, good luck!"

His words sent a tiny shiver of hope through me as he moved on to Bald Joe. If I really was that "golden" and "brilliant" . . . surely they'd want to keep me on camera longer? It was just enough to break through my fog of indecision and force that car back on the road, and yes, I was mixing my metaphors, but I was mixing cuisines, too, damn it.

So. My pen hit the paper. My protein was salmon. I closed my eyes, thinking back to—lox. Smoked salmon we often ate on bagels. My eyes popped open. I didn't have bagels, or ingredients for bagels, but I did have rice. What if I ground some of the rice to make a crispy crust on the salmon, then smoked the salmon in a play on lox? The seaweed had the same briny notes as capers,

and I could pickle these radishes the way I'd pickle red onions . . .
I'd need some kind of creamy sauce, too. Maybe I could use the
rice for that again, cooking it up and blending it, since there
wasn't any dairy in Bald Joe's basket?

Way too soon, Adrianna told us to put our notebooks away.
Maz got in front of the camera, like he'd been there the whole
time. "Chefs, you will have ninety minutes to give us you on a
plate," he said grandly. "And your time starts . . . now!"

I sprang into action. The world shrank into the radius of my
tiny kitchen; my knife became an extension of my arm, the counter
an extension of my brain. I had no room for thoughts besides
what was going into that blender. What was sizzling on the stove.
What was cooking in the smoker.

By the time the buzzer sounded, I was literally dripping with
sweat. I stepped back from my station, breathing hard, swiping
at my forehead with a *Chef Supreme*-branded hand towel. It was
extremely absorbent. Still, when I blinked, my eyes stung with
salt.

The world around me returned in dribs and drabs. Production staff whisking away one plate from each station to bring to
a separate table and photograph from every angle. Maz complaining about how the cameras were purposefully focusing on
his tiny bald spot. The smells of tomatoes and black bean sauce
and roasted chickpeas and chocolate, a combination that you'd
think would be terrible but was actually quite nice. Or maybe
that was just the delirium speaking again.

Time for judging. Maz always ate, as well as the two other
judges. Though John Waterford wouldn't be returning, I remembered. I hoped he was doing okay.

Lenore Smith came in first. She looked, if anything, even

more imposing than she did on TV. Which was hard, because she looked extremely imposing on TV. Probably close to six feet tall even in flats, she had a sleek helmet of silver-white hair, blue eyes sharper than any chef's knife, and pale, strangely wrinkle-free skin, even though her Wikipedia page said she was in her late sixties. Either insane genetic luck or even insanely better Botox. She was known for being one of the preeminent women chefs of the American West, right up there with Alice Waters and Nancy Silverton.

Beside me Nia hopped up and down on the balls of her feet, eager to see who the second judge was going to be. He took his time, his footsteps clacking slowly behind Lenore Smith as she looked over her shoulder to tell him to hurry, and then there he was, at the head of the room.

"Oh, I know him," Nia breathed.

All of my muscles tensed. Including my chest. I couldn't breathe.

I knew him, too. More than knew him. I'd kissed him

"Hello, chefs!" said Luke.

6

HE WAS JUST AS HANDSOME AS I REMEMBERED. MAYBE
even more handsome now that he'd been through the gamut of
TV makeup and someone had dressed him in a tailored navy
blue suit that hugged every line and blade of his—

No. *Stop it, Sadie.* This was a disaster. A monstrous disaster.
Worse than the time I hooked up with a one-night stand after
chopping a bunch of jalapeños sans gloves (the burning sensa-
tion didn't go away for hours). If Adrianna or any of the others
found out that I'd made out with one of our supposedly impar-
tial judges . . . what would they do? I'd bet my painstakingly
smoked salmon that finding a new contestant at the last minute
would be a lot easier than finding a new judge.

Oh em gee. I'd officially discovered something worse than
being the first one kicked off: being asked to leave in disgrace
because I'd tried to curry favor with a judge beforehand. And
not the good kind of curry, like with coconut milk and lemon-

grass. Come to think of it, I was starving. I could really go for a good panang curry right now.

I was officially losing my mind.

I held my breath as he looked around the room. Beside him Maz was introducing him to the cameras. "... Luke Weston, son of acclaimed restaurateur and three-Michelin-star chef Charles Weston and one of the world's most preeminent experts in French cuisine! Having only just opened, his new restaurant has already received three stars from the *New York Times*."

All of the breath whooshed out of me. *That* was why he looked familiar. Everybody knew who Charles Weston was, at least everybody in the culinary world. He'd won the first season of *Chef Supreme: Best of the Best*, a spin-off that focused on chefs with lots of awards already under their belts. The Arlington Restaurant Group, one of the biggest and most well-known restaurant families, had partnered with him on multiple restaurants. I wondered if *Chef Supreme* had called him up first for the open judgeship, and he told them, *no, I'm too busy, but you know my son is a chef, too, and he's*

Looking at me.

I could see the surprise spread over his face, but only for a split second before it disappeared. The cameras probably wouldn't pick up on anything. Unless he said something right now. What if he said something right now? Announced it to the cameras and all the other chefs and Adrianna?

The worst happened. He smiled and said, "I know you!"

I forgot how to breathe.

He was walking toward me. My entire body tensed in preparation for the explosion sure to follow. He was almost here, and I could feel the warmth of his body even from feet away, or maybe that was just my stove I'd forgotten to turn off, and then he was looking me in the eye, and an echo of his lips touched mine, and I leaned toward him, involuntarily, and even as I was furious at myself I couldn't stop it . . .

And then he was walking past with not even a cursory nod in my direction, his eyes trained on Kel. "Chef Kel, it's been a few years," he said, holding out his hand. "Though wasn't your hair green then?"

Kel nodded, their cheeks nearly matching the purple of their hair. "It's great to see you, Chef."

I took a deep, shuddery breath as Maz asked the two how they knew each other, then splayed my fingers on my station, trying to stop my arms from shaking. "I worked for Chef Weston when I first moved to New York," Kel was saying to Maz and the cameras. "At one of his dad's restaurants. He was kind of a mentor to me. He really took me under his wing. I don't know if I'd be here without his guidance."

"That's so kind of you to say," Luke said, and for a moment I got a glimpse of that sun-breaking smile I'd seen in the Korean speakeasy before it returned to bland TV polish.

"But don't expect any special treatment!" Maz said heartily, and the three of them laughed. Beside them Lenore Smith pursed her lips, as if the mere idea were blasphemy.

"Of course not," said Kel. Their cheeks were still a little pink.

Maz and Luke gave them a nod before moving on. The farther Luke got from me, the easier I found it to breathe. "We'll start with Megan Qin," Maz proclaimed. He stared Megan down over what looked like plates of hand-torn noodles. How did she make hand-torn noodles like that under pressure in an hour, with Kaitlyn's basket?

I was so out of my league.

"Chef Megan, please tell us about your dish."

As the judges tasted Megan's dish (the noodles were excellent; the sauce was too salty), I racked my brain for what I remembered about the Weston family. I vaguely recalled watching Luke's father celebrate his *Chef Supreme: Best of the Best* win with his entire family. Maybe that was why I'd thought Luke looked familiar when I met him.

The judges moved on to Kaitlyn, who'd made ravioli with minced pork and egg yolks inside them. Both she and Megan must have been planning on making pasta, which was lucky for them in terms of switching baskets. Resentment simmered inside me as they exchanged cheeky grins. Though of course I should've expected it. Everything came easily to Kaitlyn. I was kind of surprised Maz hadn't just told her she didn't have to switch baskets at all.

The judges liked Kaitlyn's ravioli but thought the dish could use more color and texture.

And then it was my turn. There they were. Maz, Lenore Smith, and Luke, standing in front of my station, looking appraisingly at me. And my food.

Had Luke always had a dimple in his right cheek?

When I opened my mouth, I was seized by the absurd fear I'd blurt something like that out. That I would suddenly lose the ability to control my mouth. But all I said was, "I've made for you a smoked salmon with a rice crust, atop some pickled vegetables and a creamy rice porridge." I took a deep breath. It came in a little shaky, but so far so good. "I cook Jewish food with a twist, and this dish was inspired by bagels and lox. And Joe's Japanese-themed basket."

That drew a little laugh from Maz. Luke smiled as he met my eyes. My heart thudded, and my face heated up, but I did my best to keep a pleasant smile on my lips. "I hope you like it."

Knives sliced cleanly through the salmon, pink flesh flaking on either side, the crust giving way with a satisfying crunch. Lenore Smith and Maz were eating, too, but I kept my eyes fixed on Luke's fork. He tried a bite of the salmon plain first, chewing thoughtfully, then swept up some of my rice porridge with the seaweed-pickled vegetables, then returned for a bite of everything together, pink salmon and white porridge and pops of green and red all entering his parted lips.

He closed his eyes as he tasted my food. He didn't open them again until he swallowed. "The salmon is perfect," he said. "Flaky and tender, with just the right amount of smoke, and the crunch of that crust is just . . ." He paused, those bottomless eyes on mine. The tip of his tongue darted over his lower lip. "Incredible."

I didn't mean to smile, just nod appreciatively at any praise, but I felt it curl over my lips anyway. "Thank you."

"I agree," said Lenore. "The salmon is something quite special. Is the crust rice alone?"

"No," I said. "It's ground rice with some panko and a little nori."

She nodded with approval. "And these seaweed-pickled vegetables are stellar. Bright and tangy, a lovely pop of acid against the richness of the salmon and the porridge."

The smile spread wider. My cheeks were beginning to hurt.

"Oh!" Luke leaned over his plate. "Did you arrange the porridge to resemble a bagel?"

"I did," I said. Right at the minute mark, before the timer

went off, I'd swept the porridge into circles on the plates and scooped holes out of the middle. I hadn't been sure anyone would notice.

"The one thing I don't love is the porridge itself," Maz said. My smile slipped a bit. "It's a tad gummy. I don't love how it's sticking to my teeth."

"I disagree," said Lenore. Okay, smile back on. "I like that it has some chew to it. It makes me think of a real bagel."

They bickered over my rice porridge for a couple more minutes. I kept expecting Luke to weigh in with the deciding vote, but he only stared at my plate, blinking at it like it might suddenly come to life and jump at him. The verdict on my rice undecided, they finally nodded at me, thanked me for preparing a delicious dish, and moved on to Bald Joe.

With the cameras off me at least for a moment, I let my shoulders sag in a big sigh of relief. They liked my dish. They liked my dish! That meant I probably wouldn't go home this week. Going home the first week was usually reserved for someone who messed up in some drastic way, like serving the judges a raw protein or not getting anything on the plate at all. Not every chef was suited for the time constraints and spontaneous thinking of *Chef Supreme*. As the weeks went on, and I was working under less and less sleep and more and more pressure, held to higher and higher standards, I might feel that way, too.

But not this week.

I watched the other contestants' judgings and Luke's back as he judged them. Bald Joe had taken my basket and created some kind of okonomiyaki by shredding and frying the potatoes and the herring. A kind of okonomiyaki-latke, if you will. He got high marks for creativity and a few dings because the pancake was greasy and not crispy enough around the edges, sure signs it needed another minute or two of cooking.

Luke's eyes flickered to me after judging Bald Joe's dish, as he was circling around to Nia's station. They were dark and inscrutable, pinning me briefly to place like a butterfly to a corkboard. *He could still say something about me*, I told myself. *Maybe he didn't want to ruin the take or make a scene in front of everyone, because he's a fundamentally decent person, which makes it even worse. Maybe instead of making a big stink about it, they'll do an edit to make it look like my porridge was inedibly sticky, or like the salmon wasn't creative enough, and I'll go home.*

Sweat popped out along my hairline, dampened my armpits, trickled down between my boobs. Who was I kidding? Of course I was going home.

The judges loved Nia's dish, some kind of crispy fried shrimp with a sweet and spicy barbecue sauce, and liked Vanilla Joe's fried chicken and biscuits, though they said he'd showed a lack of creativity for using Nia's original idea. I shifted from foot to foot as they went down the line, finally finishing up with Mercedes. The judges left without a backward glance, presumably to deliberate.

From there, we were ushered into what Adrianna described as the "stew room," named because we'd be sitting here stewing while awaiting judgment, slowly breaking down emotionally the way tough beef breaks down under low and slow heat. I recognized it from past seasons of the show. "Chill out and try to relax," she told us. "There's wine and beer in the fridge. Keep in mind that you're being filmed the whole time."

She promptly exited, leaving us to sit down in the circle of folding chairs and stare at the blank white walls. Vanilla Joe immediately cracked open the fridge to pass around drinks. I took a beer, wishing that we had something a little stronger on tap to smooth my frazzled nerves. As I took a long sip, surveying the others around me, I was pretty sure we all felt the same way.

Kel broke the silence, slapping their knee hard. "Well, that was something."

That was all it took for everyone else to bust open. "It's so much harder than it looks on TV," said Nia. "I didn't prepare for that!"

"Half of my raviolis burst open in the water, and I didn't have time to do another batch," Kaitlyn said mournfully.

"What was I *supposed* to do with a vegetarian basket?"

"My lamb was overcooked."

"I couldn't find the grill pan!"

We bitched. We drank. We drank some more. Old Joe slid off his chair and stretched out on the dirty tile floor, claiming the folding chairs were bad for his back. We toasted and accidentally spilled some beer on Old Joe.

And conversation turned to the judges. "I've always thought Lenore Smith was one of those women who didn't support other women, you know?" Megan said conspiratorially.

Kaitlyn nudged her with an elbow, looking scandalized. "Don't forget they're filming us!"

But either Megan didn't care, or she'd drank enough to think she didn't care. "You didn't notice? She was way harsher on the women than the men."

"Not for me," I said. "It was Maz who was tough on me. He didn't like my rice."

Megan sat with her legs open wide, her burly arm dangling between them as she leaned onto her elbows. "Then maybe it's that she doesn't like gay people or something."

"How is she supposed to know you're gay?" said Kaitlyn. "That's probably not in the biographies they're given of us."

Megan scratched her buzz cut, flexing the arm muscles beneath her men's T-shirt. Then snorted. "You're sweet."

A blush flowed down Kaitlyn's face, temples through cheeks through throat. She was left looking almost as if she'd been steamed.

Oliver butted in. "I'm gay. She was perfectly nice to me, and she liked my dish," he said. He ran a hand through his neatly coiffed hair. "How about Luke Weston, though? Can you even believe?"

I slumped down in my chair, a little tipsy from all the beer. I was definitely *not* chiming in during this conversation.

"I'm about as straight a guy as you can get, but even I can say he's a pretty good-looking man," Vanilla Joe said.

Eyes, don't roll.

"Hey, Kel," Kaitlyn said. "Were you making that up in there about him being your mentor for the cameras, or was that true?"

I wanted to remind Kaitlyn that there were cameras in here, too, so whatever Kel said couldn't be trusted, but Kel spoke first. "It was true," Kel said. "I grew up in western Pennsylvania. Appalachia. Lived the stereotype: dirt-poor childhood in a hometown hit hard by the opioid epidemic, learned to cook because nobody else in the house was going to do it. Developed an appreciation for the food of the land by foraging and scavenging what I could. Have you ever tasted ramps with dirt still on them?"

Vanilla Joe leaned back in his chair, clasping his fingers over his paunch. "She didn't ask about your childhood. She asked you about Chef Weston."

Kaitlyn tossed her hair so that it fell over her back in a shimmering brown waterfall. "Sure, but I'm happy to hear about their childhood, too."

"I was getting to Chef Weston," Kel said, exasperated. They scratched the bridge of their nose. "I got the hell out of there as soon as I turned eighteen, moved to the city, was young, scrappy, hungry, and all that. Chef Weston saw something in me. Gave me a job washing dishes and let me work my way up." The exasperated look faded into a nostalgic smile. "He was only a couple years older than me, having just started heading the kitchen at one of his dad's restaurants, but I saw him as a mentor, because he saw something in me."

The sound of the old-fashioned wall clock suddenly seemed especially loud. *Tick, tock, tick, tock*. I looked up at it and squinted, wondering if maybe the producers were somehow making it louder for the effect; the movement was enough to make my head spin. I leaned over and rested my forehead in my hands.

"Sadie, you okay?" Kaitlyn asked.

"I'm okay," I said, voice muffled by my hands. "Just feeling a little sick."

"Worried you did badly?" Vanilla Joe said. I glanced at him from my lap. I bet anything that, when Maz asked him the question about who his greatest competition would be, he'd only named the male chefs.

I pushed myself back up with some effort. It seemed important that they hear what I had to say. "No, I think I did *great*," I lied. Then moved back to our previous topic. "Trust me, it doesn't matter how perfect someone is. If you're working together, you do *not* want to get involved."

I wasn't sure exactly who I was talking about anymore, Luke

or Chef Anders. Derek. But everybody else was staring at me like I'd told them I preferred hot dogs to Ibérico ham.

I stood, wobbling only slightly. "I have to go to the bathroom," I said. "They have to allow us access to a bathroom, don't they? It's probably legally required?"

"I don't think it's a legal requirement, depending on how long they have us in here," Nia said, but I was already moving toward the door. It swung open easily. Sure enough, I could see a bathroom sign down the hall.

As the door closed behind me, I could hear Kangaroo Joe start bitching about how the judges hadn't given his pork a fair shake, that pork production was safe enough now that it was okay to serve pork a little rare. I breathed easier not to hear it. The only thing that might drive me crazier than sitting there and going through all of our dishes again might be sitting there and dissecting Luke's looks. His looks, which, yes, were impressive, but on the inside he was so much more—

There.

He was *there*. Standing in front of the bathroom. Because of course the judges would have to go to the bathroom, too. I saw him before he saw me, which meant I had a head start on him. "Luke," I said, stopping an arm's length away.

What I wanted him to do: rush to me, circle his arms around my waist, lift me into the air and spin me around, lower me back to the ground, and kiss me passionately, kiss me until he took my breath away (literally) and left me dizzy.

What he actually did: stared at me like I was a vampire swooping in on him. Even though he was the one who looked like a vampire, his face all ashy and pale. He didn't even say hello.

I didn't reach for him. He stepped back anyway, almost violently, slamming his back into the wall. "Judges and contestants aren't supposed to fraternize."

"They should have considered that when they told us to use the same bathroom," I said back.

"The men's bathroom in the judges' hallway was actually being cleaned, so they told me it wasn't a big deal to run out and use this one, because I really had to—"

"Luke." I interrupted before I had to hear the details of his bathroom emergency. "Did you tell them anything?"

His face was purpling now, like he'd been bitten by the vampire and all the blood was pooling in his cheeks in preparation for exiting his throat. "About what?"

I only now realized there might be cameras in the hallway. I glanced around belatedly, then leaned in closer to Luke. If there *were* cameras, hopefully they wouldn't pick up my words. "About us," I whispered. His face didn't change. "What happened between us after the airport? When we ate Korean food and made out in a doorway?"

His face did change now. Something flickered over it: I couldn't tell exactly what it was, but it looked like sadness. And then it tensed up all over, twisting his lips into a scowl. "You shouldn't have read into that, Sandy."

Him calling me the wrong name made me prickle all over with the heat of shame. I thought I'd sweat out my entire body's supply of liquid during the challenge and the judging, but apparently the beer had replenished it. *Well, that's good,* my tipsy brain told myself logically. *If you sweat everything out, you won't have to pee anymore, right?*

But I didn't want to show up to judging all sweaty and rumpled and reeking of alcohol. And I really didn't want to feel shame right now. Why was I feeling shame, anyway? *Did you really think he'd like you? Don't you know better than that by now?* said my brain, suddenly stone-cold sober. It was speaking to me with Derek's voice. *Of course you should be ashamed. You should shrivel away into a shame ball.*

Luke was already going on. "I'd entirely forgotten about that whole thing until I saw you in the judging line." That slight British accent was creeping in again, making everything he was saying sound a tad more posh and infinitely more infuriating. "So there was really no reason to go bringing it up with Adrianna or Maz. We're both here to do a job, so let's do our jobs and forget all that other nonsense, yes?" When I didn't respond, just tried to force the shame back down my throat so that it didn't erupt in a camera-shattering screech, he prompted, "Right, Sandy?"

The shame built up with a pressure, forcing my lips open, forcing out—

A burp.

Well, that was embarrassing. But at least now my face was boiling for a reason other than shame. "It's Sadie," I bit out. "My name is *Sadie.*" I pictured him saying my name outside the Korean restaurant, those dark eyes melting into mine, those two syllables lingering on his lips as if he were tasting the most delectable chocolate truffle. I pictured him saying my name just before I kissed him, my own lips swallowing the last syllable, and yes, in his mouth, my name tasted like nothing else I'd ever tried before, spices from a night market shimmering with gold and smoke and mystery. "Two syllables. Five letters. Not so hard. *Sadie.*"

The shame was back, making me feel like all of my insides were crumpling in on themselves like a sheet of paper in Luke's hand. Had I seriously imagined our connection? Was I so desperate or hungry for attention that I'd totally made up the heat in his eyes, the—

"Sadie, yes," Luke said dismissively. "Right, I believe the last girl I brought there from the airport was named Sandy." He stepped back in the direction of what I assumed were the judges' chambers. "I won't let any of it affect my work on the show, and you shouldn't, either. Good luck to you."

Before I could shriek or punch or anything, he hurried back down the hall. I watched him go, all the words evaporating in my throat. I wanted to yell after him that he'd meant nothing to me, either, but he disappeared through the door.

And then I was alone in the hallway, aside from my throbbing bladder. I couldn't tell what ached more: that, or my heart.

I HAD TO GO TO THE BATHROOM TWICE MORE TO PEE
out all my beer before they finally came and knocked on the
door. Which was fortunate, because by then I'd mostly sobered
up. As had the others, which left us sitting in the stew room in a
morose kind of silence. None of us had really been happy with
our dishes. All of us thought we might go home. Nobody wanted
to go home.

That wasn't entirely true. Right now, I did kind of want to go
home and curl into a ball under my covers, the same way I had
for the three days after I'd gotten dumped and fired by the same
person at once. But just as that didn't make me feel any better
then, it wouldn't make me feel better now. And if that meant getting fired on national television by a guy I'd made out with and
then got spurned by, so be it. It would only torment me for the
rest of my days. Which would probably be short, since I'd waste
away of embarrassment.

Maz swung the door open and stood silhouetted in the entryway. It must be late by now, I realized. I could have looked at the clock, but I purposely stared Maz in his bright green eyes instead. We existed in some timeless, liminal space between fates. "The judges would like to see Nia, Kel, and Sadie," he announced, his voice smooth.

Me? My stomach knotted with nerves. *Chef Supreme* usually called out the top three and the bottom three in each challenge, but they didn't tell each group which was which until they were standing in front of the judges and enough sufficiently dramatic pauses had passed. I took a deep breath. It shook. Then I realized the others were in front of me and I had to jog to catch up as they walked quickly down that interminably long hallway.

"Oh my Lordy Lord," Kel breathed as I fell in line with them and Nia. "My heart is going to burst right here."

I squinted at the two of them, trying to remember if the judges had liked their dishes or not. The second half of judging had been a blur. I'd been too busy frantically worrying about Luke. "I thought they liked mine," I whispered. I didn't want this caught on camera. I didn't want to get the stuck-up villain's edit. Or worse, the oblivious loser's edit. There was always someone who talked a big game about how the judges had loved their dish and they were definitely going to win, when everyone at home knew their dish had been bad. The audience loved watching people's faces fall.

Nia, meanwhile, was mumbling what sounded like a mantra under her breath. And then I realized it was mostly numbers. ". . . the last three seasons, the winners were called first sixty-eight percent of the time. Statistically, we are more likely to be the winners than the losers. In the first three seasons, the person whose name is spoken second won forty-eight percent of the . . ."

Maz stopped in front of a door at the end of the hallway. He leaned in, voice hushed. "The cameras will be filming you as you walk into the room, just FYI." He sounded different when he was speaking off camera. Less confident. More nasally. "You'll walk in and stand in a row in front of the judges. Follow the tape on the floor."

I was glad we were given tape to follow, because the effort of looking confident—but not arrogant—plus following floor markings kept me from looking at Luke until I was standing on my designated X of tape. Then I looked up. My eyes locked onto his. He looked startled, almost, like he was surprised to see me here. Something sparked inside me. I wasn't sure if it was pure fury or if I wanted to dive over the judges' table to kiss him again. Or both.

His eyes slid away. The spark went cold and died.

We had to do three more takes of us walking in and lining up in front of the judges, because we kept staring at the floor. By the time we moved on, I was pretty sure all of my body had dissolved into sweat aside from the nerves sending white-hot tingles of panic from my shuddering heart to my swimming bowels.

Was it too late to go pee again?

"Chef Nia, Chef Kel, and Chef Sadie," Maz said in his announcer voice. I wondered if the camera was catching sunspots off the sweat glittering all over my face. "We've asked you here because you made our . . ."

Dramatic pause.

Dramatic pause continued.

Seriously, did all sound waves stop working or something?

Maz cleared his throat. ". . . *favorite* dishes of the night!"

I didn't consciously smile, but I felt it spreading over my face.

My focus was mostly on the rest of me, which was collapsing with relief. It was like my nerves had been a scaffolding, and now that they were gone, busy celebrating my top-three finish, the rest of me was ready to melt into a hot, loose pile of goo.

"Nia, your fried shrimp dish was what I can only describe as transcendent," Lenore Smith was rhapsodizing. She'd changed clothes since we saw her earlier, maybe to suggest that the judging was taking place on a different day, and was now wearing a navy blue tailored suit with a red bow tie. Maybe she hadn't wanted to accidentally drip raw pork juice on her fancy suit. "They were so light and tender and crispy, and you balanced it out perfectly with your sides. I might go so far as to say it was the best fried shrimp I've had all year."

Nia's face was positively glowing. I was at once happy for her and annoyed that her food was so good.

Luke went on. "And Chef Kel, your barbecued lamb was most impressive for having made it in an hour, but the real star of your plate was that chowchow. It was bracingly spicy and crunchy and tart and sweet, all at once. I want to feature it in my restaurant."

"Thank you," Kel said. Their cheeks were pink.

Maz turned to me. "Chef Sadie, that salmon was luscious and tender and tinged with the perfect touch of smoky flavor. That rub was crunchy and contrasted perfectly with the softness of the inside, and those nori-pickled vegetables provided the perfect bite of acidity. I only wish you'd left that slightly gummy rice porridge off the plate."

My cheeks were frozen. "Thank you!" That was really all you could say to judges' critique; anyone who argued with them got frowned at by the judges and endlessly vilified online. In my mind, Grandma Ruth snorted and shook her head, sending her short white curls bouncing before falling precisely back into place. She'd used so much hair spray, her house was pretty much a fire hazard. *Nothing wrong with a good argument now and then. Adds some spice to life*, said the woman who'd once fought a woman at the grocery store for the last package of American cheese even as she derided American cheese as plastic. American cheese might have been plastic, but I, her eldest grandchild, loved plastic cheese.

So it had been for me. And just the fact that someone had once fought a woman in the grocery store for *me* made me stand a little taller, gave me the courage to receive judgment from Luke the enormous asshole.

"While all three of your dishes were excellent, there can only be one winner," said Maz. I held my breath. "This week's winner is . . ."

He paused for so long I had to start breathing again or else I'd pass out. *Say Chef Sadie*, I urged him in my head, though I knew they'd already decided on the winner before we even stepped foot in this room. *Sadie, Sadie, Sadie!*

". . . Chef Nia!"

My face slipped into disappointment for just a moment before I remembered to push a smile onto my lips. With my luck, the camera would have focused in on me at that one moment and I'd be painted as a sore loser. *Better take care of that, then.* I turned to Nia and gave her a quick side-hug, that big, fake smile plastered on my face. Her elbows and shoulders felt even sharper and pointier than they looked. "Congratulations!" I gushed. "You deserve it!" Too much? Too much. Oh well. It wasn't like I could say, *just kidding, you don't actually deserve it.* And she did. My being here was probably a fluke, whereas she'd obviously studied like crazy. And her dish had clearly been amazing.

Kel, too, evidently had the same strategy as me, also smiling and saying congratulations. Or maybe they were a genuinely kind human being and I was garbage. Either one.

Nia was smiling so big it looked like her face might actually break in two. A light shone out her eyes. "Thank you so much," she said.

"You're one to watch," said Lenore Smith. The way her silver hair didn't move reminded me a little bit of Grandma Ruth. They both wore hair like a helmet.

"Now," Maz announced, his tone somber, signaling a shift. "Unfortunately, I'm going to have to ask you to send in some of your colleagues."

Our walk back down to the stew room was buoyant, the three of us floating above the tile floor. "I'm so excited to be in the top three," Kel said. "Even if I didn't win."

"I *did* win," said Nia, like we'd forgotten, but it was hard to hold it against her with that smile. "You know, approximately thirty-three percent of the chefs who win the first challenge go on to win the whole show!"

I wasn't sure exactly what to say to that. Fortunately, we arrived then at the stew room door. I took a deep breath. "Ready?"

Nia pushed the door open without waiting for a response.

The room was crackling with anticipation, all of them obviously hoping that we'd been the bottom three. "Well?" Vanilla Joe demanded, standing up. I had no idea why he stood. Maybe so he could jump up and down if one of us had gone home.

"I won!" Nia said. She was back to smiling, but it was a more cautious smile this time, taking into account the feelings of everybody else, who had to deal with the double whammy of knowing they didn't win and that they might go home.

A murmur of extremely insincere congratulations went up around the room. Kaitlyn actually came up to us and gave Nia a hug. "Congrats!!!!" she said. I could hear the exclamation points.

And then she turned to me. "You, too!" she gushed. "I'm really happy for you!"

Sure she was. She probably just wanted more camera time. Still, it felt good to have the upper hand. I might have just been crushed personally, but I was crushing it professionally. "Thanks," I said, grinning back at her. Did you know that, in apes, sometimes showing your teeth in a smile is actually a sign of aggression? I kept that in mind as I looked around at our circle, everybody smiling away.

Nia sobered. "They asked us to send three of you back," she said, and the room hushed, because everybody knew what that meant. The bottom three. "They asked for Mercedes and two of the Joes. Um, Joe Martinez and Joe Johnson?"

Kangaroo Joe and Old Joe stepped up alongside Mercedes, their faces grim. Vanilla Joe and Bald Joe smiled with relief. "Good luck, guys," Kel said as they all headed out.

The mood felt lighter as we took our seats again, waiting for the verdict. Nothing heavy was hanging over our heads. Even those who hadn't won knew they wouldn't be going home. "I don't know why you didn't make top three, Kaitlyn," Kel said. "Your ravioli looked so good."

Kaitlyn shrugged. "All of your food looked really good, too!"

Everybody murmured polite agreement . . . with one exception. Vanilla Joe slouched down in his chair, making what sounded like a scoff. I was ready to ignore it, not wanting to provoke a fight that could be twisted by the cameras, but Kaitlyn didn't seem to mind. "What?" she asked. "Is something wrong?"

If Vanilla Joe was wise, he'd say no, that of course all of our food looked delicious and he was absolutely not just a sore loser.

Vanilla Joe was not wise. He said, "It just doesn't seem fair. I was stuck with Nia's basket. Of course she won with *Southern* food. Southern food is easy to make from any basket. You can throw together some fried stuff and drown it in butter any-where." He lifted his chin in what looked like a challenge. "Not the case with *my* food."

Nia's eyes widened. "Excuse me?"

"Hey, fuck you," said Kel. "Not you, Nia. You, Vanilla Joe. Don't be an asshole."

Vanilla Joe didn't look bothered by being cursed out. I would. Not so much from the cursing out itself—I'd experienced much worse as a woman on the line—but from the fact that cameras were watching our every move, recording our every word. The producers were probably salivating: they had their villain of the season. Even if Vanilla Joe apologized to Nia right away, they'd have a fight to air.

Not that he was showing any signs of apologizing. "Not try-ing to be an asshole," Vanilla Joe said with an elegant shrug. "Just being blunt and honest."

Aka, the calling card of assholes everywhere.

Nia's eyes narrowed, and I got ready for some statistically driven defense . . . but the door eased open. The bottom three were back.

Mercedes and Old Joe entered with sheepish but relieved smiles. Kangaroo Joe entered with a grimace, his hands raised in front of him. "It's me," he said. "I'm out."

Everybody descended on him with hugs and reassurances. Nia, Kel, and I hung back, not sure if he'd want kind words from the winners. I wasn't sure if I wanted to give any kind words, really. The guy had served the judges rare pork. He should've known better than that.

It seemed that pork was harder to cook than kangaroo.

By the time we were told our schedule for the next day and to leave, it was dinnertime. Had we eaten lunch? I didn't remember. Our cars drove us home in the same formations we'd come there in. I stared dreamily out the window as we went over the bridge, watching the lights of the city sparkle in the water. Nia stared holes in Vanilla Joe's neck from the back seat. Vanilla Joe fell asleep.

Back at the *Chef Supreme* house, nobody wanted to cook. Kel and Kaitlyn and Old Joe threw together a massive cheese board from what they found in the fridge, scattered not only with cheese and crackers and bread but various fancy mustards and dried fruits and pickled things. We fell upon it like wolves on a carcass. I could practically hear the cheeses screaming.

The mood was festive—we'd all made it through!—until Ernesto ran to his room to grab a cigarette from his bag and found the bunk under his totally stripped and empty. "The kid's stuff is gone already," he said. Megan was laughing heartily, but she trailed off into a cough. "Like he was never here."

And soon enough it would be another one of us. I wondered who'd packed. Had they ushered Kangaroo Joe back here while the rest of us were getting instructions, to grab all his stuff and run out before we could feel sorry for him again? Or had they sent some unpaid intern to pull his underwear out of the drawer and throw it into a garbage bag so that an eliminated contestant wouldn't sully the threshold of our house?

As much as I wanted to get a good night's sleep before being woken up at the crack of dawn again tomorrow, my mind was racing and my stomach was churning. Maybe it was stress, and maybe it was too much cheese. Either way, I jumped in a quick shower, where long hairs of all shades already streaked the tile walls, then went out to the terrace.

I wasn't the only one who had that idea. Kaitlyn was out there smoking, as usual; from the ashtray in front of her, she'd been out there for a while. Nia sat upwind, her face turned toward the Manhattan skyline. Lights glittered up into the dark sky.

"Want a smoke?" Kaitlyn asked. I shook my head. She knew I didn't smoke. "Congrats again."

"Thanks."

We sat in silence for a bit, the wind ruffling our hair. "What do you think they'll do to us tomorrow?" I asked.

Kaitlyn shrugged. Nia said, "There's an odd number of us, so it won't be a team challenge."

"Makes sense," I said, but Nia wasn't done talking.

"I don't know enough about the new judge," she said. "I did a lot of research on John Waterford to know as much as possible about his likes and his dislikes and his history. Like, I've planned a whole bunch of recipes around not using raw red onion, because I know how much Chef Waterford hates it." Her brows knitted in dismay. "But what if this Luke person *loves* raw red onion? What if it's his favorite food, and I've doomed myself before I could even get started?"

"You just won the first challenge," Kaitlyn said dryly. "I wouldn't call you doomed."

They debated Luke for a while, going back and forth about what he might like, neither of them bringing up the idea of just asking Kel, as I sat there and seethed with anger. At that bastard. I couldn't believe he'd faked our connection that well. He was worse than . . . well. Than Derek.

Or maybe not quite that bad. Still, he was a giant asshole. Maybe he'd helped out Kel's career, but being a good boss meant nothing when it came to being a dick to the girls he dated. See: Chef Derek Anders. Ran an efficient kitchen; was a terrible boyfriend.

I'd just have to harness this anger. Pretend this was a horse race. My anger might have been bucky and stomping, but it would take me far, fast. Luke thought I was worthless? My old boss thought I'd never get another job—that I didn't *deserve* another job? I'd show them.

I hoped.

I'd gone too long without talking. Kaitlyn and Nia were both looking at me expectantly, waiting for me to chime in. I said, a bit too loudly, "I am completely and entirely in the dark on Luke's likes and dislikes to the point where I don't know if he even has any likes and dislikes."

Nailed it.

Kaitlyn squinted at me. "Ooookay."

"Anyway," I said quickly. I knew Luke didn't like fennel from our conversation on the plane, but maybe that had just been one more of his lies. "It feels a lot different being here than it does watching it on TV, doesn't it?"

"Yeah," Kaitlyn said quietly. Nia was still turned away, looking out over the sea of lights. Hoots and hollers drifted our way from the dark streets below, maybe people leaving a bar or kids out running the streets. I shifted in my seat. I liked New York City, liked the energy I'd seen so far and the fact that so much seemed to be going on all the time, but I was not a fan of this heat and humidity. Give me Seattle's dreary mist any day over the feeling that I was sitting inside a dog's mouth.

Nia looked back at us, frowning. "I can't believe Vanilla Joe said that about my food."

About it being easy to cook Southern food, because you could drown anything in butter and fry it and easily make it taste good. "He's an ass," I said sympathetically. "Just ignore him."

Nia rubbed her chin. "I don't just make Southern food. I figured I'd do Southern food for the first challenge because statistically, that seems to be what the judges like best coming from Black women. It's what they expect when they see us, especially since I'm actually from the South."

"You are?" Kaitlyn said quickly. "Where?" Was it my imagination, or did she seem eager to change the subject?

"Near the Georgia–South Carolina border," Nia said. "My family owned a barbecue joint. I started out there, cooking the sides—that was the women's work—then moved on to the city. Atlanta. Cooked there for years in all types of restaurants. Of course, what I really want is to open my own where I have full control over the menu."

"Of course," I said wistfully. Me, too. But for that, I'd have to do well in the next challenge, and the next. So I sat out there, watching curls of smoke disappear into the night sky, running through today's challenge in my head, remembering where different ingredients were placed and thinking about what I could have done better.

I would, after all, recount it for my confessionals tomorrow. And then do it all over again the next day.

8

I WOKE UP THE MORNING OF THE SECOND CHALLENGE to a camera in my face.

"What?" I fought the urge to punch it as I recoiled, squinting at the cameraman's light. "What . . ."

"Good morning!" the cameraman said jauntily. "Rise and shine!"

I fought the urge to punch *him*.

A whirlwind of toothpaste and dry toast and coffee later, we were filing into our shiny black cars. Adrianna was at the head of the line, pointing us into each back seat. "We're mixing it up this morning," she said, and was it my imagination, or was I getting a little bit of stink eye? "Wouldn't want anyone getting *overly stimulated* by their company."

So she *had* watched our video from the morning of the first challenge. Somewhat bashfully, I ducked my head and avoided her eyes as she pushed me into a back seat behind Bald Joe and Megan. Two of the larger people on set to be crammed into a back seat with, but I'd survive. Vanilla Joe hopped in the front seat. Again. I scowled at the back of his head.

Megan elbowed me as we pulled out. At first I figured it was an accident, considering how tight it was back here—so tight I could feel just how rock-hard Megan's right thigh was beneath her jeans—and then she did it again. "Hey, Sadie," she said. "So what's the deal with Kaitlyn?"

"The deal with Kaitlyn?" I repeated slowly.

"Yeah, Kaitlyn," she said, shifting around in her seat, or trying to shift, anyway. "You're friends, right?"

Friends? How exactly was I supposed to answer that? "Um, we used to work together. At Atelier Laurent," I said. "So we got to know each other pretty well there, I guess. But it's not like we're hanging out all the time or anything."

We'd tried, once. We'd even gone on a double date. Her and me with two of the waiters. Her waiter was obviously deep in the closet, and she'd gone home with mine.

"Well, anyway," Megan went on. She ran a hand over her buzz cut. It was starting to grow out a little, getting shaggy on the sides. "What is she? Do you know?"

I blinked, then jumped as our driver honked at a car taking too long to move after a green light. "What do you mean, what is she? She's a . . . chef? She's a . . . person?"

Megan heaved a disgusted sigh. "I mean, does she like women? Is she a lesbian? Bi? Is she—"

"I get it," I said quickly. Beside her, Bald Joe was smirking. I could only imagine Vanilla Joe's face in front. I didn't want to, but it forced its way into my head anyway. "Um, I don't know. We're not that close." I smothered a sigh with my hand. Of course everybody was in love with Kaitlyn. Jealousy flared in my belly. Everybody was in love with Kaitlyn, with how pretty and funny and charming she was, which hurt, especially given how everybody in my life was actively not in love with me.

Megan settled back into her seat, faintly disappointed. "What am I supposed to do, ask *her*?" She sighed. "I can't even stalk her social media while we're here." She settled until the point it became a slouch. "I feel like I'm missing a limb."

I felt a little bit that way, too, but I kind of liked it. Yeah, it was like I was missing a hand, but it was also like I hadn't realized the hand had been clenched up in pain all the time. Sometimes literally, because it had been wrapped around my phone for too many hours as I scrolled through people's feeds, catching up on all the things I wasn't invited to because I was busy working. That was what happened when you worked in a kitchen: you ended up hanging only with other people that worked your same off-hours. I was more likely to be cooking for one of my pre-restaurant friends than to be at the table with them myself.

At the *Chef Supreme* kitchen, we went through the same rigmarole as we had with the last challenge: hair and makeup; them picking apart our outfits; us lining up at our stations. I didn't even have to look for my name card when I got there; the station already felt familiar to me. Maybe not like my own kitchen, in which I could cook with a blindfold on, but like a friend's kitchen. I wondered which contestants had been at my station in previous seasons. It would be really cool if I were cooking at Julie Chee's station. The chances were only one in twelve, but I decided to pretend it was true anyway.

Once the cameras were ready and the lights were making us all sweat, Adrianna stepped away—the signal that we were going on camera, because she might run this whole thing, but she'd be damned if she let the public know it, she told us—and the door at the front of the room opened. Maz stepped through, every inch of him sculpted, plastic perfection. I didn't understand how there was enough hair spray in the world to make his black hair into a wave that high.

And behind him came the judges. Lenore Smith, today in a bright green pantsuit and a little too much blush, which made her icy blue eyes pop. And Luke. I hated that my stomach did a little jump when I saw him. They'd trimmed his black hair, I noticed today. He didn't look at me, of course. Those endless dark eyes of his scanned the entire kitchen, but over our heads. Like we didn't matter at all to him.

I fought back a scowl. Didn't want it on camera. Instead, I tried to beam thoughts in his direction. *You're going down. So down. So far down you'll burn in the earth's crust.*

It didn't entirely make sense, considering he wasn't actually competing, but it was still pretty early in the morning.

"Hello, top eleven!" Maz proclaimed. I tried to smile, demonstrating how happy I was to be here. Kaitlyn was beaming so hard the rays of light reflecting off her big, shiny teeth might burn out Maz's eyes. How were her teeth even that white with all the smoking? "We have a special surprise in store today . . ."

Oh no. Surprises were never a good thing in the *Chef Supreme* kitchen.

". . . for one of our judges!" Maz finished after his dramatic pause. Lenore Smith's overly sculpted eyebrows lifted in surprise. I wondered if it was real. If the judges were as much in the dark on each challenge as we were.

Luke's face didn't change at all.

Maz angled himself toward the door at the front. That also

happened to be his best angle, where you could clearly see all the defined lines stark in his cheekbones and jaw. "Please welcome today's guest judge, Chef Charles Weston!"

Charles Weston. That was Luke's father. I was busy watching Luke's face, so I missed his father's entrance. Luke certainly didn't; his eyes were trained on the door. An enormous smile was plastered cheek to cheek, but I could see the muscles twitching in his jaw even from where I stood. It looked as if they were trying to jump out through his skin.

I tore my eyes away from him as I realized what I was doing. Why did I even care where he was looking or what he was feeling? The only extent he should matter to me anymore was how to get him to like my food enough to vote for me over any reservations. I should kiss those stupid dreams I had in the doorway of that Korean place goodbye. No, not even kiss them. I should kick them out the door and leave them shivering in the cold.

I realized Charles Weston was talking. *Focus, Sadie. Remember the most important thing here.* ". . . excited to be here for my seventieth birthday," he said in a crisp, posh British accent. He didn't look seventy. Yes, he looked distinguished: old white man with sculpted bone structure and silver hair, but his skin was still fairly smooth, and his stomach didn't stick out too much. "I wanted to spend my seventieth with my only son, which meant also spending it with all of you."

Maz confirmed my suspicion. "For your next challenge, you'll be in charge of catering Chef Weston's birthday celebration. Each one of you will be responsible for one hors d'oeuvre to serve one hundred guests."

Okay. So that would be tough, but I could do it. I waited for some twist he could throw in—*you'll have to cook them balanced on one another's shoulders in a human pyramid!*—but he only asked Charles to share his personal tastes.

"Well," Charles Weston said. "I don't want to sound like a food snob, because I like my street cart sausages as much as the next man, but my guests will be expecting dishes that are exciting and sophisticated at the same time. I'd like you to push the boundaries. Show me what's possible in a small, bite-size package." He winked. On most older men it would've looked creepy, but he pulled it off. "Oh, and I absolutely can't stand beets. They taste like dirt and sadness."

I found that offensive, because beets were delicious, but everybody else laughed, so I did, too, so that I wouldn't be the only one scowling on camera.

Though I noticed, to my satisfaction, that Luke didn't look thrilled, either. He must also love beets.

"So you'll have three hours to prep here in the kitchen, and ninety minutes to finish up on-site tomorrow," Maz said. He went on to tell us that each hors d'oeuvre should be approximately one bite and should reflect our unique culinary perspectives, and that we had to make enough to feed one hundred people and the judges. "Chefs, you may start your cooking!"

It took me a while to tease out my idea, but I was really happy with what I came up with. I mean, as happy as I could get while still being absolutely sure I was going to go home.

The train of thought went like this: I scribbled down the most "sophisticated" foods I could think of. Foie gras. Truffles. Expensive wine. Caviar. Ibérico ham. The one that struck a chord with my Jewish brain was caviar. Caviar served with blinis, little pancakes hailing from eastern Europe. In Russia they served blinis with caviar and sour cream. But even if I could make a hundred and fifteen blinis in the time allowed (since we had to make a few extras for beauty shots and mistakes), I couldn't just serve them with caviar and sour cream. That wasn't transformative enough. Original enough.

What else was served with blinis? I tapped my pen thoughtfully against my *Chef Supreme* notepad. We were getting to the end of our planning session, and the way the others around me were nodding and whispering to themselves was making me nervous. *Sadie, they all know exactly what they're doing, and you don't,* I thought to myself. And then I nodded, confirming it.

Jam. Blinis were served sweet-style with jam. But even if I made my own jam, that wouldn't be enough. I needed a wow factor. What if . . . what if I made sweet blinis, but disguised them as savory blinis? Ideas ran through my head as we were driven to the grocery store. I wasn't hugely into molecular gastronomy, but even I knew how to take a liquid or an oil and turn it into small gelatinous pearls not unlike fish eggs. I could take jam, thin it out, and turn it into caviar. Then what would be my sour cream? A sweetened mascarpone whip? And then I needed something to keep all the sweetness from becoming overwhelming. I'd have to make the jam nice and tart. And maybe add a savory element. A fried sage leaf? That could be interesting . . .

At the grocery store, I threw a wild variety of things into my cart, doing calculations in my head to make sure I stayed within my budget. What I had to do during prep time today: make all of my mini-blinis (an adorable word I resolved to say on camera multiple times). They wouldn't be as good as they would be if I made them to order at the event tomorrow, but I couldn't make them all tomorrow and also do everything else I had to do, and what if the stove top there wasn't working and I had to share heating space?

No. I had to make my tart berry juice today, too, so that it could cool overnight. If I had time left over, I'd do my mascarpone whip.

The prep time flew by. I didn't stop moving even to wipe the sweat off my face; hair slipped out of my ponytail and stuck itself in lines all over my forehead and neck. My arms ached as I mixed and stirred, as I poured careful circles of batter onto the griddle, as I boiled berries and carefully strained out all the seeds. By the end of our allotted time, I was sweaty, satisfied, and coated in a thin layer of jelly, which also described one of my past late-night flings with the owner of a local doughnut stand.

He'd ghosted me after two weeks. Hopefully, I'd have more success this time.

THE DAY OF CHARLES WESTON'S PARTY DAWNED BRIGHT and clear, which was fortunate, as I'd watched enough *Chef Supreme* to know that disasters came along with rain. I snoozed most of the hour and a half to the event site, even though our wake-up time was later than it had been the past couple days—a generous eight thirty a.m. But I'd had trouble falling asleep last night, my stomach eating itself over all the possible things that could go wrong with my dish.

Also, Kel snored like a mofo.

I woke up with a few minutes left in the car ride, enough time to notice how the crowded streets and tall buildings of the city had turned into rolling green lawns and massive houses with pillars framing the doors. Between houses I caught sight of the ocean, meaning that these houses had private beaches. "Where are we?" I asked the car. It was hard to believe we were still in New York.

"The Hamptons, I think?" Kel was goggling out the window, too.

Well, that explained it. Most of what I knew about the Hamptons came from episodes of *Gossip Girl*.

The event was to be held in the great lawn behind what looked like a country club mansion. I wouldn't know if it belonged to a country club or a real person, as nobody told us what it was, and we weren't allowed inside. When I had to nervous pee as soon as I got there, I was directed to a cluster of porta potties hidden behind a tall hedge. I held my breath as I tried not to let my dress touch anything in there. Wardrobe had pulled me aside last night and warned me against wearing my usual jeans, since this party was so fancy and everything. Hence this sleeveless green and yellow flowered midi dress.

I emerged from the porta potty to find my spot. Our eleven stations were arranged in a wide semicircle facing the building; waiters were setting up cocktail tables in the middle, and at the other side a bartender was laying out lots of shiny glass bottles. Like our stations in the *Chef Supreme* kitchen, our locations were assigned. Mine was situated in the middle of the group between Vanilla Joe and Kaitlyn. I didn't have time to think about how this must be some kind of twisted revenge from Adrianna, because our prepared carts from yesterday were arriving. I still had to distill my juice into caviar bubbles, and make my mascarpone whip, and fry my sage, and un-chill my mini-blinis (heh) so that they didn't taste like refrigerator, and assemble everything. This was going to be a tight ninety minutes.

I was so in the zone, focusing hard on everything I had to get done, that I didn't notice the cameras until they were right in my face. Like, literally—I unbent myself to go turn on my deep fryer and found myself staring into the blank black lens of a camera. "Chef Sadie!" Maz boomed from somewhere behind it. I took a step back. The camera followed me. "Can you tell me a little bit about what you're doing?"

Now he was somehow next to me, staring intently at my setup. I wanted to curse him for shattering my focus, all of which I needed to finish on time, but I forced myself to smile instead. "My grandma Ruth used to make us blinis for breakfast in the mornings when we'd sleep over her house," I told him. "They're like little pancakes, and you can make them either sweet or savory. One of the traditional eastern European ways to eat them is with caviar and sour cream, so I'm doing a play on that."

Grandma Ruth was cackling in the background. *I never in my life cooked you a blini, dear.*

I knew that. Obviously, I knew that. But what was I supposed to say? *Chef Supreme* loved family stories, the sappier the better. The contestant competing to prove something to their estranged dad who looked down on their career choice. The contestant striving to live up to the example of their dead mom. More than anything, they loved family recipes—chefs pulling out things older relatives made them as a child, fulfilling a family legacy, cooking the food of their heritage and history.

I ignored the imaginary protestations in my head. "We, of course, used to eat ours with whipped cream and jam."

Maz said, "Just don't serve us whipped cream and caviar."

I raised an eyebrow in what I hoped was an amused way. It just made my head echo with my grandmother's laughter.

"Thanks, Sadie," Maz said, and moved on. Thankfully, leaving me more room to maneuver my trays.

That moment of split focus made me realize there was a conversation going on behind my head. Kaitlyn was calling to Vanilla

Joe, "You think pigs in a blanket are going to be enough to get you a win?"

I flicked a few drops of water into my fryer to test the temperature. Vanilla Joe called back, "They're elevated. I made my own sausage!"

The fryer still wasn't hot enough. Was it the morning chill in the air? I gritted my teeth.

Kaitlyn was laughing like a seal. "Keep your sausage out of it!"

"You're welcome to a taste of my sausage anytime."

Were they . . . flirting?

I gritted my teeth even harder. I did *not* have time to parse what was going on here. And at least they were loud enough to mostly cover up Nia shouting from her station that she couldn't find her measuring cups, and that she needed those particular very specific measuring cups, and who stole them?

After what felt like just a few seconds later, I raised my head from where I was dropping a careful spoonful of berry pearls atop white mascarpone pillows and noticed clusters of distinguished-looking older men and women in fancy suits and dresses beginning to trickle into our semicircle of stations. I glanced up at the clock, flicking sweat off my forehead. Five minutes left. That was better than I thought, actually. I had most of my—

The sage. Crap, crap, crap. My fryer still wasn't as hot as it needed to be, but I dropped a handful of sage leaves in anyway.

And then promptly forgot about them.

I pasted a smile on my face as I turned to my first customers, a man and a woman. They were both older, both white. The man wore a silk tie with a pattern even I, an unfashionable person, recognized as being from a very fashionable designer, and the woman had glittering diamonds in her ears that probably cost more than my parents' house. "Good afternoon and welcome to the party," I told them. "I have for you today a mini-blini with jam caviar and a mascarpone whipped cream, topped with . . ."

I trailed off. Heard the fryer sizzling. *"Shit."*

"I'm sorry?" said the woman, as the man said, "It's topped with what?"

"Not shit!" I called over my shoulder as I ran to the fryer, leaving their mini-blinis on the counter.

Crap crap crap *crap crap*.

But it was too late now. I pulled the sage leaves out of the fryer, all black and bubbly and unusable, and dumped them in the grass. I stood there for a moment, calculating. Did I have time to throw in some more? Would it look worse to leave the ingredient off my dish or to serve inconsistent plates?

"Excuse me?" the man said from the front of my booth. I spun around. A line was already forming, several people deep.

I clenched my jaw, that voice echoing in my head again. *A real Chef Supreme wouldn't burn her garnish. A real Chef Supreme is just better than you are. The Arlington Restaurant Group is going to laugh in your face.*

I was unable to bring that forced smile back. I dropped mini-blinis into the hands of the rich couple, unable to meet their eyes, either. I saw a few caviar pearls roll onto the ground. Great. Just great.

When I saw the cameras approaching, I knew the judges were close. I tried to ignore them as they swooped in for some action shots of me placing my mini-blinis on napkins and chatting with guests as they tried theirs, pricking my ears in hopes of overhearing what they were telling Maz over there. Hopefully, that they loved my dish and found it creative? Not that I'd barked at them that my blinis were topped with shit?

I raised my head to Lenore Smith's gleaming smile. My stomach did a flip, not from seeing her, but from knowing who would be there with her: not just Maz and Chef Charles Weston, but Luke.

Luke wore a tux today, one that had clearly been tailored to his slim form. His black hair had been gelled until it went slick, but not in a sleazy or gross way. It made him look like a nineteenth-century oil painting. I lifted my lip in a snarl as heat rushed through me again. Good. Harness that hate. Because hate was *definitely* what it was.

Still, my mouth went dry as the judges lined up before me. "Hello," I said, forcing a smile. I stared at Maz's hair. How exactly *had* he gotten it so high? Was it actually a wig? The thought made me slightly less nervous. Slightly less focused on how I wasn't sure I had what it took to advance in this thing.

"Tell us about your dish," said Lenore Smith, and I launched into the presentation that had grown tighter and funnier over the twenty times I'd given it already. They laughed in all the right places. My grandma cackled in my ear.

"Looks delicious," said Chef Charles as I handed him a napkin. He turned to his son. "Doesn't it, Luke?"

Luke cleared his throat as he waited for his own serving. I handed him a blini in a napkin, and my fingers brushed up against his. His skin was dry and rough; the feel of it zapped my own skin, nearly made me drop his food on the grass. "It's hard to tell without tasting it."

I had to hold my eyes back from rolling. What an *ass*.

In unison, they all took a bite. I stared at Luke's lips closing around the soft pancake, the creamy mascarpone, the dark red pops of jelly. The camera zoomed in, too, catching the single caviar pearl that tumbled down his chin and caught in his elbow. I was seized with the urge to pull it off before it popped and stained that custom tux, and maybe let my fingertips linger against him a moment too long . . .

But he relaxed his arm and it tumbled away to the ground, where it would get stepped on by some other guest. "It's a nice mixture of sweet and sour and salty," he said, talking to the other judges as if I weren't there. I was torn between the desire to thank him for what he was saying and hate him for being him. "The tart, sour jam, the rich, creamy cheese, the soft, doughy pancake—it's a luxurious mouthful."

"I enjoyed the playful presentation," said Maz. "I mean, it looks like caviar and sour cream, and then you bite in and your mouth is totally surprised!"

So far, so good. But I knew they typically praised people before tearing them down, so I braced myself.

Sure enough, they went on for a bit more about what they liked before the clincher. "When did you make these blinis?" Chef Charles asked. "Did you make them to order?"

I drummed my fingertips on my counter. *Do you see a long flat-top grill?* is what I wanted to say. But I told him that I did indeed make them ahead of time.

"I thought so," he said dismissively. My cheeks heated up. "There was a slightly stale texture to them, a little bit of a dried-out feeling, that came from being made yesterday and chilled overnight."

"I thought the cheese and the jelly mostly made up for that,"

Luke said. He took another bite, as if checking to make sure. He closed his eyes as he chewed, and the midday sunlight glanced off his cheekbones.

"I agree with Chef Charles," Lenore Smith said. "And I felt that the textures were all soft, soft, soft. We needed something crispy or crunchy or hard to break it up."

Like a crispy sage leaf? It was like hearing about my slightly gummy rice porridge all over again, but taken up a notch with the knowledge I'd had a plan to fix it. The other judges nodded to agree about the textural problem.

Maybe they would feel better if they knew I'd known about it. "I was going to add a crispy sage leaf to each blini, but the time got to me," I said. I was going to add more about how that would have solved their problem, but my voice faded into nothingness at Lenore's contemptuous glare.

"We can't and won't judge you on that," she said. "Only what makes it onto the plate."

I wanted to wither up and crumble away like my overfried sage leaves. But I forced a smile onto my face and spoke in a voice that felt like eating glass. "Thank you so much for your feedback."

Once the judges left, the pressure on me eased a little bit. I stopped worrying about the precise amounts of tiny caviar pearls that went atop each pillow of cheese, and started looking around me to see what the other chefs were doing. As I knew, Vanilla Joe on my left was handing out his homemade pigs in a blanket, his hand-ground sausages wrapped in what looked like hand-rolled pastry, all served with a variety of dipping sauces he must also have made himself (including vanilla aioli, obviously). The judges were at his station now. From the big, cheesy grin on Vanilla Joe's mustached mouth and the rhapsodizing tones of Charles Weston's and Maz's voices that floated my way, they loved it. I scowled.

On my other side, Kaitlyn looked to be handing out arancini balls atop a bed of crisp greens and pickled vegetables. Probably tasty, but hard to eat in one bite—the judges always took that into account. She was laughing and talking with each guest, assembling her dishes in a way that looked totally effortless; was she even sweating at all?

Guests wandered by with charred meat on a skewer, alternating with ripe chunks of watermelon and tomato. In the distance I could see Kel cooking up spoon bread with what looked like mushrooms. Megan was frying dumplings, which made my mouth water thinking about the inner mixture of pork and cabbage and water chestnuts. When I saw somebody eating takoyaki balls, I assumed that was Bald Joe's work—after all, the tender balls of fried dough and octopus were a traditional Japanese street food. Somebody else had soup shooters.

As I squinted into the crowd, flaring my nostrils to try and pick up any distinctive smells, what floated to me instead were quick, hurried voices to the side. Very familiar voices. I pricked my ears toward the overhang, trying not to make it obvious I was listening.

". . . being ridiculous." The older man's voice dripped with disdain. "I thought your palate was better than that."

"I'm not being ridiculous." The younger man's was defensive. "The dumplings' filling was tender and savory, soft with just a bit of crunch, and the wrappers were crispy and chewy all at once. And that dipping sauce? It took the dumplings from being simply very good to transcendent, in—"

"Dumplings, though?" said Chef Charles. I couldn't see him, but I pictured his thick silver brows forming a V over those pale blue eyes. "Son, I asked for sophistication. For class. For these chefs to push the boundaries of what they can do with food—"

"And pigs in a blanket does that?" Luke. Arguing with his father over what dishes they were going to vote for, it sounded like. "Those dumplings took just as much skill, if not more, to make than—"

"End of discussion." Chef Charles's voice was colder than the salmon fillets I'd once forgotten about in the back of the Green Onion's walk-in freezer. They'd burned my fingertips when I went to throw them away. "It seems you still have learning to do about your palate."

The silence that resulted sounded as if he'd walked away. I snuck a glance behind me to confirm. Chef Charles was somehow already in conversation with a guest, a warm smile on his face as if he hadn't just frozen his son into a statue of ice standing only feet away.

As if he could feel my eyes on him, Luke uncracked and spun on his heel, stalking off into the grounds in the direction of the porta potty hedge. I watched him go, feeling a heavy weight settle into the pit of my stomach. That hunched posture, that bowed neck, those balled fists? All after someone you cared about yelling at you?

Me, bowed over, panic scrabbling at the insides of my rib cage, everything inside me screaming to go somewhere no more specific than "away." Derek's words hanging in the air like knives aimed in my direction, cruel and sharp and ready to slice skin till it bled. I had to get out of their way, and I knew running would make me look weak, but I didn't care. I just didn't want to get cut.

My feet were moving in Luke's direction before I could consciously decide anything. *What are you doing?* my brain asked furiously. *He's a jerk! And a judge! You shalt not fraternize with either one!* Don't ask me why my brain suddenly decided to sound like one of the Torah tablets Moses dragged down from Mount Sinai. *Maybe you would know the answer if you'd continued going to temple after your bat mitzvah, Sadie.* Thanks, brain!

As much as my brain wanted to stop me, the rest of my body was totally on board. My legs obediently followed my feet, and my hands set down their pile of napkins, and my mouth shouted to the nearby Adrianna, "Bathroom!" She looked faintly disgusted at the idea of any bodily function, but nodded. I'd gone through my hundred appetizers already. The party was over, at least for us.

My Converses sank into the grass as I walked toward the porta potty hedge, which made me wonder how all those fancy women wearing fancy heels were managing. The thought of this pristine lawn being poked full of high-heel holes when this was over kept me occupied until I rounded the hedge and found Luke. He melted back against the hedge beside the porta potties, his arms crossed tightly against his chest and eyes staring so intently at the ground that I wondered if he was thinking about high-heel holes, too.

"Hey, I overheard your conversation with your dad," I said, and then those intent, blazing eyes were on *me*. I had to steady myself against taking a step back. "Are you okay?"

His eyes shifted up to the sky. It was clear blue, not a cloud in sight. It actually kind of worried me how close he was looking to the sun. You weren't supposed to look directly at the sun. It would burn your retinas into cinders or something. "I'm fine. Go to the bathroom."

"I don't have to go to the bathroom," I said, even though I

SADIE ON A PLATE

kind of did. I always kind of did, despite the fact that I'd purposefully dehydrated myself today so that I wouldn't have to pee during the challenge. I should really drink something, actually. My mouth was parched.

"Then what are you doing *here*?" He gestured at the porta potties. A smile twitched at the corners of his lips. Not enough to make them actually stay up, though. "This isn't exactly the scenic part of the property."

"What if I like the smell of sewage?" I asked. The smile twitched again at his lips, and I found my heart twitching with it.

That idiot, said my brain disapprovingly. *No sense, all emotion.*

You're the one being an idiot, said my grandma Ruth, just as disapprovingly. I shook her away.

"Then you're funny in the head." The trace of that British accent came out again. The same as his dad's, I realized. "Besides, you shouldn't be here with me. We're not supposed to fraternize."

I shrugged. "I'm going to the bathroom. Maybe *you* should go back."

He didn't move. I didn't move. He sighed as I moved closer to him, putting my back up against the hedge and wrinkling my nose. "God, you're really downwind right here, aren't you?"

He didn't answer, just sighed again. "Let me wallow, Sandy." His heart wasn't even in the wrong name. It just sounded pathetic. He was actively trying to be a jerk, and somehow that made the whole act less offensive.

"You know perfectly well my name is Sadie."

"I do now that you've reminded me." He squinted at the bright sky. Maybe he was *trying* to burn his retinas out. Those seemed like self-destructive tendencies to me. I admired it a little bit. When I'd had the opportunity to go self-destructive, I'd just lumped into a sad, weepy heap of blankets. "What do you want?"

I opened my mouth to respond, but the words stuck in my throat. Maybe because even they weren't sure what they were trying to say. What *did* I want? Why had I even come here? "Just to make sure you're okay," I said. I looked around, checking that there were no cameras on me. I'd already switched my mic off just in case, which didn't arouse any suspicions, considering I was supposed to be in the bathroom.

Even so, I whispered, in case they'd set up super-illegal hidden cameras in the porta potty hedge. "Your dad seems like kind of an ass."

The laugh that burst out of him made me jump; it was that deep and full and resounding. He laughed until he had to rub his eyes, which were tearing up. I'd saved them from being burned out. Success! "Yes, that's putting it kindly," Luke said. "I'm pretty sure he's a full-on ass."

"A hairy one," I said, because I wanted to see him laugh like that again. I got my wish.

He shook his head once he was done. "Is it really wise of you to criticize your judges?"

I shrugged. "Nobody's ever described me as wise."

"I'm not surprised," Luke said dryly. "But you're wrong about that last one. My father waxes every bit of his torso."

"I definitely did not need to know that."

"Neither did I," said Luke. "But I had no choice. Now you, too, have no choice but knowledge of my father's gleaming bald ass."

I shuddered. "Really, though," I said. "Don't let him get to you. *You're* the official *Chef Supreme* judge. You know what's best."

He squinted at me. "It's not that easy. My dad . . ." He trailed off, and I remembered everything he'd told me back when he thought I was just Sadie, some random cook he'd met on an airplane. That his dad didn't approve of what he wanted to do.

And it all clicked. "He's a food snob," I said. "Isn't he? One of those guys that doesn't see 'ethnic food' as food that can be sophisticated or high-class. That's why he wouldn't give Megan's dumplings the win over anything else, no matter how good they were." I knew I was right by every centimeter Luke's face fell as I spoke. "He's the kind of guy that would actually, unironically call her dish 'ethnic food,' right? And he's why you won't go after your dream of opening that unfancy Korean restaurant experimenting with your halmoni's recipes. Because there's no way he'd approve."

His face stopped falling and froze solid. I held my breath, afraid he'd explode with anger at my presumption, at my guff, at my daring to speak the truth.

But when he finally spoke, it was in barely more than a whisper. "I have to get back to the party." His movements were jerky, as if his legs and arms were being controlled by an invisible puppet master overhead. I watched his movements smooth as he walked. By the time he worked himself back into the clusters of conversation, he was laughing.

THE PRODUCERS SEQUESTERED us behind another set of hedges for ages as the judges deliberated, and then they judged us all together out there on the lawn. They had us line up in the order of our stations. I took my place between Vanilla Joe and Kaitlyn. Everybody smelled like sweat and stale oil, and even though the sun wasn't fully down yet, I ached to my bones with exhaustion.

"I'm thrilled with my birthday celebration," Chef Charles said, all white teeth and shiny forehead and gleaming bald ass *no Sadie stop don't think about it*. He had his arm draped loosely over Luke's shoulders. I bet it felt heavier than it looked. "Thank you for such excellent hors d'oeuvres, chefs. What a way to enter year seventy."

Blah, blah, blah, everyone is a winner, blah blah. "We'd like Chef Joe Hennessey, Chef Kel, and Chef Megan to step forward, please."

Vanilla Joe, Kel, and Megan stepped forward, leaving the rest of us to marinate in a pungent mixture of our own fear and stress and, yes, more sweat. "Chefs," said Maz. "You made our . . . favorite dishes!"

My stomach gave an unpleasant lurch. I hadn't won. No more top three for me. I forced what I hoped was a pleasant and interested look onto my face so that the cameras wouldn't catch me looking upset.

Nia wasn't making such an effort. She was outright scowling, her brows crunched over her nose, her lips moving as she whispered to herself. Maybe she was trying to figure out what she'd done wrong. Beside me, Kaitlyn wore a frozen smile that made her whole body stiff.

I turned my attention back to the judges as they praised the top three's food. "Chef Kel, your spoon bread and trumpet mushrooms were so rich you almost didn't need to add those shavings of ham on top," Maz said, then added a hearty laugh. "Though I'm sure glad you did. Almost as glad as I was for those bracingly vinegary sumac-pickled onions in the mix. They kept the dish from being over-the-top rich."

Lenore Smith went on to gush over Megan's dumplings, and then Chef Charles rhapsodized over Vanilla Joe's fancy pigs in a blanket with their surprisingly delicious side of vanilla aioli. *Win, Kel,* I thought to myself. *If I can't win, let it be you.*

Luke didn't say a word.

Maz turned to face the camera, his eyebrows raised high. "For one of the only times I can remember, the judges' panel was evenly split across the top three. Each of us urged the others to choose a particular dish." He turned his megawatt smile on Luke. "It came down to our *youngest* judge to be the tiebreaker."

I was so interested in what was going on that my interested expression was actually natural. It sounded like Maz's favorite was Kel's dish, Lenore liked Megan's dumplings, and Chef Charles obviously preferred Vanilla Joe's sausages. So it really came down to whether Luke had it in him to stand up for Megan's dumplings, or whether he'd cave to his dad and pick—

". . . Chef Joe and his pigs in a blanket!"

Vanilla Joe stepped forward and took a mock bow, nodding his head in thanks at Chef Charles. Looking at them together, it was kind of funny how similar they looked. Charles was Vanilla Joe in thirty or forty years.

As the winning chefs stepped back into line, I tried to catch Luke's eye. But you can't catch what isn't swimming near you. He managed to look everywhere but at me, which was quite a feat, considering I was right in front of him.

Stop thinking about him, I told myself. *Not only are his daddy issues none of your business, and not only is he a giant ass, your name could be called next.* My heart hardened again.

I held my breath as Maz spoke the bottom three's names with an exaggeratedly solemn frown. "Chef Mercedes, Chef Joe

Johnson, and . . ." He paused dramatically. If he didn't get on with it, I was legit going to pass out. ". . . Chef Nia, please step forward."

I exhaled in a whoosh, but Nia sucked her teeth so loud I could hear her over it. She was still scowling as she stepped forward. *Stop*, I thought at her. *Play nice. Or they'll cast you as the villain.*

Mercedes's play on balut—Filipino fertilized duck egg—where she'd mixed duck and egg was not popular. One-note, the judges said, and too sour. Old Joe's gazpacho shooters hadn't been creative enough and had felt way too simple for the task at hand. "And Chef Nia," Maz said. "Technically, your beef and beet tartare was tasty. The pickled beets had a nice acidity to them, and the spices were interesting—was that five-spice powder you used?—and the beef was cut well."

"But," Charles Weston said, "I specifically told you all that I do not like beets."

Nia lifted her chin, looking determined. The camera did a swan dive at her face, gleefully anticipating the drama. "I know you don't like beets. I thought my dish would make you like them."

None of the judges answered her, just looked at her with raised eyebrows. She pressed her lips together. "Maz just *said* it was a good dish."

"*Chef Supreme* isn't all about a technically good dish," Lenore said kindly. "It's not just about the ratios of ingredients, or the proper amount of salt. Not totally. It's about knowing your audience, and your heart, and cooking what will sing for them."

"Exactly," Charles Weston said, raising his chin so he could look down at her with an imperious air. "Being Chef Supreme is more than just being able to follow a recipe. It's about cooking from your heart to someone else's heart. It's about being vulnerable, and putting who you are, all you've got, on the plate, but ultimately it should be as much about the other person as it is about you."

That was word salad even less impressive than the desperately sad kale and lemon juice bowl I'd once thrown together for a customer who didn't want anything with meat, gluten, fat, or sugar in her meal. But I understood what it meant.

Nia was shaking her head. "One of my line cooks hated beets until I made her that dish. Now she loves them."

"Nevertheless," said Charles Weston, "you should have respected my wishes."

Maz waited a few seconds to see if Nia was going to respond, but she just slumped back, a sour expression on her face. He gave his usual doom-laden spiel about how one of them had to go, blah blah blah, and then, "Thank you, chefs," he was saying. I fixed my face into a somber expression. "The chef who won't be moving on into the top ten is . . ." Dramatic pause. "Chef Mercedes. The dish just tasted off. Please remove your apron and go."

Mercedes sniffled for a bit as Old Joe and Nia pretended not to be totally relieved. For Nia it might not have been a show, actually. She was still cursing under her breath as Adrianna ushered us into the back seat of our black car. This time I was stuck in the middle of the back seat between Nia and Kaitlyn, with the front seat empty. I didn't think to ask about moving up there until the car was already moving. This time, being awake, I could see the big houses and expansive green lawns turn into smaller houses bunched closer together turn into taller buildings side by side as we reapproached the city.

"You okay, Nia?" I asked.

She was glaring into the dashboard camera. "That was *bullshit*. My dish was *great*."

"I bet it was," I said. "But cooking's not just about making something that tastes great."

"Yeah, whatever," she mumbled.

"He did explicitly say he didn't like beets," Kaitlyn said. "Was it really about trying to make him like them?"

Nia slouched lower in her seat. "I decided beforehand that I was going to make the beef and pickled beet tartare for an hors d'oeuvres challenge," she said. "I knew one would be coming. I didn't . . . I didn't factor in the variable that the judge might not like beets."

Sounded to me like Nia needed to loosen up more. To stop relying on her plans and statistics and measuring cups. But it wasn't like I could say that. I just said, "That sucks," and let her continue to glower at the dashboard camera until she sat upright.

"You know what sucks?" she spat. "This car. This is the worst piece of shit car I've ever been driven in."

And then she slumped back in her seat, her arms crossed tightly over her chest, and refused to say another word.

10

LATER THE NEXT NIGHT, AFTER FILMING OUR CONFES-
sionals on the hors d'oeuvres challenge, my eyes were already
bleary and it wasn't even dinnertime yet. Days of waking up at
the crack of dawn, being on your feet and under high-stress conditions for sixteen hours straight, grabbing a few hours of sleep
on a bunk bed that might as well have been made of cardboard,
and consuming mostly cheese and coffee weren't actually that
good for you, as it turned out. From the way all of us remaining
contestants were slumped around the dining table, listlessly
picking at tonight's array of cheese and crackers, I didn't think I
was the only one ready to go to my room, pull my thin, scratchy
blanket over my head, and black out. At least, until Bald Joe said,
"It's Sunday tomorrow."

"Today is Saturday?" asked Kaitlyn. "Go figure."

I rolled my eyes, but I had no idea what day it was, either. The
days were all blending together. Hopefully, Bald Joe wasn't about
to suggest that we all go to church. Though if it meant getting to

sleep later than six a.m., I might be willing to violate centuries of rabbis' edicts about staying out of them.

But what he had to say was even better. "We have tomorrow off."

My eyelids popped open. A rush of energy zipped through my veins. When Kaitlyn raised her fist in the air and hollered, "PARTY!" I answered with a holler of my own.

I might have been losing my mind a little bit, but at least I could do it out on the terrace, with my belly warm and full of wine.

Before drinking the wine, though, we had to make a toast with it. Us top ten assembled, the fairy lights twinkling overhead, the lights of the city sparkling over the water. I wished that I had my phone so hard it hurt. Not so that I could stare at it and pretend I was somewhere else, but so that I could take a picture, or a recording, and ensure I'd be able to remember exactly what it was like to be here at this moment, with the lights glittering over our skin and the smell of heat and asphalt in the air.

The show cameras were here, of course. Most of the camerapeople had gone home for the evening, but Adrianna had conscripted one of them to follow us around for dinner. I didn't know his name—he hadn't spoken to us aside from the occasional apology when he bumped one of us with a piece of equipment—but I knew what he was here for. Every season liked to humanize the contestants, make the viewers feel like they knew us in ways aside from what they saw on set.

But what he was recording wasn't *real*. I kept my expression appropriately somber as we poured out a little wine in tribute to Mercedes when what I wanted to do was whoop and celebrate because I'd made it through another week, not pretend to be sad for a woman I barely knew. Maybe the others were sincere; I didn't know. They could be better people than me.

We made toasts to one another and the two dearly departed, smiling toothily at our reflections in the camera lens. Even Nia only sulked in the back for a minute before wising up and making herself look sympathetic.

I drank, but not too much, as aware of the lens on me as I was of people passing behind me on the line. We chatted about our food, our restaurants, the TV shows we all not-so-secretly wanted to have one day. I slapped Kel on the shoulder as a congratulations for being in the top three again, maybe a little harder than I had to. They slapped me back, definitely harder than they had to.

As I glanced to the side, I noticed the cameraman whispering something in Kaitlyn's ear. She nodded, then turned back to the group, flashing us all a warm smile. "So, you guys, do your parents approve of what you do?"

Adrianna must have wanted us talking about this topic. I remembered it as a popular one from seasons past, but I guess I'd always assumed the topic had come up organically. Maybe it had come up organically in the past, and *Chef Supreme* had noticed that viewers liked it.

Well. If the viewers liked it . . . "My parents weren't thrilled at first." I spoke loudly, in case anybody else wanted to be first. "I went to college but dropped out after two years to go to culinary school. They wanted me at least to graduate. But then they saw how much I loved food, so . . ." I trailed off, because I really had loved it for so long. I'd worked my way up the ranks, and I'd loved every part of it, all the late nights and the aching bones and the backbreaking work, until . . .

"Same with my parents," Kaitlyn said. She hadn't technically interrupted, since I'd trailed off, but I bristled at it anyway. "Neither of them went to college, and they were really hoping I would. But I hadn't done great in school, and I didn't want to take out loans, so I fell into cooking. Thought I'd get my own TV show someday."

A laugh went up around the circle as she tossed her silky waves of hair, her big blue eyes glittering with suppressed mirth. "I guess it came true!"

"Well, it's not really *your* TV show," I muttered, but nobody heard me.

Vanilla Joe stretched out on his lounger, folding his hands on his round belly. From this angle, it was evident how far his hairline was receding. "My sisters are both doctors. I was supposed to become a doctor, too."

"You were?" Kaitlyn leaned in, propping her chin on her fist.

"Yep." Something decidedly different from his usual smug expression flickered over his face. He looked almost . . . sad. "My dad and my stepmom have been hounding me about it for years." He cleared his throat, sat up straight, crossed his arms over his chest. "Being on *Chef Supreme* is my chance to prove to them that I made the right choice." Cracked a smile. "I probably wouldn't have gotten into med school anyway."

The circle shared another laugh, including one from me.

"Well, my family loved that I became a chef," said Megan. "I loved cooking and eating since I was really young, and they know it was the right decision."

"Mine did, too," said Bald Joe. "In fact, when I was . . ."

As he spoke and spoke and spoke, I migrated over to Nia, who was sitting on the edge of the crowd, nursing her drink. She looked up at me. "I could only look social and interested for about a half hour before my head started to hurt."

I held my wineglass up for a toast. "I feel you."

She toasted me with what looked like a glass of water. She tucked her feet under her on the chair, folding herself into a pile of sharp angles. "I don't drink very much. I'm not a good drunk. Unless you consider 'on the floor crying' to be good."

"I definitely do not," I said. And neither would the cameras. "How are you feeling? I know being in the bottom is hard, but—"

"It's not that I was on the bottom." Her words came out like bullets. "If I'd made a bad dish, or if I'd made some mistake in my cooking, I would understand. But I didn't make a bad dish."

She took another sip, crunched on ice with such vigor I worried she'd crack a tooth. "I'm just glad they aren't pigeonholing me as a Southern chef, the way they do all the time for Black chefs on this show. Or any non-white chefs who get pigeonholed in their 'ethnic cuisine.' It's a pleasant surprise."

I, too, had noticed some of the non-white chefs in seasons past got asked why they'd decided to cook a different cuisine than the cuisine of their heritage in a challenge, got told that the judges didn't feel that their heart was in a dish because of it. Ironic, considering Luke's unmet desires. I wondered how Bald Joe had escaped that trap with his Japanese cuisine.

"So really," Nia said, her head lolling to the side. She might only have been drinking water, but she looked drunk. "I'm going to keep on keeping on. I have my roster of tried-and-true recipes I want to do, and I'm going to do them."

I got ready for her to elaborate more on what she wanted to do, until she wrinkled her nose, looking behind me, and I glanced over, too. Kaitlyn was straddling Vanilla Joe's lap on his

lounger. They were both reclining—into each other. He was de-
vouring her face with the passion I'd only had consuming a
three-hundred-dollar-per-person omakase dinner Derek had gotten me as a birthday gift.

"Gross," said Nia. The camera did not agree. It zoomed in on
them, practically bumping up against those thrashing tongues,
getting what I imagined would be an excellent close-up of Vanilla
Joe's pores.

Kaitlyn moaned, and I cringed. "Maybe we should move
inside."

Nia, Kel, Megan, and Bald Joe followed me in. Bald Joe closed
the door behind him, and, even though the noise level was even
louder inside, with HGTV buzzing companionably in the background and something beeping in the microwave, it felt like something had just been hushed. Like a crying kid disturbing everyone
at the restaurant had finally been scooped up and taken outside.
And then I realized it was because the camera was gone, that for
the first time in this house outside of sleeping and showering
and using the bathroom, my movements were going unfilmed. I
jerked my head to the side, then wiggled my hips. All my own
movements. A small smile spread over my lips.

"What are you doing?" Nia asked.

Okay. Maybe not entirely all my own.

"Nothing," I said. I glanced at Kaitlyn and Vanilla Joe
through the big window. They were basically one conjoined being at this point. A flailing monster with two heads. Clearly, Kaitlyn was not interested in Megan the way Megan had wondered.
"Hey, Megan," I said. She looked over at me, a flicker of annoyance in her eyes, but I couldn't stop. "Guess this answers your
question."

That flicker of annoyance turned into an eye roll, and she raised her hands in front of her. "It was a stupid question." Her middle fingers flicked up, but she didn't seem too angry. She only held them up for a minute before her arms went limp and her hands fell into her lap.

"What was the question?" Kel asked. They were reclining dangerously low on one of the barstools; one slip too far and they'd be sprawling on the floor. Beside them Bald Joe quietly nursed a beer, staring into the opening of the can like there might be treasure in there.

Megan didn't answer, so I did it for her. "Nothing."

Kel took me at my word and also took another sip of their beer. A lip piercing clanked gently against the metal of the can.

I turned my attention back to the group as Bald Joe started to speak, his voice a low rumble in his chest. "Your dish looked good, Nia. Beets and all."

Nia frowned down at the counter. "What do you think it means to cook from your soul? Obviously, it doesn't mean only to cook Southern food the way my most recent ancestors made it, since they're not pigeonholing me so far." She dissolved into grumbles, but Bald Joe seemed to take her seriously, cocking his head in contemplation.

"I don't know. I do know Japanese food *is* my heart and soul. My mentors were Japanese, and I made my career cooking in Japanese kitchens. Just because I didn't grow up eating my mom's sushi or my dad's ramen doesn't mean that my heart and soul can't be there."

That made sense to me, even as it wasn't my truth. Or Kel's, I didn't think. The both of us cooked the foods of our heritages, the same basic recipes our ancestors had cooked, using some of the same ingredients our forebears had dug from the ground. It was funny, because we both had a similar twist on it: upscale and fusion, trying to make people take Jewish and Appalachian food seriously, because they were foods that hadn't really had their big renaissance yet. That people didn't always think of as fancy or upscale.

"But what if my heart and soul aren't in any particular place?" Nia asked. "What if they're in the recipes I've honed over the years? In the ratios I've memorized?"

Bald Joe shrugged and rubbed at his goatee. "Then maybe you won't be Chef Supreme."

She slumped over the bar. "But I want to be Chef Supreme."

"We all want to be Chef Supreme." Bald Joe took another long drink of his beer.

"That is true," said Kel. "How about the judges, huh? Have they been like you imagined?"

"Lenore Smith and Maz Sarshad are exactly like I imagined them," said Nia immediately. She moved on seamlessly from her last topic to this one, not so much as blinking. "They're like marble statues, both of them. So polished. So shiny. Like if you pushed them too hard, they might fall over and shatter on the ground."

I could see what she meant. They were both a little bit too perfect to be human. I couldn't picture them relaxing on the couch in front of the TV, or microwaving a baked potato for dinner because they were too tired to cook, or going to the bathroom. Not that I generally made a habit of picturing people going to the bathroom.

Now I was picturing everyone around me in the bathroom.

"Charles Weston reminded me of my second boss." This was

Kel. "Old white guy who refused to call me by my pronouns but also didn't want to get sued, so called me nothing at all until I got sick of it and left."

I considered telling them what I'd overheard between Luke and Charles. It wasn't like I had any particular reason to keep it a secret. I didn't owe Luke anything. Maybe I should share his secrets. That jerk.

And yet I kept my mouth shut.

"I really don't know how Luke came from *that*," Kel continued. "He was probably the best boss I've ever had."

So what? Again, you can be a great boss and a shitty person. And yet I asked, "Really?"

"Really," said Kel. "I didn't start until after it was his kitchen, but from what I hear, before his dad gave him that position, the exec chef was pretty much your typical bro. Ran the kitchen like a frat. Then Luke started and changed it up. Brought in me, obviously, and a few women." Kel pressed their lips together. "The sous-chef gave me and one of the women trouble once, made us feel uncomfortable, and Luke put a stop to it at once. Fired him and told everybody else that behavior like that was not acceptable."

"Wow, basic human decency," I said, but my heart gave a squeeze.

"Eh, I don't know if that's fair," Kel replied. "It can be really hard to stand up to people you don't know well, especially when you're new and green. And not only did he stand up for us, he made sure our kitchen ran fairly. He made sure we all got vacation days and sick days, even when it meant he had to take our place on the line."

"Whatever," I grumbled.

Nia shrugged. "I don't care if he's a good guy. Kel, do you have any inside knowledge on his tastes or preferences you can share?"

"'Fraid not," said Kel. "And if I did, I probably wouldn't share them with all of you."

"Fair enough," Nia said.

Megan said, "At least he's cute. I might not be attracted to him, but I can appreciate his aesthetic appeal."

"I think he's ugly." The words jumped out of me before I could think them through. "Not just ugly, hideous. I don't see it at all." I sat back against the counter, for some reason panting for breath. I hoped there were cameras mounted in here. I hoped someone on the production team would tell Luke what I'd said. I didn't care if it meant I'd probably go home next episode.

No, actually, I did. "Maybe I shouldn't say that," I said hastily. I could always wait until this competition was over and I hopefully had my money and title and notoriety and could ride that wave of publicity into my own little restaurant, and then I could talk to the cameras. Maybe they'd even pay me for some controversial words.

I wouldn't even have to say anything actually negative; I'd seen how previous seasons' contestants did it, usually about the other chefs. They'd start by gushing over their favorite people on set. *Oh, Julie Chee was a delight to work with. You saw the episode where she shared her curly parsley with me, didn't you? And Karnam Singh's cooking was an inspiration. I learned so much from him.* And then you just delicately avoided the subject or gave bland platitudes when asked about someone else. *Jen Mauro? She . . . hmm, I don't have anything to say about her.* The gossip sites and *Chef Supreme* subreddits would run with it, and by the end of the day the headlines were, *Chef Alex Riley of* Chef Supreme *dishes on his spicy rivalry with Jen Mauro!*

"He's not everybody's type," said Bald Joe. "But maybe there's someone else here who's yours?" He raised an eyebrow.

I knew something was going on, but yes, I was dense. So dense it took Nia clapping her hand to her mouth to realize what it was. Of course, her words helped. "You like Sadie!" she blurted, eyes shining as satisfied as if she'd just solved the mystery of why her dish tasted flat despite proper salting and acid.

He was a good-looking guy. Older than me, but not like, gross creeper old. A square jaw. The cut of his T-shirt promised a good, hard body beneath.

Why not have a fun night? mused Grandma Ruth. *You deserve at least that.*

Maybe I did need a fun night. Maybe if I released all this pent-up energy, I'd stop seeing Luke in that way. I'd stop worrying so much about him. I could stop hating him so much.

I smiled at Bald Joe. He smiled back, and his face transformed into Luke's: those lines by his eyes; that dimple in his cheek; that black hair flopping into his face.

My stomach lurched. I stood, pushing my chair back. "I'm just tired," I said. "Nothing against you. Um, I think I'm going to go to bed." I couldn't seem to look Luke—Bald Joe—in the eye. "Maybe we can do something tomorrow, when we have the time off?"

"We can't leave the building without an escort and express permission," Nia said. Someone had read our contract fully. "But let's cook something reasonably good for us for lunch and dinner. With vegetables that aren't potatoes. And there's a gym in the basement—let's go to the gym! And maybe we can get out for a walk. I think there's a park nearby."

I nodded along, and nodded along, and then I nodded to sleep, and I slept through my entire Sunday.

WHICH MEANT I should have been refreshed when it came time for the next challenge, but I wasn't. I was groggy and hazy and stumbling as we got into teams that would prepare competing themed menus for a movie premiere that sounded like an extended *Downton Abbey* episode, but honored that I was Kel's second pick. Two days of prep and cooking later, we were unfortunately on the losing team, though I got a special callout from Lenore Smith on the quality of my everything bagel potato gratin. We said congratulations to Megan, who won judges' hearts and stomachs with her five-spice pork pie, and goodbye to Old Joe, who'd tried to make beef Wellington in ninety minutes.

And then, before I could get more than five hours of sleep multiple nights in a row, the next one was upon us. I could feel the edges of my mind fraying, and I understood why a pregnant chef had decided to leave on season five after only four episodes. Even though I cut myself and bled into my diced onions, I rallied, had the medic wrap me up, and ended up in the top three for this soup challenge (my matzah ball ramen, obviously), though Kaitlyn took home the win with her light, fresh green soup. I pasted a smile on my face and gave her a congratulatory squeeze even as I wanted to peel her face off and throw it in the fire flickering in the corners of my vision, and did I mention that I was tired?

Oliver went home. Bye, Oliver, hardly got a chance to know you.

During these two challenges, I barely saw any of Luke. Every time I went to the bathroom—and there were a lot of times, considering how much coffee I was drinking—he wasn't there. Though once I did walk in on Lenore Smith leaving without washing her hands, which, if I had my phone to take a picture, probably would've sold to the tabloids. (Maybe the real reason they took our phones away?) He didn't say anything about any of my dishes during these challenges, leaving the critique and praise to the others. He was effusively complimentary about Megan's pork pie, like it would make up for not allowing her dumplings to win.

After filming confessionals for the top nine episode, we got home slightly earlier than usual, and Adrianna announced that we'd each be allowed to call a chosen family member or friend. I'd listed my sister, Rachel, on the form. They must have told her to expect me, because she picked up on the first ring, something she has never done in her entire life.

"Sadie!" she trilled from the other end of the phone. "You're alive! I've been thinking about you literally every day!"

There's nothing that quite warms the heart like an adoring little sister, even if she was only being so adoring because the cameras were there recording her every word. I felt my cold, dark one thaw slightly. "You, too!" Which was a lie. "How are my plants doing?" I'd tasked her with watering them.

She paused just long enough where I knew she'd totally forgotten. "They're doing . . . great!" she said brightly. A scratching noise from the other end, probably her scribbling a note to herself. "How are you doing? Are you Chef Supreme yet?"

"You know I'm contractually silenced from telling you anything show-related," I said. "But I can tell you that I've been
thinking about Grandma a lot." Or more accurately, she'd been
butting in on my thoughts. "I really feel like she's been here with
me as I've been cooking." Out of the corner of my eye, I noticed
Adrianna nod approvingly. I knew they'd love that.

"I hope none of Grandma's spirit is coming forth in your
cooking! She'd make you burn and under-season everything,"
Rachel said. Adrianna's nod turned into a frown. They'd probably cut the footage before that. "So I know everything is supposed to be a secret, but I've been googling *Chef Supreme* every
day and following along on all the fan sites and some information has leaked. Not your name, but I know your old pal Kaitlyn
is there." She'd probably leaked it herself somehow. "And Joe
Hennessey looks cute."

I barely held back a snort. She could do better than Vanilla
Joe. Anyone could do better than Vanilla Joe. "Okay."

"And I saw *Luke Weston* is coming on as a judge?" Her voice
glowed with awe. "You know I went to one of his restaurants
once when I was in New York? Eric took me there for our first
anniversary. It was extremely fancy and expensive."

"Sounds right," I said, but Adrianna made a warning gesture
at me. Either I was coming close to my time limit, or I was getting too close to subjects I wasn't supposed to discuss.

Rachel continued, oblivious. "He's been all over the media
circuit in preparation for this new stint." How did he have the
time? I guess he had to be doing *something* on our shopping and
prep and confessional days. "He's soooo hot. Does he smell as
good as he looks?"

"You have to stop talking about this," I said as Adrianna

leaned over, her too-tight ponytail swinging menacingly close to me. "Or I'll get in trouble and you'll have to hang up."

"Okay, whatever," she said. "Hey, just out of curiosity, where did you buy your plants? Just in case I want to buy some exactly like them for . . . myself?"

Rachel's words kept rolling around in my head as I lay down in my bunk bed, even more strongly than I physically rolled around in the bed thanks to Kel's rolling around below. Luke was out playing the media, probably telling people how excited he was about his new fancy restaurant. Lying. *That's not fair, Sadie.* It wasn't like I wasn't playing the media myself. Though I thought there was a pretty significant difference between thinking about what would play best on the show versus totally misrepresenting myself and who I was. It was kind of an unnerving thought, that I could be presented on TV as Sadie, but not Sadie. Me, but not me. How much control did I really have over how the world saw me?

Also, Luke *did* smell as good as he looked.

There was only so much time I could spend thinking about it before the ZzzQuil kicked in. Tomorrow was the top eight, and I was determined to make it through.

11

A QUICK SEVEN HOURS LATER, WE WERE LINED UP IN front of our stations. Maz was doing his trademark dramatic pause after telling us he had a surprise, which was never good news. "Surprise" in real life might mean a surprise party or a surprise proposal. "Surprise" on *Chef Supreme* meant time limits or ingredient restrictions or some other way to torture us.

And from the way Maz's face settled into a somber frown, I knew it would be bad. "Today will be a double elimination, chefs."

I could hear the gulps around the room. One of them came from me. There were eight of us here. A double elimination meant that two of us would be leaving. That was a one in four chance. Twenty-five percent. Way too high for my liking. I didn't think they'd ever done a double elimination before, which made it even scarier.

And getting eliminated at this stage wouldn't be good. I mean, getting eliminated at any stage wouldn't be good, but this was still too early. You really had to make it into at least the top four to attract outside interest and investment in your restaurant. You could market a restaurant coming from a *Chef Supreme* semi-finalist. It was a lot harder for a contestant in the final eight.

"Chefs, today you'll be competing in the Duel of Spatulas!" Maz announced, a slick smile spreading over his face, bright green eyes gleaming. "A *Chef Supreme* tradition you know and love."

I tried not to groan out loud as Maz explained the rules of Duel of Spatulas for those who were just tuning in for the first time. Basically, we would divide into two teams of four and get twenty-four hours—an insanely short amount of time—to open our own restaurant, which would compete against the other restaurant in a head-to-head battle where the judges would look at both the quality of our food and the quality of our service. Each team of four would need to take on different roles: someone would need to be the executive chef, in charge of the kitchen with two other team members under them, and someone would need to take over the front of house to take care of guests, making sure service was running smoothly and that guests weren't waiting too long for their food. Exec chef and front of house were high risk/reward positions: the winner of Duel of Spatulas was almost always one of them . . . but so was the person going home. They just had way more on their shoulders.

This year, Maz told us, we would need to serve three different courses—appetizer, entrée, and dessert—with at least two options for each course, for a total of six dishes. They could come from any member of the team, though everybody had to contribute at least one. I took a deep, shaky breath. So much of this challenge would end up being about my team. If we worked together well or turned into a disaster tornado.

Well, I'd find out soon—Maz was bringing out the spatulas. I chose mine with trepidation. It felt way heavier in my hand than a wooden spatula should be.

Blue. I looked around for the other three with blue spatulas. I spotted Kel first, which made my face break out into a smile. Our cuisines weren't so different, and I already knew we worked well together. So, good. Then I saw Bald Joe—our cuisines were different, but he was an excellent chef and a good team player. Good again. Who was fourth? Hopefully, Megan or Ernesto, both of whom—

Vanilla Joe waved his blue spatula in the air, a cocky smile on his face. "We're going to rock this, blue team," he said. "Come on, let's huddle." We'd have a half hour to come up with a menu theme, food ideas, and a name before they sent us out shopping.

Damn. So close. But it wasn't like I had a choice. I followed Vanilla Joe, Bald Joe, and Kel to the other side of the room, while the red team of Nia, Kaitlyn, Megan, and Ernesto bumped heads where we'd been.

"So, guys," Vanilla Joe said without preamble. "We need a theme and a name. I'm thinking we do modern New American food, with a one-word name. Something like Table, or Chair."

Kel scoffed. "So we should all get on board with your style of cuisine? Why don't we do a modern Appalachian restaurant, then?"

"It's not just that it's my cuisine, it's that you've all cooked New American before, while I've never made sushi or anything," Vanilla Joe said.

I cleared my throat. "But that's not where we're at our best," I said. *It's not where our hearts are.* "Why don't we theme it around a particular type of food? Like seafood restaurants always do pretty well on Duel of Spatulas because there are seafood recipes in most cuisines? Or we could do vegetable-focused dishes?" I swallowed hard. "That really seems more fair?"

Vanilla Joe tsked. "I really think we should do New American. It's a lot more cohesive. I hate it when the judges say a menu doesn't come together."

I went to argue, but he looked so sure of himself. And I wasn't. Yeah, I thought I was in the right, but I'd thought I'd been in the right a lot. Like back at the Green Onion, and I'd lost everything.

So I stayed quiet as Vanilla Joe decided we'd be doing modern New American cuisine, and that our restaurant would be called Table, because we'd all be eating on tables or around the table or something corny like that. "I'll be exec chef, if nobody else wants to do it," he said. He didn't give anyone else time to speak up. "Great. Who wants to be front of house? Sadie?"

I bristled. "Are you saying that because I'm the only girl?"

"Of course not," Vanilla Joe said. "I was just thinking you'd do best up there."

"Because I'm the only girl," I said. "I've never worked in front of the—"

"I'll do it," Kel said. "No worries." They nodded at me. I nodded gratefully back, knowing that if they hadn't stepped in, I'd be wearing a dress and escorting people to their seats, taking charge of the waitstaff and schmoozing with all our guests.

We'd spent so much time arguing over the restaurant that now we had limited time to figure out our menu. I glanced over my shoulder at the other group, who were sitting in a circle laughing like everything in the world was just wonderful. I turned back with a scowl.

Usually, in Duel of Spatulas, the exec chef and the front of house each took on just one dish of their own, since they were handling other things besides cooking, and the other team members each did two. Our team was no exception. "I'll need to pick a dish where I can do most of the work ahead of time and then trust you guys to assemble it," Kel said. "So I'm thinking either a dessert or an appetizer, something where I wouldn't have to be cooking protein to order. Is dessert okay? Maybe some kind of bread pudding with homemade ice cream—simple, but hearty and good?"

We all nodded. "I'd like to do a raw fish appetizer," said Bald Joe. "Maybe a crudo with hamachi?"

"And I'd like to do an entrée," Vanilla Joe said. "A beef dish. Which means our other entrée should probably be seafood."

I nodded. "I can do a slow-cooked black bass." We'd done one at the Green Onion that I loved. It had a preserved tomato broth and cauliflower and a pile of nutty grains. I could do farro.

That left Bald Joe and me to divide another appetizer and a dessert between us. "I can do a dessert," I offered, thinking about a deconstructed baklava, but Vanilla Joe shook his head.

"No. Joe here is already doing one appetizer; we can't make him do two. He'll get overwhelmed."

"I really don't mind," said Bald Joe. "As long as Sadie helps me put everything together. I'd rather do an appetizer. I'm not great at pastry."

Vanilla Joe shook his head before I could speak up and say of course I would help. "Joe, I want you doing a dessert, so Sadie, you pick an appetizer."

Fine. Whatever. I hashed it out with the rest of the team, decided I would make a sunchoke soup with bacon and thyme. Vanilla Joe squinted at me. "I didn't think bacon was kosher."

"I don't cook kosher food," I explained patiently. I actually didn't mind; I was used to it. Kosher cooking had a long list of rules: no pork, no shellfish, no combining meat and dairy, among many others. Grandma Ruth had kept kosher, and I had total respect for everyone who did, but it wasn't me.

"Okay," Vanilla Joe said, shrugging. "Joe, how about your dessert?" Bald Joe decided on a fancy cheese course.

Okay. Table. It would have to do. Half of our team would need to check out our space and go to the restaurant supply store to choose furniture, place settings, and everything else with our budget, while the other half would do our whole team's food shopping. "I'll go to the grocery store," I said immediately, because I didn't want to take the chance of somebody forgetting one of my ingredients . . . but of course we all had the same idea.

As executive chef, Vanilla Joe made the executive decision. I was getting really sick of him playing that card, but there was nothing I could do about it. Nothing that was going to make him listen to me. "Joe and I will go grocery shopping," he said. "Kel and Sadie, you'll go to the restaurant supply store. Make sure our space looks pretty."

I ground my teeth. "Make sure *you* get everything on our list."

"*Everything*," Kel said.

"Of course," Vanilla Joe said. "We're a team."

I kept those words running through my head as Kel and I drove to the restaurant supply store right behind Kaitlyn and Megan. *We're a team. We're a team.* We'd win together or we'd lose together.

No matter how disgusted Kel's sigh was. "Check out this fish knife," they said, holding it up with a flourish. Though the shelves running through the big, warehouse-like space were tall, the ceiling light still glinted off the knife's hooked, nasty top. "Bet I could fillet Vanilla Joe like a trout."

"I would not advise that," I said. Kel's face dropped, until I held up a cheese grater the size of my head. "How about grating him instead?"

That was perhaps a tiny bit of overkill for his general level of douchebaggery, but we shared a grim laugh anyway. We made our circuit through the store, choosing tablecloths and wall art and the various types of plates and bowls we needed for our three courses. We ended up stuck behind Kaitlyn and Megan in line as they bickered over the precise shade of blue their napkins should be, but it wasn't a big deal—we were ahead of schedule anyway.

I glanced at the *Chef Supreme*–provided flip phone we'd been given to communicate with our team at the grocery store. It hadn't rung at all. "I hope their silence means they found everything we need," I said.

"Yeah. Me, too." Kel stretched their arms over their head, making their shirt ride up. White belly flashed at me. "Hey. What will you do if you win? You know, with the money?"

I glanced around automatically for the cameras, but they were all focused on Kaitlyn and Megan. "My own restaurant." I didn't even have to think about it. "Easy. I'm ready to work for myself. To not have to worry about having a bad boss." Kel was looking at me curiously, and I wasn't ready to share what had happened with Derek, so I went on hastily, "And I want to be able to be creative with my dishes. I've gotten to do my own specials sometimes and conceive my own dishes, put my own flair on the menu. But I've never really gotten to cook what *I* want to cook, because it's always had to fall in line with everything else the restaurant serves. And I think there's space in the market for a Jewish-inspired menu. Last time I was here in New York, I went to this Jewish-Japanese place, Shalom Japan, and it was incredible. So creative. But most of the Jewish restaurants in the city are your standard Jewish delis. I want people to know that we have thousands of years of cuisine on offer. And so many different kinds! We were part of the Diaspora for so long, living in places as diverse as India and Yemen and Italy and Poland for thousands of years, and each community developed their own cuisine, and then they all came together again in Israel and America and fused with each other, and there's so much potential for a fine-dining restaurant. And then the fast-casual chain branching off . . ."

Kel laughed. "I feel you. Appalachian food doesn't get the respect it deserves." They ran a hand through their choppy purple hair. It had grown shaggy, with reddish roots, over the last couple weeks. "Just before we cloistered ourselves in here, I was reading this article—in the *New York Times*!—about how Appalachian food was experiencing a major resurgence in restaurants. And I was like, well, I better get in on the ground floor or I'll just be one in the crowd."

"And you don't want to be crowded into an elevator." It took Kel a minute to get it, but then they laughed again. "Someone always farts."

"It's true," Kel said. "It's true."

I glanced off to the side, "Hey, do you still think we're okay with those white plates? Maybe we should go with a pop of color. Since the tablecloths are white, too."

Kel shook their head. "I feel like that might distract from the food, don't you think?" I shrugged. They had a point. "That was

what Luke said back when I worked for him, anyway. He had the
restaurant switch from colored plates to clean white plates. And
I don't think we want to go against the ideals of a judge."

I scowled. Hearing this was Luke's philosophy made me
want to get plates in bright red and purple and yellow, the most
garish colors we could find.

No. Kel was probably right. I had to focus on winning. Not
on Luke.

But then I glanced to the side, and for a moment it was like
he was there, leaning casually against a display of deep fryers.
The corners of his lips quirked into a smirk. *You can do this, Sadie.
You can win.* I stepped toward him. Toward the arms crossed over
his chest, the edges of the tattoo that peeked out from under his
T-shirt sleeve. I believed him. Just for a moment.

"Where are you going?" Kel asked me, which broke the spell.
I blinked, and he was gone. And yet somehow I still believed
what he'd said. That I could do this. That I could win. The con-
fidence in me he'd shown over the course of the show . . .

No. He's a jerk, remember? I told myself firmly.

Except I wasn't sure if I totally believed this one.

Kaitlyn and Megan finally finished up, letting us check out.
When we left we drove not to the *Chef Supreme* kitchen but to the
Duel of Spatulas space, which was out in Queens, not far from
the *Chef Supreme* house. This area was more industrial, the side-
walks mostly empty of people, trucks idling on the curb. From
the outside the space looked like all the other unassuming warehouses, but on the inside . . . well, it still looked kind of like an
unassuming warehouse. A wall divided the big, gray, empty
space in two, with a door at either end through which I could see
the shiny chrome of a kitchen. Kel and I left the people from the

restaurant supply store to unload and set up our furniture rent-
als, then headed into the back.

It was actually a really nice space: big and expansive, with all
the major appliances on wheels. They must have rented this space
specifically for Duel of Spatulas. Vanilla Joe and Bald Joe were
already here, unpacking what they'd gotten from the grocery
store. "So I assume you got everything on our lists?" Kel asked.

Vanilla Joe nodded. "As much as we could."

Those imaginary spines along my back bristled again. "What's
that supposed to mean?"

He raised his palms to us, raising his pale eyebrows. "I called
you. You didn't pick up."

"You didn't call us at all!" Kel cried. They took a long, deep
breath, rolling their eyes up toward the ceiling. They puffed out
their cheeks, making their round face even rounder. "Oh my Lord.
Okay, Kel. Calm yourself. What didn't they have, Vanilla Joe?"

"Well . . ." Vanilla Joe rolled his shoulders, as if procrastinat-
ing. "It's not so much as them not having something. It's about
how we may have bought too few eggs."

Kel's eyes widened. "But I need a ton of eggs for my bread
pudding and my ice cream!"

"We'll make it work," Vanilla Joe said. Bald Joe pressed his
lips together and shrugged as an apology. "Don't worry."

And we worked. We worked and worked and worked. I made
everything work. Our day of prep time passed in what felt like
the sizzle of water splashed in a hot pan. I wiped sweat off my
face, dabbed under my arms, pureed sunchokes and de-leafed
thyme and jumped back to avoid being splattered with bacon fat;
started my preserved tomato broth simmering, my farro cooking. I hopped to the side a couple times to help Bald Joe butcher

hamachi and advise him on which jellies and jams to make for his fancy cheese plate, but by the end of the night, I'd prepped as much as I could. I stepped back from my station, shaking my hands out to the sound of Kel advising me and Vanilla Joe how to plate their dish tomorrow.

We slept for about five minutes, then rolled up the next morning to the restaurant space. My head was throbbing, and the amount of coffee I was drinking—way too much—wasn't helping. It was just making me jittery. So I jittered through the process of us arranging our restaurant to our liking, dragging tables and chairs here and there, approving the signs and menus the graphic designers had whipped up overnight, figuring out where to hang the art on the walls. I had to blink extra hard every time my eyes closed, considering they didn't want to open again. And it took me several hours to notice that my jeans were unbuttoned. Hopefully, my long, untucked button-down had done a decent job at hiding it from the cameras.

I didn't even know how the day flew by. All I knew was that I was in the back cooking again in my crisp chef's whites, with Kel coming in and out between training the servers. "What's in your beef dish?" they asked Vanilla Joe.

"Come back later," Vanilla Joe snapped. "I'm not totally sure yet. My sauce isn't working." He stirred it, tasted it, sighed. "I might need your help to get everything done on time."

A storm passed over Kel's face. "I don't have time."

Vanilla Joe's voice might as well have been thunder. "I'm not going to finish my appetizer and my entrée in—"

"What do you mean, your appetizer?" Kel said tightly. "I thought you were just doing an entrée."

"We decided at the store that we should have a red meat appetizer in addition to the two we already planned," Vanilla Joe said. "We should've mentioned it to you, I guess. Too late now. In any case—"

"In any case, I'm busy getting things sorted up front and trying to get my own dish done," Kel snapped. "Maybe you should have—"

"You're only doing one dish," hissed Vanilla Joe. The veins were standing out on the sides of his thick neck. "How hard is it really to tell some servers what to do?"

My heart was pattering away. Should I step in? Try to mediate?

The light flashed off Kel's facial piercings like lightning. "Are you joking me? You're joking me, right?"

"Man, I can help you," interjected Bald Joe. "I have time."

But Vanilla Joe didn't look over at him. He was glaring at Kel. "We're a team."

"And I'm doing my part for the team," Kel said acidly. "The part we agreed on."

I shot Kel a sympathetic glance as they stormed out. I should have said something. Stepped in. But it was too late now.

Over the next hour, my arms moved with such a blur of activity I hardly noticed the cameras. Bald Joe and I moved in a synchronized dance, managing to weave around each other without stabbing anyone with a knife or spilling boiling water on ourselves. Slowly, our dishes came into shape. Too slowly. Because tickets were already starting to come in.

Kel was storming back into the kitchen, lightning not just glinting but crackling over their face. "What in all hells is going on back here?" they cried. "I have tables waiting a half hour for their *appetizers*. What are you doing?"

I wiped beads of sweat from my forehead before they could drip into my eyes and burn. Kel wasn't yelling at me. I'd been keeping up with my sunchoke soup—all I had to do with it to order was dump it into a bowl and arrange the garnishes on top.

"Vanilla Joe!" So he was the problem. Was he chopping each plate of tartare to order? "People are grumbling out there. You need to get your ass moving."

"I'm moving," Vanilla Joe said. "And you can refer to me as *Chef.*"

I ground my teeth. That was the least of our problems right now.

Kel rushed back out. Vanilla Joe dropped a plate. It shattered all over the floor. He shouted. I ground my teeth harder. They were going to turn to nubs by the end of the night. "I'll go find Kel and let them know," I said.

This reminded me of when I worked at the Green Onion, before everything had gone down there. I'd been the sous-chef—the vice president of the kitchen in that I was second-in-command always and first-in-command when the executive chef was out, not that I would take over for Derek if he died. I usually kept the kitchen in pretty good shape, making sure everyone was moving, but that was a while ago. I didn't know if I could do that now.

I followed Kel out into the restaurant. I wished I could slow down and really take it all in, but I was moving so fast and with such purpose that I could only catch flashes: tables set in crisp monochrome silver and white; the stark TABLE logo hanging on the wall; the clink of glasses and ice cubes as people toasted.

As I was moving past one table, someone stopped me with a tap on the shoulder. I turned with a growl. *"What?"*

It was a guest. One of a pair, sitting at a table, both of whom looked vaguely familiar and extremely rich. Where had I—oh! They were the people from Charles Weston's party . . . the ones who I'd told my mini-blinis were topped with shit. I tried to force a smile for them, but I was pretty sure it came out like a rictus grin. "Sorry. Your food will be out soon."

"We have our food," said the man with the designer tie. "We just wanted to tell you that we—"

I sighted Kel's purple hair bobbing across the dining room and missed whatever the man told me. I was already moving as I said, "Sorry, please address any concerns to your waiter!"

My stomach was swimming uneasily as I noticed how many tables didn't have their food, how many people were impatiently checking their watches. So I didn't blame Kel when they turned to me with a snarling, "*What?*"

"They're having trouble back there," I said faintly. "Wait . . ." I noticed waiters emerging from the kitchen, bowls and plates stacked on their shoulders. The nicest thing I could say about those bowls and plates was that they were a little sloppy: my sunchoke soup was spilling over the rims of their bowls, and the cuts of Bald Joe's fish were all different in shape and size.

This was *not* good. The night was already spiraling out of control. I raced back toward the kitchen, bumping into chairs on the way, just in time to hear someone yell that the judges were here.

This was even more not good.

Back in the kitchen, the Joes were in the weeds, throwing food onto the plate to get out from under the deluge. Entrée tickets were starting to come in, and I wasn't anywhere near ready to start plating my black bass. And Vanilla Joe didn't seem to have a solution to any of this; he was frantically trying to plate his own dishes, while machines were buzzing in the—was that the ice cream machine? "Is that Kel's ice cream overchurning?" I said furiously to Vanilla Joe, who was not supposed to have an appetizer and was therefore supposed to be prepping Kel's dessert. If he ruined Kel's dessert, he'd cause Kel to be sent home. "I thought we were supposed to be a team?"

He just shrugged.

And I snapped. It was like I'd removed a film over my vision; the kitchen around me took on a crystal-blue tint, and everybody started moving in slow motion. I couldn't chicken out and let Kel down again.

I'd been the sous-chef of the Green Onion, and I *knew* how to take charge of a kitchen. At least I had once.

I might not have been a *better* option, but I was the *only* option. I *had* to reach back and harness those skills I'd once had.

I slammed my hand on the metal counter, making everything around me shudder like a small earthquake had just shaken the venue. "Listen up!" I shouted. This was probably the loudest I'd spoken since coming into the competition; both Joes raised their heads in surprise. "Hey! I'm taking over here."

Vanilla Joe opened his mouth, but I shut it by slamming my hand on the counter again. "We're going to lose if we don't turn this around. So I'm going to tell you how we're going to make it work."

Vanilla Joe's eyes narrowed. "You can't just do this! This is a coup! Sadie!"

"That's *Chef* Sadie to you," I said.

We both looked over at Bald Joe. He looked back at us, then

shrugged. "Man, we're in the weeds. If Sadie—Chef Sadie—can pull us out . . ."

And so the coup was bloodless, unless you counted the "blood" that ran out from Vanilla Joe's beef, which wasn't actually blood at all but myoglobin. I stayed on my fellow chefs, directing Vanilla Joe and Bald Joe and myself as we frantically assembled our dishes, trying to catch up. Kel checked back in a couple times and swore at Vanilla Joe about their ice cream, which resembled butter more than the smooth, creamy dessert. I told them I'd do something about it—make a new batch of ice cream if I had to—but there were no more eggs. So they brushed me off, their face bright red, and stayed in the kitchen to tinker with it themself.

It took a lot, but we finally made it to dessert. I paused for a moment while helping Bald Joe assemble his fancy cheese plate and looked around. I was gasping for breath, but a proud smile tugged at the corners of my lips. I'd done this. *Me.* And I'd been so busy doing it that the usual constant stream of *You suck You're worthless You don't deserve to be here* had actually gone quiet for a little while.

Look at the way those boys are taking your orders, said Grandma Ruth, her voice thick with pride. *You did good, kid.*

I had no idea if we'd won, but I kind of felt like I already had.

OF COURSE, THAT voice started up again as we assembled back in the *Chef Supreme* kitchen the next day for confessionals and then judging. At least I'd slept well, better than I had since the start of the competition. Which was surprising, considering the way Kel was tossing and turning beneath me.

I woke up before the alarm and brushed my teeth and washed my face in the empty bathroom without waiting in line, which was nice, and then padded out into the living space. Kel was already there, sitting in their usual spot at the bar, a glass full of light brown liquid before them. I eyed it. "A bit early for a drink, isn't it?"

They cracked a tiny smile. "It's tea." They took a sip, then their smile cracked slightly larger. "With maybe a little bit of whiskey in it."

I couldn't fault them for it. This was the first part of the competition where we didn't know anything the judges thought about our dishes and our service. I assumed I'd find it disconcerting, but I found that I actually preferred it. Less obsessing over every little word and gesture they'd given us, less comparing our dishes to the other team's. Maybe that was why I'd slept so soundly.

Kel took a long sip of their drink. "I think I'm going to go home."

"Don't say that!" I punched them in the arm. They held their drink steady, like a pro. "You have no idea who's going home."

They shook their head. "It's just a gut feeling."

"That's indigestion from drinking whiskey first thing in the morning," I said.

"Maybe."

"Probably."

"Good morning!" the voice came from an armchair. "I got a better night's sleep in this extremely comfortable armchair than I did any other night in the bed!"

"The cameras aren't here yet, Kaitlyn," I said.

Kaitlyn's head popped up over the armchair and frowned at me. "Oh. Oh well. I'll just save it for when they get here. Actually . . ."

She hopped up with an energy that was almost scary at this hour, even though she was wearing what looked like the most frayed, comfortable sweatpants in existence, and headed up the stairs. We watched her go, shaking our heads.

Then I turned to Kel. "Wow," I said. "That glass looks excellent for holding liquid and transporting it to your mouth."

Kel quirked an eyebrow. "I'm only able to use this spectacular glass thanks to the convenience of this barstool, which, though it looks like every other wooden barstool I've ever seen, is somehow so much more comfortable."

We shared a laugh. Everybody was sick of Adrianna urging them to talk up everything that we ate and drank and sat on and drove in. Even though, as she continuously reminded us, we wouldn't have a show without our sponsors. One of us definitely wouldn't be taking home a quarter of a million dollars without those advertisers paying for it. "Kaitlyn seems made for this," I said. "She's faker than the plastic food in the pictures on the McDonald's menu."

"When's the last time you ate at McDonald's, Sadie?"

The answer was embarrassing. I'd eaten multiple meals at McDonald's after I got fired from the Green Onion, not just because it was within walking distance of my apartment but because it was the only food place I knew for sure I wouldn't see any of my fellow chefs or food people. So I only shrugged in response.

"And she doesn't seem too absurdly fake to me. Not faker than the rest of us. Aren't we all acting differently for the camera?" Kel continued.

I shrugged again, toeing at the carpet.

"You just don't like her," they said.

"It's not that I don't like her," I said, an automatic response. "It's just that . . . that . . ." I realized I didn't know how exactly I felt. Because Kel was right: Kaitlyn really wasn't that much more incredibly plastic than the rest of us. So why was I so annoyed by everything she did? I couldn't think of anything else to say.

Which ended up being fine, because our conversation was interrupted by Kaitlyn striding back into the room. She'd changed out of her comfy-looking sweatpants and into a tight T-shirt and striped pair of men's boxers. More significantly, she was towing Vanilla Joe behind her; he was stumbling along in an outfit that pretty much matched her own, his mouth creaked open in an endless yawn. She stopped before the armchair and put her hands on her hips. "You lie down first," she directed. "And then you can spoon me. We pretend to be sleeping and that the cameras wake us up."

The two of them curled into the armchair and around each other. I turned back to Kel. "Like I said," I told them assuredly, though really I didn't feel sure at all. "Plastic."

THE NERVOUSNESS WAS back full blast by the time we finished our confessionals and lined up before the judges in the *Chef Supreme* kitchen. My stomach squirmed with it even as my mind was oddly clear. Even as Maz reminded us that two of us would be going home.

The camera did a dramatic pan over our final eight faces, then settled on Maz. He talked a little bit about how hard it was to open a restaurant, much less open a restaurant in twenty-four hours, and how we'd all risen to the challenge and performed admirably under the circumstances. "However, we felt that one team outperformed the other by a considerable margin," Maz said, his voice low and full of tension. I crossed both sets of fingers. *Say blue team, say blue team, say blue team* . . . "And that team is . . ."

Blue team, blue team, blue team . . .

"The red team! Congratulations, Chef Nia, Chef Kaitlyn, Chef Ernesto, and Chef Megan!"

My shoulders sagged as my team and I stepped to the side. The winning team was whooping and hollering, slapping one another on the back and high-fiving so hard I could hear the smacks from over here. The judges started rhapsodizing about how they'd absolutely loved the red team's focus on seafood, how they had a cohesive menu because of that even despite their different cuisines and styles, and of course how the—

An elbow hit me in the side. I glanced over to see Vanilla Joe frowning at me. Because all the cameras were currently focused on the judges and the winning team, I felt safe spitting, "What?"

"This is your fault," he whispered furiously. "Because you mutinied. If you'd just let me stay in control the way I was supposed to, then—"

"Then we'd still be here," I said. A daring little thrill ran up my spine. Who was this Sadie, this one so confident in herself that she was interrupting?

Then again, if this Sadie was really that confident, would there be that line of cold sweat trickling its way down the back of her neck?

"She's right," Kel whispered. They sounded angry, but their face was bleak. "We were so behind by that point she was doing triage. And you're the one who killed my dessert."

"Your dessert was fine in the end," Vanilla Joe said back. "That's what matters."

The judges pronounced Nia the ultimate winner, both for her fine food and her iron rule as executive chef, then motioned us back over. The trickle of cold sweat turned into a flood. "Unfortunately, that means that you, the blue team, lost this challenge," Maz said somberly. "And two of you will be going home."

Okay, now I felt a little bit like I was going to throw up.

"Your menu felt cohesive, if a bit unoriginal," Lenore Smith said, her hands folded neatly on the table before her. "My favorite dish of my meal there was the short rib with those crispy yet pillowy gnocchi. Who made that?"

Vanilla Joe smugly raised his hand, a smile playing on his lips.

"It was fantastic," Lenore Smith said. "The texture of the short rib was just unbelievable, meltingly soft yet with those crispy edges. I don't know how you got that texture without drying out the inside. And those gnocchi sopped up that sauce so well. I'd say it wasn't all that exciting, except for the hints of five-spice powder in that red wine sauce. The roasted broccolini on the side was well seasoned, too, and necessary for breaking up the richness on the rest of the plate. Just so well-done, Chef Joe."

"Thank you," he said. He bowed his head, but I could still see him smirking.

"We also really enjoyed the sunchoke soup and the slow-cooked black bass," said Luke. "Which chef made those?"

My fingertips tingled as I raised my hand. "I made them."

Luke nodded, his face serious. "The sunchoke soup was creamy, earthy, and smoky all at once, and those bacon croutons were crunchy and added some much-needed texture. We all liked the hint of thyme—it was just enough, as any more would have sent it over the edge.

"And the slow-cooked black bass was so tender it almost

melted in our mouths. The preserved tomato broth was a touch salty for our tastes, and we thought the cauliflower could have been cooked a little less, but the texture of the nutty farro stood up against the broth and the fish quite well." He swallowed hard and looked me in the eye. What was that I saw now? Admiration? "Very nice, Chef Sadie."

I gave him the barest nod in response, but I felt like jumping up and down.

"We didn't like the other dishes on your menu quite as much," Maz said, and then he tore everything else apart. Vanilla Joe's beef tartare was bland, and the cut of the meat wasn't precise. The hamachi crudo was underseasoned and lacked acid or zing or pep or anything to make it stand out ("I may as well have been eating a napkin," said Lenore Smith, which made me do a full-body cringe). Bald Joe's fancy cheese plate was okay, but not creative enough, and the ratio of cheese to other ingredients was off. And Kel's ice cream had an off texture, though the bread pudding was rich and sweet. A little too sweet.

"The biggest problem with your team, however, was the service," said Maz. "It was inconsistent, took too long, and guests said they felt abandoned. It took fifteen minutes for us to be seated, and when we looked around for you, Chef Kel, as the front-of-house, you were nowhere to be seen. Why weren't you up front greeting tables and making sure everything in the front of house was running smoothly?"

Kel drew in a deep breath. I wanted to reach over and grab their hand in support, but I kept mine clasped at my front, since that would involve reaching around Bald Joe's broad back. "There were issues with how Chef Joe as executive chef was running the back of house," they said, their voice steady. Tiny spots of red boiled on their otherwise very white cheeks, and while their hands were clasped before them, they were shaking. "I spent a lot of time racing back and forth between the back and the front trying to keep things going. Sadie took over halfway through service and got things running smoothly, but by then I realized there were issues with my ice cream, and I had to stay in back to fix it."

"I see," said Maz. "Unfortunately, it was still your responsibility as front-of-house to make sure everything up front ran smoothly, and we were sorely disappointed with how that went."

Kel let out a puff of air like they'd just been punched in the stomach. "I understand."

Maz nodded somberly. "Chef Sadie . . ."

Me? Every muscle in my body seized up tight.

". . . your food was excellent, and we were impressed with how you righted your sinking ship," Maz continued. "You are safe. Please step back with the red team."

I was shaking, but I leaned over and gave Kel a quick hug before moving to stand with the others. It was as much to hold me up as give my friend comfort, honestly. I felt as if I might fall over.

I glanced over at Luke once I was firmly situated, my legs no longer feeling like they were going to give out under me. He was looking over at me with a little half smile, though it disappeared as soon as I saw it. Which left me wondering if it had ever really been there at all.

Did it matter, though? I was safe. And not just safe because I was lucky—I was safe because I'd spoken up for what was right, because I'd made excellent food.

Maybe I deserved to be on *Chef Supreme* after all. Maybe.

"It was difficult to decide among the other three of you," Maz said. "But ultimately it came down to the food. Chef Joe Hennessey . . ."

Vanilla Joe took a deep breath.

". . . your short rib saved you," Maz said. "You are continuing on to the final six. Which means that, unfortunately, Chef Kel and Chef Joe, you'll be leaving us tonight."

I hugged my arms tight around me. Kel. Going home. This was the first elimination that really hurt.

Though of course it didn't hurt me as much as it hurt Kel and Bald Joe. Bald Joe actually looked pretty composed, a crease between his eyebrows the only indication that he was upset, but Kel looked as if their face had shattered into pieces. "Thank you, chefs," they said weakly. "I've learned so much."

My insides were a jumble. Sadness for Kel. Annoyance that Vanilla Joe had squeaked through. And yes, a little bit of relief that two serious contenders for the title were out of the running.

I gave Kel a quick, weak smile, and then they were gone.

12

I KNEW TO EXPECT IT, BUT SITTING BY THE BAR AT HOME that night without Kel was pretty depressing. I had a drink of whiskey in their honor, wrinkling my nose every time I sipped what tasted like dying in a fire. I had to make fun of Kaitlyn and Vanilla Joe in my head now, and slept soundly that night without Kel's tossing and turning below me.

More confessionals later, it was finally another Sunday, and my plan was to sleep through it, thanks to both my Kel-related depression and non-Kel-related exhaustion. Which meant that, when somebody knocked hard on my door at—I cracked one bleary eye to check the clock—ten a.m., I was crabbier than usual. "Go away." I rolled over and pressed my ear into the pillow, trying to muffle the sound. "I'm sleeping."

The voice that responded wasn't any of my fellow competitors': it was the perky *Chef Supreme* assistant's. Didn't she ever get a day off? "Fun surprise time," she chirped. "Get camera-ready and come downstairs!"

A *fun surprise* in *Chef Supreme* parlance probably meant a challenge. "Even on our day off?" I grumbled to myself as I got dressed and brushed my teeth, swiped on some lip gloss and mascara. None of the other girls were anywhere in sight. Nia was probably at the gym after a healthy, nutritious breakfast. Kaitlyn and Megan? Probably chain-smoking on the terrace.

Two cameras and Maz were waiting downstairs. Vanilla Joe, Ernesto, and Nia were sitting on the couch, the first two slouched back into the cushion like they were hoping it might swallow them up, Nia perched on the edge of her seat. She swiveled to face me as I entered the living space. "Finally," she said. "Now we're just waiting for Kaitlyn and Megan and we can find out what this 'fun surprise' is."

She actually sounded excited, and I didn't want to burst her bubble, so I just took a seat on one of the armchairs where I could keep a good eye on the cable box clock. Every minute Kaitlyn delayed us was one more minute I could have been sleeping, and was one more reason I could have a valid reason to be annoyed at Kaitlyn.

She and Megan finally stumbled down the stairs laughing seven minutes later. I glanced at them sidelong as Kaitlyn apologized to the *Chef Supreme* assistant for making her wait. "I was just upstairs," I mumbled to Nia. "And they weren't in their bedroom or the bathroom."

She shrugged. I didn't have any more time to ponder the mystery of where they'd been, since the assistant clapped her hands "I know that 'fun surprise' usually means a challenge, but today it actually does mean a fun surprise," she said. "The judges know you had a hard challenge in Duel of Spatulas and that you just saw two of your friends leave, so they decided to come and cook you brunch!"

As if they were waiting outside for a cue—they probably had
been—the judges filed in through the front door. First Lenore
Smith, her silver hair just as stiff and immovable as it was on set,
though she'd eschewed her usual pantsuit in favor of tailored
jeans (creased down the front) and a blue silk blouse. Then Maz
Sarshad, who'd chosen a bright green designer sweatshirt that
matched his colored contacts.

And finally, Luke, of course. He wore jeans, too, and a plain
white T-shirt, and somehow it looked as suited to him as his
tailored tuxedo. Suddenly, I felt self-conscious of my leggings
and oversize shirt.

The cameras followed them, too. I sat up straight. This might
be something "fun," designed to give viewers a few minutes of
levity after a particularly bruising challenge, but it was still work
for us. I still had to consider how I'd look on camera, how my
personality would come off.

I'd really been looking forward to a day's break from that.

But it was what it was. I forced a smile as Maz stepped forward and basically repeated everything the assistant had just
said, only a few more times for the camera. "So lie back and relax while we cater to you!" he finished with every time. After
another take, the judges headed into the kitchen.

Where, naturally, we all followed them. Because we had two
of the country's top chefs—and Maz—here with us in our
kitchen. Of course we wanted to take the opportunity to learn
from them . . .

. . . and maybe make them like us a little more as individuals
so that they might hesitate before sending us home.

"I love your blouse," Kaitlyn gushed to Lenore, her smile
sparkling as she rested a hand on her shoulder.

"You have to tell me where you got that sweatshirt," said Vanilla Joe to Maz, attempting a similarly sparkling smile.

"I can't wait to see what you cook," Nia said to Lenore. "I've memorized the brunch menu of your last restaurant for inspiration on any breakfast or brunch challenges. Are you going to make one of your signature galettes?"

Let's be real: I wanted to suck up to them as much as anyone else. But the other contestants had all beaten me to Lenore and Maz—maybe they seemed more influenceable—so as the smells of frying garlic and onion and the sounds of dough mixing in glass bowls rose into the air, I found myself beside Luke at the other end of the counter.

I glanced at him sidelong. Why weren't the other chefs flocking to him the way they were to Lenore and Maz? I could understand the appeal of Lenore Smith: she was a legend. Maybe they saw Maz as easily manipulated when it came to judging or something. Or maybe they were really interested in his Persian breakfast. "You're being ignored," I said quietly, hopefully quietly enough where the cameras wouldn't pick it up. Though the cameras seemed to be focused on the other end of the kitchen, where actual cooking was happening. Maybe that was why the other chefs were focused on Lenore and Maz: because they were actually cooking and not just standing there, their plain white T-shirt tight against broad shoulders and the edge of that tattoo that had been tickling my dreams peeking—

Why wasn't Luke cooking? I raised an eyebrow at him, and it was as if he read my mind. "I have a whole menu planned out," he said. "Based on the brunch menu of my new restaurant. But it seems like they have it covered over there." He shrugged.

"You're full of shit," I needled. Okay, definitely hoping the cameras didn't pick *that* up. But as they were currently occupied filming Nia quiz Lenore Smith on her galette dough and Vanilla Joe helping Maz theatrically crack about a million eggs into a giant bowl, I thought I'd be okay. "You just don't want to cook your fancy French food. Why don't we cook a Korean-inspired brunch the way you'd do at your dream restaurant?"

The words were out of my mouth before I could stop them, or ask them why they cared so much about what a jerk like Luke was doing. I should have been watching Lenore make her galette. That would've been a way better use of my time.

Luke shrugged. "Korean breakfasts aren't so different from Korean lunches and dinners. It's mostly the same food, and I imagine many of the ingredients I'd need won't be stocked here. And I've never been all that passionate about brunch food in general."

My mouth dropped open. "Then clearly you've never had *good* brunch food."

He raised an eyebrow, obviously amused. That tiny gesture made something hot tweak below my stomach. *Down, girl.* "I've eaten brunch at some of the best restaurants in the world."

"But not from *my* kitchen," I countered. Now it wasn't so much about caring about how he felt: it was about proving I was right. "Come on. We're going to make a full Ashkenazi breakfast spread. I'm talking blintzes. I'm talking challah French toast. I'm talking bagels and lox and shakshuka. I'm talking matzah brei."

"I've never heard of that last one."

"See? You *have* never had a good brunch." I cast my gaze around the kitchen, searching for space and materials and tools. All were in short supply. Lenore Smith was using just about every bowl in the kitchen for her galettes and fillings, the sure sign of someone who hadn't had to clean up after themselves in a very long time. And Maz was now playfully swordfighting Vanilla Joe and Megan with a trio of spatulas while the cameras looked on. "Okay, maybe we're not going to be able to cook up that whole spread. But we're at least making matzah brei, since you've never had it."

I reached out to grab a stainless steel pan from the counter while Lenore was busy explaining the filling's consistency to Nia, but I stopped when I noticed Luke's lips twitch. My arm hung in the air, like it was waiting for somebody to hang a coat on it. "What are you smirking at?"

"Nothing." But his lips were still twisted like he was trying not to laugh, so clearly, there was something. I lowered my arm, then reconsidered, reached back out, and stole the pan before Lenore could turn around.

"Bold of you to lie to the person making you food," I said. "What is it, really?"

"You're not supposed to be making the food. You're supposed to be relaxing on your day off."

I shrugged, "Maybe I find cooking brunch relaxing." Most of the ingredients I needed were already scattered about on the kitchen island, and it only took a few trips to gather them all: eggs, salt, butter, sugar, cream. The only thing missing was . . . "Could you see if there's matzah in the cabinet? Hopefully, they have some." Considering Passover was fairly recent, at the end of which matzah would've been on a fire sale, I was hopeful whoever'd stocked the pantry had been cheap.

"I'm not sure if I've ever eaten matzah." But he turned to check the pantry anyway, treating me to a view of his back. The

T-shirt clung to every muscle, outlined that divot running down the center where I could see myself tracing my fingers. And then of course there was his ass in those dark jeans.

That warm spot throbbed. *Damn it, Sadie. Focus.* "Matzah is terrible. It's like a dry, stale cracker." Was I talking weirdly loud? "But matzah brei makes it tolerable. No, not just tolerable. Delicious."

He turned around with a big cardboard box of matzah in his arms. I looked down for a moment to hide how red my face was.

When I looked back up, Luke was casually leaning against the counter with his arms crossed. From this angle, I could see a little more of the tattoo on his upper arm: a black outline of what appeared to be a chef's knife. The blade was pointed down toward his elbow. Staring at it, I grabbed the box of matzah from him and opened it up. A puff of dust came up with the cardboard top, making me think this matzah had been here for way too long, but it wasn't like it could get any harder or drier than it already was. No mold. We were okay. I set sheets of the matzah into a bowl, then covered it with cool water for it to soak.

As we waited, I said, "I like your tattoo."

"Thanks," he said. "Do you have any tattoos? Like, where I can't see them?"

My back stiffened, and for a second that was all that was in my mind: Luke's hands ranging up my shirt to see if any tattoos were hiding up there, warm skin on warm skin down below, parting my legs to see if any decorated my inner thigh . . .

"That came out wrong, sorry," he said hastily. I swallowed hard and cleared my throat, realizing his face was bright red. Good. We matched. "I've just, I've looked all over the parts of you that were showing, and I didn't see any, so I figured that if you *did* have any, they would have to be where I couldn't—"

"It's okay," I said, turning my back to grab a pan. And maybe so that he couldn't see the little smile on my red face. "So you've looked all over me, have you?" The flame flicked on under my pan. I had to reach awkwardly over a bubbling pan of spinach, onion, and garlic in order to dump the butter in mine. Two tablespoons. Hesitated, then added two more. You could never have too much butter.

He cleared his throat. "Um, that didn't come out the right way, either. What I meant was . . . um . . ."

For a moment I enjoyed letting him stammer. Then grinned. "I don't have any tattoos. I've thought about getting one, but I'm too indecisive. I know I'd change my mind after getting something permanently inscribed on my body."

"That's why I got a chef's knife," Luke said. "I knew I'd never regret that."

I handed him a bowl. "Could you whisk a bunch of eggs while I brown the matzah?" I took each damp, soggy sheet from the water, shook off the excess water, and tossed it into the bubbling butter, where it sizzled and spat. A few droplets bounced into whatever was going on in that spinach pan, but that wasn't a big deal. Again, no such thing as too much butter. "Once it's brown, we'll chop it up and scramble in the eggs."

Watching Luke work was like watching a professional dancer dance. I actually risked letting the matzah burn so that I could take it all in. The graceful flex of his fingers as they deftly cracked eggs against the flat surface of the counter, then held back any shell as he deposited each egg into the bowl, all one-handed. The flick of his wrist as it whirled the whisk around the bowl, keeping the contents swirling quickly, but not so quickly that they'd slop over the bowl's rim. The careful look in his eye as he calculated whether the resulting pale yellow liquid was light and foamy enough. The crease in his brows as he glanced up and asked me, "Is your matzah burning?"

Yes. Yes it was. I flung my attention back to the pan; the matzah was a bit browner than I would have chosen, but it was still good. I carefully poured the eggs in, whisking them so that they blended with the pieces of matzah, then sprinkled some salt and sugar on top. "They won't need long," I said, continuing to stir. "Why the chef's knife, though? There are plenty of things you could've gotten to symbolize being a chef. Loving food. I knew people with tattoos of bacon, or vegetables, or even one with a turnip, which looked a little bit like a rash on his arm."

He didn't hesitate with his answer. "I couldn't cook without my chef's knife. It's like an extension of me at this point. And it doesn't matter what I'm cooking, what I'm doing. It's there no matter what."

Over the course of saying that, the matzah brei was done. I immediately removed it from the heat, glancing around for a serving platter. Somehow Lenore Smith was monopolizing all of them, too, but her hair was shaking as she debated Nia over proper galette folding techniques, which I figured meant she was fully distracted. The one I nabbed had traces of what tasted like butterscotch coating the ceramic, but that would only make the matzah brei better.

"And served," I said, turning back to Luke. He was gazing down at me, his eyes unreadable. And I suddenly realized he'd stepped closer to me while I was turned away. I could feel the heat of his body now. If I reached out only a few inches, I could cut myself on his chef's knife.

The cameras were here. This was dangerous. Extremely dangerous.

I couldn't take a step back, since my back was up against the counter, but I didn't want to step away anyway. The edge of the granite was digging into my spine, but the rest of my body was tingling. "We shouldn't be doing this," I said softly, so softly he probably couldn't hear me.

He ducked his head. I nearly swooned. Like, literally swooned, which would've made me face-plant in the matzah brei (swooning was not as sexy as it sounded unless you were appropriately positioned in front of your fainting couch). "Sadie," he said quietly, and just from the way his voice shook a little on that one word, I knew exactly what he wanted. To lean in only a few inches more and kiss me. To kiss me until we weren't sure who was who anymore. To trace every inch of my body with his lips to make sure I didn't have a secret tattoo anywhere.

I took a deep, shaky breath, inhaling the spice of Luke's smell, and even though I knew that he was a jerk, that my spot on the show was worth so much more than a kiss, I was thinking with the wrong head right now, and I—

I couldn't do this. I stepped to the side. It took a moment to speak, considering how hard my heart was pounding, how heavily I was breathing. "What do you think you're doing?"

Luke had stepped away now. The gulf between us was cold, and I had to fight the urge to fill it. "I shouldn't have gotten so close," he said roughly, angling his head down. "Shit."

My face was blazing. "Of course you shouldn't have. You barely even remember my name."

His face shot back up, his eyes widening. "Sadie . . ."

Maz clapped his hands, which broke whatever was going on between us. "The cameras want some good shots of us all sitting around the table enjoying our feast. Preferably laughing," he said. "Anyone got any good jokes?"

Luke leapt back from me like I'd burned him. For a moment I could only describe his face as open: eyes wide and vulnerable; lips slightly parted. Like anything I said in that moment would hit him hard.

But I didn't say anything. I *couldn't* say anything. The cameras were here, focusing on all of us. Besides, he was a jerk, even if he didn't always act like one. And so his face closed up again, took on that hard, polished countenance I'd seen at all our challenges so far. Lenore said to Maz, "How about your hair?" Vanilla Joe laughed but cut it off when he realized Maz's pursed lips and stormy eyes meant he wouldn't join in.

Fast-forward ten minutes, and we were all sitting around our long dining table. Through the big picture window the sun blazed and white puffy clouds floated on a crystalline blue sky. It reminded me a little bit of being on the airplane here, and only partially because I was sitting beside Luke again. Our instincts had been to scatter to opposite sides of the table, but the *Chef Supreme* assistant in attendance had seated everyone in a designated order.

The *Chef Supreme* assistant also went around and put some of all the food on everybody's plates, so that eagle-eyed Internet commentators couldn't form conspiracy theories about anybody secretly hating another chef because they didn't eat any of their food. It took a while for her to do so, during which the food grew cold. "But that's okay," she assured us when Nia brought it up. "The camera can't tell how hot or cold the food is, so it doesn't matter."

Lenore's galettes, one savory with a filling of fresh summer tomatoes and basil and one sweet with caramelized peaches, were tender and flaky and buttery and perfect. Maz's nargesi, an egg and spinach dish similar to shakshuka, burst with flavor on the tongue, especially when eaten beside the fresh watermelon and soft cheese salad he'd brought. They'd catered in bagels from the local bagel place, and whatever empty boasts New York City made about its food, they were right in that they had the best bagels anywhere. Especially when heaped with lox and cream cheese and capers and red onions sliced so paper-thin light shone pink through them.

And my matzah brei. Not going to lie, people made some skeptical faces as it was spooned out on their plates. Even Luke. He took a bite, then tilted his head and considered. "I wasn't sure when you were first making it, seeing the sugar go in with the scrambled eggs, and I may have said some regrettable things about it . . ." He had? ". . . but I shouldn't have. I'm sorry."

Oh. He wasn't talking only about the matzah brei.

"I think," I said carefully, "that I was maybe a little harsh. On the matzah brei. When it was browning, I let it go a little too far. Because I really wanted to eat it, too."

"I wanted that matzah brei more than anything else in the world," he said, taking a deep breath, holding his eyes with mine. My forkful of nargesi stopped halfway to my mouth.

I stared at him. He stared at me. Maz stared at the both of us. It took me a minute to realize he was trying to wrinkle his forehead in confusion, but all the Botox wouldn't let him wrinkle at all. "It's just eggs and matzah."

Luke took another bite. His eyes were still on me. "But have you truly tasted the lushness of the egg custard, how it gives way for your tongue? The sweetness that hits just before the salt?"

I was definitely flushing hard. What the hell was he doing? He shouldn't be putting me in this position. Flirting through my food. *He's a jerk, don't forget,* I tried to tell myself, but my racing heart didn't want to listen.

"I don't get much salt," Maz said dubiously.

I dropped my eyes to my plate. "I think that my food should *stay on my plate where it belongs.*"

"Where else would it go?" Maz scratched his head. "I'm so confused."

"You're not the only one," I muttered under my breath. When he asked me to repeat myself, I raised my head and forced a smile. "I said, your nargesi is delicious! What's the recipe?"

13

WE SPENT THE NEXT FEW DAYS FILMING CONFESSION-
als about the brunch and then some general material I thought
might eventually be used for promos. The morning after our last
shoot, we arrived at the *Chef Supreme* kitchen to find it decked out
for Halloween. Orange and black streamers dangled festively
from the ceiling, far enough above our stoves so that even the
most vigorous bananas Foster wouldn't light them on fire. Thick
cobwebs featuring comically oversize plastic spiders hung in the
corners. Pumpkins and gourds were piled along the walls.

Which was odd, considering it was still June. Where did they
even find gourds this time of year? And not just any kind of
gourd, but those fancy green ones that looked like swans?

"Hello, chefs!" Adrianna greeted us from the front of the
room. A pair of glittery black cat's ears perched atop her tight
black ponytail. "And happy Halloween. At least it'll be Halloween for our viewers. That's when this episode's going to be
airing."

Ah. That made more sense.

"Your challenge is going to be Halloween-themed, too. So get ready to make a spooky dish. And when you talk up our sponsors, feel free to use Halloween-y language. 'This oven heats up scarily fast!' That sort of thing." She exited, and out came Maz to tell us this officially. He was wearing a glittering teal bodysuit, platform heels, and a wig teased with what looked like so much hair spray he'd better stay far away from our stoves. I was so distracted by his fake eyelashes, which were longer and thicker than any of the plastic spiders' legs, that I missed his corny Halloween introduction, complete with menacing laughter. I wasn't that upset. I'd get to hear it at least twice more.

"Your task today, chefs, will be to create a *spoooooooky* dish to serve fifty guests at the *Chef Supreme* Halloween party tomorrow," Maz said.

Okay. That wasn't so bad.

But Maz stopped and considered, teetering on his high, high heels. "You know what? That's not a scary enough challenge for Halloween. So . . ." He let loose with a sinister-sounding laugh. "You're going to create *twoOoOo* dishes for our Halloween party."

They made us fake horror at that announcement for two more takes, but it wasn't all that real; this still wasn't too bad a challenge. And my mind was already churning. This could actually be fun.

The obvious solution would be to make something that *looked* scary. Deviled eggs that looked like eyeballs. Noodles that looked like worms. Anything spattered with red stuff that looked like blood.

The noodle/worm idea was appealing to me. I hadn't made

pasta in the competition yet. And noodle kugel was a traditional Jewish dish that held tight to my heart . . . and could also be made to look extremely disturbing. To be honest, it could be a little gross-looking on the best of days. Noodles submerged in a creamy cheese base, some of them sticking up top to get crispy in the oven. Raisins or other fruits flecking the kugel like little bugs. Maybe I could make the whole thing graveyard-themed.

If I was going to make something so rich and heavy and creamy, my other dish should balance it out by being light and savory. And spooky, of course. Maybe organ meats? Chicken feet were extremely scary-looking, maybe with some kind of beet sauce . . .

I rubbed my hands together in anticipation. Yes, this was going to be fun.

The next day, the day of the actual event, the ingredients of my noodle kugel made a sick squelching noise as I stirred them. I kept half an ear on that, and half an ear on Maz talking to the other contestants, getting some brief sound bites for the camera. It was easier to hear now that there were only six of us: fewer buzzing machines, less clattering of kitchen tools, not as many knife sounds on cutting boards.

I wasn't sure which way I preferred it.

"Chef Joe," Maz was saying. Vanilla Joe could be simply Joe now, since he was the only Joe left. Though he'd always be Vanilla Joe to me. "Who do you think your biggest competition is now that the field's half the size it was at first?"

"I'm my own biggest competition," said Vanilla Joe. Of course he would say that. "The girls had better watch out!"

That didn't even make any sense considering Ernesto was still in the competition; I just rolled my eyes. Nia shot him a death stare over her cutting board. Kaitlyn let loose a trilling bray of a laugh. "You're your own worst enemy, you adorable lunkhead," she yelled at him. He blew her a kiss with a wink.

I mimed vomiting into my kugel bowl. Hopefully, they didn't catch that on camera.

THE PRODUCERS HAD gone low-budget and decided to host their Halloween party here in the *Chef Supreme* kitchen rather than rent a decked-out venue, which explained the festive decorations. Guests ranged through the room, trying all of our dishes and sipping murky-looking potions.

I beamed at the judges as they came by my booth, all dressed up for the occasion. Lenore Smith made an extremely convincing Maleficent, looming over us great and terrible, her ice-blue eyes glowing eerily. I almost worried she'd swoop in and curse one of us for not using enough salt.

And Luke. Luke didn't look all that different from his usual self, wearing a tailored black tuxedo and a black cape sweeping behind him, his dark hair slicked back. I was about to ask if he was supposed to be a maskless Phantom of the Opera before he opened his lips to smile at me and I saw the pointed teeth.

"Can you eat with those in?" I couldn't stop myself from asking.

He stared at me, poker-faced. "No, but I can suck your blood."

I imagined him leaning in, the scrape of his chin on my jawline, his lips brushing across my skin, his teeth nipping my throat.

He coughed. "I've been taking them out to taste." From the

way he leaned back, almost unconsciously, I wondered if he'd been thinking the same thing as me.

"Tell us about your food, Chef Sadie," Maz said. I had to strain my neck to look up at him.

Right. The food. I cleared my throat, wishing away the phantom imprints of Luke's teeth grazing my skin. "Tonight I'd like you to imagine yourself stepping through the gates of a graveyard," I said. "There's no moon above. Around you, it's pitch-black. And then you hear the scraping ahead of you . . ."

I stepped back, gesturing at my station like I was a magician pulling a rabbit out of my hat. "We set the scene with our graveyard noodle kugel. Noodle kugel is a traditional Ashkenazi Jewish dish, basically a baked noodle pudding. I grew up eating it around the family table."

"My word!" Lenore Smith exclaimed, leaning in. I had to step back to avoid getting speared by one of her horns. "I can't imagine eating this around the family table."

"Well, I gave it a Halloween-y twist, of course," I said, cracking a grin. "The kugel is the graveyard, to set the scene. The crust on the outside represents shards of bone."

The judges looked it over with an appraising eye. I'd used vegetable dyes to color the entire thing a purple so deep it was almost black, the effect of which was fairly unappetizing . . . but perfect for Halloween, I hoped. I'd turned up the richness of the filling, aiming for a luxurious mouthfeel without being sickening, and made the whole thing more savory, dialing back on the sugar and adding garlic and onion and lots of fresh herbs to cut through the richness. I then rolled bites of it in a potato chip crust and deep-fried them, which sounded bizarre but worked.

At least, I thought so. I held my breath as the judges crunched in and chewed thoughtfully.

"I love this." Lenore Smith was blunt as always. "It's bizarre, but in all the best ways. The inside is melty and rich and savory, and the outside is perfectly crunchy and salty. It makes me think of an arancini."

I was familiar with the fried Italian risotto balls, but I hadn't connected them to my dish until now.

"I don't want to ask how many calories are in this," Maz said with a mock frown.

"Even better than matzah brei," Luke said with a hint of a smile before finishing his entire kugel ball, which I hoped was a good thing.

By the time they'd finished, all of their mouths were stained purple. I declined to mention that as I introduced my second dish. "So you've heard the scraping in the graveyard. Your terror is mounting, when—AHHH!" I jumped toward them, hands outstretched into claws, face twisted into a terrific frown. Lenore and Maz jumped, Maz stumbling over his heels. Luke raised an eyebrow, his face inscrutable. "A claw breaks through the earth at your feet!" I presented my plate with a flourish. "I have for you braised and fried chicken feet, served with buffalo sauce, a salad of cauliflower rubble and grated celery, and a blue cheese mascarpone cream."

Luke's face lit up as he saw the chicken feet, the exact opposite expressions of Lenore and Maz, who looked very much as if they were at an actual graveyard and had seen an actual claw shoot up from the grave. "It reminds me of dakbal," he breathed, and he sounded for a moment as if it were just the two of us sitting side by side in that Korean speakeasy, shoulder touching shoulder. Unconsciously, I took a step toward him. "My halmoni used to make dakbal as a snack when we visited her in Korea. She'd steam them first, then panfry them until they were charred, and then there was the secret sauce she made, all garlicky and gingery and tingling with gochugaru . . ."

As he trailed off, I could almost taste his grandmother's chicken feet. The chew of the meat after the crisp of the char. The caramelization of the sugars on the skin, and the nose-running spiciness of the sauce.

"I didn't know you were Korean," said Maz.

That broke the mood. I stepped back, clearing my throat.

Meanwhile, Lenore Smith was crunching away. "I was worried about eating these fried chicken feet right after that deep-fried noodle kugel, but this bracing, vinegary salad underneath really cuts through the fat and the richness," she said, swallowing. "I love the chicken feet, but I almost love this salad more. Is that crazy?"

"Yes," Luke said. "The chicken feet are delicious. Cooked so that they're tender and also crunchy on the outside, and that sauce is the perfect amount of spicy and vinegary."

"The dish is saved from an overabundance of vinegar by that cream underneath," said Maz. "Luke, are you really Korean? Why did you never tell me?"

Luke looked skyward, sighing through his nose. "We should move on to the next station."

I watched them walk over to Kaitlyn's station, then did a quick fist pump. *They liked it. They really liked it.*

As I did my fist pump, my hip bumped out, too, and hit a corner of my station. "Ouch!" I winced and flung myself back, away from the pain, which was maybe a tiny bit of an overreaction. But a reaction it was, and my back hit the front of my station, where I'd set out plates.

I'd gotten a C in physics class in high school, but I still remembered that the definition of momentum was the quantity of motion of a moving body, measured as a product of its mass and velocity. The front few plates were heavy with mass, and I'd just given them velocity by smashing right into their surface. So they had plenty of momentum, which sent them sailing off the table and onto the guests waiting next in line.

"Oh my God!" I cried. It looked like a very small massacre. Purple kugel juice had splattered all over a woman's expensive-looking pale pink dress. Buffalo sauce had stained a man's designer cream-colored tie. A chicken foot had clawed its way down his pants, streaking them with more sauce. "I'm so sorry!"

Both the man and the woman wore very strained grins. Which was why it took me a moment to recognize them as the couple I'd accidentally cursed at at Charles Weston's party and the people I'd blown off during the Duel of Spatulas. These people really had the worst luck. Maybe I should grant them a restraining order from me for their own protection. "It's all right," the woman said, but her cheer was clearly forced. A little painful. "We'll hit Adrianna with the dry-cleaning bills."

Great. One more reason for Adrianna to love having me on this show.

"I'm so sorry," I repeated. Thank goodness I'd only lost a few of my plates. I quickly plated them new dishes of food just to get them to go away. The other people in line kept a safe distance as I continued plating. I couldn't blame them. Though it meant I had to really prick my ears to hear all the nice things they were saying about my food. And they *were* nice things, aside from some initial dubiousness about the chicken feet. Once they'd tried it, I didn't hear a single grumble.

So when the judges asked us all to line up at the end after our time in the stew room—now that we were only six, there was no more being in the middle—I was confident. Well, mostly. My stomach still felt like one of those nasty Jell-O salads from fifties dinner parties with tuna and mayonnaise and pineapple in it, but that was just part of standing before the judges. "Chef Nia, Chef Sadie, and Chef Kaitlyn, please step forward."

We stepped forward. I held my breath, which made the Jell-O salad stop quivering for the moment it took for Maz to say, "The three of you made our . . . *favorite* dishes today!"

I preened like a bird in the sun as the judges went over their praises for my fried potato chip kugel and buffalo chicken feet. Then smiled respectfully as they gushed about Nia's pork candy and lobster claw with biscuits and Kaitlyn's eye meatballs and beet pasta.

"But only one chef both truly encapsulated the spirit of Halloween *and* served us such good food we're still dreaming about it hours later," Maz said. "Congratulations . . . Chef Sadie!"

Me. That was me.

He'd said my name.

It took a minute to sink in. Kaitlyn grabbing me from the side and squeezing me tight helped. "Yay, Sadie!" she squealed. Her arms crunched my rib cage. I fought back the urge to gag.

Nia patted me on the back. "Congratulations,"

I'd won. My first solo win. It came with something like five thousand dollars, but that hardly mattered right now. Fireworks were exploding inside me, and not just because Kaitlyn was close to strangling me. This was another sign that I was really a contender. That I was going to be in the top five. That I might actually achieve my goal, and get to have the restaurant I'd dreamed of.

That Chef Anders might have blacklisted me in Seattle, but there was only so much weight his word could hold against the *Chef Supreme* brand.

I stepped back with a huge smile that didn't dim even as the judges called forth Megan, Vanilla Joe, and Ernesto. Though of course I tried to look sad as they sent Ernesto home. I *was* sad, honestly. I would have rather seen Kaitlyn and Vanilla Joe go before him. But he was a talented chef, even if he'd messed up and served the judges rubbery octopus, so it was good to have one more obstacle out of my way.

Surprisingly, Nia seemed just as upbeat as me on our drive home. We were down to two cars now, and she and I had ended up in one by ourselves, allowing Kaitlyn, Megan, and Vanilla Joe to take the other one. Next week, I realized, we'd be down to fitting in one car.

Assuming I was still here.

Somehow my nerves were rattling even more than they had last week. Because I'd won this week. Because I was so close to the final four. Because this whole experience was zooming by and I was somehow doing this on four hours of sleep a night and I thought I might break down at any moment. "Hey," I said. "We have confessionals and then it's Sunday, right? We should do something." I didn't know if I could handle another day sitting in the *Chef Supreme* house, closed in by those four walls, which only made the rattling of my nerves seem louder. "Like, go somewhere. We're in New York City, and we've barely seen any of it. We should make the most of it."

Nia stretched, clasping her hands over her head. "I guess we can request an escort. Let's ask Adrianna tomorrow when we get home."

Home. It startled me that hearing Nia call the *Chef Supreme* house home *didn't* startle me. Maybe it was the delirium resulting from my lack of sleep, but the apartment was actually starting to feel like a home. Or maybe it was that the people inside the apartment felt like home, like a family. I'd even dared to finish unpacking my stuff the other day, holding my breath the whole time like I was cursing myself. Nia, naturally, had unpacked the first day, filling her drawers with neatly folded clothes and covering the surface of her portion of the dresser with thick books she'd brought from home and framed photos of family members and friends. Kaitlyn was still living out of her overflowing suitcase, clothes scattered all over her side of the room.

It was a home, if a member of your family was kicked out onto the streets every week. I felt a pang as I thought of Kel, wondering what they were doing right now. I'd done enough research on the show to know that eliminated contestants might have "gone home," but that they didn't actually get to go home for real, because then it would be obvious when the show started airing who would go home and who would stay in for the finale. Kel and Bald Joe and the other eliminated contestants were most likely cloistered in a hotel or Airbnb nearby, consoling themselves with a full bar.

I shook my head, both to chase away thoughts of my dearly departed friends and to answer Nia's idea. "I don't want to deal with that. I want to get away from the cameras for a night."

"But we can't go out without an escort. It's against the rules."

Right. The lack of sleep was getting to me. I blinked hard, trying to get the sandy feeling out of my eyes. "You know, never mind."

But I kept thinking about it the next day as we filmed our confessionals. How nice it would be to get away from the cameras for a little while. And maybe it was the lack of sleep that made me bring it up again, only not just with Nia, with all the others.

"I wish we could spend a night without the cameras," I told them in our apartment. I couldn't even look up toward them; it was like they were sucking the life out of me. "But we can't leave this apartment, or we'll get kicked off the show."

"That's not actually true," Nia said. She cocked her head to the side, rubbed her black halo of hair. "They keep it quiet, but I read on the gossip blogs that, pretty much every season, the contestants sneak out at some point. As long as they're not too obnoxious about it, they don't get in trouble. Or kicked off."

"Seriously?" Megan said thoughtfully. Why hadn't she mentioned that yesterday in the car? Vanilla Joe cocked his head, considering.

"That doesn't mean I think we should do it," Nia said quickly. "No. We should stay right here, where we belong."

"If we all sneak out, we can't *all* get in trouble," said Vanilla Joe.

"True," Megan said. She stood up from where she was lounging, put her hands on her hips. "And if you're saying past seasons have done it, then really we're continuing a *Chef Supreme* tradition."

Kaitlyn twisted her lip as if she were thinking. I twisted my lip, too, because I definitely was thinking. Thinking about how maybe this wasn't such a terrible idea, if we all did it together . . .

But Nia's lips were still pinched up. "It's almost ten thirty right now. Where exactly are we supposed to go? None of us have phones, so an Uber is out, and the bus and subway this late are a crapshoot as far as running on time goes from what I understand. They do a lot of construction overnight on weekends. Besides, we'd have to jump the turnstiles since we don't have our wallets, and that doesn't go well for people who look like me."

Kaitlyn waved her hand like she was trying to push Nia's concerns away. "Aren't we in the city that never sleeps?"

"That's Manhattan," Nia said. "We're in Queens. We might be able to find somewhere, but we don't have our phones to look anything up. Plus, like I said, we don't have any money."

"I have some cash," Kaitlyn said. "Snuck it in my bag in case of an emergency. You can all pay me back later." She gave us a wolfish grin. "Though I won't need it after I get my two hundred and fifty thousand dollar check."

Everybody laughed, but Nia had made good points otherwise. I slowly felt myself begin to deflate, like a soufflé left on the counter too long. Maybe she was right. We shouldn't risk it. Not if it was going to be this difficult.

Except . . . I had an idea. The smile spread over my face. The soufflé pumped itself back up.

"Guys," I said. "Follow me."

14

"WOW," NIA SAID, HER EYES WIDE AND ROUND. "I DON'T know if it's the adrenaline from breaking the law or if this place is just that cool, but . . . wow."

We'd stepped through the front door of the Korean speak-easy. The other four's jaws had dropped as I walked confidently into the convenience store, its fluorescent lights flickering over-head and dust lying thick on the boxes of tampons and cans of peas, and opened up the back wall. As with the last time I was here, the colored lights dazzled and the random paintings on the wall made the whole thing feel like a grunge bar, except without your foot sticking to the ground with every step.

"We're not breaking the law," Kaitlyn said dryly. "Rules aren't laws." Her voice sounded different off camera, I realized, and it wasn't just the dryness. I mean, it was still raspy as all hell, but the syrupy sweetness that had coated every word for the past few weeks had crystallized, grown rough edges. "So let's go wild."

Everybody in the bar was staring at her; she'd gone all out for this trip and had dressed herself in her fanciest clothes, a tight glittery top and an even tighter pencil skirt. She'd given herself a smoky eye and the longest lashes I'd ever seen, and even though I didn't like it, I couldn't stop my eyes from lingering on her a little too long.

The rest of us had thrown on jeans and T-shirts. Except for Vanilla Joe. He was wearing sweatpants.

"I mean, maybe not too wild," I replied hastily, tearing my eyes away from the impossible heights of Kaitlyn's contoured cheekbones. "I think we'd get in, like, a *lot* of trouble if anyone passed out here or was put up on Instagram?" Vanilla Joe was not listening; his eyes were gleaming as he strode off to the bar, which was sparsely populated for a Saturday night. "So let's not go too wild. Let's just chill and celebrate."

Kaitlyn gave me a crafty smile. It reminded me of the time we were at Atelier Laurent together, and she'd just finished solemnly telling the chef that the shipment of cutting boards he'd been planning to use as plates had never arrived. "You think I'm going to let this place serve food on a chopping board?" she'd told me later out in the alley as she sucked on a cigarette and I ranted about the customer who'd told me he wanted me to cook his tuna tartare. "That trend peaked in, like, 2015."

Megan grabbed her hand. "Come on. Let's get *crunk*."

That slang had also peaked in a time long past, but Kaitlyn didn't seem too bothered about that. She clutched Megan's hand tight as Megan towed her along. Like, really tight. Like, strangely tight. I eyed them curiously, eyed even more curiously the distance between Kaitlyn and Vanilla Joe, who was already seated at the bar, laughing and talking with the bartender.

The bartender. My eyes widened, all thoughts of Megan and Kaitlyn and Vanilla Joe flying out of my head like a napkin at a barbecue. It was the same guy I'd met when I came here with Luke only a few weeks ago.

And just like that, Luke was everywhere. I could smell the tinge of spice on him that had lingered even through our airline dinner of overly sweet chicken on a metal tray, and hear the rich bubble of his laugh float over from the bar, and feel the heat radiating off his skin. The brush of his forearm against mine, his hairs soft on my skin, as he bought me a drink. The way his lips closed slowly around a bite of food, tongue flicking out to catch a crumb caught on the corner of his mouth. The animated sound of his voice as he talked about the food he loved, eyes bright with want.

I wanted him here.

Not the jerk. But the guy he'd pretended to be when we were here.

"You!" said the bartender, pointing at me, and for a second my chest seized, sure he could see exactly what I was thinking, what I was wanting. But of course not. That was absurd. So I assumed instead that I was doing something wrong, violating the dress code or stepping on somebody's toes. Vanilla Joe, Kaitlyn, Nia, and I *were* the only non-Asian people here. Also, including Megan this time, the only people here under sixty. Maybe seventy.

But then his eyes crinkled in a smile, and I pushed my anxiety away. "I know you," he continued. "You were here with—"

"My old college friend, Sandy!" I shouted. Everybody in the bar turned to stare at me, and sweat popped along my hairline. I hated being stared at for shouting, but I'd hate being exposed in front of the other chefs more. If they knew I'd kissed Luke before the show, they'd assume he was helping me win, and they might run straight to the producers to inform them. Vanilla Joe and Kaitlyn would, anyway. Maybe even Nia, not to spite me but because she was such a stickler for the rules. "Sandy, she loves this place, yep. What a good friend."

To his credit, the bartender didn't rat me out. He managed not to even look surprised or skeptical. He just nodded, then winked, which was charming in a way that it can only be coming from a very old man. "Yes, Sandy. Good girl."

Everybody ordered drinks: Megan, Vanilla Joe, and Kaitlyn did shots, Nia got a soda (caffeine-free, she informed me), and I approached the bartender and leaned in. "I don't know what it was, but I got it when I was—"

"Yes, I know," the bartender nodded. I was skeptical that he would remember exactly what I'd ordered weeks ago when he must have served hundreds of people in between, so I was surprised when he slid over that foggy green glass brimming with crushed herbs.

"You remembered!" I exclaimed, then glanced around. Megan, Vanilla Joe, and Kaitlyn were huddled at the other end of the bar, doing some kind of obnoxious drinking game that involved a lot of hooting and a small bit of hollering. The other patrons would probably be giving them dirty looks if they hadn't been captivated by Nia, who had wandered over to one of the tables and was asking questions about all their food; when I looked over a second later, she'd slid into the booth and was snacking with them, as much a part of their circle as if she was a seventy-five-year-old Korean man. There were only two other people sitting at the bar, both old men focusing intently on the TV overhead playing some kind of Korean drama. Which meant I could say whatever I wanted without worry.

Still, I lowered my voice as I leaned in. "Please don't tell any of them I was here with Luke."

The bartender frowned at me, deepening every one of the many wrinkles carved through his face. He crossed his arms. "You are ashamed of him?"

"No, no!" I waved my arms to drive the point home. "Not at all. But . . ." I leaned in even farther. "You know he's a judge this season on *Chef Supreme*, right? We're competitors. I'd be in a lot of trouble if they knew I'd met him before."

All at once, the wrinkles relaxed into a cheerful grin. He was missing two teeth on the side. "Ah. Well, that's better. Luke is a good, good boy."

I settled onto a barstool, resting my fingertips against my glass. They made little circles in the condensation, miniature windows into the forest of a drink. "Is he? How long have you known him?"

"Since he was this tall." He crouched. I couldn't see over the bar, but I assumed the bartender's hand was hovering close to the floor. When he popped back up, he was beaming. "I am his . . . how do you say it, a family friend. My sister was friends with his halmoni when they were that small. He grew up in New York. His father has many, many restaurants here."

"I knew that." I dropped my hands, resting them on the surface of the bar, which was shining clean. "What was he like as a little kid?"

I shouldn't have been asking this. I should have nodded, smiled, and gone off to hang out with Nia and her new friends, or slammed shots with Kaitlyn and Megan and Vanilla Joe. I shouldn't be entangling myself with Luke any further than I already was. I shouldn't *want* to, considering the way he'd spoken to me. I knew all this.

And yet I asked anyway.

"A good, good boy," the bartender said again. "A chubby little potato." The thought tickled my insides, made me smile. "He always wanted to be in the kitchen, but he also wanted to be out here, giving people their food. Sometimes he would volunteer as a waiter, but he never only took tables their food. He would stand there as they ate and ask them questions—What did they think of the dish? How about this part? How about that part?—and take down notes. Then he'd go in the back and tell us how to make it better. Add some crunch here. Use less sauce there."

"So it sounds like he was born to be a judge on *Chef Supreme*," I said.

"He was born to cook," replied the bartender. "He cooks from his heart. From his soul." A pause, where I took in his words. "That is, when he is not drawing."

That was a surprise. "Drawing?"

"He draws little comics," the bartender said. He disappeared down below the bar again. This time when he popped up, he was holding what looked like an old menu. "Look."

I took the menu and flipped through. Yes, it listed various dishes and their prices. But the artist—Luke—had doodled all over it, tiny pictures of the food, wavy lines of steam rising over bowls of rice specks and eggs, and slightly larger pictures of the people enjoying them as elaborate anime characters: their eyes enormous, little strings of drool slipping from the corners of mouth slashes, frizzled lines of movement showing their frenzy as they dove through the menu categories looking for more food. "This is adorable," I said with some surprise. I hadn't pictured Luke, with his posh accent that slipped out when he wasn't paying attention and his buttoned-up fancy restaurants, drawing cartoons.

"Yes," the bartender said. "Adorable."

I spent another few minutes flipping through the menu, absorbed in Luke's artistry as I sipped from my drink. Before long, my straw slurped at the bottom. "This drink was delicious, too. Did Luke create it?"

"No. That is mine." The bartender slid the glass toward him, and, in one smooth motion, pushed a full glass back toward me. "This is on the house, for you. For my Luke's little lady."

I quirked an eyebrow even as I took a long slug of the new drink, just as sweet and tart and refreshing and herbaceous as the last one. Strong, too. Which is maybe why I said, "How many 'little ladies' has he brought here?"

The bartender's face was open with surprise. "You."

I waited for the admonition to follow—*you dare be this disrespectful; you will be paying for this drink after all*—but he didn't go on. "Me what?" I said, a little impatiently, just to get it over with.

He shook his head. "You are the first woman he has brought here in a very long time," he said. "How else do you think I remembered you?"

Then why had Luke called me Sandy, made me feel like an herb crushed into this drink?

You little putz. Of course he'd try to drive you away. Grandma Ruth nodded self-importantly. *He didn't want you to be focused on him or feeling like you had to leave the show.*

In my head, I frowned at her. *Why couldn't you have told me this sooner?*

Because I'm a figment of your imagination and could not possibly have known before you figured it out, said Grandma Ruth.

I shook my head, sending her away. "Are you sure?"

The bartender laughed softly. "Absolutely, positively sure, my dear."

There was no Sandy. Sandy was fake. That jerk version of Luke was fake.

"He was so happy here with you," the bartender continued. "The light that shone in his eyes as a child, that made him interrogate every diner and draw pictures on my menus, it faded away when I saw him with his father. But when he came charging in here with you, breathless and sweaty and lugging two suitcases behind him?" His smile was like a shadow. "It was back."

I had no idea what to say to that. Except that I wanted to kiss him. Not the bartender—Luke. I wanted to put on a flowy white dress and run toward him in a park at midnight like in a nineties romantic comedy so that he could scoop me up in his arms and spin me around.

That was an absurd idea, though. For one, I didn't have a flowy white dress with me—big flowy clothes were a danger in the kitchen, so I hadn't bothered bringing any other than pajamas, and I wasn't going after Luke in my big flowy pajama shirt I'd stolen years ago from my dad. And two, I wasn't going after Luke at all. Not only did I not know where he lived, but because if I did go after him and confess my feelings, I didn't see a way that I could stay in the competition. I was already pushing it, having made out with one of the judges. If I had an ongoing romantic connection with a judge? I'd be asked to forfeit. The integrity of the entire season would be thrown into question. They might even scrub my name from the competition altogether, find a new chef at the last minute to take my place, and bring back the eliminated contestants for a do-over.

I *needed* this jump start from *Chef Supreme*. I needed my own restaurant, where I had total control of everything that happened inside. And the only way I could foresee having that within the next few years was through *Chef Supreme*. Otherwise I'd have to move somewhere like New York or Boston or DC and get a job at a restaurant and work my way up from the bottom again, considering I had no references I could use now.

I was already in the top five. I just had to make it one more episode, and then I'd be in the final four. The semifinals. I could name a bunch of really successful past contestants who'd come from the final four.

The bartender was looking at me expectantly, like he was indeed waiting for me to kiss him. Or thank him. Or something. I wasn't sure I could open my mouth without crying, though. Maybe it was the turmoil of emotions gurgling within me. Maybe it was having downed two strong drinks within too short a period.

So I just gave him a froggy sort of smile.

And then something hit me on the shoulder. It sent me forward on the barstool, slamming my chest up against the bar. It didn't hurt, but it kicked the rioting emotions, told them sternly to stay down. Maybe it was just what I needed.

I turned to find Nia grinning at me. "Sorry, didn't mean to hit you that hard, but you didn't hear me every time I said your name." Hopefully, she hadn't been standing there long enough to hear the bartender's and my conversation, but I had a feeling she wouldn't be grinning that hard if she had. "You *have* to come try these banchan! Or I guess you've probably already tried them with your friend Sandy. But anyway! There's a kimchi made out of cucumbers stuffed with chili and onions and some kind of garlic chives? Whatever it is, it is amazing, and you must put it in your mouth right now."

I still felt bad about not answering the bartender. But when I turned back around to apologize or at least say something, he was off polishing a glass at the other end of the bar, conversing with one of the old men about the K-drama.

So I went with her and put it in my mouth right then. And not just the stuffed cucumber kimchi. We ate seaweed salad with sweet vinegar, and crunchy sesame lotus root, and dried shredded squid with a spicy sauce, and steamed eggs, all with sticky white rice, and then we had bulgogi, thin grilled slices of marinated beef. It was all fully drool-worthy. I imagined I could taste Luke in every one: the extra shake of vinegar that took the seaweed right to the edge of being too tart but stopped just in time; the intentional lack of spice on the steamed eggs, necessary for a palate cleanser between all of the bright and spicy and sour. His hands in every one.

Nia's eyes as she consumed this food were luminous. She was quizzing the men about the ingredients, about the recipes, and let out a shout every time they shrugged or cocked their head or said the specific ratio didn't matter. "But that can't be," she kept saying. "Of course the recipe matters, of course the ratio matters. How else do you know when you've gotten it right?"

One of the old men shook his head. "You need to trust your tongue."

Nia looked skeptical. "Trust my tongue?"

The old man nodded. "Your tongue, and your heart. That's how you'll know it's right."

Nia perched her chin on her palm, eyebrows frowning like she was thinking hard.

I, too, got caught up in the sampling, guessing ingredients and recipes. At least until I glanced over my shoulder at a noise and noticed Kaitlyn and Megan on a barstool. Like, a single barstool. Because Kaitlyn was perched on Megan's lap. Straddling

Megan's lap. And they were kissing. Like, not two-girls-dared-to-kiss-at-a-bar kissing. There was definitely tongue involved.

Where was Vanilla Joe in all this? I searched for him to find him sitting between the two old men at the bar, fully absorbed in the K-drama with them. Did he see what was going on? Whether they were exaggerating their relationship for the camera or not, Kaitlyn seriously had some nerve. Not that I should have been so surprised, after what I'd seen from her back at Atelier Laurent. Once she'd called out sick three days in a row, making me cover her shifts, only to confess giggling later on that her married lover had flown her off to Bermuda for an impromptu getaway.

I got up from the booth and marched over to Vanilla Joe, tapping him on the shoulder maybe a little bit harder than necessary. "What?" he asked as he spun around on his barstool. The men on either side of him gave me dirty looks for disturbing their TV watching.

I flailed my arm in Kaitlyn and Megan's direction. It felt like it was moving slower than usual and faster than usual all at once. Yep, I was definitely a little bit drunk. But it didn't dampen the urge to take Kaitlyn down a notch. To be quite honest, I didn't care very much about Vanilla Joe. I just wanted to see Kaitlyn's face sag with the knowledge she was doing something wrong. "Do you see what is going on there?" I shouted in his face, just to make sure he heard me. "You're being cheated on!"

The two men beside him spun around so fast I swear their stools smoked.

Well, I wouldn't let them down. "You're being cuckolded!" I really liked that word, so I said it again. "Cuckolded, I tell you!"

Vanilla Joe blinked lazily at me. He was a chill drunk. "Oh no." He took a leisurely sip of his drink. "I'm heartbroken."

I blinked at him. The room spun just a tiny bit when I opened my eyes. I had to lean heavily on Vanilla Joe's shoulder to make sure it didn't spin me right off my feet. "You don't seem heartbroken."

"Has anyone ever told you you're excellent at reading people?" Vanilla Joe said dryly. "Truly, a master."

My tongue felt very large in my mouth. "I feel like you're making fun of me."

Vanilla Joe patted me on the shoulder. "Why don't you have a glass of water?"

But I wasn't *thirsty*.

"I got this," said a voice from behind me. My upper lip curled with a snarl. Kaitlyn! The cheater herself! Before I could snarl at her, an arm tucked itself through my elbow and pulled me toward the door. I lurched along, like my arm had gotten stuck in a bus door and I was trying to keep up. Yes, that was a terrible metaphor. In my defense, I was drunk. "Come outside with me, Sadie. Let's get some fresh air."

Of course, she lit up a cigarette as soon as we stepped onto the sidewalk. So there really wasn't very much fresh air to be found.

And yet somehow the muggy night air soothed me. I took a deep breath, then another. A pair of young men stumbled by us, leaning on each other and laughing loudly. Heading home for the night, probably. I went to go check my phone for the time before realizing I didn't have one anymore.

Kaitlyn had taken a step away; she looked like a magazine ad for perfume, with her thin arms folded over her chest, her light brown hair blowing in the wind as she exhaled a thin stream of cigarette smoke above her. "So," she said. "You're a pretty obnoxious drunk, Sadie."

I narrowed my eyes. "You're a pretty obnoxious *person*. Cheating on your new boyfriend, and—"

She interrupted me with a sigh. "You always get right to the point, don't you? I've always liked that about you." She liked something about me? I was going to ask her to elaborate, when she went on. "Can it really be considered cheating if you're not dating?"

"Even if you're not exclusive, he clearly likes you," I said solidly. Or at least I hoped it was solidly. "It was pretty rude of you to hook up with Megan right in front of him."

"Oh, Sadie." Kaitlyn draped an arm around me. I wrinkled my face at her. She wrinkled hers right back. "I have zero interest in Vanilla Joe, and he has zero interest in me, either."

Really? They'd been pretty convincing, the way they made out all the time.

"Nia's not the only one who did her research," Kaitlyn said. "Contestants who get involved in a romance in the *Chef Supreme* house tend to stay longer than those who don't. My theory is that the producers like the drama it brings. And the het romances do better than gay ones." She shrugged. "So I talked to Vanilla Joe and he was game. He wants to stay longer, too."

"Seriously? Is that true?" I stopped and considered. Maybe I should've hooked up with Bald Joe while I had the chance.

Kaitlyn nodded. "Megan and I have been hooking up for, like, two weeks now. You really haven't noticed?"

"No!" I gawped. "I didn't even know you were gay."

"I'm not. I'm bi."

"When did you start?"

"Being bi?"

"No, hooking up with Megan." I remembered Megan asking

me if I thought Kaitlyn might be interested and then . . . nothing. Literally nothing. Maybe I'd been too focused on the competition, but shouldn't there have been smoldering glances, hand brushes crackling with electricity, Megan jealously bumping Vanilla Joe in the pantry with her shoulder and making him drop all his eggs on the floor? But then I remembered how Kaitlyn and Megan had been late together to brunch, and they'd appeared from the second floor even though I'd just been up there . . .

"Two weeks ago. I just told you that," Kaitlyn said. "Have you ever been in that room in the house all the way at the end of the hallway, next to the linen closet?"

"No, it's locked." I'd assumed it was a storage closet for camera equipment or something.

"Well, I'm excellent at picking locks, thanks to an old boss who didn't give me keys but still expected me to be in first every morning to open." Kaitlyn dropped her cigarette on the ground and smashed it with the heel of her ankle boot like she was killing a roach. "Turns out it's like a half bedroom, a tiny little windowless office space. It's illegal to sleep in a room without a window in New York, just like in Seattle, so the producers probably decided to bar it rather than trying and failing to convince someone not to claim their own space."

"So that's where your forbidden romance blossomed."

Kaitlyn pretended to gag. "Gross." Stopped gagging. "But yes."

I shook my head. Maybe it was the strong smell of smoke, maybe it was the quiet, maybe it was the friendly but matter-of-fact way Kaitlyn was speaking, but I was sobering up fast. "And she's just . . . okay with everything with Vanilla Joe?"

She shrugged. "She knows it's for the show."

"Oh." I felt a part of me shrivel away. But not the part that had been so eager to watch her fall down. That part was as big as ever, as noticeable as ever.

But why? Why was it there?

I tried to push it down. "Whatever," I said. "I think it's pretty gross of you to fake a relationship like that."

Kaitlyn let out a short laugh. An abrupt laugh. "Of course you do."

"What's that supposed to mean?"

She laughed again. "I've tried so hard with you over the years. Maybe we're not meant to be friends, but I thought I'd try anyway. But you were always so . . ."

She trailed off, but it seemed very important that I hear the rest of what she was going to say. "So what?"

She pulled out another cigarette, lit it, breathed in deep. "So . . . judgmental of me. Like no matter what I said, you'd find a reason to look down on me."

That wasn't true . . . was it? I was just sick of hearing all about her, of watching her do things so easily, all those things that came easier to her than they did to me . . . and she'd never liked me, either. Everything she did, everything she said, was through a veil of not liking me. Unless . . . I'd just been interpreting them that way. But why?

It clicked. Jealous. I was jealous. I was jealous of Kaitlyn. I'd been jealous of Kaitlyn this whole time.

I opened my mouth to tell her I hadn't meant it that way, only what came out was a sob.

And of course she put aside what she'd just said and pulled me in for a smoky hug, murmuring reassuringly in my ear, "It's okay. It's okay."

But when I pulled back, I knew it wasn't really okay. "I've been jealous of you ever since we met, I think," I said. "Because you're beautiful and everybody likes you and you're an amazing chef, and it all seems to come so easily for you in a way that it doesn't for me. And so I convinced myself that everything you say to me is putting me down."

Kaitlyn's blue eyes softened. The little wrinkles stretching out from them eased. "Oh, Sadie. I wish I could see myself through your eyes. Not the putting-you-down part, the rest of it."

Did that mean she didn't see those things in herself? The way I could never see anything good in myself?

"If they're true, none of them come easily," she said. "I have to work for them."

And it wasn't fair to be jealous of her for being a nice person who people liked. If I really wanted to be liked by everybody, I could work harder at it, too.

"You know," she said, but I interrupted her.

"I'm sorry," I said. "It wasn't fair of me to act like that toward you because I'm jealous. I'm going to try to be better going forward."

"Thank you," she said. "I appreciate that."

We were both quiet for a moment, and then she said, "Sadie, do you know what my cooking style is?"

I thought back and . . . I had no idea. She'd made all sorts of dishes over the course of the show. "Um . . ."

"Right," Kaitlyn said quietly. "I don't really know, either." She tilted her head back and looked up toward the stars. "I'm jealous of all of you who know exactly what you want to cook.

You with your Jewish food. Bald Joe with his Japanese food. Nia
with her extensive collection of memorized recipes. And then
there's me. Cooking is showing what's in your heart, right? So if
I don't know what I want to cook, does that mean I don't know
what's in my heart?"

That was deep. Or at least it seemed that way to my slightly
drunk self. "What's your last name?"

"You know my last name," Kaitlyn said. "It's Avilleira."

"I know what is is. I meant, where's it from?" I couldn't believe I'd never asked this before.

"Cuba," she said. "Half of my family fled Cuba years ago,
and none of them took the food with them. I didn't grow up on
Cuban food. I grew up on pasta and lasagna and eggs, because
they were easy and cheap."

"You still have a right to cook it," I said. "It's still your heritage."

She shrugged. "But do I want to? I don't have to cook my
heritage, especially if I don't feel connected to it. Bald Joe's not
Japanese, but look at the love and passion he has for Japanese
food." She brought her chin down and looked me right in the eye.
I wasn't sure when was the last time I'd looked Kaitlyn in the eye,
which was kind of sad. "One of the reasons I was so excited to
come on *Chef Supreme* was because I hoped I'd . . . God, this sounds
so cheesy, but I hoped I'd find myself in the kitchen. That it would
help me figure out where my heart is. But so far it hasn't helped."

I tried to break the heaviness of the moment with a joke.
"What about the glamour?"

Her laugh was short and dutiful. "That was why I *became* a
chef. Of course I realized quickly it's not as glamorous as it looks
on TV. You were right there with me every time we got yelled at

and overworked and burned and cut, every time we got handed our tiny paychecks."

She was quiet for a moment. "I stayed a chef because I liked making people happy. And it makes people happy when you cook for them. I like wowing them and impressing them with what I can do, whether it's in the kitchen or in bed. I just . . . I've spent all this time cooking for other people that now I'm not sure how to cook for *me*."

I didn't know what to say to that besides something unhelpful like *I think you can do it* or *I hope you'll figure it out*. So I stayed quiet. Kaitlyn sighed. "We should go back inside."

She turned to go, but I stayed put. "You go ahead. I need to sober up a bit."

She nodded, then leaned in and gave me a quick, tight hug. "Don't wander off," she told me. "You don't have a phone, so we'd have to call the police and risk the wrath of Adrianna."

The door to the convenience store swung behind her as she entered. I stared after her. Had that all really just happened?

"It's you."

I turned back toward the street, and there he was. The gritty city wind fluttering his mussed black hair, the ghost of someone else's laugh echoing in the background.

Luke.

"What are you doing here?" I asked, then realized. "Wait. This is *your* place. Of course you'd be here."

He leaned back on his heels, flexing his hands in his pockets. He was wearing dark jeans tonight, a casual look to go with his casual hair.

I wanted to devour him. But first . . . "Hey, you'll never guess what I learned tonight." I'd come out here to sober up, but the drunk fuzziness had fallen over me again as soon as I'd spotted him. "It turns out that you're not a jerk after all! You were just pretending to be one to help me."

He raised an eyebrow. "Is that so," he said. It wasn't a question, because of course he already knew the answer. "You know, I should be the one asking *you* what you're doing here. Aren't you not allowed to leave your apartment?"

"Yes, but we snuck out." I giggled a little. "We are very bad."

"We? Does that mean the others are here, too?" He craned his neck as if trying to see through the fake wall at the back of the convenience store.

"Yes, but it doesn't matter. They're all back there." I took a step toward him. His Adam's apple bobbed in his throat, but he didn't take a step away. I took that as permission to take another step. A couple passed us, splitting a set of headphones between them, swaying as they stepped and not giving us a single strange look. Why would they? Out here, we weren't Sadie the contestant and Luke the judge. We were just two regular people out for the night. Probably for a date, because of how close we standing. And what did two regular people out for the night on a date do?

Not what a *Chef Supreme* judge and contestant should be doing, that was for sure. And I knew that well. But I was tipsy. And that tipsy fog was shrouding the consequences from my brain.

I leaned in, close enough where I could feel his breath warm on my face, smell the chocolate he must have had for dessert. I wanted to taste that chocolate, too. "I want to kiss you," I said, and he didn't say anything back, and he didn't move away, and his eyes sparked with how much he wanted to kiss me, too, so I—

—had bad aim because of my drunkenness, which meant I

missed his mouth. My lips brushed against his jawline, which made him shiver, which made *me* shiver. So I leaned in again and—

—he caught me by the shoulders. "Sadie, this is a bad idea. Not because I don't want to kiss you—I really, really do—but it's too risky. Remember? The brunch?"

"It's not even risky," I said, tossing my hair over my shoulder. Some of it stuck to the sweat on my neck. "They're all still inside. Nobody will see us."

He'd *said* he really, really wanted to kiss me, so I leaned in again. Only he leaned back, which made me stumble. I barely managed to stay up by grabbing on to his arm. Somewhere in the back of my mind, beneath the blanket of fuzziness, I was aware that I was embarrassing myself.

And maybe because I was embarrassed, I said, "You're being a square."

His lips tightened. "Fine, I'm a square. You'll thank me later."

Would I? Yes. The part of my brain that wasn't drunk was firm about that. It even suspected the rest of me was exaggerating my drunkenness in order to have an excuse to throw my inhibitions away. "I'm sorry," I said weakly, but I hoped sincerely. "That was a stupid thing to say. You're right. Totally right. We can't take the chance, and I do not blame you for turning down this mess."

An eyebrow quirked. "You're quite the hot mess." And his face blanched. "I didn't mean that in its . . . traditional meaning. I was attempting a play on words in that you said you were a mess, and that I think you're quite hot."

"I get it." And I loved it. I smiled up at him, and he smiled down at me, and I could kiss him, all I had to do was lean forward a little more . . .

No! I lurched back, shaking my head at myself. *This is the exact thing you're not supposed to be doing!* At least this time I kept control of myself. Still, my face heated up as the door of the convenience store clanged behind me.

"Oh my God, look who it is!" Kaitlyn swooped around me, stopping beside me to place a hand on a cocked hip. "What are the odds?"

Nia, suddenly on the other side of me, looked skyward, probably calculating the exact odds of running into a *Chef Supreme* judge on the streets of Queens.

"Amazing, isn't it?" I interjected before she could say anything. "So weird. Anyway, we'd better be going."

Kaitlyn tossed her hair over her shoulder. None of it stuck to her at all; it went cascading gracefully through the air like she was on a shampoo commercial. *Which is good for her, because she is a good person,* I told myself sternly. "So, obviously, we're not supposed to be out here, and we could get in big trouble if we were found out. If we go straight back to the house, would you consider not telling on us?"

Luke looked at us sternly. The whole effect was kind of ruined by his lips twitching. "If you go straight back and swear not to sneak out again, I promise I won't tattle on you."

"Thank you so much!" Kaitlyn linked her arm through mine. "Come on, everybody. Let's go home."

I only looked back once, as we were about to round the corner. He was still staring after us, hands in his pockets, somebody else's laughter floating on the breeze.

15

I'D PLANNED ON SLEEPING THROUGH MY ENTIRE SUN-
day again, but I was woken up rudely early—eleven a.m.—by a
slam of my door. "Get up." Adrianna's voice was sharp.

I shuffled out into the living room in my fluffy bunny slippers, blinking blearily against the light streaming in from the
full window. Nia was already up, sweaty and dressed in workout
clothes. The other three contestants looked just as unhappy to
be awake as I did; Vanilla Joe had red lines pressed into his face
from his pillow, Kaitlyn's eyes were half-lidded, and Megan
looked as if she was close to dozing on the barstool, keeping
herself partially awake through sheer fear of Adrianna.

"I found these in your fridge." Adrianna thumped our take-
out containers onto the counter. The plastic lid popped off one,
splattering kimchi juice all around it. "Which was strange, as I
didn't get a notification that the *Chef Supreme* take-out account
had been used last night." The glare she gave all of us made my
legs feel weak. "So I reviewed the security footage to find that

you'd left the apartment all on your own last night. Where did you go?"

"Sadie took us there," Vanilla Joe said. Adrianna's glare turned to me, and now that it was solely focused on my skin, I felt my feet start to shrivel in my slippers. Thanks a lot, Vanilla Joe.

I cleared my throat, trying to force words out. "We just wanted to blow off some steam. It was a tiny local place, there wasn't even anyone there—"

"You are not supposed to step out without an escort." Adrianna's voice was so cold it burned. "If one person in that tiny local place takes a picture and posts it online, it will circulate on all the *Chef Supreme* blogs and spoil the entire season. Is that what you want? Is it?"

Unable to speak, I shook my head.

Adrianna raised her phone. "I'll need the name of the place, immediately. You'd better hope I can do damage control."

I said a silent apology to the bartender about the dragon I was sending his way and hoped he wouldn't take it out on me by sharing my secret. If Adrianna was this mad about us sneaking out for a night, she might literally explode if she knew about me and Luke.

As if she were punishing us, the hot water went out. Which actually was to my benefit when waking up at the crack of dawn Monday morning. Nothing, not even coffee, wakes you up like water so cold it literally takes your breath away.

I figured that I'd be a total wreck going into the top-five challenge, especially with Adrianna pissed at us—like, a ten out of ten on the nervous scale. Or a twelve out of ten, even. But it was like those extra couple points somehow reset the scale back to a two out of ten, and I was almost scary calm. No shaky hands. No sweat dripping into the food. No worry I'd vomit when I opened my mouth to talk.

Even though the challenge ended up being vegetarian, everybody's least favorite challenge every year. I didn't get the hate—I ate vegetarian a lot at home, considering it was a whole lot cheaper than buying racks of lamb or large shrimp or steaks on a regular basis. I almost laughed at the way Vanilla Joe's lip curled as Maz announced what we'd be doing: a five-course vegetarian dinner, with each of us doing a course. Since I won last week, I got to choose which course I wanted; that gave me an advantage right off the bat. I chose the appetizer—I'd get to go first and set the standard, and not have to worry about presenting a full plate or large portions.

As much as I really wanted to give the judges my take on gefilte fish (which was and is SO much better than that slimy, mealy garbage you get in the jar), obviously, that wasn't going to work for a vegetarian challenge. So what did I have up my— latkes! Of course. I hadn't made latkes yet. And I could easily gussy them up. I made an excellent version with parsnips to go with the normal potatoes and onions. I could make a fancy cream to complement it, and homemade cranberry applesauce, and make sure the edges were perfectly lacy and crisp . . .

To make a long story short: I came in second to Kaitlyn, who wowed the judges with her not-chicken potpie. Nia came in third. Vanilla Joe and Megan were in the bottom two, and we had to say goodbye to Megan, who'd been hit by the dessert curse.

I sat next to Kaitlyn on the ride home. She was silent the whole drive, staring out the window, watching the buildings go by.

SO HERE WE were. The top four. I'd made it exactly where I needed to be, I thought the morning of the next challenge as I threw on my jeans and a plain black T-shirt. All of my clothes smelled like food and sweat, but it didn't really matter, considering the camera couldn't capture smell. Even if I went home today, I still had a realistic chance of having investors interested in me, of having my own restaurant, of shoving my success in Derek's face.

And yet. And yet. Now I wanted to go all the way. The sheer want of it burned inside me like the stove in my first apartment, which had one temperature and that one temperature was five hundred degrees. I wanted to stand up in front of those judges and have Maz proclaim that I, Sadie Brooke Rosen, was Chef Supreme. I wanted to hug Julie Chee and Kevin Harris and know I belonged in a kitchen with them. It was like I'd gone so long hoping I'd just get into the top four, and now that I was here it was no longer good enough. Wasn't that always how it went?

It wasn't just that, though. I had to prove myself to Luke. To prove that I was worth the massive blunder we'd made that would bring us down if Adrianna found out. To prove that I was on his level. That I was worth more than what Derek told me I was, both personally and professionally.

We all fit in one car now. Nia, Kaitlyn, and I crammed into the back, while Vanilla Joe claimed shotgun. I scowled at the back of his head.

"So here we are," he said. For a minute I wondered if that

was some kind of a prelude to a fight, and then he said, "The final four."

"The final four," Nia said solemnly. Our car sped up as we coasted over the bridge, the dark water shimmering beneath us. The sun was beginning to rise over it; by the time we reached the other side, the water was awash in oranges and reds. "Each of us has a twenty-five percent chance of winning it all."

We all knew that, but somehow hearing it made it all more real. Twenty-five percent. That was the odds of flipping two coins and having both come up heads. Hell, I'd flipped three coins before and had them all come up heads. I could do this.

Of course, the other three were all thinking the same thing.

The car dropped us off at the sidewalk; men rushing by in business suits sidestepped us like we were all part of a choreographed dance, and the sound of cars honking followed us into the building. Inside, the wardrobe assistant took one look at me, made a clucking sound with her tongue, and pulled me into her little dressing room. "We're changing this up," she said, and winked. "You'll want to look extra good today."

That was strange. But I wasn't about to complain about looking extra good, even if I wasn't being judged. Because I had to get dressed again—the wardrobe assistant put me in leggings and a long but clingy dark green shirt— I was the last one into the kitchen. The other three were arranged already at their stations, Kaitlyn shifted across to me at Bald Joe's old station to condense us and save space. She gave me a wave, cocking her hip in her little denim shirtdress. I was pretty sure she was the only one of us never to get pulled out of line and redressed by wardrobe. Which was kind of funny, considering how wrinkled all her clothes were from being piled all over our room's floor. "Looking hot," she said.

"Thanks?"

Adrianna clicked in on her heels, a line between her eyebrows and a few hairs escaping her slicked-back ponytail. She gripped her clipboard in her hands. "Morning," she told us. Ever since she caught us sneaking out, we hadn't merited a "good." "Today you'll be making a dish inspired by your favorite chef."

My favorite chef? I rubbed my hands together in anticipation. I had so many chef role models. Maybe I should stick with the *Chef Supreme* brand and make something inspired by Julie Chee—I did really admire her farm-to-table ethos. Or I could go old school and make something inspired by the chefs I'd watched on TV growing up. I kind of wanted to do a woman, though. There were Brooke Williamson and Stephanie Izard and Kristen Kish and Melissa King and Nina Compton and Nini Nguyen and and and . . . Or I could choose one of the restaurateurs I aspired to be like myself. There were so many.

"When each of you filled out your applications months ago, you indicated your favorite chef on the page," Adrianna continued. My hands fell to my sides. I didn't remember exactly who I picked . . . but given the timeline, that I'd been in the throes of admiration for Derek at that point . . . "You'll be using that chef as inspiration. In case you forgot, Kaitlyn, you picked Julie Chee—" Of course she had. Adrianna reminded Nia and Vanilla Joe who they'd selected, Nia a mentor I'd heard her talk about in glowing terms, and Vanilla Joe Bobby Flay, naturally.

And then me. "And last but not least, Sadie, you selected Chef Derek Anders."

My stomach turned to ice, shivers rippling through me. "Is it too late to change my choice?"

Adrianna eyed me like I'd suggested making our next challenge a feature of Spam and broken glass. "Yes. It's too late."

I knew I should just let it be, but I really, *really* hated the idea of making a dish inspired by Derek. I'd rather make something out of Spam and broken glass and eat it down to the last slimy, stabby crunch.

So I pushed. "But why?" I hoped I didn't sound too whiny. "Can't you just pretend I wrote something different?"

She blinked at me, irritated. Especially irritated, considering she'd pinned me as the ringleader of our Korean bar expedition. My heart sinking, I knew I'd burned every last bit of goodwill she might once have had toward me. "No."

Okay. So be it, then. I stood there behind my station as Maz announced our challenge a few times, my fake smiles and fake surprise coming just a few beats too late each take. It wasn't so much the making of the dish I was dreading—there were a lot of dishes I loved from the Green Onion's menu, ones I could easily put my own spin on and still pull off in the time limit, considering the number of times I'd made each component of each dish.

I was dreading the parts where I'd have to gush about Derek on camera. I'd never seen this exact challenge done before on the show, but whenever they did dishes inspired by another chef or mentor or person, the contestants were expected to talk all about them. I knew they'd want me to tell the camera all about how wonderful Derek was, how much he inspired me, how much I wanted to be just like him one day.

And the thought made me want to vomit up all the Spam and broken glass I'd figuratively eaten before.

No, I told myself. *If you start throwing up, they'll make you sit out the challenge and you'll probably have to forfeit.* And I would *not* forfeit. Especially not because of *him.* I gritted my teeth. I could do this. I'd say vague things like, *I am where I am because of him* or *I really loved cooking his food,* both of which were true. The best revenge was to look forward.

"Go!" Maz announced. I jumped as the other three peeled off their stations and raced toward the pantry. My legs carried me after them just a minute too late. *Shit, shit, shit.* I hadn't taken advantage of the time to think about what I was going to make. And now here I was, standing stock-still in the middle of the pantry, watching my time tick down second by second as the other three whirled around me like I was the dud on a dance floor.

Quick! Quick! Think! But the more I racked my mind, the only thing I could see was Derek smirking at me. *Of course you can't think of something to cook. Could you ever? I made you, and I destroyed you.*

Don't listen to him! Grandma Ruth said, letting loose a string of curses that probably would've given her a heart attack in real life, cocks and asses and fucks and shitheads. The mental image of my grandmother cursing like a line cook in support of me was enough to make me laugh, just enough to break me free from this paralyzing fear.

When I had only three minutes left for planning. *Quick, what was my favorite thing to cook at the Green Onion that I can make in this time limit?*

The Green Onion's menu had been plant-focused, not much red meat, with lots of fresh Pacific Northwest seafood. Which was good, because I didn't have a ton of time to spend roasting a full rack of lamb or simmering a brisket. A salad was too simple, falafel was too complicated, and—

Scallops. My mind whirred, gears clicking into place. Scallops cooked quickly. The Green Onion had a scallop special that people really loved. Seared scallops with a green, herby broth and tempura-fried vegetables. I could put my own spin on it and do a fried artichoke instead of the tempura, and make the broth more of a buttery green sauce. Yes. That would be delicious. I raced through the pantry throwing ingredients into my basket, praying with every step and every stumble that nobody else had taken the scallops. My prayers were answered. I had artichokes and scallops and lemons and herbs and lots and lots of rich unsalted butter threatening to overspill my basket as I skidded out the pantry door.

Maz had told us we had ninety minutes to cook, and that we had to plate eight dishes. I calculated what I had to do and when. It would be tight, but manageable. Especially if I pretended that every stab of the knife went through Derek's ribs, and that every time I scooped a spoonful of fuzz from an artichoke heart, I was scooping out one of his eyeballs.

I usually retreated into my head as I cooked, totally focused on my own counter, keeping track of where everything was in its cooking time and when things had to go on. But today I couldn't stop seeing Derek's face everywhere I looked, which took me out of my head. Or maybe made me sink even deeper into it.

I wanted to get the scallops and the artichokes cooking, but I knew I had to wait till the end of the cooking time, otherwise they would get cold and soggy. So I'd work on the broth and the sauce. I tossed some onions and garlic and carrots and celery into a pot and set it to boil. I leaned over the pot to make sure the water level was right, and Derek was sneering up at me. I jumped. *Your broth is going to be watery and bland,* he hissed.

Not once I blend in all the herbs, I argued. Why was I wasting time arguing with myself? I gritted my teeth and put the lid on the pot before I remembered that I'd decided to make the broth into a butter sauce. *Ugh*. Derek had rattled me, throwing all of my thoughts off-kilter. I'd already put the broth on, but I could still blend up a nice green herb butter and smear it around the edges of the plate. Would I need something vinegary or tart to balance out all the richness and herby notes?

You're a tart, said Derek. I could practically see him standing in front of me, his smirk leveled at my forehead. The thing about Derek was that he hadn't been especially handsome: he was short, not much taller than me (and I was only five-three); he had a broad face with pits of acne scars scattered over his forehead; his eyes were a bright blue, but the rest of his features were unremarkable. And he wasn't nice. He was sarcastic, and snarky, and always had something nasty to say.

And yet I'd fallen hard for him anyway. So hard it had given me bruises.

Shut up, I told him. I went to grab the butter, then eyeballed the time. *Shit. Shit shit shit*. How had so much time passed already? I had to get my pan heating up for the scallops. And my oil was cold. I had to heat the oil or my artichokes would be soggy disasters.

I whipped the butter frantically, my heart thumping. I spared a glance over at Nia's station, where she was literally whistling while dropping crawfish into a huge pot of boiling something, steam beading pearls of water all over her face. Doubt hollowed out a hole inside me. She was doing fine—better than fine—while I was scrambling.

Naturally, that was when the cameras showed up at my station.

I forced a smile as cold sweat broke out over my forehead. I still had to whip up the butter, and cook the scallops and the artichokes, and finish up the broth with the herbs, and plate it all . . .

"Chef Sadie! It smells great over here," Maz said. If that was true, it was because of the savory duck meat Vanilla Joe was shredding nearby. All I'd done so far was clean and prep my artichokes and scallops, and start my broth. *Shit. Shit. Shit.* I was so behind schedule. "You chose Chef Derek Anders, owner and executive chef of the Green Onion in Seattle, as your inspiration. Tell me a little bit about why."

That cold sweat prickled not just over my forehead, but everywhere else, too. I definitely had nasty sweat circles marring my nice new shirt. I knew I had decided on vague enough things to say, but my mind was totally blank. I couldn't remember what they were. "Um, good food," I said, turning. My pan was probably hot enough for the scallops now. I'd have to be very careful not to overcook them. Nobody wanted rubbery scallops.

"Lots of chefs make good food!" Maz said heartily. "There must be something besides good food that made you pick him!"

How about the way he looked at me when he told me I wasn't like other girls? ("That's a toxic mindset," my sister, Rachel, had said disapprovingly, but I'd known he didn't mean it like *that*. He just meant that I was special.) The way he'd press up against me in the walk-in freezer and kiss me to the point where I thought our steam might melt the frozen stock and ice cream. ("Isn't that unprofessional?" Rachel had said. I'd rolled my eyes. Clearly she'd never been in love.)

I realized my forced smile had fallen right off my face. I tacked it back on. "Um, I worked for him! For a couple years! Learned a lot!"

I had. It just hadn't all been about food.

Food. Shit! My pan! It was definitely hot by now. I spun away from Maz, hoping he wouldn't take it as a snub. I dumped a big cube of butter in the pan. It melted and sizzled, spitting flecks of fat on me. *Shit.* My pan was too hot. But I didn't have enough time to get another one hot, not if I wanted to get my artichokes done on time. So I just threw in my scallops along with more butter I hoped would cool down the steel, crossing my fingers it would all work out.

Now the artichokes. I flicked some water into the pot of oil to make sure it was hot enough; it spat and sputtered, which was good. Though maybe I should use the deep fryer instead. I glanced at the station with the deep fryers to see Nia hovering over them, chanting something under her breath like she was casting a spell. Okay, no deep fryer, then. I dumped the artichokes into my own pot and watched them bloom for a second, hypnotized by the sight of their little leaves opening up. At least one part of my dish was going right. The way this dish was coming together was an excellent metaphor for my relationship with Derek, actually. Everything going wrong at once, and then me in the middle trying frantically to keep it all together.

Stop, stop, stop thinking about him. You need to focus on your dish, Sadie. While the scallops and the artichokes cooked, I should get the broth ready. I pulsed a bunch of fresh green herbs—basil, mint, and parsley—with olive oil in the food processor until they were the consistency of a pesto, then turned the heat off my broth and picked out all the now-shrunken, flavor-depleted vegetables. Then I went to mix them—

Wait. The scallops. How long had they been in the pan? I'd been too busy thinking about Derek. I set the herb slurry down

on the counter, teetering precariously on the edge, and bustled
to my scallops. My heart leapt into my throat as I flipped the first
one . . . and found it blackened. I held back a groan. Could I spin
this? Tell them my intention hadn't been a nice, brown crust, but
to blacken them, like blackened shrimp? That was a dish. The
only problem was that the scallops were almost certainly overcooked now, which meant I couldn't cook them as much on the
other side . . .

I tossed in another chunk of butter once I'd flipped them all,
hoping it would lower the temperature of the pan just enough. I
turned back to the herb slurry, still on the edge of the counter . . .

. . . and knocked it off. "No!" I shouted at it, but that didn't
stop it from falling. The plastic container didn't break as it hit
the floor, but the herb slurry oozed out, making a slippery pud-
dle. I grabbed for the container. Most of the herb slurry was on
the floor; maybe a third of it was left in the container.

You are going to go home, Sadie, said Derek.

I mixed that third of the herb slurry into the broth, then
jumped back to the scallops. The crust on the alternate side was
pale and wan, but it would have to do. I turned off the heat and
went to plate them on the edges of the wide, flat bowls I'd chosen, then stopped to consider. Which side did I want to plate
down in the broth? Did I want to judges to be confronted first
with the pale wan non-crust, or the black side? I sighed. If Derek
saw this dish come out of his kitchen either way, he would frown
at me, send it back, and then probably mock me in front of the
rest of the staff.

At least the blackened side was *a* crust. I plated that side up,
then poured in the broth. It was pale, with little bits of herbs
floating in it rather than the thick herb soup it was supposed to

be. That was not appetizing, but it was already on the plate with my too-dark scallops. Maybe I could spread the herb butter on top of the scallops to hide some of that blackness. I smeared it on them, then dolloped a healthy amount on the edge of each plate where the artichokes would go when I plucked them from the oil at the last minute.

I pursed my lips as I looked at my dishes. I might get dinged for not having something to cut all the fat, all the freshness of the herbs be damned. Did I have enough time to quick-pickle some shallots or something to strew on top?

Not according to the clock: we were down to two minutes, and I still had to remove, drain, and plate my artichokes. I set my last artichoke into its buttery home with shaky hands just as the clock ticked down to 0:00.

I sighed heavily and pulled off my apron, using it partially to wipe the sweat and oil off my face and partially to hide from the cameras and the other contestants that my eyes had started to water. This was not a great dish. Definitely not worthy of the *Chef Supreme* top four.

I just had to hope that one of the other three did worse. Or else I'd . . .

I took a deep breath, feeling it shudder in my chest. I didn't want to lose. Especially not on my Chef Anders–based dish. I could only imagine his smirk as he watched this episode. *Not only did I rattle her into a subpar dish, I made her cry, too. What a pathetic little girl.*

That put a fire in me. It roared up in my belly, drying my eyes to a crisp. When I lowered my apron, my eyes were a little red, but clear. I could do this. I had to. I didn't even need my mental manifestation of Grandma Ruth to tell me that.

Naturally, Adrianna called my name first. I took deep breath after deep breath as I and a team of waiters walked my dish into the judging room. I held my head high as I turned the corner and the table of eight revealed itself to me.

"Hello, Sadie," said Derek, a smile curling over his lips.

I dropped my plate.

16

BRIGHT GREEN BROTH SPLASHED UP FROM THE BRO-
ken shards of the bowl I'd dropped, soaking my shoes in mint
and basil. The scallops slip-slid under the table, having given
their lives up for nothing. The artichoke sat proudly in the middle of it all, greasy with butter.

All because I'd frozen totally up at the sight of Derek sitting
there at the table like he belonged. Smirking at me like we were
back there in his kitchen. I'd run in after receiving that awful
firing-by-text just so he could look down at me, tell me that of
course he had to let me go, he couldn't keep me on now that
everybody had seen me like . . . *that*. He'd mouthed the word
delicately, like he hadn't been the one who'd put me in that position in the first place. Literally.

I stared at him, unable to process what I was seeing. It was
like I'd dropped my plate directly onto my brain.

"That's okay!" Maz said, giving me a gracious smile. "That's
why we had you make an extra."

I couldn't bring myself to thank him. I couldn't stop myself from staring at Derek, who was staring back at me. He looked as if he were watching his favorite team play some kind of sports game. He rubbed his hands together with anticipation. "I can't wait to taste your food, Sadie," he said, and winked. "It's been so long."

The rest of the table murmured their appreciation as well. Lenore Smith and Maz were there, along with Bobby Flay—who looked exactly the same as he did on TV—Julie Chee, Kaitlyn's selection and former Chef Supreme, and an older man I assumed was Nia's mentor. The fact that *Chef Supreme* had flown them all out explained why they hadn't let me change my selection.

And Luke was there, too, of course. The others were all chuckling over my mishap—clearly assuming I'd been shocked by how thrilled and excited I was to see my "favorite chef" here, but he was frowning. Not too much, but enough where I actually let my eyes meet his. He cocked his head, blinking, and raised his eyebrows just a tiny bit. I could almost hear him mentally transmitting, *You okay?*

No. I briefly considered shaking my head, then running out of the room and out onto the street and out of New York City and probably drowning trying to swim across the Atlantic Ocean, just to get as far away from here as I possibly could.

But that wasn't an option. I couldn't let Derek see me sweat.

Well, not more than he already had.

So I inclined my head toward Luke, just slightly, and I forced a smile onto my face. "Chef Anders," I said. "I didn't know I'd see you here."

"Surprise!" Maz butted in. His own smile was gleaming and white, probably just as fake as mine. "We wanted your favorite chefs to taste the dishes inspired by them! Sadie, can you tell us a little more about why you chose Chef Derek Anders of the Green Onion in Seattle? You worked for him, correct?"

Derek smiled like a wolf. He always had.

I pretended I hadn't heard Maz's question. "Today I made for you seared scallops with an herb broth and herb butter, with a crispy fried artichoke," I said. I spoke directly to Luke. Somehow looking into his eyes soothed the fire in my insides. Not killed it, or I'd probably shrivel up like a beached hot-air balloon, but lowered it to manageable levels. "One of my favorite dishes to cook at the Green Onion was the seared scallops with herb broth. I added my own spin on it with the herb butter and the artichoke. Please enjoy."

I kept watching Luke, though with less joy now, because I knew he'd grimace as he realized how bad my plate was. But he kept a poker face as he chewed and swallowed. It was Maz who tipped me off beside him as he scraped the butter off the top of a scallop. "These are very black," Maz said. "Too black, I'd say."

"Unfortunately, my scallops are overcooked," said Derek. He didn't sound disappointed; he sounded gleeful. I took a deep breath and fought the urge to crawl under the table and hide. "They're rubbery, and they taste charred in an unpleasant way. I hope you never served scallops like this in my kitchen, Sadie."

Clenched the jaw. Bared the teeth. Tried not to scream.

"I'm afraid I have to agree," Lenore Smith said. She, at least, sounded appropriately sad, even as the elegant lines of her face didn't move. "I loved your fried artichoke. It was cleaned perfectly, very crispy, and sang in combination with the herb butter. But I'm not sure how well it went with the overcooked scallops and this rather wan herb broth." She turned to the rest of the table. "What does everybody think of this broth?"

Bobby Flay liked it, at least. Thanks, Bobby Flay. And Luke was silent. But the other three agreed that it was bland and under-seasoned. "Like, is it a soup?" Julie Chee wondered. "Am I supposed to dip the scallops and artichokes in it? Because it makes them soggy. Or is it a sauce? Because it's too liquidy and doesn't cling to anything on the plate. And there aren't enough herbs."

Hearing her words felt a little bit like dying, but I made myself say, "Thank you, Chef Chee." It hit me now that the older chefs were referred to by their last names while we were all referred to by our first names, even though we were all chefs. Why? It suddenly felt very important that I spend my time thinking it through.

"Thank you, Chef Sadie," Maz said. "Chef Anders, anything you would like to add before your protégé heads off?"

I didn't look at Derek, but I could hear the reptilian smile in his voice. "I would say the *Seattle Gazette* would be disappointed by this dish."

Maz said, "Wait, what?" at the same time as Luke said, "What did you just say to her?"

Derek grinned. "Are you aware of why Sadie here left Se-attle?"

A sob crawled its way up my throat. I had to get out of here. Right now, before it burst out and got all over everyone. As embarrassing as it was, I spun on my heel and rushed out of the room before Maz told me I could go . . .

. . . and nearly ran right into Kaitlyn. "Whoa!" she cried out, jumping back and somehow managing not to spill her plate of food. My eyes were so blurred with tears I couldn't even tell what she'd made.

"Sorry, sorry." I tried to get past her before the tears over-flowed, but she stopped me with a gentle hand on my arm.

"What happened? Are you okay?"

I couldn't swallow over the enormous spike in my throat. But out of everybody here, Kaitlyn was from Seattle like me. She knew exactly what had happened. So, come to think of it, might Julie Chee. The spike grew even larger. All I could get out was, "Chef Anders."

Her face darkened. "You're upset you had to make a dish that reminded you of him?"

I shook my head. "He's here."

Her fist, the one patting my arm, clenched. She stepped past me and, though Maz or Adrianna hadn't called for her, stalked into the room.

Whatever she was going to say or do, it was too late for me. So I fled. Into the bathroom. Where else?

There were three stalls, and all were empty. I shut myself into the larger accessible stall, locked the door, and closed the toilet lid so that I could sit on top of it. I rested my elbows on my knees and put my face in my hands.

And then I finally let myself cry. I cried out of shame, out of anger, out of helplessness. I cried until my throat was raw and clear snot smeared my cheeks and my head thumped with a dull, pounding ache. I cried because my past had followed me here, and now I was going to go home for it, and it wasn't fair. It wasn't *fair*.

The outside door creaked open. I tried to stop crying, but it was like trying to stop salt from hitting the meat once you'd already loosed it from your fingertips. So instead I tried to muffle the noise, smashing my hands up against my mouth and nose until I felt like I might suffocate. Hopefully, whatever person had to pee would just go pee and leave me to my misery.

"Sadie?" It was not a woman's voice. That was definitely a man. A familiar man.

Luke.

I unclamped my hand from my face. It made a sticky noise as it pulled away. "What do you want?"

Footsteps thumped over the tile floor. They stopped at the door of my stall. I could see his shoes under the door, shiny brown leather. "Are you okay?"

I let out a barking sound that was somewhere between a laugh and a sob. "Thanks to Derek, you all know about the nude photos now. Do you *think* I'm okay?"

A beat of silence. "The . . . what?"

My heart thudded to the ground, making a sound in my head like one of Luke's footsteps.

"None of us know what's going on," he said. "You ran out of there, but we assumed it was because you were upset about your dish and because your mentor was being . . . well, kind of a jerk. And then before he could say anything more, Kaitlyn ran in snapping and snarling, calling Derek every name in the book and asking him, and I quote, 'why the fuck he showed his face in this studio.' Then she threw a meatball at him."

I blinked. "She threw a *meatball* at him?"

"Yes. Hit him right on the cheek. He's lucky it was soft and broke apart upon impact, as a good meatball should."

Despite everything, I felt a smile twitch at my lips. "Can you stop judging for one second?"

"I can't help it. I'm a natural." The door creaked as he leaned against it. From the direction of his shoes, I could tell his back was to me. "But really, I don't judge. Not you. Not when it isn't about food."

That was a lot of double negatives in one sentence, but I gathered his meaning. He was telling me he wasn't judging me for the nudes. But he didn't know what had happened.

Thank goodness we were in the bathroom. That was the only place the cameras weren't allowed to go.

I pulled my feet up onto the toilet lid so that I could bury my face in my knees. That seemed the only way I could talk about it, if my voice was muffled. "He was my boss. I always had a crush on him, and then he finally turned his attention to me. I was so happy. I felt so special. We had to keep it a secret from the rest of the restaurant, of course . . . but that was okay."

Luke was quiet, but I could feel the patience and the kindness radiating through the door.

"It was stupid, I know it was stupid," I rushed to add. "He was my boss, and he wasn't really that nice to me, and—"

"Who hasn't done stupid things in the name of love?" Luke said darkly.

That gave me enough courage to go on. "And of course he asked me to take pictures for him, and of course I did. Again, I know it was stupid. Taking nude pics for anyone is stupid, just having them out there, and much less for your boss who isn't very nice to you."

I swallowed hard. "And then the restaurant reviewer from the *Seattle Gazette* came by. Frank Morrison. I don't know if you know him, but basically he's *the* premier restaurant reviewer in Seattle. And he gave us a glowing review. Which was great for the restaurant . . . except that the dishes Frank Morrison specifically called out in the review were all dishes I'd conceived and come up with. Not Derek's. And Derek didn't like that.

"The next day I came into work and everybody was snickering at me. Because everybody had the pictures, of course. Derek claimed that somebody had hacked into his phone and sent them out to all his friends, but he was smirking as he said it." My face burned at the memory, at the remembered rage and helplessness and betrayal I'd felt. Still felt. "It wasn't long before pretty much every chef in Seattle knew what I looked like naked."

I should've known better. My life had that pesky habit of changing entirely while I was in the nude, after all.

"He fired me because, and I quote, 'You're a distraction to the other guys, Sadie.' The word got around to all his friends at the other restaurants, and I knew nobody would hire me there, either. And I was way too embarrassed to go beg a job off someone like Julie Chee, who knew everything that happened. And why would she hire me anyway? I'd just been fired. It wasn't like I was someone exceptional or famous." I blinked hard, trying to stop crying. I'd have to go back out there eventually. "And then I got the call from *Chef Supreme*."

Luke's shoes squeaked as he shifted. "I'd argue with that. From what I've seen, you *are* exceptional."

Okay, if I let myself answer that I'd definitely burst into tears. So I continued, "For a while I thought I could start over again. That *Chef Supreme* would help me take off, and I could just pretend this whole thing never happened." I blinked harder. "I was naive to think I could really get away."

A beat of silence, and then Luke said, "You're not the one in the wrong. *He's* the one in the wrong. Why do you think he got meatballed in the face?"

A smile tugged at the edges of my lips, pulling them up a little higher this time.

"Fuck him," said Luke. "Not literally. Though you already

did literally, I guess." I could practically hear him smack himself in the forehead. "Forget I said that. Seriously, he's a giant ass, and everybody out there knows it. You trusted him, and he betrayed that trust. It's him who should be embarrassed. It's not like nude pictures are so shocking. I think we all know what naked women look like."

This time I actually heard the smack, which made me giggle. It was a small giggle, but a giggle nonetheless. "Sorry! I'm bad at this. What I'm saying is, he's an ass, and all the chefs who wouldn't hire you are asses, too."

Though come to think of it, I hadn't actually *tried* to get another job in Seattle. There hadn't been time for that. I'd let Derek spook me. Maybe . . . he was wrong? "But a lot of people still wouldn't hire me now that it's all out there," I argued anyway.

"Well, if that's true, they're wrong," Luke said. "Just because there are a lot of them doesn't mean they're not all wrong."

I flattened my palm up against the inside of the stall door. I pictured him with his palm against the other side. I really wanted a hug right now, but I knew we couldn't do that. So I settled for, "Thank you, Luke."

"You're welcome, Sadie." He hesitated, his feet shuffling. I held my breath, reached for the door, wanting to see his face . . .

And the bathroom door opened, heels clicking inside. They stopped short. "Luke?" It was Adrianna's voice, and she sounded surprised. "What are you doing in here?"

"Is this not the men's room?" Luke said. He also sounded surprised. I was seriously impressed by his acting. "Oh, well. No harm done. See you in a bit." His footsteps hesitated for a fraction of a second, then headed out the door.

Before Adrianna could knock on my stall door, I pushed my

way out. I couldn't bring myself to fake a smile, but I didn't think my face was that red anymore.

"Splash some water on your face," Adrianna said impatiently. "We're behind schedule, and you're going to need to stop in makeup quickly so you don't look quite so . . . puffy."

I nodded. I wasn't even freaking out anymore. Instead, I felt a kind of calm resignation. What would happen would happen.

I wish I'd felt this way before destroying my dish.

I was almost out the door when Adrianna cleared her throat. "For what it's worth," she said, very quietly, "I'm on your side."

She let me hug her for a good two seconds before stalking away.

MAKEUP DID INDEED make me look slightly less red and puffy. By the time judging rolled around I was resolute, my chin held high. Hopefully, one of the others had done worse than I had. I really didn't want to go home because of Derek. Kaitlyn had said much the same thing in the stew room, right after I gave her the biggest, tightest, most sincere hug I thought I'd ever given someone in my entire life. "You didn't get in trouble, did you?" I asked her.

She shook her head. "They said they'd edit out the whole meatballing incident, and then Chef Anders left in a huff," she said, snorting. Even her snorts were dainty and delicate. "I think he was waiting for someone to run after him and beg him to come back, but fuck him. I hope they edit him out altogether."

In the background, Nia and Vanilla Joe were dissecting their dishes, but I tuned them out. I didn't want to know anything they'd done, have to weigh every word they said against mine.

"Thanks for defending my honor," I said. "I didn't . . . honestly, I wasn't even sure if we were friends."

Her face opened with genuine surprise. "What?"

"We're just . . . really different. And you know, after what I said to you outside the bar . . ." I blurted. Maybe I shouldn't have said something after all, but now it was too late to stop. "I mean, you're . . . great, but I wasn't sure if we . . . ever, um—"

She held up a hand to stop me. "That's enough," she said dryly. "So we aren't platonic soul mates. So what? That doesn't mean we can't be there for each other. To stand up for each other, and for what's right. And to respect each other as excellent chefs."

That was so profound it stole all my words from me. I blinked back tears again. She laughed. "No! Don't start crying again! Adrianna's going to kill me."

But just then Adrianna knocked on the door, sticking her head in before we could answer. "Come on, folks," she said. "Time to get judged."

We filed into the kitchen and lined up in front of the judges' table. The guest judges were gone, leaving the usual lineup of Maz, Lenore Smith, and Luke. Luke was cool as a cucumber gazpacho, carefully avoiding my eyes as I looked at him. Good on him, making sure it wasn't obvious how well we knew each other.

Or was he avoiding my eyes because he knew they were about to give me bad news?

For all the zen I'd talked about earlier, my heart was thumping awfully hard. I tried to swallow it down, but it kept pushing up like it was trying to leap out my mouth.

Maz gave us his usual preamble about how tasting our food

was a delight and it was so exciting to be at the final four and we
were all extremely talented, before saying, "Chef Kaitlyn and
Chef Nia, please step forward."

I knew they were the top two, but some tiny, illogical part of
me hoped they'd be on the bottom until Maz actually congratu-
lated them. I gritted my teeth and stared down at the ground as
Maz gushed about their food. My intestines had transformed
into a bundle of snakes, all squirming around one another into a
giant knot.

"Your take on a crawfish boil was both old and new, something I'd never had before and something I'd eaten a million
times," Lenore Smith said to Nia. "Was it one of your mentor's
recipes?"

Nia's smile curled slowly over her face. "No. I tried something different this time." She coughed slightly. "I threw the
recipe book away."

They pronounced Nia the winner, and Nia and Kaitlyn
stepped back in line. "Chef Sadie and Chef Joe, it's your turn."

I took a step forward, not meeting Vanilla Joe's eyes. I almost
wanted to grab his hand for some comfort, but of course I didn't
do that. He'd probably try to squeeze mine until it broke, anyway.

"Chef Sadie," Maz began, and he went over again how much
they'd hated my dish. The overcooked, rubbery scallops. The
weird texture of the broth, and the oiliness of the herb butter.
"We did like your artichokes, but we questioned how exactly
they fit into your dish."

I pricked my ears as Lenore started talking about Vanilla
Joe's dish, hoping she would announce that Vanilla Joe's chile
rellenos with barbecue duck and smoked red pepper salsa had
been bland and dry and desiccated and made all the judges run

to the bathroom to immediately vomit them up. "We all enjoyed the spice rub on the duck—it was pleasantly spicy and smoky— but unfortunately, the duck was overcooked and therefore tough," said Lenore. "And while the chiles were wonderfully charred on the outside, the red pepper salsa was too sweet."

So we both overcooked our proteins, I thought to myself, frantically trying to compare our dishes without having seen his, much less tasted it. *There's still a chance. There's still a—*

"Chef Sadie," Maz said. The entire room funneled into the sound of his voice. I could barely hear the clock ticking, Vanilla Joe's nervous breathing, my own pounding heart. "Chef Sadie, I'm very sorry, but you'll be leaving us tonight."

17

I WAS FROZEN. INTO A STATUE. OF ICE. BECAUSE AS hard as my heart had been beating, it had now stuttered to a stop.

How long could you live without a beating heart?

Somewhere distant I heard Maz and the judges saying how much they'd miss me, how I had such a bright future ahead of me and blah blah blah, but it was like I was underwater and they were talking to me while I was drowning. How could I focus on what they were saying when I couldn't breathe?

I felt Kaitlyn's arms squeeze me, then Nia's squeeze me even tighter, and then a very bro-ey backslap from Vanilla Joe. I nearly tipped over, because my legs had gone entirely numb.

This was it. I was done.

I raised my head to meet Luke's eyes. His face was creased in sympathy, a genuine twist of pain to his lips. But had he voted to send me home? I had no way of knowing.

I turned and walked out.

Be proud of yourself, Grandma Ruth told me. *You achieved your goal, didn't you? You made it into the final four! The semifinals! Investors could be knocking down your door!*

It was true—I'd achieved my goal. And yet it still felt shitty to go home now. Especially on such a bad dish. It left a taste in my mouth like I'd just bitten into a peanut butter sandwich and found that it was actually Vegemite, the devil's condiment. I didn't want the last that America—and investors—saw of me to be *that* dish.

Adrianna met me in the hallway. "Sorry and everything," she said without preamble. "We're going to zoom you back to the house to get your stuff, okay?"

I'd only had to make it *one* more episode till the finale. Tears pricked my eyes again, but this time I let them come. I knew I'd have to film one final confessional, but I didn't care anymore if the cameras saw me cry. At least they let me do it now rather than making me come back in tomorrow.

Indeed, I cried through my talking head, but I said all the right things about how I was grateful for the experience and I wished the final three well, and then Adrianna whisked me out. I sat in the front as she drove. It was our same sponsored black SUV, which looked oddly naked without the dashboard camera. This was one of the only times in weeks I wasn't being filmed. I felt reckless, like anything might burst out of my mouth without control.

"This really fucking sucks," I said, then held my breath from the daring, like Adrianna might yell at me for cursing. But there were no cameras around! No consequences! She merely glanced at me sidelong.

"You *must* have come into the competition assuming you

wouldn't win," she said. "Eleven out of twelve of you wouldn't. It's simple math."

It's funny. I *had* come into the competition assuming that.

When had I changed my mind?

My heart squeezed extra hard as I walked into the *Chef Supreme* house. The rays of the setting sun greeted me as I paused in front of the big window. One last look over the city skyline, my future going dark just as all those lights started blinking on.

"Hurry up," Adrianna called, interrupting my profound moment. "The others can't come back until you're gone."

And so it was my turn to rush upstairs to pile my clothes into my duffel bag and carefully pack all my toiletries into my suitcase. I hesitated in front of the *Chef Supreme*–branded bathrobe that had been waiting in the bathroom for each of us, unsure if I was allowed to take it, then stuffed it into my bag anyway. It was really warm and fluffy and would be perfect for the next few days I'd spend curled up in bed eating everything in the hotel mini fridge.

At least I'd get to see Kel again.

Marginally more cheered, I dragged my stuff down the hallway and stairs. Adrianna watched me silently through her heavy eyeliner as my suitcase bounced off each step. "It's about time," she said. "Do you want to grab something to eat on the way?"

I shrugged. "Can I just eat with the other eliminated chefs?"

"Not tonight," Adrianna said vaguely and . . . mysteriously.

What the fuck did that mean? Because I had no more cameras on me, I let myself say it out loud. "What the fuck does that mean?"

"You've got quite a potty mouth away from the camera,"

Adrianna said mildly. "It means that you're going to get there so fucking late they'll probably all be sleeping."

"It's, like, eight o'clock," I said.

"Do you like Thai food?"

"Sure," I said, and that's how I found myself sitting across the table from Adrianna at a local Thai joint. The walls were festooned with lanterns and colorful maps of Thailand, and the tables were crammed together so closely I nearly bumped elbows with the woman next to me. I looked the whole menu over back and front, scanning the specials and deliberating over my choices, before just getting chicken pad thai.

Adrianna sighed extra heavily.

The noodles were bland and generic, which was fine. I was too tired to appreciate good food now anyway, so I just shoveled it all in, grateful for the carbs. Adrianna picked at her papaya salad, grimacing at her first bite. "I told them not spicy."

"You shouldn't have ordered a spicy salad then," I told her. She made a face in response.

I stuffed a bite of noodles into my mouth and chewed thoroughly before speaking again. "So, who do you think is going to win?"

She shrugged. "You're all very talented," she said. "I haven't gotten to try any of the food, so I can't exactly pick a favorite."

"The viewers at home don't get to try any of the food, either, but they all have favorites!" I cried. Maybe too loud, because the woman next to me glanced at me sidelong. "Sometimes to an unhealthy degree. At least you get to *smell* the food."

She shrugged again. "It's the truth. I'll tell you something, though. I'd love to see another female Chef Supreme."

SADIE ON A PLATE

"Me, too," I said, though that was tipped by really not wanting the only male chef left to win it all.

We ate the rest of our meal in silence. I was actually starting to believe myself when I thought it wasn't so bad to get eliminated now. I was still top four. A semifinalist. I'd be on TV for a lot of weeks and show America a lot of good food. It was likely I'd still attract some investors interested in funding a restaurant.

And then Adrianna said, "Every season of *Chef Supreme* has ten episodes. Every season."

I had no idea what this had to do with the situation. "So?"

"So, this season is no different."

Again. No idea what this had to do with me. "Okay?"

"I was waiting to see if you'd figure this out, but you're just as dense as the rest of them." She sighed. "Sadie. Ten episodes. One elimination per episode, with the final three competing in the last one."

"Okay?"

"Do you not know how to do math? We had a double elimination in episode five. Do you know what that means?"

My brain was starting to knock at the inside of my thick skull, telling me Adrianna was trying to say something important. "That . . . um . . ."

"We're trying something new this year," she said, and chose the absolute worst moment to take a big bite of her papaya salad. I sat there on the edge of my seat, chewing the inside of my cheek impatiently as she crunched the bite down, grimaced at how spicy it was, and slowly drank half a glass of Thai iced tea to mitigate the burn. After what felt like a million years, she continued, "We're giving eliminated chefs a chance to return. In the next episode."

I sucked in a deep breath of excitement. My heart hovered from my feet up to somewhere around my knees as she told me about the top secret *Chef Supreme: The Comeback*. Apparently, while I'd been assuming the eliminated chefs were kicking up their heels and crying into their hotel bathrobes, they'd actually been competing in a shadow battle of their own filmed while the rest of us were doing our confessionals. "Each week, the reigning champion goes up against the most recently eliminated chef in a challenge," Adrianna said. "And the winner moves on to the next round, with the idea that the winner of *Chef Supreme: The Comeback* returns as part of the top four."

That deep breath caught in my throat. "But that's next episode!"

"I said that already," Adrianna said impatiently. "But yes. Since you're the most recent eliminated chef, you only need to win one battle against the reigning champion to make it back into the competition."

My mind raced. I could do this. I could redeem myself. "Who's the reigning champion?"

She smiled smugly, seemingly appreciating my desperate attention. "You'll find out tomorrow at the challenge."

"You can't give me even a little hint?"

"Nope. It wouldn't be fair to the others."

As we finished our dinner and got in the car to go to the hotel, I went over the possibilities in my head. The chances of a contestant eliminated early on—Kangaroo Joe, Mercedes, or Old Joe—making it this far were unlikely, but in the event that they did, it would make them even more formidable, considering how many other chefs they'd bested. Same with Kel and Bald Joe, but to a slightly lesser extent. Though I hoped Kel had done well. My heart twisted at the thought of my friend. Maybe I'd get to see them at the hotel.

The most likely opponent I'd see tomorrow was Ernesto or Megan, both excellent chefs.

You're an excellent chef, too, said Grandma Ruth.

The hotel was not as nice as the *Chef Supreme* house, which was kind of insulting. I wasn't sure if the run-down carpets and old bubble TVs were given the thumbs-up because they wouldn't be shown on camera or if the measly two pillows and overly soft mattresses were some kind of punishment for being eliminated. I got my own room, though, which I knew was either because they didn't want me finding anything out about *Chef Supreme: The Comeback* or because the other rooms were full, so the scratchy sheets seemed like the most luxurious thing in the world as I kicked and tossed myself to sleep.

The next morning, Adrianna showed up to wake me. I wrinkled my forehead at her, ruining the effect by yawning hard. "Shouldn't you be with the real competition?"

"They did their confessionals already. Now we're giving the 'top three' a so-called rest day before the finale." She smirked. "Really, it's so we can film this and get one of you ready to go back into the game tomorrow."

I squared myself for battle. "*Now* do I get to know who I'm going up against?"

She shook her head. "Go get dressed."

I threw on my usual jeans and Converses—this was not the time to shake things up—and forced down some of the stale mini muffins at the hotel breakfast bar, mind whirling the whole time. I peeked into every half-open door I passed, thinking I might catch a glimpse of one of my fellow competitors.

"Is this going to be on TV?" I asked Adrianna as she escorted me outside into what was, again, my very own black car. I could get used to this.

She shook her head. "Web series."

She pulled up outside the *Chef Supreme* building. Upon seeing it, my stomach did a funny little flip. I never thought I'd be here again.

Even though I'd last been here literally less than twenty-four hours ago, I still felt strangely nostalgic as I had my makeup done and walked through the hallways to the *Chef Supreme* kitchen. *Don't feel nostalgic. Get ready to come back.*

So I walked into the *Chef Supreme* kitchen with my fists balled, ready for battle.

And was met with a series of gasps and applause. The eliminated contestants were all sitting in chairs at the head of the kitchen, everything in view, an audience to the future battle. I smiled tightly and waved at them, and then my smile turned more genuine, because it really was good to see everyone again.

The camera zoomed in on them as it captured reactions. I realized just now that they must not have been told who was coming here, either. Maybe that was why I hadn't seen anyone at the hotel—because they were all somewhere different, somewhere they couldn't catch even a glimpse of me at the breakfast bar or investigating the pool.

"I didn't expect to see you, Sadie!" Kel said. Their purple hair had faded a bit with the days. They smiled sympathetically at me, facial piercings glinting in the light. "I really thought you'd go all the way."

The other contestants said similar things, with Megan running over to give me a quick slap on the back. I wondered while we were hugging if they said the exact same thing with every eliminated contestant. I mean, nobody wanted to hear, "Hey, I thought we'd have seen you here already, considering you're such a shitty cook."

"Since this is a web series, we don't have a host; we'll just be adding a voice-over in edits," Adrianna said. "So I'm going to back away, and then you guys wait ten seconds, then I need the champion to stand up slowly and dramatically."

She backed away. The ten seconds we waited were the longest of my life. My eyes flitted from eliminated contestant to eliminated contestant, wondering who I'd see stand up.

Three Mississippi . . . two Mississippi . . . one Mississippi . . .

Kel rose from their chair, smile wide over their face. "Sorry in advance, Sadie," they said.

I smiled back at them. My teeth covered steel. "You have nothing to apologize for. Except maybe how loud you're going to cry when I beat you."

They whooped with laughter. When they swooped in to give me one of those half hugs, half back pats, I returned it to them with equal enthusiasm. I wanted to win. I really wanted to win.

But at least if I didn't win, it would be Kel.

We took our places at our stations. Because there were only two of us here they put me at Nia's kitchen, which threw me off the tiniest bit. Everything from my station was there—the same instruments, the same utensils and plates, and of course my knives, which traveled with me—but everything felt just a little bit off.

"And, cut!" Adrianna stepped forward. "We'll have the voice-over discuss your challenge, but here it is from me. Both of you left the competition because of substandard dishes. To-

day, you'll be re-creating that dish, but doing it better. Feel free
to create a new dish using your old dish as inspiration, if you'd
like. Two plates' worth." I wasn't sure why Adrianna couldn't just
host. She was pretty and polished, and she talked like a teacher in
front of a classroom. I would think viewers didn't like to be
lectured to, but people love Alton Brown. "Show us that you
learn from your mistakes. Show us that you deserve to be back
in the competition."

All of my insides clenched. Could I really handle revisiting
that wound so soon? I'd just left Derek behind, and now to go
back to him, revisit his dish, let him back in my head? I could
practically see him smirking at me from his seat at the judges'
table. I swallowed hard.

And then, like magic, I saw a meatball splat him in the face.
I felt Luke's mental hug from the bathroom. I heard Adrianna
telling me she was on my side.

It wasn't just me versus Derek. There were so many people
with me.

"Take fifteen minutes to plan, chefs," Adrianna announced.
"Good luck."

I pulled out my notepad and uncapped my pen with renewed
vigor. I wouldn't make the dish from the Green Onion. I could
take the inspiration and truly make it mine. Like I did with my
experiences there.

I reviewed the instruments on my station with a practiced
eye. If I was going to make it through this round, I'd need to take
risks. I noticed the ice cream machine—scallop ice cream? No,
that sounded revolting (though Hiroyuki Sakai's trout ice cream
from *Iron Chef America* would remain forever #iconic). There was

the microwave—definitely not touching that. The pasta machine?

My mind started to tumble, much like fresh pasta dough rolls its way through the machine. I hadn't made fresh pasta yet in this competition, and if I could pull it off, I could see it being a real winner. That way I could turn the herb broth and herb butter into an herby butter pasta sauce—maybe with white wine, maybe with some fried capers to cut through the richness with their briny bite. My scallops would go well with that, being perfectly seared this time, of course. And the artichokes? Maybe I didn't need to fry the hearts whole. I could chop them smaller and fry them like that, crispy little flowers to add some crunch to the soft pasta and meaty scallops.

I didn't see Derek's face at all. All I saw were my own two hands, scribbling away.

Through the rest of the challenge, my feet were sure beneath me. My hands were steady as they made a well in the pile of flour on my cutting board, as they cracked eggs into the well and kneaded the pasta dough out until it was smooth and silky. I made a checklist with minute marks, to make sure I put my scallops and artichokes and pasta on to cook at exactly the right moments.

"Hey, Sadie," Kel called over. "How you feeling?"

I tossed my wild curls over my shoulder. "Better than you," I called back. "Because I'm going to win."

The chefs watching laughed and clapped. Kel scoffed, but they were smiling. "You wish." A beat of silence, and then Kel was moving toward me, hand casually over their microphone. "I really am sorry to see you here, by the way."

I held my head up high. "Honestly, I deserved to go home when I did."

Kel shrugged. "Maybe. Maybe not. You're a great chef."

I smiled, and my response came out strong and clear. "Yeah. I know."

I pulled out long, shallow plates for serving, just in time to drain my pasta and spill it, along with some of the starchy reserved pasta water, into the pan with my herby butter sauce and crispy fried capers. I tossed it, pleased at the glossy way it shone under the light. Once all my sauce was clinging to my pasta and it was hopefully a perfect al dente, I pulled out healthy servings with my tongs and spun them into fancy little twirls on the plate. Arranged my scallops, their crusts a nice dark brown, around the edges of my pasta, then poured some of my extra sauce over them. Garnished everything with my crispy fried artichoke croutons (the judges loved when we called something a crouton) and a handful of chiffoned fresh herbs.

It was me. It was beautiful. It was worthy. Even if it didn't win, even if I didn't return as part of the *final* final four, I'd redeemed myself. At least to myself.

That glow didn't dissipate at all even as I smelled what was coming off of Kel's station. They'd remade their bread pudding as French toast with homemade ice cream (not scallop-flavored), and the smell of the berries and the sugar and the cream all together was heavenly. But my dish was a lot more technically difficult. I'd made my own pasta; Kel hadn't made their own bread.

Even though we didn't have a host, we did get a judge. He walked out of the door and stood in front of us, smiling genially. "Hello, chefs."

It was John Waterford, the OG judge who'd had that heart

attack that had stopped him from being a judge on the main show. He looked a little gaunter than he had in earlier seasons, his suit hanging maybe a little bit looser on his six-foot-plus frame, but he still had a twinkle in his blue eyes, and his silver hair was still thick and full. Though this close, I could see the speckles of dandruff on his shoulders.

"Chef Waterford," I said. "It's an honor."

Chef Waterford stopped before Kel's plate first. Kel introduced it. "Chef, I went home after working front of house during Duel of Spatulas, partially because of my substandard bread pudding with ice cream. Today I've remade this dish for you, turning the bread pudding into luscious French toast, topped with a basil ice cream and fresh macerated berries." It looked delicious, the glossy, shimmering buttery stack of bread topped with the smooth, perfectly pale green orb of ice cream and glistening jewel-bright berries. "Please enjoy."

Sweat shone all over Kel's forehead. I wished we were close enough to grab each other's hands, whether we were in this together or not. Or at least that we'd been able to knock back a glass of whiskey first.

John Waterford chewed slowly, his mouth open just enough where I could hear the slurp of the ice cream, the crunch of berry seeds between his teeth. "It's very tasty," he said finally. "The French toast is perfectly moist and fluffy, and the ice cream adds a delightful herbaceous note. I'm enjoying the tart berries, and think they add some necessary brightness and freshness to the plate. However . . . do you think this dish is challenging enough to put you back in the game?"

"Yes." Kel's eyebrows were bunched up anxiously on their round face.

"Hmm. It feels a bit safe to me. But overall, the dish is quite good. I'd say you've redeemed yourself."

Kel's cheeks were ruddy. "Thank you, Chef."

John Waterford turned his sights on me, walking slowly in my direction. "Chef Sadie, welcome to *Chef Supreme: The Comeback*. I'm looking forward to trying your food. Why don't you tell me about your dish?"

I smiled in a way I hoped said, *I'm looking forward to you trying my food, too* and not a nervous, terrified, *Ahhhhhhhh*. "Thank you, Chef. Um, I was eliminated based on my scallops with herb broth and fried artichokes." I paused, wondering if he'd ask me to elaborate at all on the dish or the challenge, but he just patiently waited for me to continue. Right—viewers would probably tune in to the web series right after watching the episode on TV, so they wouldn't need a refresher. "I decided to make handmade pasta to soak up the delicious herby, buttery sauce, and added capers to give it a bit of a bite. And then, of course, there are scallops and artichokes." It wasn't the most elegant introduction, but it got the point across. I held my breath as he twisted some pasta onto his fork and brought it to his mouth.

And kept holding my breath as he slowly chewed, then went to slice off half a scallop.

And kept on holding it as he crunched into an artichoke, then went in for a bite of everything all together.

Then sucked in a deep breath, because if I kept on not breathing I'd pass out.

"Chef Sadie, this is lovely," John Waterford proclaimed, which made me dizzy with happiness, or maybe it was the whole not-breathing thing. "Everything on this plate is cooked just perfectly. The pasta has this great chew to it, and each pop of a caper is like eating caviar." My cheeks heated with pleasure. "The scallops are like butter inside, but I do wish you hadn't put your sauce directly on top of them. It softened the crust there, as it also did with your artichokes. But overall, exquisite. I'd say you've certainly redeemed yourself as well."

My cheeks split into a big grin.

John Waterford held my gaze for a moment longer . . . and then Adrianna yelled for us to cut. John Waterford strode off as she motioned us over to the center. "We'll announce the winner here," she said to me. Not to Kel, because they'd won so many challenges already they surely already knew. "After he's deliberated."

I turned to Kel as Adrianna stalked away. "It's been an honor to battle you."

Kel gave me a mock bow. "And you."

"I wish we could both go back," I said, and meant it.

Kel nodded back. "But at least if I don't win, it'll be you."

I cracked a smile. "And same with you."

We stood in silence for what felt like an interminable amount of time. Even the eliminated chefs didn't speak, just stared at us. I'd expected my stomach to dance and fizz with nerves, but it might as well have been flat soda for all the bubbling it was doing. I was at peace.

And yet, when the door opened and John Waterford came back in, Kel and I grabbed each other's hands.

"Chefs," John Waterford began. "I was incredibly impressed with both of your dishes today. If the question is whether you were able to redeem yourselves in regard to the challenges that sent you home, the answer is yes. You should both be proud."

I held my breath. Maybe they *would* send both of us on.

"But only one of you can reenter the competition."

Well. So much for that.

Every second seemed to last an hour. John Waterford inhaled for a year, and then took a month to open his mouth. "The winner of *Chef Supreme: The Comeback*, and the chef rejoining the competition, is . . ."

18

THE NEXT MORNING DAWNED BRIGHT AND CLEAR. I
packed up my hotel room—not that I'd unpacked so much to
begin with. I put my hair up in a ponytail tight enough to rival
Adrianna's, leaving my face free of makeup. And then hopped in
the back seat of the black car.

I didn't know the driver, and I was the only passenger, so we
rode in silence. If I had my phone, this is the time when I
would've been checking it. I propped my head against the window, watching the other cars and bodegas and food carts fly by.

The SUV coasted to a stop outside the *Chef Supreme* studio. I
thanked the driver and hopped out, taking a deep breath as I
looked up at the building. As I strode through the familiar halls,
my feet padding over the gray carpeting and passing smiling
portraits of former contestants. As I stopped for makeup and
wardrobe. As I paused right where they'd told me.

The door opened. I walked inside, beaming, in time to catch

the tail end of Maz's speech. ". . . returning to the competition is Chef Sadie Rosen! Welcome back, Sadie!"

The three contestants' faces in front of me ran the gamut of expressions. Kaitlyn looked as happy as I felt—and for once, I didn't feel like she was faking it. Nia was frowning, but thoughtfully, not in an angry or upset way—more like she was recalculating her odds in her head after this unexpected variable. And Vanilla Joe's jaw had dropped with dismay. I held my smile in his direction for an extra moment, just to rub it in.

I wanted to swagger in all *I'm back, bitchez*, but I didn't think that would go over well. So I just walked in normally and shook all of their hands, even Vanilla Joe's. His handshake was limp and soggy. Naturally, Nia's was the firmest handshake I'd ever felt, and Kaitlyn forewent the handshake altogether and wrapped me in a hug.

And then Adrianna made a motion at me from off camera, and I stepped back in line with the other chefs, and I was just another *Chef Supreme* contestant again. Back in the final four. Back in the game. I was in it now, fully in it, and I expected no survivors.

Maybe don't poison the judges, said Grandma Ruth.

I sighed.

"Today, chefs, we'll be taking a field trip!" Maz said. "So hop in your favorite SUVs, the pinnacle of comfort and sustainability, and let's get moving."

"It was a lot less crowded before," Nia said as we crammed ourselves into the back seat, since of course SUVs meant literally one SUV. Kaitlyn had claimed the front, which meant Vanilla Joe was finally assigned to the back. I got stuck with the middle— apparently, they'd worked out a shotgun schedule last night while

I wasn't there. But it was okay. I didn't mind. I got a little nauseated sometimes sitting in the middle, but if necessary I'd just
aim the vomit stream at Vanilla Joe.

"Love you, too, Nia," I said. I would've hugged her, but my
right thigh was kissing her left thigh, and I thought that was
enough physical contact for now.

Our black SUV took us downtown into what Nia said was the
Lower East Side. We passed tattoo shops, lots of little Japanese
restaurants, souvenir racks on the sidewalk hawking I ♥ NEW
YORK T-shirts and paperweights of the Statue of Liberty, which
was nowhere in sight. Then we passed a park and started seeing
NYU banners. "There are lots of good restaurants around here,"
Nia said, scanning our surroundings. It was easy, since we were
moving at a crawl. "I wonder if we're going to one of them?"

"We haven't done one of those outside challenges yet," Kaitlyn
said, turning from the front seat. "You know, where we, like, have
to cook over a bonfire or something? Or have to scavenge our
materials from somewhere else? We might be leaving the city."

"No, we're going the wrong way," said Vanilla Joe authorita-
tively, even though he hailed from California.

Nia was right: the SUV put on its blinkers and told us to hop
out in front of a sleek, shiny building with a sign saying West.
From the lack of a menu in the window and the unassuming
signage, it was obvious this place was expensive. And not just
"date night" expensive, but "getting engaged" expensive.

Going inside didn't do anything to dispel my assumptions:
the seats and banquettes were made from the softest, most sup-
ple leather I'd ever felt in my entire life, and I actually recognized
some of the art hanging on the walls. We dragged as we walked
through the empty restaurant because the cameras wanted some

B-roll of the space, so I snagged a menu off the host stand. Sure enough, West was indeed extremely expensive. It served various French tasting menus only, with a small selection of à la carte dishes, and each tasting menu ranged from five courses for $125 to ten for $235. I could only imagine the wine list.

Maz was waiting for us in the kitchen . . . as was Luke. He was facing away from us, pointing out something in the direction of the walk-in freezer. I held my breath as he turned.

It was like watching the sun rise on ten times speed, his face brightened that much. "Sadie, I'm so—" He stopped, cleared his throat. He clasped his hands before him as his smile dimmed a few notches. "Chef Sadie, welcome back to the competition. I'm glad to see you here."

"I'm glad to *be* here," I said. I wanted to thank him for being there for me in the bathroom, for that mental hug that lingered even through the hard, cold door of the stall, but obviously, I couldn't. No matter how much my fingers flexed with the want.

I wasn't sure if his hands were dealing with want, too, but they unclasped themselves and settled onto the gleaming silver counter before him. The whole kitchen was gleaming silver and chrome, spotless and so shiny I was glad there were no windows back here, as the sun reflecting off all this might have actually burned out our eyeballs. It was pretty big, too. The four of us contestants, plus Maz, Luke, and two cameramen with their equipment, all fit comfortably. I wondered where Lenore was.

I stared at Luke's hands on the counter and remembered how they felt in mine. How my fingers slipped perfectly between his, how the texture of satiny smooth burn scars contrasted with the roughness of calluses on every finger. The counter must be cold under his fingertips, and—

"Chefs, welcome to my new restaurant," Luke proclaimed.

My eyes shot up to his face. He was giving us all a strained smile, every tooth on full and awkward display. It was like he thought if he faked it hard enough, it would turn into something real. This place, this fancy, absurdly expensive French restaurant, was almost exactly the opposite of the dream restaurant he'd told me about. The one where everyone would feel welcome as he served them food inspired by his halmoni's recipes and the things he'd learned since then.

"At West, my goal is to make my guests feel awe," he proclaimed. "Awe at what we're able to accomplish with the best-quality ingredients and some of the most impressive cooking techniques in the world." He paused to let his words sink in, but that only made them feel more wrong. Like he'd just squeezed half a bottle of chocolate syrup—the best-quality chocolate syrup, of course—onto a pile of garlicky mashed potatoes. "I'm sure you're wondering why you're here."

I wasn't really wondering, honestly. Obviously, this was going to be the location of our next challenge.

Maz went ahead and said it. "Tonight, Chef Luke Weston has been kind enough to hand the reins of his restaurant over to you. The four of you will become executive chefs for the night, serving a normal dinner service to his guests." He went on to tell us that we each had to conceive and create an appetizer and an entrée. Guests in the dining room would peruse our menus and choose one appetizer and one entrée to order. We'd have to prepare as many plates as necessary, and get them out before people began complaining or the food started to grow cold. "And, chefs," Maz finished, "the judges won't be the only ones making decisions tonight. To convince you to create the most enticing-

sounding dishes, the chef who receives the most orders total—
appetizer and entrée—will be safe from elimination and go
straight into the final three."

Well, that was tempting. It didn't even matter if the dishes
were good or not, just as long as they sounded good. Which
probably meant not doing the gefilte fish appetizer I'd been
dreaming about this entire competition. While I knew it would
be delicious, I'd seen too many people reflexively recoil at the
sound of ground-up mystery fish.

"You'll have full access to all the ingredients in Chef Weston's
restaurant, which of course are only the best," Maz said. "And
your time starts . . . NOW!"

I exchanged glances with the other three. They also looked
mystified. Should we start running to the pantry? Or running
out of the restaurant from the pressure?

Maz cleared his throat. "Your time doesn't start now, of
course," he said. "I had to say that for the cameras. You've got
some time to plan, and then you'll have all day to prep and start
cooking. Dinner service will be at seven."

So there I was, poised over my trusty notebook yet again.
Luke and Maz and the cameras went off somewhere, which was
fine, because I didn't need the distraction of their presence. Nia's
whispering to herself as she scribbled away was bad enough.

Okay. So. This was my do-over. What to make?

Appetizer. I wished I could do a fried artichoke, but I'd literally just done that, so it was out. Something with hummus would
be tasty, but I'd get dinged for simplicity. What hadn't I done yet?
I ran through my dishes in my head, and—

A knish. I'd wanted to make a knish in that very first challenge but had gotten thrown off my game after switching baskets

with Bald Joe. I'd have to make mini-knishes for an appetizer or I'd get dinged for making too much food, but that was perfect—it would take less time to fry them. I tapped my pen against the page. The knishes I'd eaten growing up generally had some form of mashed potato or beef filling, but I'd have to amp it up if I wanted to win. I could deconstruct the idea of a knish—make a cracker out of the dough, make some kind of potato salad on the side?

Or how about a homemade quick-pickled sauerkraut? I could balance out the sourness with caramelized onion and add richness with a buttery dough and lots of whipped potatoes, cream, and cheese. I could serve one or two little knishes on an appetizer plate with something on the side to make the plate look pretty, since the knishes themselves wouldn't be the most photogenic things in the world. Maybe some pastrami or some form of beef? No, that would take the dish too close to an entrée. A dipping sauce, then. Something mustardy, in an homage to the traditional dipping sauce for a knish, but not mustardy enough where it would draw vinegary attention away from the sauerkraut.

I smiled, satisfied with my appetizer. Now onto the entrée. I would want something less rich to balance out the extremely rich knish. Which meant I should stay away from beef. How about lamb? I hadn't done anything with lamb yet, which was surprising, because it was one of my favorite meats. *Lamb it is, then.*

Being in a restaurant kitchen and having to get dish after dish out, I probably didn't want to spend a lot of time pan-searing lamb to order. Too easy to get stuck in the weeds. So what if I braised it? In red wine, the way Grandma Ruth used to, and with spices like cinnamon and coriander and ginger, the way . . . well, not the way my grandma used to, but the way Sephardic Jews—whose ancestors had lived in Spain and North Africa during the Diaspora—did? Sephardic Jews also liked to pair meats with fruits. Dried fruits like apricots and prunes would be meltingly delicious cooked in the wine with the lamb; my mouth was watering just thinking about it. It would need some spiced couscous to soak up all those delicious juices, and maybe something else. I had sweet, sour, umami, and bitter, so maybe something salty. Something pickled? Pickled cherries could make the whole dish pop.

Under the table, I gave myself a fist bump. Really, considering each of my fists got bumped in the process, it was like getting *two* fist bumps. If I could just make these dishes come out the way they looked in my head, I'd move on to the finals with no problem.

We had a few minutes before Maz returned to officially kick off cooking, so I nosed around to see what the other contestants were doing. All of their menus sounded excellent, which struck some fear into my heart.

Eyes on your own plate, said Grandma Ruth sternly. *That's the only thing you can control!*

She was right. So I turned my attention into writing up descriptions of my dishes, hopefully making them sound as delicious and appealing as possible. Obviously, I wanted to win based on the merit of my dishes, but I had to say, it would be nice to be safe right off the bat by winning the audience vote.

Maz returned to the kitchen . . . with Luke. I blinked in surprise, because the judges usually weren't present during a challenge. "I have one more surprise for you, chefs," Maz announced.

"Our very own judge Luke Weston will be here in the kitchen with you, making sure everything stays on course. He doesn't want any of you to disappoint his *regular customers*." From the way he emphasized those last two words, I could tell they were part of tonight's script. Part of whatever story they were writing up for Luke. It had to be, considering the restaurant was new. He wouldn't have many regular customers yet.

"That's right," Luke said. He was wearing that strained smile again. It might as well have been a tie fastened so tight it was choking him. "My customers' enjoyment is paramount. If you disappoint them, you disappoint me."

I stood up as straight as I could, like that would demonstrate how serious I was about this.

"Well, then," Luke said. "Get to it!"

We had longer than usual to prep and cook, since we were in an entirely new environment and didn't know where anything was. So I took my time exploring the pantry and gathering all my ingredients, checking my basket against my list as I went. The pantry, which had a refrigerated section and a non-refrigerated section, was gorgeous, a pocket tucked tight into the corner of the kitchen bigger than my apartment, overflowing with jewel-bright fruits and earth-toned vegetables and meats in every shade, scented with a dizzying array of herbs and spices. I kind of wanted to come back here after the challenge was over and roll around in all the organic leafy greens.

Back to my station. Even though we were all technically supposed to be working as one, each of us had carved out an unspoken little section of counter space and shelving space to prep. We'd have to share stove tops and fryers and everything, but hopefully, that would all work out. Maybe we should've figured out beforehand whose stuff needed to go into or over the heat and when, but nobody had raised the subject. It would be a free-for-all, then.

And so it was. I did all my prep first: putting the red cabbage on to pickle as long as possible (it wouldn't have the funk of sauerkraut fermented for days, but that was fine); caramelizing an enormous batch of onions; rolling out the knish dough; putting the cherries on to pickle; giving the lamb a good, hard sear before the braise. I had to bargain over oven time and temperature for my lamb with Nia, who was baking corn bread, but we worked it out with our words. Then I battled over counter space with Vanilla Joe as I prepped my lamb and he formed what looked like burger patties, which we worked out with our elbows, surreptitiously stabbing each other with them as much as possible until he gave me a dirty look and moved over.

I was forming my knishes when I felt rather than heard someone approach me. Luke. He stood by my victorious elbow, now battered and bruised, and bathed it with the warmth radiating off him. It could've been the ovens, but I swear there was a gentleness to the heat, a kindness that pushed me to work as hard as I could. Or maybe it *was* the ovens and I was delirious from lack of sleep again. "How are you doing over here, Chef?"

That was his formal voice, which meant—I looked up—that the cameras were nearby, filming. "I'm making sauerkraut and caramelized onion knishes for the appetizer," I said. "I'm forming them right now." I stepped back to allow the cameras a shot of my knishes being formed. They were tiny and adorable, each a little smaller than my palm. I'd decided to form them like little bags of treasure, which gave the top a frill I'd have to watch carefully to keep from burning, but they would make my plates ex-ponentially prettier.

Luke leaned in to see them more closely, brushing his shoulder up against mine. It was like he'd zapped that circle of skin with an electric shock that shuddered into my chest. He glanced sidelong with a small smile. "Tell me about the filling."

He didn't move as I spoke, his shoulder still up against mine. I had to focus very hard to keep my hands moving, to keep myself from stopping and just leaning up against him, fitting the whole side of my body against his. *No.* I had knishes to make. So I filled and patted and twisted, filled and patted and twisted, saying something about sauerkraut, not even totally sure of the words that were coming out of my mouth. I just knew I could be happy standing here with Luke at my side, making food with my hands, for the rest of my life. Or at least another few hours.

When my words finished flowing, I expected him to step back and move on to the next contestant. Instead, he leaned in farther and palmed one of my little babies. The one I'd been rolling, which meant his hand overlapped the memory of mine. He looked up and met my eyes, that little smile still on his face.

Was he *trying* to fluster me? I jerked back so hard a knish went falling to the ground. Which was fine, because I had extras. "I'm going to deep-fry them for around thirty seconds, which should be sufficient," I said forcefully. "I want them crispy and golden and screaming."

He blinked, pulling back. "Screaming?"

"What?" I pretended I hadn't heard him as I turned back to my knishes. I still had a bunch more to form before checking on the lamb braising in the oven.

The rest of our prep time flashed by. But it was smooth running, every step sure and even beneath me. I even finished a little bit early, which left me hovering over my station with the disconcerting feeling that I should be doing something else. But I couldn't decide on anything but fluffing the couscous and trying to give it a little bit of a crisp on the bottom before Luke called time and gathered us to the center of the kitchen. "Orders are about to start coming in," he said. "I hope you're ready." He glanced up at the camera above him, then turned back to us with a frown, deepening his voice. "You'd better not disappoint any of my *regular guests.*"

I put a hand to my mouth with dramatic shock, covering my mouth mostly so the cameras wouldn't see my grin. It was obvious Adrianna had given him directions to act as menacing and stern as possible and keep focusing on his *regular guests.* And, well, he was doing his best.

Sure enough, the appetizer tickets started flying in. Luke pinned each one above each of our little stations, shouting out the order as he went. *One bacon brussels and one nachos! Two nachos! One knish and one bacon brussels!* My hands worked in a mad rush, dropping the knishes to order in the deep fryer, my face growing so oily from hovering over it that I'd need to exfoliate my face like three times tonight if I didn't want to break out tomorrow. Each golden-brown knish got dropped onto a small plate with shaky hands and a prayer that the fragile knot of pastry up top wouldn't shatter, accompanied by a mustard sauce and a few microgreens to add color to the plate.

I'd assumed I'd be trying to keep track of who was getting the most orders, but it was hard to tell. At one point I glanced around at the tickets hanging over each station, but they were torn down as soon as they were fulfilled, which made it hard to tell if someone was getting a lot of orders or if they were just backed up. And I heard all of our appetizers shouted by Luke over the din in the kitchen . . . except for Kaitlyn's calamari churros. I didn't hear very many orders for those. I felt kind of bad as I looked over and saw her standing at her station, biting her lip with worry. But I couldn't go back in time and tell her to pick something that sounded more appealing to the general public. I expended more energy wondering which tickets were going to the judges; they mixed theirs in with the other guests', to make sure we didn't know which ones were theirs. They didn't want their appetizers given any special or extra attention. I just hoped it wasn't the knish whose top broke off as the waiter was whisking it off the counter.

By the time the appetizer tickets slowed to a crawl and ended with one last ticket for nachos and bacon brussels, I was panting like I'd run a 5K. Which my sister, Rachel, had made me do once. I'd gotten out of work at three a.m. and had to wake up three hours later to jog slowly behind her and pretend I didn't want to die. It was not an experience I was really looking to repeat.

We were granted a short break to use the bathroom and collect ourselves while the diners finished up their appetizers. Once I peed—the bathroom back here was a cramped single stall, so there were no run-ins with Luke—I meandered back into the kitchen, next to Kaitlyn. She turned to me with woe in her big blue eyes. "I don't think that went well."

I nudged her in the side. The cameras were behind us, I tried to signal with my eyes, but she just squinted at me like she was having a seizure.

I gave up. "Things always go better than you think."

"But really, I don't think they did," Kaitlyn said gloomily. "I didn't get very many orders. I heard way more tickets coming in for you guys."

"Maybe that's a good thing!" I said, trying to sound as chipper as I could. "You got to give each dish extra time! The number of dishes ordered only matters for whoever comes out on top. As long as your dish tastes good, it doesn't matter if you come in last in orders."

She sighed. "I tried out a Cuban twist for my menu, but it didn't feel any more right than the others."

"Maybe that's not where your heart is," I said. "Maybe you have to keep looking."

She shrugged and turned to her prep space, where fish bones were scattered. It looked as if she'd be frying the meat. I left her to her prep and walked over to check in on Nia.

Nia looked almost manic, her cheeks glowing. "Halfway through!" she said breathlessly. "Still so much to do! Plantain chips to fry! Fish to sear! Why did I decide to sear it, Sadie?"

She sounded so plaintive that for a moment I thought she actually expected a response. But then she turned and started scribbling numbers in her notebook. I blinked and moved on.

The only person left in the kitchen was Vanilla Joe, who alone looked at ease. "Hey, Vanilla Joe," I said.

He frowned. "I think you can stop calling me Vanilla Joe now. I'm the only Joe still here."

That was a fair point. I nodded. "Got any nachos left?" I was suddenly starving.

"Sorry," Vanilla Joe said. "Served them all." He smiled like the cat eating the canary. "I didn't have *any* left over. It was lucky I'd made extras. It seemed like everybody wanted nachos tonight. So sad I didn't get a snack afterward."

"Epic humblebrag, Vanilla Joe," I said. His smile disappeared. "What are you making for the entrée?"

"The best burger you've ever had," Vanilla Joe said. "Not that you'll get to try one. I expect they'll go fast, too."

I cocked my head. "It had better be a damn good burger." Burgers were kind of the joke of the restaurant world, at least in the kinds of restaurants I'd worked at. Every restaurant had one, but there was only so much you could do with them. The people who ordered them were typically the picky eaters, the ones who stuck their tongues out at the fancier foods and techniques.

Then again, that could be his goal. People liked burgers to the point that every restaurant had one. Was Vanilla Joe staking his entire future in the competition on winning the numbers game? I looked at him with a new respect. Kind of. It was a big gamble he was taking—he was unlikely to beat the rest of us judges-wise with a burger—but there *were* probably a lot of people out there who'd been dragged along by partners or parents or friends. People who might really appreciate a good burger.

"As I said, best burger you've ever had," said Vanilla Joe. His eyes lifted over my shoulder. I turned to see the cameras were back. Luke, too, with tickets in hand.

The rest of dinner service didn't just fly by, it careened over my head like an egg thrown at a house. My couscous didn't just crisp up on the bottom, it crisped up a lot. Like, too much. As in, it burned. So I had to scrape around the unburnt portions, trying frantically not to let any burned bits fall onto the plate.

Which led to my plates being delayed. Luke came over, followed by the cameras, his eyebrows raised high and his scarred hands also raised high before him. "Chef Sadie, you're holding up service!" he said. Though I knew he was trying to sound angry or upset, he sounded mostly strained. "Your fellow chefs' dishes are sitting under the heat lamp, and they're going to have to remake them if you don't hurry up! And your guests are hungry!"

Tears prickled at my eyes. They weren't tears of sadness, but tears of frustration. Fortunately, my face was already so red and sweaty I didn't think anyone would actually notice if any leaked out. "Sorry, Chef. I'm moving."

I turned back to my pot, and then, to my tremendous surprise, Luke stepped up beside me, ladle in hand. He leaned over and scooped a spoonful of unburnt couscous from the bowl, spreading it out on a nearby plate with flair. "Go. I'll take care of the couscous."

Was this allowed? At the moment, I didn't care. I scuttled over to the stove and focused on plating the lamb and dried fruit, topping it all with the ruby-like pickled cherries. I found I worked faster without focusing on the mistakes I'd made, when all that was in front of me were the things I knew would be delicious.

Five plates went out, and then Luke was at my side, handing me my ladle. "Good luck," he said, and then he was gone. The cameras followed him, which allowed me to sag against the counter, exhaling my frustration into empty space. I'd sent the plates out. I'd gotten a good number of tickets.

The rest was in the judges' hands.

I held on to that ladle for the rest of the night, even though the rush of orders never got as intense as it had during that one crush. Luke's hand had held it, and for a moment, it was like he was holding mine.

19

ONCE ALL MY TICKETS HAD GONE OUT, I STOOD IN THE kitchen with the other three chefs and obsessed. About the plates I'd sent out. About what I'd put on those plates. If my food had been creative enough, technically skilled enough, impressive enough. Delicious enough. It was enough to make me want to scream.

Get out of your head, Sadie.

I stepped up to the opening between the kitchen and restaurant and peered through. The diners were all finishing up their entrées—I knew it was a bad idea, but still I tallied the orders mentally as I looked around.

I saw a lot of burgers.

A bad feeling settled heavy in the bottom of my stomach. Much like I'd just eaten a giant burger, the best damn burger I'd ever had.

The judges sat at a three-top at the edge of the room, all on one side of the table, facing us. Adrianna beckoned us out, and we followed. We lined up before them almost instinctually, me between Kaitlyn and Nia. Kaitlyn caught my eye, and she gave me the barest nod and a smile. I felt myself instinctually begin to scowl, because we'd just been through the ringer and of course *she* was *smiling* . . . but then I told myself to stop. And I just smiled back.

Luke was the first of the judges to speak. "Chefs, I trusted you tonight with my VIP guests and the kitchen of my flagship restaurant," he said in a voice like he was reading this speech off a teleprompter. I actually looked to see if there was one hidden among the hanging plant vines on the wall across from him. There was not. "And I have to say . . ." He gave a dramatic pause worthy of Maz Sarshad himself. ". . . I was very impressed with your work!"

His smile actually made me feel worse. If we were *all* impressive, that set the bar higher.

"My guests were very impressed as well," Luke continued. "I almost regret bringing you here. I think they might prefer you to me."

That sent up a big laugh around the room. Luke smiled in response a second too late.

"Thank you, chefs," he said, sitting down. "You'll be judged later. For now, enjoy some food and wine."

A yawning pit opened up in my stomach. All of a sudden, it roared to be filled. Nia tittered at the sound. The diners eyed us as Adrianna sidled up to our sides. "You may mingle with the diners," she said, then added, more sternly, "You may not say anything about the show. *Anything*. You may not tell them who's been voted off, or what your favorite moment was, or what time you fucking woke up. Nothing. Nada. All you may say is 'no comment.' Get it?"

I nodded meekly. So did the others. And then, as if by magic, our waiters showed back up, balancing trays on their shoulders. They bore what looked like various little chocolates, cakes, and pastries, with dessert wine following.

I ate what probably amounted to a bakery's entire Valentine's Day stock and then downed a goblet of wine, everything settling together in my stomach in a way that somehow didn't make me feel any more nauseated than I already was. Then I glanced around to see what everybody else was up to. The judges were gone, maybe off deliberating somewhere. *Okay, now I'm officially more nauseated.* The other three contestants were already circulating through the room, talking to diners who had their empty plates on their tables.

I was already behind the others, but just going and stopping at a random table nearby somehow felt awkward. Like I was asking for praise. Fortunately, I was saved from the awkwardness when two diners at a nearby table motioned me over. I followed the motion automatically before I realized who they were. Yep, it was them again. The wealthy older couple I'd insulted and spilled food on. I cringed inside even as I forced a smile on the outside. Hopefully, they weren't calling me over to yell at me.

"Chef Sadie," the woman said. "We very much enjoyed your dishes."

Indeed, they'd scraped my plates clean. I noted with some satisfaction that they'd left a few bites of Kaitlyn's fish behind. But not too much satisfaction, because I immediately felt bad about it. "Thank you!"

The man leaned forward on one elbow, his eyes trained on mine. They were a deep blue, somehow familiar. "My mother-in-law is Jewish."

"So's my mother!" I chirped. Awkward.

He gave me a half smile. "What would your mother say if I told her the top of my knish had fallen off as it came to my table?"

Of course. Of course they would get the *one* defective plate. "I would say, 'Shit, that sucks,'" I said. The man's half smile became rather frozen. Of course I'd said the wrong thing again. Of course. Then again, I was so exhausted and so drained that he should feel lucky to get actual words out of me instead of random gibberish. "I mean, even if it wasn't the prettiest knish in the world, I hope it was still delicious!"

I gave him a quick smile and moved on before he could rag on me more or I could manage to insult them or destroy any more of their clothing. After circulating through a bunch of diners, delighting time after time at how much they said they enjoyed my food, I noticed Nia alone in the corner, arms wrapped tight around herself. I moseyed over that way, smiling absently as a woman leaned almost all the way out of her chair to ask for the recipe for my braised lamb so that she could make it at Passover next year. "Hey," I said, nudging Nia gently with my shoulder. She swayed gently back and forth, a soufflé about to collapse. "Are you okay?"

She bit her bottom lip, looking troubled. "I did a great job tonight," she whispered. I leaned in to hear her better. "Like, extremely well. My record has been getting better and better over the past several weeks. I have an actual shot at winning this whole thing."

I blinked, waiting for the punch line, but she left it at that. "I hope you don't want me to express sympathy for you?"

"I don't want you to do anything," Nia said gloomily. "I didn't ask you to come over here and talk to me."

Point taken. "Okay, I guess I'll get back to the others."

I spun to head back into the scrum, but she caught me by the shoulder. "Sorry, that came out wrong. Sometimes I say things and they come out wrong."

"Don't we all?" I moved back to face her. "So, you're doing great and for some reason you're unhappy about it."

She scoffed, barely audible over the hum of conversation all around us, the clink of glasses, the cozy rustle of skirts and suit jackets. "I'm not unhappy about doing well in the competition. I'm . . ." She sighed and rolled her neck, cracking it so hard I instinctually cringed. "I'm a little bit scared, to be honest." She turned her face away from me so that she was staring at the wall. "I've spent my life as a chef mastering technique after technique, memorizing recipe after recipe. And yet I'm doing my best as I throw caution to the wind and *improvise*. I can't control improvisation, but I might need to do it to win. And not having that control scares me."

I rubbed her arm in what I hoped was a comforting way. "I think that means you're doing it right."

"How can it be right if I'm scared?"

"Taking risks *should* scare you," I said. "And you need to take risks. Otherwise, what's the point?"

"Winning the competition," Nia said, but her tone said, "Duh."

"I can't think of any *Chef Supreme* winner who's played it safe." My own words struck a chord deep inside me. I'd been playing things safe my whole life, letting Derek scare me from looking for a new job because I was afraid of what might happen, letting Luke keep his distance because I didn't want to lose what I had.

What if I needed to heed my own words to win?

Nia blinked at me, eyes thoughtful. Before she could respond, Adrianna's sharp clap split the air. "Time for judging! Sadie, Nia, Kaitlyn, Joe, come back to the judges' table. Everybody else, please take your seats and stay quiet."

I walked past a woman whispering excitedly to her dining companion. Adrianna snapped, "I said *quiet*, for God's sake!"

"She'd better watch it," Kaitlyn whispered to me as we took our places. "She's going to *disappoint* the regular *guests*."

I snickered as the judges filed back in. Maz, Luke, and Lenore Smith took their seats, all folding their hands in front of them like they'd rehearsed the motion in the back room. Their faces were impossibly grave. "Chefs, we've tallied the votes and made our decision," Maz said, those bright green eyes solemn beneath his crest of shellacked dark hair. I went to hold my breath, then decided against it. It always seemed to end with me almost passing out. Instead, I made a point of breathing deeply and evenly, of anchoring my feet to the floor. "First, I'd like to announce the results of tonight's orders. We had one hundred diners tonight, not counting us judges. Out of one hundred, our winning chef claimed thirty-four of the appetizer orders and thirty-seven of the entrée. Congratulations . . ."

Okay, I couldn't help but hold my breath.

". . . Chef Joe!"

I deflated. Vanilla Joe hollered and pumped his fist in the air.

"Chef Joe, while we didn't find your dishes especially original, the guests were clearly excited by your elote nachos and your Brie burger," Maz continued. Damn. His risk had paid off after all. I hoped Nia was taking notes. "Chef Joe, you are safe from elimination and may step to the side. Welcome to the final three!"

To Vanilla Joe's credit, he didn't spend any more time whooping and hollering and rubbing it in. He took a big step to the side with a relaxed, lazy grin. I'd watched enough *Chef Supreme* to know this was a moment where the cameras would do a dramatic zoom on my, Nia's, and Kaitlyn's faces, close enough to catch every drop of sweat glistening on our foreheads and the throb of our pulses beneath the thin skin of our throats, set to a frenzied drumbeat and shiver of strings. "Chef Sadie, Chef Nia, and Chef Kaitlyn," Maz said. "One of you will be leaving us tonight, while the other two will be joining Chef Joe in the final three."

First, they looked to Nia. "Chef Nia," Lenore Smith began. "When I saw brussels sprouts salad with corn bread on my menu, I will not lie to you, I sighed. But when that plate was put in front of me, my heart sang. That candied maple bacon you did was something entirely exceptional, and your corn bread was moist with the perfect crust. I would say that I barely noticed I was eating brussels sprouts, but I *wanted* to eat your brussels sprouts because of how crunchy and lightly sweet they were. I thought your salad could have used a touch more vinegar, but otherwise it was excellent. It made me think of you as a little girl standing by your stove, carefully taking notes as your grandmother pulled that maple bacon out of the oven."

"Thank you, Chef," Nia said. "My grandmother never made those. I made that dish up on my own."

Lenore Smith nodded, her silver eyebrows arching high in a way that looked impressed. "And your entrée was very good as well," the judge went on. "Your curry sauce was maybe a little bit too spicy for most of our tastes, but the flavors were complex and went well with your moist salmon and your plantain chips. The one thing I wished was that you'd left the skin on the salmon—some crispy skin would have been the perfect complement to the plantain chips."

"Thank you, Chef."

All the judges' eyes swiveled to me. I swallowed hard. My turn to be under the microscope.

Luke spoke for me. "Chef Sadie," he said, and God, I loved hearing my name come out of his mouth. Even if he was about to put me on the grill and light it. "We all loved your knish. You should have seen Lenore's face when she saw sauerkraut on the menu—"

"It wasn't pretty!" Lenore Smith laughed. There was a tiny smudge of lipstick on her front tooth.

"Your face is always pretty," said Maz, and he actually sounded sincere. Well, that was something I'd literally never considered: whether Lenore Smith and Maz Sarshad were having a secret, torrid affair behind the scenes. Why not? They were both good-looking people. I'd say they'd make beautiful babies, but those days had obviously passed long ago for Lenore.

"Anyway," Luke said. He sounded slightly uncomfortable. Exactly the way he would if he were stuck between two people having a secret, torrid affair. "The sauerkraut flavor wasn't too strong, but it balanced out the caramelized onions and the cheese in the most lovely way. And am I to understand that you made your own sauerkraut for the challenge?"

"Yes, Chef." He already knew that, since he was back in the kitchen, but the other judges wouldn't have.

"When tasted on its own, it lacked some of the complexity that comes along with sauerkraut that's been fermented for weeks or months, but it served its purpose well inside the knish," he said. "Though we weren't all in love with your mustard sauce. Why did you choose to pickle the seeds? We thought there was enough pickle flavor with the sauerkraut, and some of us"—he glanced at Maz—"weren't thrilled with the way the seeds got stuck in our teeth."

"Some of us have paid a lot of money for veneers," mumbled Maz.

I assumed they'd edit that out.

"I just liked the flavor, Chef," I said.

Luke nodded to show that he'd heard. "And we thought your lamb was delicious; the dried fruit in the braise added a necessary punch of sourness and sweetness, in the very best way. We loved the bright pop of the pickled cherries as well. However, we thought the couscous was somewhat bland."

I flushed. "I hoped that the couscous would mostly serve as a blank canvas for the sauce, Chef."

He eyed me appraisingly. The judges didn't typically like people arguing with them. "We also felt that the plate needed a bit more textural contrast. Maybe some fried onions on top or some diced raw apple for crunch."

Damn. I ground my teeth. That made sense.

Finally, Maz looked over at Kaitlyn. "Chef Kaitlyn, we enjoyed your calamari churros. Your sauce was delicious, spicy and vinegary, but not enough to cover up the delicate flavor of the squid or the light sweetness of the dough. However, we all felt the dish was missing something—perhaps a vegetable, perhaps some seasoning. It tasted good, but was just a little bit off the mark."

Kaitlyn nodded, looking somewhat defeated.

"And in your entrée, the battered fish was fried perfectly," Maz said. "Though I found a bone in mine."

I sucked a breath through my teeth. It was never good when the chef left a bone in their fish.

"We did, however, really enjoy the spicy fruit salsa. Its freshness and sweetness broke through the richness and oiliness of the fried fish. But something about the fish and the salsa and your sides didn't quite come together as a cohesive entrée."

I could picture the camera spinning around, doing more dramatic zoom-ins on each of us. I tried to keep a poker face. I'd already been eliminated once. I could handle it again, if it came to that.

No matter how nauseated I felt right now.

"We wish we could keep all three of you," said Maz. The guests behind us were cloaked in a dead silence, not so much as a cough or a sneeze breaking it. "All six of your dishes were good. But only two of you can move on to the next round. Chef Nia . . ."

Nia sucked in a breath.

". . . you have made it into the final three!"

She didn't whoop or holler like Vanilla Joe. She just sucked in a deeper breath of relief, tilting her head back and closing her eyes just for a moment. "Thank you." She glanced quickly at me and Kaitlyn, then stepped off to the side with Vanilla Joe.

"That means one of you will be going home," Maz said to us.

I felt a hand grab mine. Kaitlyn. Warmth swelled in my chest. She and I might never be the best of friends. We were very different people. But as she'd said, that didn't mean we couldn't be there for each other. Respect each other. Support each other.

"Chef Sadie . . ."

I closed my eyes.

". . . you will be joining Nia and Joe in the final three! Congratulations!"

I opened my eyes. I felt almost crushed with relief, like I might stagger. I gathered myself together enough to give Kaitlyn a hug as she wiped tears from her eyes, and then I walked to the side.

"Chef Kaitlyn, that means that you'll be leaving us tonight," Maz said somberly. "You're incredibly talented, and I know you have a bright culinary future ahead of you. I look forward to tasting more of your food someday."

Kaitlyn nodded, sniffing. "Thank you. It's been an honor."

She had time to give us each another hug before being ushered out. But just as Adrianna was motioning at her from the nearby doorway, Maz stopped her by clearing his throat. "Chef Kaitlyn. One more question for you."

Kaitlyn turned, her eyes sparkling. It was extremely unfair, but she was a beautiful crier. The tears caught in her eyelashes, making it look like she was wearing glitter mascara, and the only parts of her face that went red were the apples of her cheeks. "What is it?"

"Who do you think will be the next Chef Supreme?"

Kaitlyn blinked, a tear trickling down the blush of her cheek. She eyed each of us, going from me to Nia to Vanilla Joe, before turning back to Maz. "They're all great, but the one who's going to take it all?" she said. Then smiled through the tears, which made her look even more unfairly beautiful. "Sadie. Sadie's got what it takes."

Before I could thank her—or do anything, really, but blink in a stunned fashion—she was ushered out the door. Nia nudged me. "Statistically, it's the winner of the second-to-last challenge who most often wins the final," she whispered. "In case you were wondering."

"I was not," I whispered back. "Nia, forget about the statistics. They don't matter anymore. The only thing that matters going forward is the food."

She blinked at me, but her mouth twisted thoughtfully.

We were freed to mingle with the guests further before wrapping up, which meant more people swarming me and wanting to pat me on the back thanks to what Kaitlyn had said. It was just the pat I needed to send me over the cliff's edge of exhaustion, the way caramel could be a perfect golden brown in your skillet one second and burnt to a charred crisp the very next. One moment I was fine with my fake smile and on-cue laughter, and the next all my insides were prickling with the need to get away. I needed to be out from under all these eyes and all these hands grasping at me. They'd already eaten my food, and now it kind of felt like they wanted to eat me, too.

Adrianna was nowhere around, probably getting things sorted with Kaitlyn, which made it easy to slip back into the kitchen— the only place around here where people were guaranteed to not be (except maybe a bathroom stall, and I was kind of done hiding in bathroom stalls). Plus kitchens tended to calm me down. Especially this kitchen, which was really, really nice.

I trailed my fingers over the counter as I walked deeper in. We'd been pretty good about not causing giant messes, but the counters were still splattered with last-minute drips of sauce and plantain crumbs. Passing by my area, I noticed a pickled cherry that had rolled out of the way and grabbed it, popping it instinctually in my mouth. Damn, it was good. I deserved to make it into the final three. I really, really did.

But that pickled cherry made me realize just how much my body was craving something other than chocolate and wine. Surely, Luke wouldn't mind if I made a stop in his pantry and ate some carrots or wheat bread or something that would help my stomach stop gurgling in this unappetizing way.

Except that as soon as I saw who was in the pantry, my stomach started gurgling anew.

"Sadie," Luke said with some surprise, turning to face me. He'd been scanning the shelves, moving things around. "What are you doing here?"

"Getting some space," I said, taking a step closer. "What are *you* doing here?"

Luke's dark eyes shimmered with something I couldn't name. Like I could just see something moving beneath the surface of a calm lake on a dark night. "We're going to be open for regular service tomorrow, so I'm checking to see what we need to restock and making sure everything's in its proper place."

"Makes sense." I took another step toward him, my wish for carrots or wheat bread forgotten. I liked the sparkling of my stomach now, how it stirred up more with every step I took.

This is a bad idea, Sadie, Grandma Ruth said disapprovingly. *Step away from the handsome man and devour some carrots instead.*

I knew she was right. The rational part of my brain was telling me the same thing. I'd held out for this long for the sake of my career. Surely, I could hold out another week or so.

But I ignored her (after considering telling her to shut up; but I couldn't do that to my grandma, even if she was only in my head right now). Because I couldn't ignore how I was feeling. Not for another second.

I stepped right up to Luke. I couldn't take another step without physically pushing him out of the way. This close, I could feel the heat radiating off his front, smell the aromas floating from the herb shelf behind him, fresh rosemary and thyme. I waited for him to move away, rustling the shelf and pushing more of that homey scent into the air, but he stayed right where he was. "Sadie," he said, his voice hoarse.

So of course I kissed him.

20

I'D DONE A LOT OF STUPID THINGS IN MY LIFE. ONCE during college I'd jumped into a book donation box to steal a copy of an Ottolenghi cookbook and gotten chased through campus by the overzealous RA on duty before losing her by jumping into some extremely thorny bushes. (The book was fine.) That was a pretty stupid thing to do, even if I came out of it with the cookbook I'd wanted for ages but was too broke to buy at the time.

But this? This was colossal stupidity. I knew it even before I pushed myself up against Luke, before I stood on my tiptoes and framed his chin with my palms, before I pressed my lips against his.

It felt at once like coming home and exploring somewhere new and utterly thrilling.

His lips weren't just warm against mine, they were hot. His arms wrapped around my back and pulled me closer. Bold of him to think I *could* get closer. I'd done a pretty solid job of melting into him, of making sure every inch of myself touched an inch of him.

But I understood. I was smaller than him, which meant that there were inches of him left in the cold. He was hungry, pulling me into him, every bit he could reach. And I responded, every inch of me sparking with heat, every single tiny millimeter glowing with delight as our lips opened as one and his tongue teased its way into my mouth.

Maybe I was stupid, but he was stupid, too.

His fingernails raked their way down my back, making me shiver in the best way. I sighed into his mouth, and he growled into mine.

I wanted him. Right now. Right here on this pile of summer squash.

We stumbled backward as one, hands grasping; my fingertips grazed a few inches of a hard back, while his teased the gap between my shirt and my pants. Every touch of his rough fingertips on my hot, hot skin made me want nothing more than another touch. His hands grabbed my hips, and I gasped at the wonderful forwardness, and then he was lifting me up, sitting me down on the vegetable counter. Zucchini went rolling, landing with a thump on the floor.

I wrapped my legs around him, raising my chin while he kissed my throat, and saw a blinking light in the corner of the room. A blinking light?

A camera.

Shit.

I zoomed back into myself. *All you had to do was wait another week.* My inner voice was furious. *You* idiot.

"Luke," I gasped into his ear. He nibbled at my throat. I swallowed hard, because I knew I had to make him stop. "*Luke.* They've got a camera in here."

He stiffened against me, and not in the good way. "What?"

"*Camera.*"

He jumped back. I teetered on the edge of the vegetable counter, throwing my hands up to cover my face. Way too late. I didn't even know why I was doing it. They'd definitely gotten more than they'd signed up for.

It was like someone had dumped a bucket of cold water onto a campfire. That was how fast my amorous feelings sizzled into cold, soggy lumps of wood and stone. "They saw us." My voice shook. "They *saw* us. Oh my God." Maybe not yet—they probably weren't watching a live feed of the pantry when none of us were supposed to be in there—but they would. Adrianna had showed us that much when she called us out for mocking the car our first day, and for sneaking out to the Korean bar. She would see us, and then . . . what?

I'd have to go, I realized with a dawning horror. I was the one who kissed Luke. And I didn't need to read the rules to know that this was *definitely* against them. We'd had to hide this whole time that we'd met and kissed before the show. But *during* the show? That was even worse. There would be no way he'd be able to judge me impartially, and Adrianna would know it. She might even see it as a ratings bonanza—the drama of a final-three contestant kicked off the show for hooking up with a judge.

My breaths came short and fast, but they didn't quite fill up my chest, which was drawing tight. They were starting to whistle in my throat. Great. A panic attack. That was exactly what I needed right now.

Luke's hands clamped on to my shoulders. "Breathe, Sadie. Breathe."

I closed my eyes, but I swore I could still see that camera's blinking light. With Luke's hands holding me firm to the ground, I took deep breath after deep breath, trying hard to calm myself.

I might get good ratings, but no one would invest in me. Nobody wanted to pay for the restaurant of the official *Chef Supreme* trollop.

I didn't realize I was crying until Luke brushed a tear away with his rough thumb. I went to pull away, thinking about the camera, and then figured why not let him do it? It wasn't like it could get any worse for us. The camera had already seen us kissing. "I'm going to get kicked off when Adrianna sees this," I sobbed. "I was stupid. So stupid."

I let him hug me to his chest, because again—why not? "It's going to be okay," he said soothingly. I could feel his words brush against my ear.

"No, it won't," I cried. "This was my chance. To prove I could make something of myself. To prove I deserved my own restaurant. And I couldn't keep it in my pants for a few more days."

He snorted. "It's not like I was entirely innocent in this, you know. You didn't ravish me against my will."

His wording was so funny I let out one giggle in spite of myself. "I kissed you first."

"But what do you think I was doing here in the first place?" He was supposed to be setting up the pantry for tomorrow's service. "I saw the way you were looking around here earlier. I hoped you'd come back." He shook his head. "If it's anyone's fault, it's mine. I've spent more time going to the bathroom than I have in my entire life in hopes of running into you and your damnably tiny bladder. I tried to drive you away at first in hopes that I wouldn't harm your career. I've done my absolute best to judge in an unbiased fashion, but I can't get your food out of my mind, because your hands worked the dough and your tongue tasted everything that went into my mouth."

His words rang in the silence. I could only hope the camera didn't pick up on sound, because if it did, we were both absolutely screwed.

"Sadie? Luke?" Adrianna's voice filtered into the back of the restaurant. As usual, she sounded impatient. "Where are you? Are you back here?"

I backed away from Luke, nearly tripping over a zucchini and breaking my neck. That would have been a terrible way to die. "I have to go."

"Wait." He reached a hand out toward me, but I was already racing back to the restaurant, where the guests had already almost all filtered out. I filed into line behind Nia and Vanilla Joe, panting from the run.

Nia glanced at me over her shoulder. "Where *were* you?"

"Bathroom," I gasped.

"Again?" She shook her head. "You've got to be in the top one percent as far as bathroom usage goes."

I faked an unconvincing laugh. Sure, top one percent. Top one percent of all the people who were completely, utterly screwed.

I DIDN'T SLEEP that night. Not like the overdramatic *oh my God, I didn't sleep last night*, where what you really meant is that you tossed and turned a little and got a few hours less than you should have. I mean, like, I didn't sleep, at all. I was a temporary insomniac. I lay awake in my bunk and stared at the ceiling, my eyes growing crusty and dry. I couldn't stop thinking about how close I'd been, and how I'd ruined it.

Maybe I didn't deserve to be here after all.

All the coffee I had to drink the next morning to keep my eyes open only made it worse: now I wasn't just exhausted and doomed, I was exhausted and doomed and extremely jittery. I'd thought about it all night, and I was still no closer to figuring out what I should do. Tell Adrianna and get out ahead of it? Because she'd see the tape eventually. Or hope that the camera had been broken or obscured somehow?

I did nothing by default. Which meant that I was a queasy mess when our black SUV dropped us off at the *Chef Supreme* kitchen for a morning of confessionals and then an afternoon starting the final challenge. I had to spend extra time in makeup as the makeup artist tried desperately to make me look less like a recently risen zombie, which meant Adrianna was able to accost me right outside the door of the makeup room without disturbing the other two contestants. "Sadie," she said, crooking her finger. "A word."

As I followed her to a door I'd never gone through before, my mind whirled with thoughts of potential escapes. I could turn and run and disappear into the city. Start a new life. I didn't need an ID or a social security number to get a job in a kitchen somewhere. It would be sad never talking to my family again, sure, but I'd always have my grandma in my head.

Adrianna ushered me through the door and shut it behind me with a click. *Trapped.* The room looked like her office, or like somebody's office, anyway—it was small and cramped, packed with a desk, a few cheap fabric chairs, and stacks and stacks of papers and tapes. I expected her to take a seat behind the desk, but she only turned to me, arms crossed over her chest and a severe expression on her face.

Maybe I could light the stacks of paper on fire and flee amidst all the chaos? Or burn to death. At this moment, that was feeling okay, too.

"Sadie," Adrianna said. "I hope you aren't considering a lawsuit."

I blinked. "Excuse me?"

Adrianna pursed her lips. I couldn't stand to look her straight in the face, so I looked behind her. Only a tiny bit of the desk was free of the chaos, but in that one small, clear space sat a framed photograph of Adrianna holding a small child. Both were smiling. "I want you to know that Luke Weston no longer works for *Chef Supreme*."

What? My jaw literally dropped open.

Adrianna's foot tap, tap, tapped against the floor. It was like she was taking up all the energy in the room, because I found myself unable to move at all despite my earlier jitteriness. "He told me that he kissed you in the back room of his restaurant against your will," she said. "I want you to know that—"

"I mean, it wasn't really against my will," I blurted. Maybe it was stupid, but I couldn't let Luke go down for this. Not like that. "He—"

"Sadie," Adrianna interrupted. She fixed me with such a heated glare that I couldn't look away. For an extremely weird split second, I wondered if she was about to kiss me, too. "This is the spin. He kissed you. He shouldn't have. You didn't kiss him back. He quietly leaves the show, and you continue on without pursuing any legal action. Don't you want to stay on the show? You're so close to the end."

"But that's not the—"

"*The truth is what we make it,*" Adrianna said with such force it actually blew me back a step. "I saw the tape. I know the truth. So what?" She took a step toward me, making me take another step back. I hit the door. "We create story lines out of nothing on this show all the time. Luke is stepping quietly back because John Waterford is making a heroic return from his brush with death. What a guy! He'll be in attendance at the dinner because otherwise the media will start rumors about him being forced out."

"But isn't that what—"

"He came to *me*," Adrianna said, emphasizing every word. "He did this for *you*. Listen to me, Sadie." She paused, as if to make sure I was hanging on to every single syllable. "Don't waste this chance he's giving you."

I could not cry right now. I could not. Partially because I didn't want to look weak in front of Adrianna, and partially because the makeup artist would blow her top if I ruined all her hard work. So I sniffed hard and looked up at the ceiling. "Okay."

"What's that?"

"I said, okay." He'd done this for me.

And that only made me want him more.

Adrianna kindly gave me thirty seconds to get myself together before leading me to the confessionals booth. I recited my thoughts and feelings during the previous challenge and answered producers' questions, hoping I didn't sound as robotic as I felt.

After a quick sandwich, it was time to hear details of the final challenge. It felt oddly empty in the *Chef Supreme* kitchen with only the three of us left, like our voices would echo when we spoke aloud. I took my place between Nia and Vanilla Joe. I had no idea how I was still awake.

Maz strode dramatically out of the front door. "Chefs, welcome to the final three!" he said. "This challenge will be the most difficult one you've faced so far in this kitchen. Only the chef who aces everything we give them will earn the title of Chef Supreme."

Basically, the final challenge would be the same as it was every year: to make the best four-course dinner of our lives, prepared to serve a restaurant full of fifty people. Two smaller courses, an entrée, and a dessert. Us on a plate. Well, four plates. No holds barred. Several other clichés about how hard we'd need to work and how much of our heart we'd need to bleed onto our pristine white plates.

"We wouldn't let you go into this alone," Maz said. "So we're going to give you a bit of help." The door opened again, and in filed nine familiar faces—the eliminated contestants. Though I still felt like hot garbage, seeing their faces did perk me up a little. Though not as much as if Luke had been at the head of their line. "Each of you will get to choose two of the eliminated contestants as your sous-chefs as you prep, cook, and serve your four-course meal."

We drew spoons to see who got to choose first. For once, I got a stroke of good luck and pulled the shiny gold number ONE. I surveyed the group. I knew from watching past seasons that choosing your sous-chefs wasn't just about picking the best cook or your best friend. It was really about whose skills would complement yours, about who would support you in the kitchen rather than undermine you, about who you could trust with the biggest moment of your life.

So the decision was easy. "I choose Kaitlyn," I said.

Kaitlyn swanned over to my side, tossing her long brown hair as she turned. It smacked me in the face, and I got a big mouthful of hair spray.

Some things would never change.

Vanilla Joe was next, and he picked tanned, leathered Old Joe for his kitchen wisdom. Nia chose Megan. When it came back around to me, I grabbed Kel, of course. Vanilla Joe took Bald Joe, and Nia rounded out her team with Mercedes for her skills at prep work. "Reuniting the Joes," Vanilla Joe proclaimed. The three Joes did a group fist bump while the reject Kangaroo Joe obviously tried not to cry.

Us three finalists and our sous-chefs assembled back in a line. Kangaroo Joe, Ernesto, and Oliver filed back out, probably to get really drunk. That's what I would have done. No, that's what the old Sadie would have done—the new and improved Sadie had new and improved ways of dealing with her feelings.

"Your four-course meals will be served two nights from now at Chef Lenore's restaurant," Maz said. Two nights. Good. That meant I'd hopefully get to catch up on sleep before the big event. As long as the guilt left me alone and didn't gnaw, gnaw, gnaw at the bottoms of my feet where they stuck out over the edge of my bunk. "You have the rest of today to plan out your menu with your sous-chefs. Tomorrow you'll go on a shopping spree for ingredients and have the rest of the day to prep. And then the next day, you'll cook and all serve your meals to the restaurant's fifty guests and the panel of judges."

Kaitlyn, Kel, and I bowed our heads over my station. My trusty *Chef Supreme* notebook sat between us. "I really want my roots to come through in this meal," I said, very conscious of the cameras filming everything I was saying. "I want to make sure viewers and diners"—and investors, please, especially investors—"see everything that the food of my ancestors can be. That Jewish food isn't just matzah ball soup and pastrami sandwiches."

So it was with that attitude I went about planning my menu. "I'm thinking my first dish is going to be a tribute to my grandmother," I said. "She was very into chopped liver. I hated it as a kid, for good reason: her chopped liver was bland and gritty." Grandma Ruth hissed in my ear, but I ignored her. "I want to make *good* chopped liver on good bread with something vinegary and acidic to cut through it. Maybe some kind of pickled fruit, because the judges really loved my pickled cherries in the last round."

"How about kumquats?" suggested Kaitlyn. "Or gooseberries?"

"I like gooseberries," said Kel.

I made a note. "We'll see what they have at the store, since we'll be on a budget. With the second course, Ashkenazi cooking has so many preserved and sometimes weird fish dishes. Think gefilte fish and pickled herring. I've wanted to do my special gefilte fish this whole competition and never got a chance, so I think now's the time."

"If not now, then when?" Kel said reasonably.

"Indeed. And I think coupling it with pickled herring and maybe some other kind of fish to make a trio will create something amazing. Maybe something fried, since the other two parts of the dish won't have any crunch. Or I could just do, like, a potato chip? I do love potatoes." I made another note. "And for the third dish, I'm thinking duck. I want to do cracklings with the duck skin and then a play on borscht, which is what the dish is really about. Beets on the plate, pickled onions, an oniony sauce, et cetera."

"Ducks and beets play well together," Kel said, approval warm on their round face.

"And for dessert, I want to do babka in some form," I said. "Not a bread pudding; that's too easy."

"French toast?" Kaitlyn said.

I shook my head. "Again, too easy. Those are the desserts everybody does on *Chopped* so much it's a cliché. The judges groan every time they see them."

"Gee, thanks," said Kel.

"Don't mention it." I looked back down at my notes. "I'm thinking beignets." I loved beignets, the fried little doughnut-like balls so typical in New Orleans. I liked mine hot and crispy right out of the fryer, ready to be drowned in chocolate sauce and caramel and chopped nuts. "A babka beignet. Thoughts?"

"I don't know," Kaitlyn said dubiously. "Babka's usually pretty heavy, but the point of a beignet is that it's light and fluffy. Will you be able to make a babka beignet light and fluffy?"

I flipped a page in my notebook. "That's what we're going to figure out."

We spent the next few hours so immersed in our heads that we didn't break even to eat. Sitting there, we decided in our scrawls on paper how far in advance we should make our liver pate and pickle our herring, how many onions we needed to buy for the whole meal, how exactly we were going to make babka light enough to fry into a beignet. By the time Adrianna shooed us from the kitchen like we were a flock of geese in her way, we realized we were starving.

Conveniently, Adrianna met us outside the building. "I've given permission for escorts to take each group out for something to eat," she said without preamble. "Nia's group, you go with Joaquin. Joes, you're with Fiona."

Kel sighed dramatically as the other two teams waved goodbye at us and left. "Does this mean we've been left to starve?"

"Oh no." Adrianna gave us a sharklike smile. "The three of you are with me."

Ten minutes later we were sitting around the table at a pizza joint, eagerly awaiting the arrival of one ham with pineapple, one with peppers and onions, and one plain (Adrianna's choice). We also had antipasto salads, which I'd insisted upon, because I found getting veggies in me when I felt like I'd been hit by a truck made me feel like I'd only been hit by a car. These antipasto salads consisted mainly of cured meats and cheeses, but it was the sentiment that counted, surely.

"So, I heard a rumor." Kaitlyn glanced at Adrianna mischievously. "Is Luke really not coming back to judge the finale?"

Adrianna took a sip of water. "It's true." Her heavily lined eyes darted to me, like actually darted, as in they were saying, *I will stab you with a poison dart if you say anything untoward.* Maybe that was why she'd elected to come with our group rather than one of the others. "John Waterford's making a surprise return for the finale, and Luke was gracious enough to step aside so he could reclaim his old place on the judges' panel."

"Oh, that's so nice!" Kaitlyn squealed, clapping her hands together.

Kel furrowed their brows. "Surely, there would be room for an extra judge?"

Fortunately, at that moment the pizzas arrived, and we were way too distracted by inhaling every single slice on the table to question her further.

Once we swallowed every bit of food and were waiting to pay the check, I asked Adrianna, "Do you cook at all?"

She shook her head, sending her ponytail swinging. Didn't say anything.

"Like not even at all?" I pried. "Not even for fun? Baking?" I couldn't imagine wanting to work on *Chef Supreme* of all shows and not having any interest in cooking, but she kept shaking her head. "What about eating? Do you like going out to different restaurants? Trying different foods? Anything?"

The head kept shaking. "Food is fuel," Adrianna said with a wry smile. "I eat a lot of boxed mac and cheese and oatmeal. And salads. Why do you look so surprised?"

Kaitlyn didn't actually look surprised; she looked like Adrianna had just told her we'd only be allowed to use canned meats in the finale. "Because you work on *Chef Supreme*. The food show to end all food shows."

Adrianna shrugged. "It's a job. A good one. It pays well, and the hours could be worse." She waved over the waiter, gave him her corporate card. "Most people don't get to work on their absolute passions. Even most chefs get into it because they have to—it's immigrant labor, backbreaking work on nights and weekends for low pay. You're very lucky that you get to do what you love and get featured on TV for it."

Kel leaned over the table. "What would you do if you *could* work your absolute passion?"

Adrianna shrugged again. "Not sure. Still figuring that out." The waiter returned with her card, and she scribbled a tip and signature on the receipt before standing. "Let's get you back. You should get some sleep before tomorrow."

I kind of wanted to talk to Kel alone and make sure there were no hard feelings about the whole *Chef Supreme: The Comeback* thing, but Adrianna dropped them off at their hotel and me off at the *Chef Supreme* house. Where, of course, the cameras were waiting. I rubbed at my eyes. As soon as that pizza landed with a thud in my stomach, I'd been ready to pass out.

Inside, Nia and Vanilla Joe were sitting around our kitchen

island with glasses of champagne already poured. "Finally," Vanilla Joe said, as impatiently as Adrianna. "Is this part of your strategy? Keep us up late and exhaust us so you can take home the win?"

I very pointedly yawned so hard my jaw cracked.

"That would be a terrible strategy," Nia said. "She'd be just as exhausted as we would."

"Whatever," said Vanilla Joe. "Anyway, the producers want a few takes of us toasting to us being in the top three and reminiscing about our favorite parts of the competition."

The perky *Chef Supreme* assistant poked her head out from behind the cameras. "And it would be great if you could work in our sponsors!"

I suppressed a groan as I sat down. This was the absolute last thing I wanted to do right now, but I pasted a smile on my face anyway. "To the top three!" I said, lifting my glass and clinking it against Vanilla Joe's and Nia's.

"To our ergonomic transportation!"

"To the incredible appliances in the *Chef Supreme* kitchen!"

I took a deep breath. My glass of champagne was nearly empty. All the bubbles were fizzing in my stomach. "To our final four-course meal!"

21

OUR PREP DAY FLEW BY EVEN FASTER THAN THE DAY
before, which was good in that it gave me no time to obsess
about Luke and the hit he'd taken for me. I directed Kaitlyn and
Kel as we cooked liver and ground it into pate, as we sculpted a
log of fancy gefilte fish, as we boiled beets with herbs and spices
and rolled out babka dough. There was stress in the kitchen, yes
(especially when I realized how bland my first batch of pate was),
but there was also laughter. And fun.

I was dying to know what Nia and Vanilla Joe were cooking,
but we'd been separated into different kitchens for prep since
there were so many of us in one place; we'd be back in the same
kitchen tomorrow for service. I'd asked a few questions last night
between sips of champagne, but Nia'd been cagey, and all Vanilla
Joe would tell me was that it would be the "best fucking food
[I'd] ever shove into [my] face hole," which, gross.

The morning of the service dawned not bright and clear, but
with a torrential downpour. I wanted to go sit on the terrace one

last morning with my coffee and watch the sun rise over the city, but the sky was gray and the rain pounded on the concrete, soaking through Kaitlyn's abandoned ashtray and the wicker lounge chairs. I tried not to take it as a bad sign.

The finale wasn't being held in the *Chef Supreme* kitchen but in Lenore Smith's restaurant. It was big enough to be three restaurants in one, which meant it was perfect for this event, and reminded me much of Luke's kitchen, everything gleaming chrome and stainless steel. The producers had already come in and marked up boundaries while bringing in our prep carts, which saved me from having to fight Vanilla Joe with my elbows again. Each of us had our own ovens and stove tops and everything.

I kept my ears pricked toward the dining room as I unpacked my cart. Kaitlyn and Kel showed up in spotless white starched chef's whites much like my own; they were stiff, and I wished I'd gotten a day or two to wear them in so that they wouldn't be so hard to move around in. Again, I hoped this wasn't a bad sign.

"Where's my pea puree?" Vanilla Joe cried from the other side of the kitchen. "Sadie, did you take my pea puree?"

"The last thing I would ever want to take is your pea puree," I told him. Nia, between us, just wrinkled her tiny nose as she rolled what looked like oysters in a cornmeal batter.

"Then where is it?"

"How the fuck should I know?"

Vanilla Joe rattled his cart as he looked from shelf to shelf. "I swear to fucking God, if my pea puree isn't here, I'm going to—"

"Dude." That was Bald Joe from the side. "I have the pea puree right here."

"Hmph," said—emoted?—Vanilla Joe.

"I accept your apology!" I called over.

As I chopped and baked and sautéed, I began to feel almost as if I were in a dream. Maybe it was the glitter of the lights off all the silver countertops and appliances and knives, or maybe it was the delirium-inducing lack of sleep, or maybe it was just my mind's refusal to accept that the outcome of today would decide everything. If I got the money. If I got my restaurant. If I became Chef Supreme.

If I deserved the sacrifice Luke had made for me. Like, if I crashed and burned today, he'd have taken the blame and lost this job for nothing.

So I listened closely to every sizzle and watched every boiling pot and smelled every hint of smoke near every oven. Because now this wasn't only for me; it was for him, too.

It felt like ten minutes had passed and at the same time like ten years had passed when the buzzer went off on the wall. "Appetizers!" Nia shouted. "Appetizer tickets are coming in!"

Kaitlyn's bread was still hot coming out of the oven; it emitted the most heavenly steam as she sliced into the golden crust. "The liver!" she called. Kel and I swarmed her, schmearing slices of toasted bread with the chopped chicken liver made rich with schmaltz—chicken fat—spicy and smoky with paprika and za'atar, and sweet with blackened, almost burned caramelized onions. I topped it with fried leeks and some microgreens. Soon enough, it came time to take our first plates out to the judges.

The dining room was a buzz of activity even greater than Luke's had been, and everybody was already chowing down on our three appetizers. I walked through with my head held high, but I almost dropped my plate when I heard a shriek. "Sadie!"

My eyes nearly bugged out of my head. "Rachel?" The judges

could wait one more second. I whirled around to see my sister sitting in a booth. With my parents! My face split into a smile so wide it tweaked some muscle in my cheek. Was I potentially the first person ever to be injured by smiling? "Hi! What are you doing here!"

"Surprise!" My dad leaned forward. Before him and my mom were plates of my appetizer, the chopped liver. "Your grandmother would be so proud of you!"

"You'd be surprised," I told him. "So what did you—"

"It was delicious!" said my mom, about as enthusiastically as it was possible to say anything. "We're so proud, honey!"

My dad nodded. "I'm glad you didn't take my advice. You belong here."

Before Rachel sat an unfamiliar plate. She looked up at me and shrugged. "This is Nia's plate. Mom and Dad said they would share yours with me. Nia's was *really good*." I blinked. She blinked back, startled. "But not as good as yours, of course!"

Great—that was a sound bite Adrianna was probably high-fiving the cameramen about. "Well, enjoy. Thanks for coming. And see you later!" As I continued on toward the judges' table, my waiters loyally in tow, I scanned the room for other familiar faces. The three eliminated contestants who hadn't been chosen as sous-chefs—Kangaroo Joe, Ernesto, and Oliver—had their own little table to the side. They all looked happy enough as they shared our plates. And there was an older Black couple I recognized from the framed photos Nia had put on her section of the dresser—probably her parents.

I arrived at the judges' table before I could spot Luke, if he was even here. John Waterford smiled up at me from Luke's spot, which gave me a sudden, irrational urge to punch him in one of those genial blue eyes. In addition to John Waterford, Lenore Smith, and Maz, all of whom were decked out fully in tuxes or in Lenore's case a glittering blue evening gown that matched her eyes, several other older people sat at the table. Maz introduced them as famous chefs and restaurateurs, most of whom I recognized after their names were given to me.

"And of course, we welcome back Chef John Waterford," Maz said, his white teeth blinding. "Chef Luke Weston was kind enough to keep his seat warm for him while he recovered from a medical emergency."

"And now that I've recovered, he was even kinder to give it back," said John Waterford with a chuckle. Nobody bothered to ask why, if so many other people got a seat at the table tonight, they couldn't both be there judging. But I knew the various *Chef Supreme* bloggers and Instagrammers definitely would, and they'd take it as some kind of conspiracy. "I've already gotten to try some of your food on *Chef Supreme: The Comeback*, Chef Sadie, and if it's any indication as to the caliber of what I can expect tonight, I'm very excited."

Behind me, I could hear the distinctive *whoop-whoop* of a Rachel cheer. My cheeks flushed hot and crimson. "Thank you, Chef. Um, tonight I decided I . . . I . . ." I was blanking on the speech I'd spent all day formulating, even though it was literally only a few sentences. I probably should've written it down on my hand. Though it would've blurred by now from the sweat and the heat. "I wanted to show you that Ashkenazi Jewish food, the food I grew up with, is more than latkes and pastrami. Growing up, my grandma liked to make us chopped liver, which I always refused to eat."

That got me a laugh. Especially from Grandma Ruth, whose laughter was the heartiest of all.

"Tonight, as my appetizer, I've reinvented the classic chopped liver, making it something I definitely would've wanted to eat as a kid," I said, and told them all about what was in it. "I hope you enjoy."

Vanilla Joe stepped up beside me. "I'm excited to serve you my food, Chef," he said. "My goal with my four-course meal was to push the boundaries of what fine dining can be. My first course is a sea bass crudo with fried sweetbreads and a pea puree. I'm hoping the sweetness and acidity of the raw fish will balance out the rich organ meat in a way none of you have tasted before."

Pretentious, but okay. Finally, Nia stepped up. "Over the course of this competition, I've gotten to cook you so much of the food I tested and refined over the years." Her voice was loud and clear. "Tonight, I want to take you on a journey of seafood. Like migrating fish, sometimes people grow up in one place and end up somewhere else. They don't always have a map, but sometimes that leads to wonderful surprises. To places they never would've thought they'd love. These are all dishes I've never cooked before, that came not from my recipe book, but from my heart." She smiled wide and clear. "My appetizer for you tonight is a fried oyster with a green tomato and pepper relish, served over a corn cake."

I angled my hand behind Vanilla Joe's back. I expected it to hover there pointlessly for a moment, but Nia got my intention, because of course she did. Her palm slapped mine with a strong high five.

The judges dug in right then and there. My stomach coiled

with wires and sparked as they chewed thoughtfully, chasing every bite down with a sip of water. They also had little cups of sorbet to clear their palates between our dishes. You wouldn't want any lingering acid from Vanilla Joe's crudo making my liver taste like metal.

Mine was the first they dissected. And they liked it! "I would eat this liver for breakfast, lunch, and dinner." "The airiness and crunch of the bread is a perfect contrast to the smooth, thick texture of the liver." "I love that these onions and leeks are hovering just on the edge of burned. It adds a wonderful complexity to the dish." "I'm enjoying the tartness of these pickled gooseberries in contrast to the richness of the rest of the plate." I gave Kaitlyn a mental high five.

Then Nia's. They liked hers, too! "Your oyster is perfectly crunchy and briny." "I like that the breading isn't too thick. The flavor of the oyster really comes through." "The relish is an excellent counterpart, though I wish there'd been a touch more acid." "The corn cake is so light and fluffy."

And finally Vanilla Joe's. Which they also liked. "Your fish is fresh and cool and nicely acidic." "I like the crunchy sweetbreads." "This pairing really isn't something I've seen before, but I don't know why. Going forward I want to eat it all the time."

I looked around for Luke again as I headed back to kitchen to prepare the second course, but I didn't see him anywhere. There were tables everywhere, little nooks where he could have been tucked away.

In the kitchen, Kaitlyn was panicking. "The gefilte fish didn't set up." She was standing over a log of it, poking at it with a spoon. My stomach clenched. We'd ground up all the fish and compressed it into a log yesterday so that it could set overnight in the fridge and get nice and compact, but that clearly hadn't worked. As I watched, it crumbled into mush.

I grabbed her spoon and took a taste. Something had gone wrong, clearly: the texture was off, too soft and yet somehow a little gritty at the same time. I must have forgotten some essential ingredient, but it didn't matter now. "Damn it," I said anyway. Kaitlyn flinched, and I immediately felt bad. "Not you. It's not your fault. Let's get out the pickled herring and see how that's doing."

The pickled herring was, thankfully, better: thick and meaty and acidic, the onions I'd packed into the jar with it still firm and crunchy. "We've got this, at least," I said, my mind already moving. "We can't serve the gefilte fish, but we can serve the herring. We'll make it work."

My heart raced as I marched back out to the judges' table with my second dish. I hoped my last-second fix would work. "My second course stems from the pickled herring my dad used to eat straight out of the jar, which I always thought was disgusting," I said. I heard my dad bark out a great burst of laughter. "What I have for you is pickled herring and onions with brown butter solids for richness, served with a dill mashed potato and a crispy potato chip."

It took the judges a few bites to speak. "I like this, but it doesn't sing the way your first course did for me," said John Waterford. "It's a little simple." I kept a smile on my face, but I cursed inside my head. The judges enjoyed the brown butter solids, but my mashed potatoes were slightly flat. They liked the crunch of the chip but didn't feel like it went with the rest of the dish, which made sense, since it had originally been intended to accompany the gefilte fish. I should've left it off.

Nia served them a Vietnamese barbecue shrimp in a shrimp broth with a fresh and pickled vegetable and herb salad; the judges couldn't stop raving about the cook on the shrimp and the richness of the broth but wanted a little more herby freshness from the salad. Vanilla Joe made a chicken sous vide with lobster sauce and a crispy potato hash, and while the judges liked all the components, they weren't sure quite how they all fit together.

On to the main dish. My stomach was still bubbling nervously as I met Kel and Kaitlyn back in the kitchen, where they were unpacking yesterday's prepped beets. "They didn't melt overnight, did they?"

"I do not think it's physically possible for beets to melt," Kel said.

"Don't say that too loud, or Nia will start telling us the exact temperature and conditions it would take," said Kaitlyn. "No, everything looks good. We'll get all this ready while you focus on getting a perfect cook on that duck."

A perfect cook on my duck was of utmost importance; it would be exceedingly embarrassing to under- or overcook my main protein in the finale. So I crosshatched the skin on my duck breasts in a neat X pattern, salting them and making sure they were totally dry before placing them skin side down in a cold cast-iron pan. I hovered over them as they sizzled away, making the skin nice and crispy; as soon as the sizzle began to die down, I flipped them over to cook on the other side. *Looking good*, I thought as I nodded approvingly at the golden-brown top, at the way the fat was beginning to render down through the dark, rich meat. I poked my testers—aka the ones I wasn't sending to the judges—mercilessly, until I was absolutely sure they were at the right temperature. As my duck breasts rested, re-absorbing all that wonderful juiciness, I paid Kaitlyn and Kel a visit to get started on the plating. "Are the cracklings in the fryer?" I asked. We hadn't had any extra duck skin, because I wanted to cook the breasts with the skin on, so we were using chicken skin instead. Hopefully, the judges wouldn't mind.

Kaitlyn saluted. "Putting them in now, Chef!"

Out of all my dishes so far, I felt most confident in this one as I walked it across the restaurant. I could see people already digging in; I craned my neck as I passed by to make sure nobody had undercooked or overcooked meat, but all looked good. I also craned my neck to search for Luke, because if he was going to try one of my dishes, I'd want him to try *this* one. I still didn't see him.

As the waiters laid my plates out before the judges, I cleared my throat. "I have for you a play on borscht: beets in a variety of forms, from fresh to pickled to pureed, with mustard seeds, onions, duck, and crispy chicken skin."

One of the guest judges poked at a beet with his fork. "You've done some form of pickled fruit or vegetable in every course. Do you think you might have an overreliance on that technique?"

I . . . had actually not noticed that until now. I tried to hide my surprise and said, as breezily as possible, "Ashkenazi food uses pickling a lot. We were frequently running for our lives, which made fresh foods inconvenient."

That brought a laugh around the table, and the guest judges couldn't argue with "running for our lives." They dove in. "I'm enjoying the beets and the duck together. It's not a combination I've had before, but it really works." "I'm not usually a fan of raw onions, but the little bits you've strewn throughout are perfect with the beets and the richness of the duck." "The chicken skin adds a nice fatty, crispy element, but I would've preferred duck skin."

They raved about Nia's, a lettuce wrap with smoked fish and pickled watermelon rind. "This fatty, oily fish with the sweetness and acidity of the pickled rind is stellar. It's Southern without being Southern." Less so for Vanilla Joe's play on sausage and peppers. "Your sausage is a bit bland."

And then it was time for the dessert of the biggest meal of my life. So much rested on this final course. My heart thumped as we lowered our first babka beignets into the fryer. "You guys, thank you." I turned to Kaitlyn and Kel, who were hovering over the fryer with me, since we didn't have much left to plate or prep. Everything rested on these little nuggets of chocolate and sugary dough, along with the cherry sauce simmering on the stove. "I know it's probably not easy, considering you both wanted to be here instead of—"

Kaitlyn thumped me on the back, nearly sending me face-first into the fryer. Now *that* would have made a dessert to remember. "It is what it is. If it can't be me, it might as well be you," she said frankly. "Besides, there's always *Chef Supreme: Back in the Fire.*"

"You won't win that, unfortunately," said Kel, mock-frowning. "Because I'm going to win."

Season four had been *Chef Supreme: Back in the Fire*, where non-winning contestants from the first three seasons had returned to compete for the title and prizes once more. There was no reason to think they wouldn't do it again at some point. Though if I didn't win today, I wasn't sure I'd want to return to compete.

Had I really just thought that?

I poked the thought with a mental finger, trying to figure out whether it was hubris speaking or delirium or a lie. But no. It was true, and it was real. I was glad to be competing now, but I wouldn't come back and do it again. Because I'd already gained what I was looking for, I realized. Yes, I wanted the prize money and the title. But I'd learned to like myself, learned all that I could do, and that was so much more important.

"It's done!" Kel shouted as the little ball of goodness bobbed to the top of the fryer. We pulled the basket out, shaking it and letting the oil drip back into the fryer. We all stared at it, waiting for it to cool enough for us to try.

No matter what, it would be enough.

22

"IT'S A LITTLE HEAVY," LENORE SMITH SAID, WRINKLING her nose. She set my babka beignet back on her plate into its pool of glossy crimson sauce. "When I think of a beignet, I think light, fluffy. This is dense and chewy."

"I agree," said one of the guest judges. "I like the taste, but the texture leaves something to be desired. I really think it needs something else on the plate to lighten it up, at the very least— some ice cream with spice in it, perhaps, or even a whipped cream."

I bit my tongue. I'd wanted to do a whipped cream, but we'd simply run out of time. "Thank you."

I could barely focus as the judges went through Nia's and Vanilla Joe's desserts. I had an idea that they enjoyed Nia's caramelized banana "scallops" with an Indian-inspired kheer—aka coconut milk rice pudding with raisins, rose water, nuts, and cardamom. They seemed to like Vanilla Joe's fancy cheese plate, blue cheese ice cream included. I was distracted, though, by an overwhelming sense of relief. It was all done. I was done. I would win, or I wouldn't, but at least I was done.

"Thank you, chefs," said Maz. "You may now feel free to mingle with your families before we head back to the *Chef Supreme* kitchen to give you the final verdict."

Of course I wanted to mingle with my family and catch up on all the gossip, but my full bladder poked at me insistently. So I swooped by to promise them I'd be right back and then bee-lined into the hall for the restroom.

Where a familiar face was waiting for me, right outside the single-person accessible bathroom. "Luke," I said.

He turned to me. "Sadie."

The chatter from the dining room faded into static behind me. "I didn't think you were here," I said. "I looked for you. I can't believe—"

He held up a finger to stop me. "Not out here. In here." He ushered me into the bathroom, then locked it behind me. As far as bathrooms went, this was the way to go: very spacious, very clean, with quiet music playing from the ceiling, a scented candle burning on the dark wood side table, and actual paintings on the wall. This bathroom was fancier than most of the hotel rooms I'd ever been in.

Though the bathroom was spacious, big enough to fit a couple of squashy armchairs if the toilet was removed, Luke and I still stood close to each other. So close I could see every throb of his pulse in his throat. "I've been here the whole time," he said. "With my dad. We were tucked into an alcove on the side. I think they wanted me far enough away where I wouldn't distract but close enough where they could get a few shots of me eating on camera."

There were so many things I wanted to say, but first things first: "Did you like my food?"

"Sadie." Luke took my hands in his and squeezed. "I *loved* your food." I would've thought nothing could make my heart flutter like those words, but then he went on. "The chopped liver melted in my mouth with the most luscious feel. The pickled herring was tart and meaty and resisted my teeth just enough to make it a battle. Your duck was so rich, the beets so succulent and slick and smooth. And the babka beignets? They were sweeter than your lips."

That was all it took for me to claim his lips with mine. I pressed myself against him with urgency . . . which reminded me just as urgently that I'd come here to go to the bathroom, and that kind of took away from the mood. So I kissed him once more, softly and gently, and then pulled away. "Can we keep doing this now that there's no longer a conflict of interest?"

"I certainly hope so," said Luke, and that tinge of a British accent reemerged in his tone.

I backed away with the tiniest of sighs, keeping myself close enough to him where our hands were still interlaced. "I wish you hadn't sacrificed yourself for me."

"You make it sound like I threw myself in front of a bullet for you," he said dryly.

"Well, you kind of did. Career-wise."

He rolled his eyes. How had I not focused on his eyelashes before? They were longer and lusher than any natural eyelashes I'd ever seen. "Truth be told, it was not such a great sacrifice. The job was a last-minute decision, helped along by quite a lot of pressure from my father. I don't have a taste for fame, and I discovered I don't much enjoy being on TV. I'm quite happy to be back in the kitchen behind the scenes." He smiled. "Also, consider it payback for being such an ass to you early on. It hurt to call you Sandy, but I didn't want to risk your participation on the show."

That didn't make me feel entirely better, but it did ease the guilt a little bit. "Maybe you should make this into a pattern."

"Not being on TV?"

I shook my head. "Not listening to your father."

He stepped back, stretching my arm, turning his face so that he was no longer looking directly at me. The mood lighting on the ceiling outlined his profile in gold. "You don't understand."

"I think I do understand." I tried to catch his eye, but he was looking stubbornly away. "You took this judging gig because you let your father pressure you. You cook fancy French food because you let your father pressure you. That restaurant, West? It's not you. It's not what you want."

He wrenched his hand away like he was going to ask me how I knew.

"You've been very clear with me about what you want." I took a step closer. This time, he didn't back away. "And it's more than that. It's the way your face lights up when you talk about your halmoni's food. The way you doodled your love for that food on the menu of that Korean speakeasy. How you loved laughing and talking and mingling with the old men there, regulars who felt comfortable and welcomed and at home."

"But you—"

"I cooked from my heart today. I cooked the food of my ancestors, with a bit of a spin, and it was good because it *felt* good. You have to cook what's in your heart, too, and it's not fancy French food. You told me that. Put yourself on that plate."

"You . . ." He trailed off. I waited for him to tell me that I didn't know what I was talking about, that I clearly didn't know him as well as I thought I did.

But he only stepped around me and out the door. Stepped, not stormed. He hadn't said goodbye.

I had no idea what that meant. I had to go after him.

But first, I really, *really* had to pee.

A couple glorious minutes of release later, I was walking back to the dining room when a familiar couple stepped in front of me. I nearly walked straight into them. Which would have been fitting, considering who they were.

The older man and woman in the always-expensive clothes who I'd cursed at, spilled food on, pushed, disregarded. The couple who would probably be better served by running in the opposite direction from me.

"I'm so sorry," I said. I figured I might as well start by apologizing, considering I'd probably somehow given them the only plate of pickled herring with scales, or unbalanced their duck and borscht so that it spilled all over their laps. "I hope you enjoyed the meal." I went to step around them to avoid any further catastrophes, but the man moved directly in front of me.

"Chef Sadie, we've seen a lot of your food over this competition, and I feel like it's finally time we introduced ourselves," he said. "My name is Harold Arlington. My wife is Beverly Arlington."

"Just like the Arlington Restaurant Group," I said. "That's funny."

Beverly Arlington gave me a gentle smile. "We own the Arlington Restaurant Group, dear."

I'd thought I couldn't possibly have cringed any more around them, but somehow I did. A whole, full-body cringe. "Oh my God, I can't believe I—"

"Enough apologies," Harold Arlington said. "Please. We've been trying to get face time with you for ages. Has our friend Lenore Smith told you?"

"No," I said, still cringing. "But she says very little to us. Conflict of interest, I think."

"Of course, that makes sense."

Could they . . . could they possibly want to . . .

"We want to invest in you," said Beverly Arlington.

Somehow I didn't short-circuit. Well, I did short-circuit on the inside—I didn't think any of my limbs could have moved, even if a brigade of chefs was trying to pass behind me with hot pans and knives. But I was legit impressed with myself that I didn't start jerking around or bashing my head against the wall, because that was literally how shocked I was. Of course, I probably would've figured it out sooner had my brain not been so exhausted.

"My family is Ashkenazi Jewish, and your food reminds me of *my* food, in the best possible way," continued Beverly Arlington. I managed to hear her words through the buzz of *whaaaaaaat*, though I wasn't sure how well they were sticking in my head. "You were right when you said there aren't enough upscale Jewish restaurants. People still think of our food traditions as bagels and latkes, when there's so much more to be seen and eaten. And we think you're the person to put it out there."

I opened my mouth to thank them, but what came out instead was, "Jesus Christ."

Beverly laughed. "No need to bring him in on this," she said. "But really, dear, you've truly made fans of us. I know you'd better be getting back to your adoring public and your family, but we wanted to make sure you knew we're interested. We'll be in touch formally once taping officially ends."

The words finally made it to my lips. "Thank you. Oh my God, thank you so much."

Harold Arlington winked at me. "We look forward to talking more, Sadie." When he shook my hand, he slipped me a business card. I lifted it up to admire it as they walked away. Part of me expected it to be an elaborate practical joke, but no—it was real. Embossed and everything. THE ARLINGTON RESTAURANT GROUP. Was that real gold on the lettering?

A shout went up from nearby, and my ears pricked in alarm. *It's the* real *Harold and Beverly Arlington shouting at the two imposters who stole their business cards and ran off.*

You need to stop all this putting yourself down, said Grandma Ruth firmly. *Haven't you proven yourself by now?*

And she was right. *I* was right. Though of course, the way I thought about myself wouldn't be a magical fix. I'd have to focus on it. Make sure I was talking and thinking about myself the way I deserved.

I knew I was worth the effort.

It turned out that the shout hadn't come from the dining room: it had come from one of the private event spaces in back, used currently as a storage space for *Chef Supreme*'s technical equipment. Was the crew arguing? I stepped closer, craning my neck to see through the half-open door, and my hand flew to my mouth as the people started shouting again.

It was Luke. And his father.

Charles Weston was in a full-on tux again, one that had clearly been tailored to him. His silver hair was practically standing on end, and his blue eyes were ice-cold. "You've lost your mind, Luke." Now that I could see him, I realized that shouting might not have been the best way to describe how he was talking—yes, he was extremely loud, but there was no spittle flying from his mouth, no chest puffing out with self-importance. He was *commanding*. "That's everything we've ever worked for. And you're going to throw it all away for . . . what? Some fast-casual joint? A bar? You'll never get reviewed by the *New York Times* again. You have three stars right now. Four stars are in reach!"

Luke replied without shouting. His voice was calm, so much so that I had to lean in to hear him. Only his rigid posture, the tendons standing out like steel cords in his neck, betrayed that he wasn't totally relaxed. "Not what *we've* ever worked for. What *you've* ever worked for. There's a difference."

His eyes looked over his dad's shoulder and out the half-open door. Found me. Softened. I stood there and tried to communicate through my eyes that I was standing with him, that I thought he was doing the right thing. That was a lot to put on some simple eye contact, but I hoped the general gist of it got across.

He turned back to his dad. "I don't care if I get reviewed by the *Times*. I don't care about my three stars. Getting those stars has made me miserable. I want to do what I love. I want to cook from my heart."

"You're making a massive mistake."

Luke stood strong. "At least it'll be *my* mistake to make."

Pride uncoiled in my heart.

His dad shook his head again. "Well, don't come running back to me with your tail between your legs when it all goes belly-up." He paused a moment, as if hoping Luke would admit how wrong he was and fall to his knees to beg for forgiveness, but Luke just stared at him. So his dad turned, surveying the empty room with his icy eyes, and stormed out the exit, not so much as looking in my direction as he stalked past me. Luke watched him go, then followed after him once his dad had disappeared back into the dining room.

He stopped before me in the hallway. I gave him a tentative smile, one that I hoped said I thought he'd made the right decision. He smiled back, took a step toward me . . .

. . . and then a hand clamped down on my shoulder. "There you are," Adrianna said crisply, right into my ear. "I've been looking everywhere for you. We have to get back to the *Chef Supreme* kitchen for judging."

Luke's eyes were dimming. "Can I just have one more minute?"

"We're on a tight schedule," she said firmly. "And you don't want anyone walking in on the two of you talking privately, do you?"

I didn't have much of a choice. So I gave Luke a tiny nod and hoped he'd understood I was saying that I'd talk to him later.

TENSIONS WERE RUNNING high as we walked back into the *Chef Supreme* kitchen for the last time. Nia had spent the entire ride here drumming her fingers on her knee in a frantic and increasingly fast cadence, and Vanilla Joe had spent the entire ride giving her increasingly annoyed looks. Even I had to admit that I wanted to rip her fingers off by the end. But now we were here, the three of us lined up in front of the judges' table, with the serious, stern faces of Lenore Smith, John Waterford, and Maz Sarshad staring back at us.

The six of us weren't the only people on camera. All nine of the eliminated chefs were there, too, lined up back to front in order, so that Kaitlyn and Megan were in front. And they'd brought our families over from the restaurant! Rachel bounced up and down on the balls of her feet with anticipation; behind her, my parents clutched hands.

They'd already taped the judges' deliberations. It was time to announce who'd won.

I was ready. Ready to hear it. Ready to know whatever would come.

Though I had a positive feeling. I'd cooked about as good a meal as I could. Yes, there were a few things I could've done differently, and that I *would* do differently if I were given time to cook the meal again. But I was happy with my performance.

Happy with myself.

"Chefs," said Maz magnanimously. "You've spent weeks here in the *Chef Supreme* kitchen. You've endured nights of little sleep and days away from your lives and families. You've fought your way through battle after battle, cooking us some of the most incredible plates of food. And all of it . . ."

Signature dramatic pause.

". . . comes down to this one moment. When one of you will be named Chef Supreme."

He looked from me to Nia to Vanilla Joe. I hoped it was a good sign that he'd looked at me first.

"The three of you should all be happy with the dishes you've made today," Maz continued. "I would gladly pay for any of them in a three-star restaurant. All of us are excited to see what you do next, and where your food takes you."

An even longer dramatic pause. I ground my teeth.

"However. Only one can be named Chef Supreme."

I crossed every finger on both hands. Crossed my toes inside my shoes. Briefly considered crossing my eyes, then decided against it what with the whole camera thing.

"The newest Chef Supreme . . . is . . ."

My heart pounded. Blood thundered in my ears.

". . . CHEF NIA!"

Nia shrieked so loud the sound might actually have punctured my eardrums. Which was fine, because it covered up the sound of my heart plummeting into my feet and thudding against the floor.

I'd told myself I'd be okay if I didn't win. And I would be.

But I'd be lying if I said I wasn't disappointed.

Still, as I plastered a smile onto my face for the cameras, it relaxed into something real. "Congratulations," I said, giving Nia a quick hug before the others could come over and swamp her.

Vanilla Joe kicked at the floor. "Congrats," he mumbled so quietly I could barely hear him. I still didn't like him, but I hoped his being in the top three would impress his parents and his doctor siblings.

Maz spoke over the din. "Chef Nia, you impressed us so much tonight with the soul, the creativity, and the plain old deliciousness of your food," he said. "Congratulations, Chef Supreme Nia!"

Nia was sobbing. The eliminated chefs congregated around her to hug her and offer her congratulations. Her family pushed their way through the pack, cheering and crying.

Rachel and my parents approached. "Sorry, Sadie," Rachel said sincerely after mashing me into her arms. My parents murmured apologies in my ears, too. "I'm sorry. I'm sorry."

"I'm not," I said, backing off. "Do you know the Arlington Restaurant Group?"

Rachel squealed as I told her about my new investors. "If you ask me, it sounds like you really won, too."

"Yeah," I said. "I did."

The popping of champagne corks took over the room as Adrianna rushed me to the side to get a quick reaction shot. Not the last one—we'd all have to return tomorrow to do our last confessionals on the finale. "I'm happy for Nia," I told the camera sincerely. "Obviously, I'm disappointed it wasn't me, but she deserves it. And you haven't seen the last of me!"

The champagne was dry and bubbly and faintly sweet in my throat. I sipped as we toasted to Nia, to Maz, to John Waterford, to food in general, and then I looked up to see Luke standing in the previously empty doorway. Just standing there. Leaning against the frame. Legs crossed casually at the ankle, head cocked to the side as he watched what was going on.

For a moment I forgot to breathe.

He noticed me noticing him. He smiled. He stepped back.

I followed, drifting after him as if in a dream. Nobody around me noticed. Everybody was busy with Nia, drunkenly making toast after toast, and my parents were busy talking enthusiastically with the parents of Nia and Vanilla Joe.

We were alone in the hallway. Finally alone. No Adrianna. No cameras. No competition hanging over our heads. "Who won?" he asked.

"Nia."

"I'm sorry."

"I'm not."

The smile he gave me was like we were sharing a secret. Which we were, I guess. When he grabbed my hand and motioned for me to follow him, I did.

"I think it was really brave what you did," I said as we walked down the hallway in a direction I hadn't been in before. "Standing up to your dad like that."

"Thanks." He rustled in his pocket with his free hand, coming out of it clutching a shiny silver key. "I'm not quite sure how to feel about it. He's never been that angry at me before."

"Maybe he needs to be angry at you."

He fiddled with the key, trying to get it in the lock of an unlabeled door while giving me a crooked smile. "We'll see. I think he'll cool down in a week or two. I just hope he understands eventually."

"I hope so, too," I told him. The key clicked in the lock, and the door swung open. It led to a narrow, dark staircase that ended high up in another door. "Where are we going?"

"You'll see when we get there." He started up the stairs. I kept up after him.

"Is it an attic?" He didn't answer. "Is it a *murder* attic?"

He paused on the staircase, turning so that I could see him raising one eyebrow. "A murder attic? Is that a thing?"

I shrugged. He shook his head, a wry smile on his face. "It's not a murder attic. Unless you're planning on being the murderer."

"Unfortunately, I left my knives at my station."

The door at the top of the stairs was unlocked. Luke pushed it open, which flooded us with a gust of warm air. I teetered on the narrow step, held upright by his hand, and kept going. Onto the roof.

The *Chef Supreme* building was not a tall one, so we didn't have a magical view of the city lights or Central Park unwinding in the distance. And this wasn't a nice rooftop with chairs and tables and potted plants flowering in the sun; it was one of those rooftops we probably weren't supposed to be on, with a ground covered in white and black splotches of pigeon crap and something industrial humming behind a heavily padlocked setup. But Luke led me to the edge, hand in hand, and the Hudson River glittered before us, the lights of New Jersey in the distance. Beautiful. I felt something inside me loosen and unwind. Maybe the part of me that was used to performing for the ever-present cameras, or the part that had tried to shoo away my feelings for Luke.

Whatever it was, it was gone now.

I approve of this boy, murmured Grandma Ruth. *Even though he isn't Jewish. You'll just have to raise the children Jewish. You are planning on giving me great-grandchildren soon, right?*

I shook her away, leaving me with only myself. So it was with full abandon that I took Luke's face in my hands and kissed him hard, kissed him so that he could feel every minute I'd been waiting for him, kissed him there under the stars. I might not have been able to see them, but I knew they were there.

Epilogue

AS I'VE SAID BEFORE, MY LIFE HAS A HABIT OF CHANG-ing while I'm in the nude. Sometimes it's a nasty habit. And sometimes it's a little less nasty.

I groaned at the sound of Luke's voice, rolling over in his bed and wrapping the sheets around my legs. They smelled like him, like warmth and calm and peace. "It's too early."

"It's almost noon." He sat down on the bed beside me, leaning to skim a hand over the curve of my hip and back. Though we'd been doing this for almost a year now, the touch of his fingers still made my skin tingle in the most delicious way. "And in case you've forgotten, today is a big day."

I popped upright. His eyes popped down to my chest, then back up. "It's today! Oh my God!" He leaned in, and his lips trailed over my jaw down to my neck, where they stopped to graze my skin with his teeth. I shivered, arching my back. "Do you think maybe we have a *few* minutes?"

He smiled at me, then leaned me back onto the bed, pushing

me into the mattress with his weight. I let out a happy sigh at the feeling of his body resting on top of me, poised to move with the slightest twitch from me. He was fully dressed in his new uniform—no more tuxes or suits, now dark jeans and collared shirts—but I could feel him hard against my leg, ready to go. "Maybe a *few*."

And yes. It was life-changing every time.

After a quick shower, I threw on the outfit I'd laid out the night before, a cute flowered dress and shiny golden Converses. My dress would be covered by my chef's coat most of the night, but I still wanted to look nice. I put on makeup and straightened my hair until it shone. Presented myself to Luke for inspection. He smiled lazily and told me he liked me better totally bare, which was almost enough to get me totally bare again. But we were already late enough, so I reluctantly rushed out the door to the elevator, him on my heels.

I'd spent a lot of time here in Luke's West Village penthouse over the past year, mostly because it was a significant upgrade over the cramped two-bedroom apartment I'd rented with Kaitlyn out in Brooklyn. He had views of the river instead of garbage bins, and an elevator to take you to his door instead of five flights of stairs, and nice clean cabinets instead of grimy cabinets visited by the occasional mouse. Which was fine with Kaitlyn, as from what I understood, Megan had been spending lots of time there in my place. I suspected both of us would make things official soon in regard to the lease.

Moving to New York had been an easy decision to make. There wasn't much left for me in Seattle other than my family—who I did miss—and the Arlingtons had really wanted me to make my restaurant debut in the food capital of the country. Though I did get messages from a bunch of restaurants in Seattle in case I wanted to stay, saying that they'd love to have me come aboard and that they'd be boycotting Derek and his food. Last I heard, the Green Onion was on the verge of bankruptcy.

I'd be lying if I said I hadn't felt a tingle of delight at the news.

Kaitlyn had come along for the ride, too. As a semifinalist, she was also in hot demand, though she'd chosen not to open her own restaurant just yet. She was currently circulating through some of New York's best restaurants, figuring out who she wanted to be as a chef. I had faith in her that she'd figure it out.

Luke and I walked briskly down the sidewalk, neatly side-stepping tourists wandering around in search of Magnolia Bakery. A few people did a double take as we passed, clearly thinking we looked familiar, but it wasn't like *Chef Supreme* had granted me instant fame in regard to the general public. Lots of people watched the show, but we hadn't become major celebrities. Which was just fine by me. The Arlingtons had tested me out with a six-month Jewish-themed pop-up restaurant, and after that closed, they'd told me they wanted to make it permanent in a new location. Which was exactly the news I'd been hoping for, of course. Avid show watchers and fans of the pop-up had already made it so that my new restaurant was booked solid for a month before the restaurant's official opening.

Which was today.

My phone chimed, as if reminding me. I pulled it out to see a text message from Kel, which made me smile. Good luck today!! I'll be making a toast in your honor. I knew they would be here with me if they hadn't been working so hard on setting up their own restaurant in Philadelphia. But it was okay. Hopefully, both our restaurants would be open for a long, long time.

I stopped in front of my new building, a thrill of pride running through me at the sight. The sign was bright and clear and elegant: Wander. Because my people had wandered all around the world for thousands of years of the Diaspora, picking up local culinary traditions and incorporating them into our own. Even if my menu had taken the incorporation in a more daring direction—some of the dishes I was most excited about were the brisket ramen and the kimchi chopped liver, a play on my finale appetizer but with Korean influences. Luke had helped me with that. It was the one dish that sat on both of our menus.

He squeezed my hand. "I'm just going to run into Halmoni's, and then I'll be back." Halmoni's had replaced West as his flagship restaurant; he'd named it after his grandmother, considering she'd inspired the food he made there, and his love of cooking. It had only been open for two months, but he was already in talks to open a second location out in LA. "She'd love you," he'd told me once, which made my grandma Ruth shriek in delight.

I kissed him goodbye. My lips lingered on his for a moment, drinking him in, and then he was off. I waved at his back, though I knew he wouldn't be able to see me. It wasn't like he had far to go—our restaurants were only a few blocks apart, which made it easy to go back and forth. It wasn't like the trip we'd made to check out Nia's restaurant opening down in Atlanta. I counted myself lucky we'd been able to get a reservation, that was how packed it was, with out-of-state license plates scattered throughout the parking lot. I'd seen pictures of lines snaking around Vanilla Joe's LA food trucks, too.

I turned the key and stepped through the door. For a moment I stood in the dark space and took a deep breath. Everything I'd worked for was here. Was now. Was this really going to work? The shadows of the tables and chairs I'd selected from several painstaking hours going through catalogs loomed in the silence.

I didn't have time to worry about it. The back doorbell was already chiming with my order from the farmers market, and my phone was ringing with the custom tone I'd given the Arlingtons, probably asking me how the opening process was going. As I picked up, balancing my phone on my shoulder as I signed for the fruits and vegetables, that was indeed what they asked me.

"I'm ready," I told them. "Let's do this."

Acknowledgments

It takes a whole lot of cooks to serve up something as complicated as a book, and I couldn't have been luckier with mine. My editor, Kristine Swartz, deserves four Michelin stars (yes, I know the guide only goes up to three. She's THAT great). Kristine, thank you so much for your enthusiasm, your love for this book, and your hard work on my behalf. Berkley is truly the absolute perfect home for me and Sadie, and I'm so incredibly grateful to everybody there who has worked to make *Sadie on a Plate* a better book and who helped the world hear about it: Dache' Rogers, Yazmine Hassan, Jessica Plummer, Elisha Katz, Colleen Reinhart, Marianne Grace Aguiar, Liz Gluck, Christine Legon, and Mary Baker. Special thanks to Debs Lim for bringing Sadie and Luke so beautifully to life on the cover!

Another four Michelin stars for my agent, Merrilee Heifetz. Thank you for everything! A big thank-you also to her assistant, Rebecca Eskildsen, and the rest of the team at Writers House.

Alix Kaye, your read and your brilliant editorial comments changed Sadie for the better. Thank you for that, and for getting your friends excited for this book before it even sold!

Thank you so much to KJ Dell'Antonia, Roselle Lim, Amy Reichert, Rachel Lynn Solomon, and Sarah Echavarre Smith for your kind words about my book. It still feels like a dream come true that you read my book, let alone liked it!

Berkletes: what would I have done without you? Thank you for your support, your kind words, and your friendship. Here's to many, many books in our future.

Finally, I have to thank *Top Chef*, from all the chefs who have cooked their hearts out to the people behind the scenes who made the show happen. This book was inspired by my love for this show, and Sadie wouldn't exist without it.

Keep reading for an excerpt of
Amanda Elliot's next novel

Best Served Hot

Coming in spring 2023 from Berkley

RUNNING DOWN A MIDTOWN MANHATTAN SIDEWALK during rush hour might as well be running an obstacle course. Leap the pile of garbage spilling out from glossy black bags. Dodge the woman weaving from side to side, eyes fixed on her phone. Zero in on the tiny opening between a row of businessmen spread out about as wide as they can go, blocking almost the whole pathway. Try not to sweat through your silk work blouse.

I leaped to a stop, panting, in front of the address. I didn't even need to confirm the restaurant name etched on the great glass window, because Alice Wong was standing in front of it. Frowning at me. "You're late."

"I've had a *day*." I drew in a great deep breath. "I woke up to a text from my bank saying that my account had been over drawn, and then there was a troll in my comments and DMs who wasn't even creative with his dick metaphors—come on, sausages have been overdone. And then Mr. Decker was grouchy all day because it's tax season, and with New York raising its tax brackets on the ultrarich, he keeps saying he might have to sell one of his yachts—"

"My God." Alice pressed the back of her hand against the blunt black bangs cutting across her forehead. "The poor man." She turned to go inside the restaurant, but I stopped her with a touch to the shoulder.

"One second. Let me make sure BiggerBoi69 hasn't popped

back up under another name." I grabbed my phone and flicked open the app. My profile, JulieZeeEatsNYC, scrolled across the screen: little shots of restaurant meals I'd reviewed and video stills of me biting into things, which, no matter how I timed them, always looked awkward. My last few comments sections were clear. Well, mostly. A small-time troll was arguing with my commenters about the optimal doneness of steak, but I could deal with that later.

I sighed. Such were the trials and tribulations of someone who published their own restaurant reviews on social media instead of doing it for real in a newspaper or well-known blog. They had a support staff for this kind of thing so that their reviewers could focus on the food.

I knew better than to complain aloud. I knew exactly what Alice would say. Not because I was psychic or anything, but because she'd said it all before. *You* are *a real reviewer, babe. You review restaurants, and you have a pretty big following, too. That makes you no less real than the others and their fancy papers.*

Alice cleared her throat. I looked up to find her staring at me, her slash of red lipstick pressed tight in a way that meant, *I'm starving.*

"Alice," I told her. "You're a genius."

The frown smoothed out. "I know. But how so?"

My phone dinged with an email notification. My heart skipped a beat as my head ducked back down. I couldn't help holding my breath as I opened it up. I'd been doing that for days now, hoping for one specific email asking me in for an interview. Dreading the email that would start with, *We regret to inform you that* . . . or, *Thank you very much for your application, but* . . .

It was my bank, offering me more overdraft protection. I sighed. It was a little too late for that. "I'm ready. Let's go in."

The restaurant was dark, narrow, and cluttered, the tables set so close together I'd have no problem leaning over and taking a bite off my neighbor's plate. The walls were hung with kitschy representations of boats and lobsters, the ceiling strung with garlands of twinkling white lights. The tacky decor was, fortunately, not a reflection of the food. I'd learned that on my two previous visits.

I didn't answer Alice's question until we were seated, glasses of tepid water before us. I preferred it tepid. Too cold and it was a shock to the system, numbed the taste buds. "You were giving me a pep talk in my head. That's why you're a genius."

"Unfortunately, I haven't mastered telepathy yet, so that pep talk was all you talking to you," said Alice. "Let me guess: 'I' was telling you that you're real and valid in what you do?"

I didn't have to nod. She knew what it meant when my eyes ducked down and stared intently at the starched white tablecloth.

"I was indeed right," Alice said. "I love saying that. It doesn't matter if you don't have a byline or a salary. You're out there doing the work, and you have a devoted following because of it."

I'd heard this before, from her and from my parents and even from one of my three older brothers, which was a surprise coming from someone whose preferred mode of communication with his younger sister had always been belching the ABC's in her face.

So what if I couldn't quite bring myself to believe it? I sneaked another glance at my phone. If the *thing* I couldn't even think about or risk jinxing came true, I wouldn't have to worry about it anymore anyway. I'd have the respect I craved. Even someone like my boss, Mr. Decker, would listen to me then.

This wasn't the time to argue with Alice, though. "How's the coding going?"

Alice's face brightened. "Fabulously. For real. My team just hired another girl! Now there are two of us."

"Compared to how many dudes?"

"Seven."

"Progress." I lifted my water glass in a toast. "To very slowly getting to equality!" By the time we clinked, drank, and set our glasses back down, the waiter had arrived with our menus. I didn't even have to page through it. "I'm ready to order, please."

As I listed off everything I wanted to feature in my post, I did my best not to cringe at the prices. If I reviewed restaurants for a real outlet, whether it was a prestigious paper like the *New York Times* or the *New York Scroll* or a blog like *Eater*, I'd have an expense account to cover these checks. But alas, all I had was a small advertising revenue. I mostly broke even, or sometimes just went broke. Hence the overdraft fee.

"So, hey," Alice said as the waiter walked away, scribbling on his pad. "How's Greg?"

I tried not to grimace. I'd gone on three dates with Greg, a thirtysomething marketing guy and surprise taxidermy enthusiast. Despite the weirdness of being watched as I slept by eight pairs of beady black fake squirrel eyes, I'd still texted him the next day. And had not heard back in the two days since. "Pretty sure he's ghosting me."

Alice swiped the back of her hand dramatically over her brow, as if wicking away a nervous sweat. "Oh, thank God. I was kind of afraid you'd end up with your head mounted on his wall."

"Whatever." I shrugged like I didn't care. To be honest, I didn't care *that* much. It was the rejection that stung more than anything. If *I'd* been the one to ignore *him*, I probably wouldn't even be thinking about it. "There are plenty of fish in the sea."

"I've never understood that metaphor," said Alice. "Are we fish, too, in this scenario? Or are we fishing for the guys, as it implies, and then killing and eating them?"

I was saved from having to answer by the arrival of the food. If I was indeed seeking a mate by fishing for him and then eating him, I hoped he'd be the lobster in the fried lobster and waffles. Anything fried well always looked delicious—light brown, glistening slightly with oil—and these chunks of lobster in their coating of crispy batter couldn't have looked more appealing atop the delicate squares of golden waffle, smeared with a sunset of sweet potato butter. "Let's take our pictures and then set up the phone to film me for a quick teaser as I eat."

Every time I had to stand up on my chair in order to snap a good angle of a plate, I said a silent prayer in thanks to my fellow millennials, who were also out there taking pictures of their food. Nobody so much as spared me a funny glance. Not that I would notice; I was too busy focusing on keeping my balance on the slick wooden chair while making the food look beautiful on my phone.

My mouth watered. The lobster and waffles was extremely delicious, but I also loved the fancy toast topped with snow crab and avocado (rich, sweet, and texturally balanced, given nice contrast by a zing of black pepper on top). And the soft-shell crab BLT, where the sweet, earthy tomato met the crisp, watery crunch of the iceberg lettuce and thick chewy smoke of the bacon, and then the sweet crispy crackles of the soft-shell crab. And Chef

Stephanie's version of New England clam chowder, which was rich with cream—but not heavy—and delicately spiced; the clams were big and briny, and the bits of bacon throughout were somehow still crispy. It would have qualified as an excellent but not all that memorable clam chowder if not for the salsify root, which had the texture of a parsnip but the taste, almost, of an oyster or a clam. It made for a marvelously interesting bite. Unfortunately, it looked like a bowl of white sludge, which meant I couldn't feature—

My phone buzzed with a push notification. My eyes flicked to it quickly in case BiggerBoi69 was back and instead caught, *New York Scroll* names new rest—

I slipped. "Eeeek!"

One of the reasons Alice is my best friend: she always catches me when I'm down, both figuratively and literally. She slipped out of her seat and caught me neatly before any soft-shell crab or salsify root could go flying onto the table next to us. "Maybe let's get our photos from a less vertical angle going forward," she told me once I was safely back on solid ground.

But my heart was thudding, and not just because I'd almost broken destiny's choice of bones. The thing I'd been dreading was staring at me from my notification list, and it had the nerve to not even be in personal-email form. A breaking news story. *New York Scroll* names new restaurant critic, Bennett Richard Macalester Wright.

Suddenly none of the food looked all that appetizing anymore.

"What is it?" asked Alice.

I sat back down with a thump. "I didn't get it," I said dully. And it wasn't like I'd expected them to read my passionate cover letter and résumé and social media stats and immediately roll out the heirloom-tomato-red carpet. But they hadn't even bothered sending me a rejection email. Or any kind of acknowledgment at all. Maybe my application had been one of a million, even though the job hadn't been listed online for the general peasantry to apply for (I'd been tipped off about the opening through an email my boss had gotten and I'd read).

Or maybe they hadn't taken my résumé seriously. Laughed about it in the office. *Who does this girl think she is? She thinks some social media followers and some videos make her suited for us?* The *New York Scroll* had never hired a critic who wasn't a white dude over fifty. They had social media, of course, but they still published trend pieces where they gaped at it and how it worked like it was a zoo exhibit. *And over here we have people—wait for it—actually getting their news on Instagram. Thank goodness the bars are here, or they might attack us.*

Not unlike my boss, come to think of it. I still didn't think he knew about my second "job," but I'd heard the way he snorted as he watched his daughters take selfies or the older one herd her kids into the perfect light for a family snap.

Alice made a sympathetic *mmm* in response. "Who'd they name? Is it at least someone good?"

The name sounded vaguely familiar, but I was already frantically googling to learn more, leaving the food to cool before us. "He went to Dartmouth," I reported. Which, if I judged by the alumni I knew—my boss and his daughters—was stereotypically rich and fratty. "And he played on the squash team." Which was basically code for "has an enormous trust fund." I scowled down at my screen. "Hobbies include skiing and patronizing art galleries."

Bennett Richard Macalester Wright had almost certainly

never budgeted incorrectly and run out of food money his freshman year of college and had to subsist on ramen and scrounged-up free pizza from various club meetings to get by.

"And then it looks like he was a food reporter at the *Times* for the last five years," I said. I scrolled through a few of his past headlines. A profile on a chef semifamous for his cooking and very famous for his string of ever-younger actress wives. A report on why high-end restaurants were trending toward smaller but more expensive wine lists. A few reviews of pricey restaurants—it looked like he'd filled in for their regular critic while she was out on maternity leave.

"At least he seems like he's qualified," Alice said. I scowled at her. I didn't want to hear that he was qualified. I wanted to hear that he sucked and that they should've hired me. But I didn't say that. I continued my googling, but turned up nothing except dead ends. Like most major food reviewers, he'd clearly done his best to take down as much as he possibly could about himself, especially photographs. No serious food reviewer wanted to tip off a restaurant that they were there, since that might lead the owner or the kitchen offering them special treatment that would bias their review. It was why I never made a reservation under my own name, though I couldn't do much about my face. Sometimes, if I got recognized on one visit, I'd go back with a wig or glasses the next time.

"Excuse me, ladies?" Our waiter smiled down on us. "How are we doing?"

"Not great, but the food is delicious," I told him.

His smile wavered, not quite sure what to do with that. "Would you like anything more to drink? We have some lovely wines on offer tonight."

"No thanks," Alice said. "She doesn't like wine."

"Alice!" I hissed. Which was always fun. Alice had a particularly hissable name.

The waiter nodded and went off to bring our check. Alice turned to me, blinking. "What?"

"We've had this discussion before," I said. "Don't tell anyone I don't like wine."

"But you *don't* like wine," Alice said.

It was true. Wine tasted like literal sour grapes to me, whether it was the cheap boxed stuff our roommates used to bring home in college or the ultrafancy kind my boss gave me last year for the holidays. It literally made my lips pucker and my cheeks suck in. I'd never been able to understand why people actually enjoyed drinking it.

But my followers wouldn't agree. Again, they were mostly young women around my age or a bit older. There was a whole meme industry around wine. The wine moms. Giant wine glasses. Social media love turned on a dime. Not like I was hiding it hardcore. It was just that I'd rather the truth not be known, because I didn't want to do anything that might alienate me from my followers. Sometimes being loved on social media meant being loved as someone who isn't really you.

"You know who I bet loooves wine?" I said, rather than continuing my lecture. "Bennett . . ." I couldn't remember his two middle names, so I made some up. "Bennett Rigatoni Mushroom Wright." Alice giggled, which made me go on. "The *Scroll* always includes a wine list in their reviews, and the wines they choose always cost a fortune."

Alice blinked for a moment, processing, then leaned in. "Bennett Ratatouille Meatloaf Wright is probably one of those guys who swishes the wine around in their mouth and then says they taste oak or cherry or chocolate underneath."

I held up my water glass and swished it around. Lowered my voice so that it honked out my nose. "Hmm, this wine is quite delicious. I believe I'm getting notes of pine and banana and . . . hmm, is that a Krispy Kreme doughnut under there?"

Alice giggled. My lips perked up in a tiny—genuine—smile. I continued, "Taking bets on if he includes that in his first review tomorrow."

"Either that, or something equally pretentious," she said. "Unlike you and your delightful videos."

I sighed. "That reminds me that I never actually *got* my video." "It's not too late."

And it wasn't. Even if I was in no mood to perform right now. But, as I'd just told myself, sometimes you had to be someone else online. So I forced myself to smile—my day job was great practice for that!—and act enthused about the lobster and waffles, which was now cold and unappealing, the grease cold and oily on my tongue, the coating soggy. "It's sooo good," I said, rolling my eyes back in my mock-orgasm face. This short video wouldn't be part of my official post, but I'd post it to my profile in advance of the actual review as a teaser. "I'm so happy to be eating this right now!"

I finished in one take, and just in time. The waiter set the check gently on our table; I grabbed it before Alice could. Though to be fair, she no longer bothered trying. Sometimes I wondered if she actually just came out with me for the free meals and not the company, but Alice wasn't that good of a liar.

"We still on for the food festival this weekend?" I asked, trying to push all thoughts of Bennett Wright aside.

The Central Park Food Festival was the most exciting day of my shooting calendar, the way I truly knew spring was here. Tons of booths and stands sent not only by some of the city's most exciting new restaurants, but by people trying to raise money to open their own restaurants or food trucks. The application process was fierce, because the heat of the attention from all the food bloggers and reviewers circulating throughout could make that investor dough rise. "Don't worry. I'm planning on doing all the research this week so we have our route plotted out exactly."

"Um, obviously," said Alice. "I can't wait."

In between all my research (and probably some expense-report filing and conference-room shining for my actual boss), I'd post a couple days of teasers, then livestream a bit on the day of, and prep some epic videos and reviews for the week after. I already knew some of the booths I'd definitely have to check out. All I had to do was figure out how to zig-zag between them to get the most food in me.

"I can't wait either," I said. "I wonder if the *Scroll* will go." They didn't usually. It was like they were saying, *We don't need to do the discovering, we'll wait for you to do the discovering and we'll do the judging.* Like they'd swish all those new exciting chefs between their teeth, straining them out, looking for undertones that I'd swallow without even noticing.

Now they had a new guy to do that for them. *I hope you choke, Bennett Ranch Dressing Milkshake Wright*, I thought fiercely, and then felt bad. *Not, like, choke to death. Just choke enough to be embarrassed, like maybe coughing up a bite of fancy food onto your boss or something.*

That mental image almost made me feel better.

Amanda Elliot lives with her husband in New York City, where she collects way too many cookbooks for her tiny kitchen, runs in Central Park, and writes for teens and kids under the name Amanda Panitch.

CONNECT ONLINE

AmandaPanitch.com
AmandaPanitch
AmandaPanitch